Sometimes the Fearless

by

James Ankrom

ISBN: 1-4107-6476-1 (e-book)
ISBN: 1-4107-6475-3 (Paperback)

Library of Congress Control Number: 2003094025

This book is printed on acid free paper.

Printed in the United States of America
Bloomington, IN

1stBooks – rev. 08/01/03

ACKNOWLEDGE

I would like to acknowledge the help I received from Ken Morris, Scott Lengle, John Loux and most of all my wife, Linda.
I would also like to dedicate this work to my three children:
Shane, Bessie and Mollie

PROLOGUE

The boy had just cleared the far tree line and was now crossing the meadow toward the cabin. Flowers blossomed around his feet and their intoxicating scent trailed by his nose as he sucked in cool, fresh air. He automatically picked up his pace, his eyes squinting into the sun as it climbed the morning sky over the distant mountains.

Then, like shattered glass, a scream echoed in his ear.

A woman's frightened scream...

Eleven year old Jack Mulligan's eyes flew open as he struggled to orient himself. He was now in his freezing cold bedroom on the second floor of the run-down house on River Street. There was no heat in the upstairs bedrooms, as he shivered violently under the thin covers. Across the street, the glow from Cromwell Steel's furnaces bathed his room in a dull orange. It was like a built-in night light. Jack didn't like the dark; so living in this location in Steubenville, Ohio, had a singular benefit.

Even with the covers pulled to his chin, Jack was cold. His starved body shivered uncontrollably as he suddenly heard the groan of his mother in the next room and the gruff sound of his father's voice.

He was "straightening her out" again.

Hatred burned like a glowing ember in Jack's chest. Why couldn't the ol' man leave them alone or better yet, die? The bastard kept beating them and the abuse never stopped. Nobody could help—not the neighbors or the cops.

Another slap echoed off the walls.

"Stop!" mimed Jack's mouth silently. "Stop…please."

"You fuckin' bitch," his father bellowed, "you been holdin' out on me. Where's my money?"

"I don't have…"

Two more slaps resounded through the paper-thin walls.

Jack could tell by the thick-tongued slur of the words that the ol' man was really loaded this time. When he was drunk, he got mean. That was always bad for Jack and his mother. The fear of his father's violence clung to him like an unwanted odor.

Jack hated his lazy, shiftless father, an out of work steel worker. He watched his mother grow frail and old as she tried to deal with the old man's drunken tirades and placate his dark, unpredictable moods. They both walked on egg shells around him. Each hoped they wouldn't be his next target. But, nothing worked. The old man was a mean drunk. Nothing could change him as he sank further and further into alcohol and violence.

This was it though.

Tonight, Jack decided, was the last time he was going to tolerate his father's cursing or his violence. Soon, his father would kill his mother. She was now breaking her back working two jobs but was beginning to get warnings from her bosses concerning missed days due to the constant physical abuse she received.

Slipping out of bed, Jack tiptoed to his closet where he had hidden the hunting knife that Warren, the junk man down the street, had given him for protection. Warren and all the neighbors knew the kind of man his father was, but all of them, except Warren, lacked the courage to say or do anything about it. At least Warren had given him a means to protect his life.

Jack dug under some boxes and old shoes until he saw the shiny, six inch blade lying flat on the floor. The handle had black tape for a better grip, and Warren, an old World War II veteran, had shown Jack how to thrust the blade to get the best and deadliest results.

Another loud slap and a dull thud sounded from the room next door. Jack's mother was now begging his father to stop. This had happened before. Didn't she know that pleading with him only made him hit her more? The old man possessed no pity or remorse.

Jack's anger intensified. Damn him! No more! The screaming and abuse had to end.

Quietly entering the dark hallway, he could see into his parent's room through a crack in the doorway. His mother was lying on the floor in a fetal position with her nightgown half torn off. His father stood over her, naked. He was a big man with a fat beer-belly, rheumy eyes and, at that moment, a large erection. The beating must be turning him on.

Warren's words echoed in Jack's mind. He had told him that if he ever used the knife, not to hesitate but go for the kill.

"If you stab to the belly, be sure to twist the blade," the junk man had instructed. "Tear things up inside, and he'll not get up then."

The knife felt heavy in his hand. Could he do it?

His breath came in quick wisps of steam and his legs shook with cold and fear.

Could he do it? The question repeated itself in his head.

Then, without warning, his father stomped on his mother's head making it sound like a ripe melon hitting the floor. He then laughed. Jack's mother groaned and slumped.

She didn't move. He couldn't see her breathing, either. Was she dead?

Panic gripped him.

NO!

Jack's temper ignited. Everything inside snapped.

With a piercing scream, he burst through the door, charged across the room where his father stood swaying over his mother. With all the strength he could muster, Jack sank the shimmering blade to the hilt into his father's pale white belly.

"SONUVABITCH!" his father roared.

Jack grabbed the blade and pulled it sideways.

The scream from his father echoed off the walls as blood came pouring out of the wound in huge red gushes. Part of his intestines, too, bulged from the gaping hole.

"FUCK!" He yelled. "You, FUCK!"

His father tried to grab the knife handle but the river of blood made it too slippery. Instead he lacerated his hand.

"Fuck!" He screamed repeatedly, his eyes zig-zagging wildly.

Jack stepped back three steps in shock, then ran to the door. He couldn't believe the copious flow of blood. It was squirting everywhere. The knife must have found an artery.

His father kept screaming obscenities as he gyrated and staggered towards the boy in an effort to surely kill him. But, too much blood was leaving his body too fast, and he fell to his knees, blood pouring from his mouth. The old man tried to talk, but the blood flow stifled his screams. Then the rest of his fat, white body hit the floor, convulsing and writhing.

Jack could only stare.

Moments passed and the old man's body kept moving; then gradually slowed. Finally, his eyes glazed and he grew still. Death wrote a look of total astonishment on his heavy jowled face.

Jack heard his mother cough and try to lift her ruined face. Thank God she wasn't dead. A line of blood flowed from her mouth and dripped on the floor. With a groan, she attempted to focus on the scene through swollen, bruised eye-slits at her dead husband and frightened son.

"What have you done, Jack?" she spat with a tooth hanging from her bloody mouth. "What have you done?"

Jack stared blankly at the body of his father and then back to his mother.

"I saved us, Mom," he replied.

She started crawling to her husband's prostrate body.

"Oh no!" she cried.

"I killed him, Mom. I did it for you," he said proudly.

Her eyes rolled wildly as she examined the corpse. Jack was shaking now, gripped in fear.

"Murderer!" she screamed.

What? Couldn't she see?

"Murderer!" She shouted, her face contorted in hate.

He'd done this for her. To help her. To help them.

"MURDERER!"

Didn't she understand?

"MURDERER!"

"MURDERER!"

Part I

Bigotry has no head and cannot think;
no heart and cannot feel.

Daniel O'Connell

CHAPTER 1

When Jack Mulligan felt the bus lurch to a stop at the entrance to Mt. Sidney College, he could see the low, tortured clouds of a fast moving thunder storm approaching from the west. The black clouds were roiling and colliding with random strikes of lightning flicking to the earth.

He had been sitting in the packed bus most of the day, and he ached. His legs and back were stiff and his feet were numb. Grabbing his cheap, prison-issued suitcase, he stepped down to the sidewalk and gazed out at the expansive green campus dotted with large brick buildings and sidewalks lined with ancient trees.

The rumble of thunder told him the storm was only minutes away from its full fury. Dark clouds already hung heavy over the buildings, and the wind was beginning to visibly pick up, tossing leaves and scraps of paper around. Several large oaks and poplar trees swayed like drunken sailors in the tempest.

Jack pulled a piece of paper from his pocket as the bus growled back to life behind him and moved away.

The housing notice said he was to go to Lincoln Hall, wherever that was.

Jack lifted the suitcase and started across the well-manicured lawn to the nearest of the ivy covered buildings. The wind, now gusting, slapped him in the face and the heavy smell of rain clung to his nostrils. Lincoln Hall had better be near, he thought, or he'd soon be getting drenched. Glancing at the sky, he automatically picked up his pace. It was then he saw a tall young man hurriedly jogging with a shopping bag full of books and looking cautiously skyward.

"Excuse me, pal," Jack said getting in the young man's path. "Can you tell me where Lincoln Hall is located?"

Annoyance creased the young man's brow.

"Why, you a student?" the black youth asked smartly. He was a head taller than Jack—broad shouldered, with large expressive eyes that didn't disguise his disgust. "You're white!"

It was more question than statement.

"Yeah."

"You sure you're in the right place, my man?"

Jack closed his inanimate blue eyes for a moment, sorry he had asked. When he opened them, the black kid was still there frowning at him. Jack frowned back and pressed his teeth together.

"Do you know where Lincoln Hall is?" he repeated slowly. "Yes or no?"

A reluctant smile came to the young man's face as he pointed. "See that big, ugly building there. It's the first building behind it."

Jack grunted a thanks and headed away. From behind him, he heard the black kid mumble, "Better hurry or you'll get wet," and then, "Well, there goes the neighborhood."

Jack knew that coming to this school would be a big mistake. An all black college would never accept a white ex-con. Superintendent Brown had said so and he was, for once, right. The moment the morons on the Juvenile Detention Board had announced their plans for him, the Superintendent had proclaimed the folly of the whole idea. It was probably the only time Jack and Superintendent ever agreed on anything.

In his office, Brown had put his flushed face inches from Jack's and told him, loudly and unequivocally, "You are a murdering scum, Mulligan. You should be rotting in hell."

Jack smiled grimly. Superintendent Brown was a real sweetheart, even if he did have bad breath. His assessment was correct, too...he had killed. In fact, he'd killed twice. There was no getting around the history or the bloody facts. Maybe Jack should have paid a higher price, but that was up to the courts, and they said he was rehabilitated.

If only he hadn't scored so high on that damn SAT test when the board had given it to the whole Institution last year. The college entrance exams were supposed to show the powers in the State Legislature that education in the State Juvenile Detention system was totally inadequate. Armed with this data, the board could then ask for more money for education.

Strange how politicians liked to appropriate money for things such as education, but never followed up to see where the money was spent or if it did any good. There was probably some bureaucrat presently lining his pockets with all that appropriated, prison education

5

money for it never reached the Inside. The lack of supplies and decent books in the classrooms he had attended was chronic and probably always would be.

The SAT results had indicated a massive failure of the prison's education system, but Jack had stood out as an anomaly.

He had scored well above the national average. In fact, his score was so impressive that the state decided to send him to college despite his past criminal record. Of course, a well placed news article by an eager beaver reporter hadn't hurt. The subsequent publicity had turned the corner away from any opposition. Soon, he became the State Juvenile Detention Board's poster boy to demonstrate how problem kids could turn their lives around with more education and more government money in the pot.

After deciding Jack's fate, the State of Ohio had canvassed an array of colleges and universities to accept him. None, however, were willing to even look at what they considered a dangerous murderer. No school needed that kind of publicity. Homicidal maniacs were not a selling point for worried parents.

Finally, however, tiny Mt. Sidney College, an all black school, said they'd take Jack but only if considerably more funding came their way. A deal was struck between the State and the college, of which Jack knew none of the details. However, there was one big catch.

Wasn't there always a catch?

If, for any reason, Jack caused any kind of problem, or if any criminal act, such as theft, rape or murder, involved him, he would immediately be taken to a maximum security prison for the rest of his life. School would definitely be out, forever.

When Jack had left his cell two days before, he had heard that the guards had bets on how long he'd last. There weren't too many takers on the long term odds, and nobody thought he'd stay clean for even a week. Jack shook his head. He'd show them. Damn straight he'd show them.

As much as he thought this school was the wrong one for him, it would have to do. He didn't have options. Mt. Sydney, Jack knew, was the only chance for a future he'd ever have. He couldn't fail—he just couldn't.

***

"Hey look, it's a white boy comin' this way," announced Keysha Jordan over her shoulder.

"Haven't you ever seen one?" laughed Danielle Myers from across the room.

"Yeah, but this one actually looks good."

Both girls were eighteen years old and had just met as roommates the day before. Fortunately, both seemed to click instantly with their shared backgrounds and spirited personalities. It was as if their lives had bizarrely mirrored one another, like sisters.

Both had grown up in upper middle class backgrounds. Keysha was from Pittsburgh and Danielle from Philadelphia. Both had gone through the same regimen of dance lessons, piano lessons and horseback riding. Both had gotten braces for their teeth the same year and had them the same number of years. In high school, both had been on the student council, were cheerleaders, honor students and were extremely popular.

The girls could hardly believe these parallels.

After talking half the night, Keysha had even blushed when she suggested they probably lost their virginity on the same night.

Despite these similar coincidences, their physical appearances were in stark contrast.

Keysha had smooth, light brown skin and an exotic beauty, her jet black hair hung in a thick braid past her waist. Wherever she walked, guys would stop and stare. Her trim athletic body accentuated her full round breasts and endless legs.

Danielle, on the other hand, was darker with short curly hair, large sensuous eyes and full luscious lips. What made her stand out was a figure that wouldn't quit. Her body was voluptuous from her large breasts, firm small waist to her perfectly shaped legs.

Her girl friends in high school had told her that every man she met couldn't help but drool. Danielle had always noticed this reaction, but considered it humorous. If boys wanted to get all hot and bothered by her passing, so be it. They could look, but they could not touch.

"I wonder if he's a student?" asked Keysha absently.

Danielle laughed from across the room, "At Mt. Sidney? Girl, he's probably a maintenance man."

"With a suitcase?"

"What?"

Danielle came to the window.

"He's definitely tough looking. Look at his arms and chest. Big, big, big. Oooh, I like him."

Keysha laughed, "I saw him first."

"He must be poor," countered Danielle. "Look how he's dressed."

"Jeans and an old blue shirt. He must think he's a hippie. His hair is sort of long, too. I think he's sexy lookin'."

"He's white!"

"So?"

Danielle rolled her eyes, "So…what's he doin' here? This is a black college. If he's here, then some deserving brother or sister is sittin' at home."

"You can't believe that, Danielle?" Keysha said, thinking how this was their first disagreement.

"Girl, get real. It's the white man's world. We is the niggers to them. There's plenty of schools for white boys to go to. Why here?"

Keysha shook her head, "Danielle, I think both whites and blacks have to get that kind of thinking out of their heads. If we don't learn to get past some things, we'll all be doomed."

"That would be fine, Keysha if we had what they have—all the money and power—but we don't. They ain't gonna let us have it either. We got to take it."

Keysha smiled at her serious new friend. "There's plenty for everyone. You'll see. Who knows, maybe this white boy doesn't have much, himself."

"That's the worst," replied Danielle smartly. "Who needs to be white and poor? How bad can things get?"

Suddenly, a bolt of lightening lit up the darkness outside and a loud crack of thunder rattled the windows. Both girls caught their breaths and stepped back from the window.

Then the lights went out.

9

***

Robert Brent cursed and shook his head one more time as he looked at the file on his desk and recalled the meeting with Dean Jans. A convicted murderer was comin' to this dorm. Shit! He rubbed the bridge of his nose and stared at the file. What was on the Dean of Admissions' mind? How could he and the Board let a murderer, such as this Jack Mulligan, into a respectable school, among good kids?

"Damn," he muttered.

Robert Brent, Head Resident at Lincoln Hall was a big man, a first year graduate student, broad shouldered and muscular, with a shaved head like Michael Jordan and brooding, sharp eyes. He looked like a former athlete. And, he had been a fair defensive end at Ohio State until a blown-out knee ended his pro-football dreams. Instead of crying about his fate though, he did well in school and studied hard. Now he was here at Mt. Sidney getting his masters degree in business administration.

Being Head Resident meant that he was responsible for this jerk Mulligan's behavior and actions. On top of everything else, this jailbird had to be white. Why didn't the Administration paint a big target on the fucker's chest and kill him now.

Sure, most of the students couldn't care less, but the handful who did...That sort of trouble was something Brent dreaded.

At least, Jans had sympathized with his plight. No one seemed to want this murderer here at Mt. Sidney. But, to everyone's dismay, the Board of Trustees had approved Mulligan's application and handed the whole matter over to Jans, who in turn, handed it to Brent. Shit always rolled downhill.

Robert hated criminals. His father, may he burn in hell, had been one, a cheap hustler who had beaten up old ladies for their welfare checks. One of the old ladies, though, made the mistake of dying, and Brent's father spent the rest of his short, pathetic life in jail. He was killed by another convict in a fight over a carton of cigarettes.

Brent could still remember the weekend visitations at the prison. He and his mother would catch a bus from Harlem for the long ride upstate. It took hours. When they got there, his father would be sullen, trying to act like he had everything under control. Brent's mother would cry in front of his father, and he'd curse at her. Then all the way back home she would weep.

He hated his father for ruining his mother's life. To her last breath, she had died loving him. People like him didn't deserve love. How could she have been so foolish? He would always hate his father for being a fucking convict who never amounted to anything.

Looking at the folder once again, Brent saw the same vacuous, institutional appearance in Jack Mulligan's mug shots as he had in his father's. Dread filled him as he studied the photo. A scarred, hardened face stared back at him. This guy had murdered his own father and then another inmate years later. What would he do to anyone who crossed him here in Lincoln Hall?

The trouble was, Robert Brent couldn't warn the kids who lived here. Dean Jans had made it clear that no one, NO ONE, was to know about Jack Mulligan's background.

"All we need is for the parents of these kids from your dorm or anywhere else on campus finding out about this white boy's past. We would be ruined."

Now Jack Mulligan was Brent's problem. Handle it, had been Jans' message to him. A determined look came to his face. The same face he'd shown to opponents when he played defensive end. Brent had gotten word that the Mulligan was arriving this afternoon. He'd just have to make the best of it.

Maybe this white boy would change his mind and not show up. Maybe the jailbird would fly. One could only hope.

As Brent shook his head one more time and closed the file, the lights went out.

***

Jack saw the lightning flash and the lights go out in all the windows and doors at once just before a wall of rain hit him. Well there goes the electricity, he noted. Fortunately, he was on the sidewalk alongside the building next to Lincoln Hall. He spotted a small doorway ahead and quickly ducked into it.

Putting his suitcase down, he looked out at the dark and now forbidding landscape of the campus. He remembered lying in bed during summer storms, such as this one, when he was small, when the sky would explode, gather itself and explode again with endless thunder claps. The lightning would flash like an uncontrolled strobe and bleach the night with hideous, artificial light. He would be so frightened, he'd duck under his covers and shake.

He then felt a trickle of water run-down his face across the scar that cleaved his once handsome features. The scar ran from his forehead to his jawbone and gave him a sinister look, one that didn't allow him to ever smile with any kind of warmth. He had almost died when it had happened. Now the long scar kept most people at a distance. Maybe there was a benefit to disfigurement, a nightmarish perk for eight years in the State Juvenile Detention Institution.

He recalled the day five years before when he had received this mark. A bad-ass black kid nicknamed Zero, real name Elvin as his Mama called him, had caused a problem for most of the white kids Inside. Even some of the brothers were scared of him. Calling him a school yard bully would have been a gross understatement. His psychosis was a deep, sick hatred of anything white.

Zero had killed at least two kids who had crossed him and had injured several others. Nothing could be proven, of course. Who would talk? No one was that stupid. Zero had his lieutenants, several brothers who would do anything for him, especially to stay in his good graces.

One day, Jack was assigned to a cleaning detail in the A wing latrine. It was a long, narrow room with blue tiled walls and floor. Fifteen toilets in stalls lined one side and fifteen urinals faced them on the other side. In the back, of the room was a passageway into a large shower room.

Jack had mopped out the shower room and was half done with the toilets, when Zero came strolling in to take a shower. With only a towel draped around his waist, he looked massive. Hours in the weight room had produced a toned, muscular body that looked dangerous. Jack stayed clear as Zero walked by. He wanted no part of him.

When Zero entered the shower room, Jack breathed easier. The shower room echoed the footsteps, and a moment later Jack heard the water go on. He doubled his efforts to get done. Zero was not someone to get noticed by, especially if you were white. Using all his strength, Jack mopped faster and faster.

Then Jack heard Zero come out of the shower and walk back into the latrine. "Hey you, motherfucker," Zero shouted. "Get me some new soap in here. Now!"

Jack gave Zero a blank look. His blood froze. He knew the Institution's policy of using up the bars of soap before more were issued. Jack also knew that there was soap in the shower room. He also was aware that Zero didn't want to use any soap that wasn't just out of the box.

Pretending not to hear him, Jack went on with his work.

"Hey you, chief," Zero warned. "You'd best get that motherfuckin' pale ass of yours in gear. You hear me?"

Jack looked up.

"There's soap in there."

"Say what?"

"I said, there's soap in there."

"Motherfucker, I don't want any soap that touched your scrawny, white ass," Zero said, stepping closer. "Now get me some new soap."

14

"No," said Jack to his own disbelief. He heard the answer come from his mouth but couldn't quite believe he had said it. Did he have a death wish? It was as though he were detached from the present, a third party observing everything from afar.

Zero's face turned to stone. Nobody, especially a white motherfucker, said no to him.

"That's a big fuckin' mistake, motherfucker," he said as he marched toward Jack. An asskicking was about to go down, and Jack knew it was his ass.

It could have been the tone of Zero's voice or Jack's hatred of bullies that caused him to react. Guys who shoved their weight around just naturally pissed him off. Besides, Jack didn't like being issued orders by this clown.

Jack readied himself for Zero's onslaught. With the floor being as wet as it was, he picked up the heavy rag mop and waited for Zero to get close. Zero never imagined that someone as insignificant as Jack might retaliate. That was unthinkable. Jack waited for the right moment to move and then whirled a shot into Zero's unprotected groin.

The mop head hit smoothly, forcefully and right on target.

The big kid looked stunned and then sick. He rolled onto the floor holding his crotch. Vomit spewed from his mouth.

Jack remembered with satisfaction the shock of seeing the baddest guy in the Institution curled up on the floor, throwing up on himself. All he could do was stare. It was a moment to be savored. Then Jack considered that at any moment, Zero might rise up like the Phoenix and stomp his brains out, so he made a hasty retreat. Besides, some of the brothers might walk in and things would get dark and ugly fast.

Backing slowly out of the latrine, Jack ran to one of the common areas, where the guards always lounged. Later that night, one of his friends told him that Zero had him on his "shit list." The list was a euphemism reserved for those individuals Zero was going to eliminate. A tingle ran down Jack's spine when he heard the news. Trouble was sho'nuf coming his way.

In the cafeteria that day, it was confirmed when he caught Zero's eyes, and Zero made a gesture with his hand as if slashing his throat. Jack swallowed hard. The die was cast. He had to do something if he wanted to live.

With the best defense being a strong offense, the first thing Jack obtained was a sharp homemade shiv from his friend, Roger. The shiv had been made from a piece of steel Roger had pilfered from a bed frame and then, over months, sharpened to a fine edge.

In his heart, Jack now knew he would have to kill Zero to survive. There would be no mediation, no reprieve. The Superintendent, the guards, not even God could stop it. This wouldn't be an innocent school yard fight. This would be a battle for dominance—prison style. Zero wanted to dominate Jack and others. He was willing to kill to achieve this power. Jack, for better or worse, wouldn't tolerate this scheme of things.

A sense of dread invaded Jack. Maybe he should try to appease Zero, but no, he just couldn't do that. Then he'd become Zero's bitch, and life would be lived without dignity of any kind. But unlike killing his father, Zero was virtually a stranger. Until two days ago, Jack had only seen him around the yard strutting like a gaming rooster. He doubted that Zero noticed or had any memory of him. That changed when the mop smacked Zero's balls.

Jack knew instinctively to keep the shiv on his person at all times. Zero would attack when least expected. If Jack wasn't ready, he'd be dead. Getting caught carrying the shiv was of no consequence next to his death.

Four days passed without incident. Then on the afternoon of the fifth day, one of the guards sent Jack to the library to fetch the daily paper. Jack hurried to get the paper but as he left the library, he paused in the hallway. Something was wrong. Call it gut feeling or intuition—something wasn't right. Quickly, he took the shiv from inside his shirt and put it inside the newspaper.

To get back to the guard station, Jack had to walk down two long hallways that were perpendicular to one another. He was just turning the corner to the second hall, when Zero stepped out in front of him. No one had to inform him that the older, bigger youth was there to keep a deadly promise. Zero's eyes were slitted under a dark brow, and his left hand was holding something out of sight behind his leg.

"You ready to die, white boy?" he asked in a deep resonant voice.

"We all gotta' go, sometime."

"Well your time is today, motherfucker."

Jack couldn't believe how fast Zero closed the distance between them. An elbow caught Jack on the chin sending him to the floor. This was followed by three or four solid kicks to his rib cage. Jack couldn't get his breath and suspected his ribs were broken.

Fortunately, Jack held on to the newspaper with the shiv inside. He'd have to hope he'd get one good shot at Zero, but now wasn't the time.

Another kick, this time to the head almost knocked him out. Jack didn't see the knife Zero was wielding. Then came the click and a metallic flash of a switchblade. Zero's brisk thrust would have taken Jack's throat out, but instead he rolled and the knife sliced his face from top to bottom. The skin of his cheek hung down in an uncontrollable flap.

Blood poured onto the floor, and Jack felt himself fainting. If he did, he would die. It was only through a timely rush of adrenalin and a clear sense of survival that his consciousness held him together.

Zero laughed hard.

"Hey motherfucker, look at chu bleed. You gonna die so ugly ain't chu?"

Jack, on all fours, spat through the blood, gripping the still hidden shiv hard. He had to wait his chance. He'd have only one.

When Zero straddled over him with the switchblade poised for his end, Jack figured the time was right.

Zero bent over and hissed, "Goodnight, motherfucker."

With that, Jack sprang from the floor catching Zero's exposed underside. Using all his strength, he plunged the entire shiv into the larger boy's solar plexus; then yanked hard on the handle to cut up Zero's insides.

Zero's eyes widened and his breath stopped as if shut off with a switch. He was stunned beyond pain. His face darkened with a blank expression.

Thanks again to Warren, the junkman, and his long ago advice.

Zero dropped his knife, made one gurgling sound in his throat and fell over. His legs kicked rhythmically, much like his father's had, but he didn't speak. Disbelief impressed itself on his handsome features. The shiv must have pierced the heart. An unnatural paleness suddenly came to Zero, like a mask of doom, and he died seconds later.

Zero's last breath sprayed blood across the floor. Then more blood poured from his mouth in an ever widening circle. That's when Jack passed out.

Several days later, Jack woke up in the Institution's hospital with his feet shackled to the bed. His face felt odd, almost wooden. He remembered the fight with Zero. Touching his face, he could feel the stitches across his cheek, a permanent reminder of his struggle to survive. He realized he wasn't going to win any beauty contests from now on, but he was alive.

Over the next several days, doctors and cops interviewed him non-stop. They wanted to know all about the fight with Zero.

Jack stuck to the fact that he had fought in self-defense. However, when the cops asked about the shiv in Zero's chest, he lied, telling them that Zero had wanted a fair fight and had tossed the shiv to him before the action took place.

Jack saw the knowing smiles on their faces and their eyes rolling toward the heavens. The tale was a stretch for anyone to believe.

No one bought it either, but Jack knew his only hope was to stick to the lie and not deviate from its untruth. There was no sense getting a lot of other guys involved.

When he was nearly recovered, an inquest was held, and Jack had an additional manslaughter charge tacked onto his sentence. He could have cared less. He already knew he'd never get out of prison. The Superintendent gleefully told him he'd be behind bars for a long, long time.

Fuck the Superintendent.

The rain was pouring hard on the buildings and trees of Mt. Sidney College.

Here I am, Mr. Superintendent Brown. Jack Mulligan, freshman at Mt. Sidney College with a major in biology. Your prediction was wrong. I'm free. I'm here you sonuvabitch.

Nothing was going to stop him, not the Superintendent, not the Juvenile Parole Board and certainly not these asshole nig…black kids.

Jack blanched at the thought of the word, nigger. It was the kind of ignorant crap he now wanted out of his life. He was starting over and didn't need any prison hate mentality. Here, at this school, he'd meet all kinds of people, some good and some not so good. But grouping them together as "niggers" wasn't right and wouldn't get him anywhere.

The time to change was now, and he would change.

Looking out at the rain, Jack waited for a lull, which gradually came about ten minutes later. He was tired of standing in the doorway. He wanted to go forward to his new home, no matter what it was like.

Grabbing his suitcase, he started for Lincoln Hall.

CHAPTER 2

Admiring himself in the mirror was one of Raymon Jackson's favorite pastimes. The handsome, black athlete was now in his second year at Mt. Sidney College with a full athletic scholarship as a stand-out tailback on the football team. His physical prowess, both on and off the gridiron, was hailed by men, boys and women—especially good looking women.

When the electricity shut down in his room at Lincoln Hall, he had been flexing his chest muscles making his enormous pecs dance on his chest. The control of every fiber of his body was so cool.

Raymon loved the way he looked. He checked out the rippling athletic body he possessed—the body he worked on constantly. The definition in his massive arms, broad chest and back and six-pack abdominals caused women, young and old, to breath hot sighs.

He knew the bitches all desired him. They couldn't help themselves.

The final touch in Raymon's magnetic love arsenal, however, was when he turned on his perfect, glowing smile. That was what made the hardest, most frigid of them, melt. No woman could resist his magical charms. None.

Raymon examined his white, even teeth in the mirror and, of course, the rest of his beautiful face. What a package. "How incredible can you get?" he thought.

Then a bright strike of lighting followed by a clap of thunder rattled the windows and the lights went out.

"Motherfucker!" he muttered irritably.

Motherfucker was Raymon's most often used word. He had developed a whole language with that one word. He could use it for practically every situation life presented to him. The word also seemed to fit into nearly every part of speech and tense.

Now he had a big problem. Raymon had to get ready for a hot rendezvous with a honey from Delta Alpha Delta. How could he do this without electricity? He needed lights to see himself. With the dusk and heavy storm outside, the dorm room was virtually dark.

Grabbing a tee-shirt from the bed, he quickly got dressed and went to the window. All the lights were off in the other buildings around the campus. Damn, he hated this mother nature bullshit. These fuckin' late summer storms always ended up knocking the electricity out when they struck.

A knock on the door sounded behind him.

"Yeah," he yelled.

The door swung open, revealing a giant man with an expansive grin on his face.

"Hey, Raymon whatcha' doin'?" said the man in a deep baritone voice.

It was his best friend, Tyrel Friday—the biggest, baddest defensive end in the Conference. Tyrel was an immense man at six-foot-six inches and two hundred eighty-five pounds. His size and strength were unprecedented. Talk of an early draft came from NFL scouts looking him over. For this, Raymon was naturally jealous. These same scouts should be keeping their eyes on him and no one else.

Raymon raised his hands, "Sittin' here in the motherfuckin' dark."

"I can see that."

Tyrel continued to smile his big toothy grin.

Raymon shook his head in disgust. "I got a sweet thing waitin' for me, home. What's she gonna think if I'm not pretty? Damn electric be fuckin' things up. Shit!"

"Hey it happens, man."

"Not to me, it don't."

Tyrel pointed at the hallway, "Hey my man, don't despair. Everyone's goin' to the lobby to party. Why don't you come, too?"

"A party?"

"That's right. I saw some fine lookin' stuff makin' their way down."

"Pussy?"

"You know it."

A party with girls was all Raymon had to hear.

"Sheeit! Then what am I standin' here talking to your ugly ass for? Let's go," Raymon said resolutely, heading for the door. "If there's some fine stuff waitin' for me, how can I deny them my humble self."

23

Tyrel laughed and shook his head, "That's what I've always liked about chu, Raymon. You always bein' so humble."

***

"What a sexy hunk that white boy is," observed Juleel Washington to himself, just before the electricity failed.

He had been watching a beautifully sculpted male creature strolling across the tree lined campus for five whole minutes. His inner gay child was piqued into immediate turmoil. Could God, not the God Reverend Watson said hated gays, be showing him his mate for a life-time. His mother had said he'd meet such a person. The irony, he had to admit, was that his mother probably still hoped his life's mate would be female.

Juleel kept up his observance, "My, my, my he is my type."

Juleel, a freshman, was slight of build and very dark with big expressive eyes. His natural and many effeminate gestures unfortunately labeled him as gay. He tried dressing like other guys but had to admit he loved feminine fashions more. The colors and textures, in his opinion, were so much more interesting.

Juleel had grown up in the small town of Walnutburg, Ohio, where he was not only the only black student in school but also the only gay person. This proved to be a lethal combination in a small, predominately white, definitely redneck town. At school, he was the brunt of hundreds of practical jokes and insults. All the white boys and girls, without exception, hated him for either being black or gay or both.

He learned to endure the cruel behavior, but the price was high. Not only did he bear the emotional scars of hatred but the physical scars as well.

He had been beaten up on more than one occasion. His nose was broken four times, his jaw twice and as near as he could tell, he only had three natural remaining teeth, the rest were caps. Seven different bones in his arms and shoulders, plus six ribs had also been fractured at one time or another. His face had one round, raised scar from the time he was held down and burned with a lit cigar. Gaybashing by the town's rednecks was considered a sport, and he knew if he didn't escape, they'd eventually kill him.

His single mom had complained incessantly to the police and to the school's principal but to no avail. He couldn't be guarded and protected twenty-four hours a day, they told her. Working two jobs, all she could do was instruct her son to be more careful and hope he could avoid attack. However, like a pack of hungry wolves drawn to blood, that hope was shattered by continued assaults.

Finally, Juleel dropped out of school and for two years studied at home under his mother's tutelage. He received his GED and after a good SAT score was able to apply to various colleges and universities. With his acceptance to all-black Mt. Sidney College, Juleel was able to at least eliminate one obstacle, his color, as a reason for discrimination.

Juleel's immediate problem was getting a roommate. His original roommate, a guy named George, had arrived just that morning and, after he and his parents had met Juleel, the father had gone to talk to Robert Brent. Juleel could sense something wrong. Twenty minutes later, Juleel was called into the hallway by Robert Brent and told he would have to pack and move to another room. A new roommate would be assigned to him.

The whole incident was humiliating. Why did he have to move? Why not George? Obviously, Juleel knew the answer to his questions. George's parents didn't want him around their precious son. He could imagine what George's father said to Robert Brent.

"No red-blooded son of mine is rooming with a faggot. George is impressionable. Why who knows what that queer will do?"

Juleel felt sad at the thought. He'd heard all this before.

Regardless of what was said, Juleel had moved his belongings to a smaller room on the ground floor. It was noticeably closer to the main desk and the lobby. Juleel surmised that Brent could therefore keep a closer eye on him. The Head Resident wouldn't want the fag causing more problems.

Juleel had just finished unpacking when he spotted the white boy and then the power went off.

Juleel stood still in the dark. Oh darn, he thought, this is all I need.

Thunder growled outside again as if to mock him.

He laid down on his bed and curled up in a fetal position. He thought of his mother who was working extra jobs back in Walnutburg to pay for his college expenses. She was the only one who truly believed in him or unconditionally loved him. Loneliness crept into his soul like an unwanted visitor, and tears started welling up in his eyes. He was homesick.

No disguise would work for him. Who was he trying to kid, everyone could see he was gay. A sign might as well be hung around his neck proclaiming it. The simple fact was he couldn't hide that part of himself.

He felt his cheeks get wet and wiped them with the back of his hand. Juleel had always been alone and friendless and probably always would be.

***

"I hate this!" screamed Danielle, her breath coming in short gasps.

Keysha looked at her new friend and saw the shocking signs of panic. "Are you alright, girl?"

Just her soothing voice seemed to calm Danielle out of a bout of hysteria. She was nearly losing it.

"Yeah, I'm okay," Danielle said, breathlessly. "It's just that I get very nervous around thunder and lightning. It's always scared me."

Keysha put her arms around Danielle. She felt her shaking and recognized the phobic panic in Danielle's voice. "Hey girl, I'm here. Nothing is gonna hurt you. We're safe in here, let's just hang out."

"What are we going to do here in the dark?" Danielle said, her voice once again quaking.

"Talk girl. Hey, we'll even have a little party."

"A party?"

"Sure, it'll be fun."

A soft rap came from the door and Mary, the accounting major next door, suddenly peeked in. "Hey you guys, want to go down to the lobby? Everyone's headed that way. It looks like fun."

Keysha's eyes brightened. This was just the prescription Danielle needed. "Sure, we'd love to go. We've even got some candles. We'll bring them."

"Great, see you down there," Mary exclaimed excitedly, shutting the door.

"See, this will be fun," said Keysha.

She jumped into action, realizing that if she got Danielle moving, the girl's tears would disappear.

"Grab the candles, Danielle, they're on the dresser."

Keysha had always been a natural leader and organization was her thing. When she saw her roommate's distress, she knew it was time to swing into action.

Danielle rose to her feet and gathered the candles, while Keysha picked out a Puff Daddy CD. Someone would have a portable boom box for music.

"Come on let's go," Danielle pronounced, her fear already disapating.

Keysha smiled.

"I'm ready!"

A party always worked wonders.

***

"Damn, we got some sweet stuff comin' here, Tyrel," Raymon observed in his usual cocky way. He surveyed the lobby for what he thought of as new pussy. These girls needed him. He, of course, was there for them.

"Thought you were more interested in what's her name from the Delta house?" Tyrel quizzed.

"She can wait, my man. This here, Tyrel," mused Raymon pointing to all the girl's gathered in the crowded lobby, "is a mission of mercy. I'm just tryin' to spread my charms around. Know what I'm sayin'?"

Tyrel shook his head at his friend's self-assured attitude.

Raymon was the first to spot several fellow ball players holding court around a couch in the center of the room. So he and Tyrel drifted over and started some friendly banter.

"Hey Raymon, you checkin' out some of these babes?" Walter Justice, the tight-end said, as he panned the crowd.

"I be doin' that, brother. But don't you be gettin' your own hopes up too high. You know these bitches all have their eyes on me."

"Shit, Raymon, they want quality, not quantity."

Raymon laughed, "Well Walter, that's true. You never would be accused of havin' quantity."

Several of the players, including Walter, laughed.

"I got enough to satisfy, my man. You just be jealous, of course, since you can't give'm anything past one minute."

"How you know that, motherfucker? You been watchin'?"

"The word be out on you, Raymon."

"Shee-it, listen to this nigger," said Raymon with a dismissive wave of his hand.

This same trash talk went on every day almost like a verbal practice. It always centered around girls, sexual prowess and sports. The verbal digs were for close-knit friends only and most times meant little to the participants.

A boom-box erupted in the room and spread a steady pounding beat of Snoop Doggy Dog through the air. Soon, Raymon forgot about his hot date at the Delta House and settled into partying.

Keysha, Danielle and several other girls walked into the lobby and sat down on the floor about twenty feet from the athletes. They chatted about school, various professors and, of course, boys. When the boom-box came on, it nearly drowned out their voices, but over the music they could still hear the athletes talking, especially Raymon.

As Keysha watched and listened, she couldn't help but notice how arrogant and self assured the well built guy in the center appeared to be. The way he talked— so loud—reminded her of several boys she had known in high school. They had worked at being the centers of attention. This guy, she observed, was the same way. She had never cared for self-centered, boastful types, but she had to admit that this guy was good looking and seemed to have a ton of charisma.

Tyrel nudged Raymon and pointed out the girls who were quietly talking a short distance away.

Raymon raised his eyebrows, "Lord have mercy."

He gave Tyrel a knowing look and as if drawn by a magnet, the two threaded their way through the crowd to where Keysha and Danielle were seated.

Sliding around to Keysha's side, Raymon tried to grab her attention by sizing up her body from head to toe with his eyes. Keysha, for her part, was embarrassed by this behavior and tried her best to totally ignore him. However, her girl friends giggled at Raymon's antics.

"Hey girl, I've got to know who you are. You be sittin' there lookin' fine...definitely got it goin'."

Keysha glared at him, "I beg your pardon?"

"What?"

"Do you want something?" She said coldly.

"Most definitely."

She heard laughter.

"Well then, you certainly don't know how to get it."

Everyone around Raymon, including Tyrel, laughed and said, "Ooh."

Raymon frowned, "Girl, don't be givin' me no white bread answer like that."

Keysha didn't even bother to answer but dismissed Raymon as a fool by turning her head back to her friends. This only served to infuriate Raymon. Who'd this bitch think she was trying to play with? Raymon Jackson was never snubbed or ignored.

***

Tyrel Friday, in the meantime, introduced himself to Danielle in a much quieter way. Just her smile and dark thoughtful eyes were enough to captivate him.

"You're from Philly?" he said shyly. "So am I."

"Where'd you go to school?"

"North Region One."

"Oh wow! I went to Barringer." she said excitedly.

Tyrel smiled, "We used to play against your team. Were you a cheerleader?"

Danielle laughed, "Yeah, how'd you guess?"

31

"You just have that way about you. You know happy, like nothin' much bothers you."

Danielle could feel herself blushing.

"Well some things do occasionally bother me."

Tyrel fumbled for words. "I didn't mean...you know...that you didn't care about anything."

Danielle smiled. She immediately liked this giant. A man with a heart, especially an athlete. Tyrel was a pleasant surprise.

"I'm amazed, I don't remember you from any of the games," he said. "I always tried to check out the cheerleaders."

"Well I wish you had taken the time to check me out," she said, warmly.

***

Rejection was something that Raymon Jackson wasn't used to and didn't care for. Girls were suppose to fall like dominoes when they saw him coming. How could this small town freshman not be thrilled to have a minor god, such as himself, even talk to her? Was she so ignorant? Did she realize that he could make or break her socially at Mt. Sidney? He'd even given her his patented killer smile.

Maybe a new, more gentle tact was all that was needed to melt her frigid exterior. He bent close to her ear.

"Listen, I'm sorry if I came on too strong."

Keysha turned so she was within inches of his face, "Maybe you did."

Ah yes, this one needed the gentler touch. Raymon lowered his voice as he squatted next to her, "I'm

Raymon Jackson. I was just messin' with you. All I
wanted to do was meet you."

"I'm Keysha Jordan." she said in a matter-of-fact
way.

"You're a freshman, I'd guess."

"Yes, how did you know?"

"I haven't seen you here before." said Raymon,
while never taking his eyes off her. "What are you here
for?"

"I'm going to study Sociology."

Raymon chuckled and pointed, "That's what Tyrel,
there is majoring in. He thinks he's going to save the
world."

"I'd say that's very noble."

"Noble?"

"Yes."

"You still soundin' like them white girls from the
suburbs."

"Well I…"

A piercing flash from outside stopped everyone's
breath, as outside a large oak tree exploded from the
impact of a bolt of lightning. The accompanying crack
of thunder was deafening and all the windows and
doors shook from the impact.

Several girls, including Danielle, screamed and
everyone stiffened from the shock.

Finally, as if to get life back into the crowd, two or
three of the students switched on their flashlights to
look outside. When the beams converged on the large
glass, double-doors another vision froze the hearts of
the gathering.

Standing on the other side of the door, as still as a
statue, was a tall, muscular white boy. How long had

he been there, no one could tell. He just stood, silently watching them? The beams of the flashlights illuminated a deeply scarred, brutal face glaring in a harsh, sinister way.

Two girls close to the door clutched their chests, screamed and backed away for safety.

Keysha and Danielle felt their lungs stop, as a chill ran down their backs.

Even Raymon's eyes widened as he whispered.

"Motherfucker."

CHAPTER 3

Thaddeus Brown was born under the poorest of circumstances in a small coal camp in eastern Kentucky. His father was a solid no-nonsense man who had labored in the mines for fifteen years, and his mother worked as a checker at the drug store.

Being an only child was lonely, but his mother had told him, she couldn't have any more children. Like his parents, young Thaddeus worked as hard as he could. At school he was one of the top students with a solid A average. He also had a part-time job at the company store making deliveries. Everyone in town knew Thaddeus and liked him. He was spirited, intelligent and most of all funny.

The young black boy always had an arsenal of jokes, which he told in dramatic fashion. He realized that the secret to telling a good story was in the storyteller's timing of events. He had listened carefully to older, retired miners who were good at yarns and had picked up their techniques. Then, he worked on saving punch lines, till just the right moment.

Thaddeus knew that if he cheered up people who were ill or just depressed, the forthcoming tip would be more generous. The extra money was a welcome relief to the family's cookie jar economy and this made Thaddeus proud.

On the day Thaddeus was supposed to graduate from high school, his mother was working on some frayed spots on his second-hand, gray suit, which had been passed to him from an uncle. It didn't seem to fit as well as it had a few months before. His mother smiled at her son with pride. He was turning into a tall, well-built young man. His grades were clearly the best of all his classmates, and his teachers were beaming with the possibility he might go to college. Not many young men or women ever made it out of the hills of eastern Kentucky. It was a time of great hope.

His mother had just resized one of the sleeves of his jacket, when a dull rumble shook the house. Mother and son looked at one another in instant shock. Fear etched every pore of their faces.

Then another loud explosion cracked the windows and sent pictures tumbling from the walls.

"Oh my God!" exclaimed his mother. Her eyes darted in the direction of the street.

"The mine!" shouted Thaddeus.

His father was at work in the mine. The explosion must have come from there. His father's shift wasn't supposed to end for another two hours.

Thaddeus ran into the street where neighbors were hurrying to the east side of town. The mine was located on a hillside there. Looking in that direction, he could see billowing clouds of black smoke rising from the mine's portal. Was his father safe or...? He couldn't think the worst. Thaddeus' heart raced, even though he had no idea what he could possibly do once he got there.

A growing crowd of women and children waited outside a chain link fence which guarded the entrance. All seemed to be chaos. Screams and shouts came from everywhere. Mine employees were racing here and there. Over a hundred men were trapped below.

All day rescuers tried in vain to enter the smoke-filled coal mine. Methane gas seemed to be the problem. A build up of the deadly gas had caused the initial blast, but now more of the volatile gas and suspended coal dust were preventing any attempt to recover survivors.

All the next day and night work went on as more and more volunteers came from the surrounding area and neighboring states. Helping each other was something poor miners understood well.

Thad's mother didn't sleep for three days until she finally collapsed outside the mine. Thaddeus carried her back to the house and laid her down on her bed. He noticed how frail and bony her body was and her gray hair seemed suddenly to be turning white. His mother was aging before his eyes becoming old and worn. Gone was her vitality, gone was her attitude of hope.

His mother slept for twenty hours and when she woke she rushed back to the mine entrance. She was angry that Thaddeus had let her sleep so long. What kind of wife was she, sleeping while her husband was struggling for his life?

Representatives from the company came eight days after the explosion and announced that there was nothing further they could do to rescue the men. Wives and children silently glared at them in grim resignation. These well dressed middle managers were the same people who allowed dangerous conditions to fester inside the deep mines. Implementing safety precautions cost too much money and money couldn't be wasted on dirty, ignorant coal miners. The executives made the big bucks, lived in penthouses in New York and dined in fancy restaurants, while men like Thad's father existed in drafty, company-owned shacks, ate beans and cornbread and bled and died of black lung and worse, down in the mines.

A decision was made, an executive order was then passed down.

The mine was sealed by a loud explosion on the tenth day. The funerals began shortly after at all the local churches.

Thaddeus' mother was broken. She became a despondent ghost of her former self and overnight seemed to wither. Working harder than ever, she did her best to forget her dead husband but sadly failed in her efforts. She had loved Thad's father too much to go on. Every day became a brave effort wrought with pain.

Her only hope was to get Thaddeus out of town before he was lured to the bottom of a coal mine.

The scholarships his teachers talked about never materialized. For their part, the teachers and counselors in his high school said they would continue to act on his behalf, but Thaddeus knew that nothing would come of it. For whatever reason, including his race, he had been turned down for every grant-in-aid.

Meanwhile, he held down two jobs: one at a feed mill and the other as a printer's assistant at the local newspaper. His mother forbade him seeking any kind of job in the mines, even though the pay was higher than other available employment. The fear in her eyes at the mere mention of the mines kept him away. She had lost a husband and didn't need to lose a son, too.

Eight months went by and Thaddeus tried to think optimistically that someday things might come his way. Then one afternoon, he came home from the mill and found his mother sitting peacefully in her favorite rocker. Too peacefully. Thaddeus knew her endless struggle was finally over. His mother had died of heart failure in her forty-first year, having worked herself to death.

Thaddeus was devastated. The day after the funeral, he quietly left town never to return. At first, he drifted west across the prairie states, getting work when he could as a laborer, dishwasher, bus boy, farm hand or any other temporary occupation. He still dreamed of going to college, but as the months turned into years and the years into many years, the dreams he had once nurtured, faded and then died altogether. Their ghosts became a mere reverie he recalled from time to time.

This didn't stop his thirst for knowledge, however. Thaddeus loved books, all kinds of books. In every town and village he came to, he haunted the local library. He read philosophy, history and literature at a voracious pace. The words of those who knew of humanity's struggle gave him comfort when all else was dark and frightening.

By the time he was twenty-seven years old, Thaddeus found himself in Oberlin, Ohio, working in a greasy-spoon diner. Oberlin College was nearby and every day he served breakfast to a stream of students and professors. He loved eavesdropping on their conversations, especially when they talked about books and ideas.

One of the regular customers was a dapper, sixty-something English professor named, Dr. Otis Westman. Westman was renowned for his literary criticism, which Thad had read and greatly admired.

One day, Thaddeus brought in one of Westman's books, Thoughts on Romantic Poetry from the Twentieth Century Perspective. *Thaddeus had read every page and considered it Dr. Westman's most brilliant book to date.*

While Westman sipped his coffee, Thaddeus shyly placed the book on the counter. "Dr. Westman uh...could you possibly, uh...autograph my book?"

Westman glanced up, saw his book in the bus boy's hand and turned his gaze to Thaddeus with astonishment. "You've read this book?"

"Yes sir. I've read all your books, but this one is your best. Your thoughts on Keats somewhat parallel mine."

Westman smiled as he took the book from Thaddeus. "Are you a student?"

"No sir," he said, bowing his head. "I can't afford that sort of thing."

Westman autographed the book, but before handing it back, he looked intently at Thaddeus. "You know it's heartening to find anyone, outside of graduate students, who read books such as this. I suggest you try going back to school, son. In fact, see me next week in my office, and maybe we can work something out."

Thaddeus' heart leaped, "Are you serious?"

"I wouldn't have said so if I didn't mean it."

For the next week, Thaddeus hardly slept a wink. All he could do was think about school and the possibility of learning. Maybe his one undying dream would come to pass.

On the day of the meeting, his nerves were raw. He prayed he wasn't getting his hopes too high. The meeting took place in Westman's office. Present were several people from the admissions department and the Dean's office. They gave Thaddeus a battery of tests, which showed him to be extremely bright. Westman was not only intrigued by the young man's intellect but also proud that he could possibly help a deserving scholar reach his potential.

The Dean of Admissions, with prodding from Westman, who Thaddeus found out later carried considerable clout at Oberlin, set him up with a scholarship grant and an on-campus job. Dr. Westman, ever true, gave him a dusty, apartment to live in over his garage. It was tiny, but it seemed like heaven to Thaddeus.

The next four years were like a dream to him. He soaked up knowledge like a dry sponge. Dr. Westman watched with satisfaction over his protégé's progress. Like a proud parent, he couldn't believe how intellectually disciplined Thaddeus became as an academian.

When he graduated with honors, a group of his friends gathered to celebrate at a bar just off Oberlin's

James Ankrom

campus. They laughed and talked into the night hours. Thaddeus told tales that enthralled and entertained everyone. He and his fellow graduates had worked hard, and the need to let go lasted till closing time, when everyone hugged and said their last goodbyes. Thaddeus was in a thinking mood and waved off offers to be driven home, opting instead to walk.

He was feeling good. The world was his at last. He owned it all. Graduate school lay ahead and then a very bright future. Perhaps teaching college would be a possibility.

But, everything crashed in a heartbeat.

With no warning, a white pickup truck stopped next to him and before he could even react, a group of men knocked him to the ground and a foul-smelling blanket was rudely pushed over his head. He was picked up then and tossed into the truck bed. Thaddeus struggled, screaming in outrage until something blunt struck his head and darkness flooded his brain.

He came back to the world later hearing raucus laughter. His head throbbed, and he couldn't seem to focus his eyes.

"Hey Billy Ray," said a deep voice, "look over there, the nigger's comin' to."

"I told you, you couldn't kill a nigger by hittin' one of'em in the head. They got them extra-thick skulls."

"Well he's gonna need his before the nights over," said a third voice.

All three laughed.

Thaddeus' eyes came back into focus, and he viewed the scene. Three white men were standing around a fair-sized camp fire warming their hands. He was next to a corn field with woods bordering on one side. The location was anyone's guess. All of the men were overweight and dressed in jeans, work boots and flannel shirts. Two of them had baseball caps on with insignias for tractor and construction equipment companies. Just three white guys having some fun on the weekend. To Thaddeus's dismay, he was the entertainment.

Thaddeus was tied with his hands behind his back to the bumper of a Ford pickup; his feet were also bound together. The pain was excruciating. He couldn't move or defend himself against these men, and chances were good, they planned to kill him.

A cold sweat soaked through his shirt and terror sent a shiver up his back. Why couldn't he have accepted that ride home from his friends? He'd be in bed now, safe and snug. Now, it was too late.

He didn't like the demeanor of these men. They appeared to be big, rough and crude, stereotypic rednecks who drank too much, ate too much, cursed and hated others, especially blacks and Jews, with no rationale or thought. What were these rednecks planning for him? Would they kill him? The situation didn't look promising.

Five minutes later, a set of headlights came into view. For a second, Thaddeus thought it might be help, but that hope faded in an instant. A fourth man arrived with two cases of beer and several bottles of some kind of whiskey. The four horsemen of the apocalypse, minus the horses. His fate was sealed, he feared. Thaddeus knew he was going to see trouble very shortly.

The four men drank for another two hours as they fortified themselves for some unspeakable task. Liquor would, of course, be their excuse. If tomorrow, they were to be asked by the police what they had done the night before, they could, to their satisfaction, say they didn't remember. They were drunk. It would be a neat, convenient excuse for unforgiveable brutality.

Thaddeus sat silently hoping they'd get so drunk they'd pass out. These were veterans of liquor consumption. An hour passed as they drank; then another hour. Finally, one of the men got up and walked over to him. He was maneuvering unsteadily as the liquor had done its job. His eyes revealed a glassy, amused twinkle.

"Where you going, Sonny?" one of the fat men at the fire asked.

"Gonna take a piss and talk to this nigger," he replied.

As soon as he stood over Thaddeus, Sonny unzipped his fly and pulled out his cock. A warm stream of acrid-smelling urine hit Thaddeus in the face. He tried to look way, but the white man kept adjusting the stream to hit Thaddeus' exposed face.

"How'd you like the shower, nigger?" he inquired in a lazy drawl. "Thought you might be a tad thirsty."

The other three laughed and came over to join Sonny.

"Fuck you!" Thaddeus shouted.

Out of nowhere, a steel-toed boot caught him in the face, smashing his nose. He saw stars, as blood gushed down past his mouth.

"Don't get smart-ass with me, nigger."

"Let's show this fuckin' nigger who's the boss," chimed in the man named, Billy Ray.

After that, all four men took turns beating Thaddeus for hours and drinking in between. Somewhere during the violent session, he lost consciousness, but came back when the men burned his face, arms and chest with lit cigars.

By the dawn, Thaddeus was hardly recognizable as a human being. His face was a swollen, bloody piece of meat and throbbing pain emanated from both his broken arms, smashed ribs and fractured legs. The rednecks had only stopped because they were too tired and too drunk to continue.

Thaddeus could pray they'd kill him soon.

"Hey Sonny, you ever hear how big these niggers claim their peckers are?" asked Billy Ray with a drunken smile.

"Yeah, the black fuckers are supposed to be hung like them apes out in Africa," Sonny said thickly.

"Why don't we see."

Thaddeus barely felt them unzip his pants. The pain he was enduring was much too intense for something so minor. He was on the verge of unconsciousness.

"Ooooowee, boy!" yelled Sonny. "Look at that. This monkey sure has a big one."

"Hell, Sonny, I got a dick as big as that one."

Everyone laughed.

"You know boys, I've heard these niggers take their hardware real serious. You know, the worthless fuckers use it to create more worthless-ass niggers."

"That's right, Sonny."

"Yes sir."

Sonny coldly continued, "Well I think we're gonna take care of this nigger's equipment right now."

With that said, Sonny pulled out a large hunting knife from scabbard hanging from his belt. He gently fingered the razor edge to see if it was honed just right. When he saw a drop of his own blood he knew he had the tool for the job.

"Bobby put a gag in that black bastard's mouth."

The man named Bobby pulled out a soiled handkerchief and roughly shoved it into Thaddeus' mouth. The sensation of gagging overcame him. His nose was so pulverized, he couldn't breath to begin with; now he fought for air. He was convinced he'd choke to death.

That's when Sonny started cutting.

The pain shot through Thaddeus like white hot iron from hell and was beyond any comprehension. Within a few seconds, he slipped into a wide pool of blessed blackness which brought him to the edge of death. Later, he would wish he had crossed into the final frontier of the grave. Why couldn't God in Heaven have been merciful and bestowed that final gift on him?

When morning came, a farmer plowing his field saw the smoke from the camp fire and decided to investigate. Thinking it some teenagers partying, he wanted them off his land. When he saw the smoldering camp fire and the bloodied body he knew something more sinister had occurred. The rednecks were long gone, but what remained must have, at one time, been a human being.

An hour later, the rescue squad gathered up his body and rushed him to the hospital. After hours of operations by a team of brilliant doctors, Thaddeus' life was saved. But for what? No-one bothered to ask him if he wanted his life saved.

His mentor, Dr. Westman rushed to the hospital and camped in Thaddeus' room for several days. Never in his life had he seen anything to compare to the cruelty perpetrated on his young colleague. Tears ran down his eyes as he watched Thaddeus come painfully in and out of a coma.

A dozen additional operations followed and were needed to set and pin bones together, wire his broken face, stop multiple internal bleeds and try to partially fix the redneck's crude castration. Thaddeus would, of course, never be able to father a child. The mutilation was too extensive.

Seven months later, he went home to Westman's house. He was physically thin and alarmingly weak, but the worst damage was psychological. He suffered from terrible dreams and episodes of paranoid delusion. Westman would run to his room at night when he'd hear his screams. During the day, the postman on the porch would cause Thaddeus to panic, and Westman would find him in a closet shaking with fear.

After two years of psychiatric therapy, Thaddeus' team of doctors felt he was well enough to get back into a regular routine. However, Thaddeus was a changed man. No longer did he feel any optimism or happiness in his life. He never smiled, nor did he cry. Gone were his funny, entertaining stories. Thaddeus was a shell, condemned to live a life of day to day tedium.

The police never caught the four men who assaulted and left him for dead. For an odd reason,

Thaddeus didn't want them apprehended. His fear of them was too great. He especially didn't want a trial in which he'd have to be in the same room with them and watch as an impotent punishment of imprisonment was given in his name. He wanted the pleasure of revenge, to castrate them, make them know what he had gone through. The Bible said, "an eye for an eye" and Thaddeus believed in the phrase.

Unknown to Westman and the others, this thought of revenge was the one emotion that kept Thaddeus Brown alive. It had started as a small fiery seed which gradually grew larger and larger in his soul. It was the one entity that, combined with his intellect, kept him going. Even Dr. Westman couldn't know how comforting and consuming this precious gift was. The beast inside was driven by pure, white-hot hatred, and in the absence of all else, this hatred got Thaddeus Brown through each and every day.

His biggest enemy would always be white people. He detested their history of slavery, he couldn't stand their culture, he was galled by the way they arrogantly spoke English and most of all he was repulsed by their pale skin and European appearance.

Neither, Dr. Westman nor his medical doctors saw any of this in Thaddeus. The young man was too smart to reveal what he really felt. As far as the professor was concerned, Thaddeus Brown was back on his feet working as a graduate student at Oberlin,

Then one day, while Westman was teaching a class, Thaddeus packed a suitcase and caught a bus out of town.

He never looked back.

CHAPTER 4

Dripping wet, Jack picked up his suitcase, opened the door and stepped in. Baffled stares greeted him. Someone turned the boom box off, and a hush fell over the packed lobby. Jack surveyed the crowd of black faces, missing nothing. A hundred fearful eyes dissected and analyzed him, much as a lab specimen.

This brought him back to his first day in the Institution. The same sort of judgmental expressions were there on the faces, sizing him up. People wanted to catagorize, find an obvious weaknesses and learn how to exploit any or all vulnerabilities. The best way to handle the situation was to give them nothing. Look everyone straight in the eye and put an attitude behind it. It was always better to be hated and feared than be considered a fool. At least with hate, you saw the bastards coming.

Across the lobby, he saw the front desk with rows of mail boxes in back of it. There was a large, scowling black man wearing a tie standing behind the counter. Jack figured him for the man in charge. Carefully, Jack started to weave his way through the crowd. To his surprise, however, the students parted like Moses and the Red Sea, giving him a clear path.

"I smell something white," said a tall young man with baggy leather pants.

"Someone musta' already whuped on his sorry white ass," said a mulatto redhead in a tight, revealing tee shirt that left nothing to the imagination.

"Hey white boy, you got the wrong address," also from the back. "You got a problem, motherfucker. We'll straighten your silly-lookin' Howdy-Doody ass out, bitch."

One of the athletes near the group containing Raymon and Tyrel said, "Hey motherfucker, somethin' wrong with your hearin'? You better head your lame ass out of here."

Jack stopped and turned to the athlete. His massive body strained under the tee-shirt. Cold-fury shot from his glaring eyes and stayed on the football player. Jack enjoyed challenging big mouths. His scarred, sinister face and veined, rock-hard arms gave clear warning. Jack Mulligan didn't take shit. Not from anyone of any color, class or religion.

The loud mouthed athlete read the danger, swallowed hard and turned away.

What a bunch of cowards, Jack thought, looking around. He had had more fun kicking around assholes Inside.

As if from an unconscious recess in his mind, the words of Superintendent Brown came back to him. "If there's one bad incident, you are back here. If there's a theft, rape or murder, you'll be heading for a maximum security prison for the rest of your sorry life."

The words struck like hammers. Jack felt his stomach knot as he thought of the tightrope he must tread. Don't let these bastards get to you. While their lives will go on, he told himself, you'll spend the rest of your life behind bars.

At the desk, Jack peered into the tired, disgusted expression of Robert Brent. The Head Resident must have been a former athlete, Jack guessed by his size and build. The man had massive arms folded over his large, deep chest. The steady perturbed look didn't go away. He wore the lined face of a bear roused from its winter hibernation. Jack was impressed. This one wasn't intimidated.

"Are you the one?" Brent asked in a deep baritone.

"Yeah."

"I saw your folder," Brent said with distaste. "Don't try anything with me. You got it?"

"Yeah."

Brent shook his head, "We have a room for you on this floor. Just behind this office here. Your roommate just moved in."

"Roommate?"

"Yes, roommate," Brent said. "We don't have any private rooms here."

Jack grunted a reply. He had been living in a barracks situation most of his life, solitude was what he craved. This guy, Brent, couldn't possibly understand.

***

Keysha's eyes were riveted to Jack Mulligan as he strolled across the lobby. She assessed his thick black hair, devastating cobalt blue eyes and a two day stubble that didn't hide his chiseled, scarred face. His six foot, plus body was massive and powerful. There was something mysterious and forbidding about him. Where had he come from and why was he here? He was white, and Keysha had been under the impression that this was an all black school. Something screamed that this was a man with a past and probably a dark one.

"Shit, now they're lettin' white folk in here," Raymon said in disgust. "That's all we need."

"He's just another student, y'all," Keysha replied.

"No, he's more than that," shot back Raymon. "You let one of those motherfuckers in, you gonna be seein' a bunch more."

"I don't think you have anything to fear, Raymon."

"I don't fear whites, they fear me. I don't like 'em."

"They probably haven't done anything to you, Raymon."

"How you know that?" questioned Raymon irritably. "You know what girl, I'd be goin' to a major college if it wasn't for white people."

He let Keysha absorb this for a passing moment. Maybe he thought she was slow or unable to understand. Keysha, however, understood and was shocked by Raymon's obvious prejudice.

"When I was in high school," he continued, "I was the highest scoring back in our conference. There be schools from all over lookin' at me. Purdue, Ohio State, Notre Dame—all of them.

"All I had to do was get out of high school with a C average. But, I had to have an English teacher who was white. Mrs. Spurlock. I hated that bitch. She rode my ass night and day. Told me I had to write papers about a bunch of dead white motherfuckers, who probably couldn't play football if their lives depended on it.

"Anyway, I told her I wouldn't need no papers in the NFL and she starts givin' me some white shit about havin' an education. The rest of my teachers understood. Know what I'm sayin'? But, this dumb, white bitch didn't get it. She gave me a D in English, and I was turned down by the big schools."

Keysha narrowed her eyes, "That's it? You blame your failure on her?"

Raymon gave back a blank look. Didn't she get it? Couldn't this bitch see?

Keysha laughed, "I think if I was this Mrs. Spurlock, I would have given you a D, too. Do you think because you're an athlete, you get a free ride?"

"Hey, we're the chosen," he said defensively.

"Oh spare me."

"What the hell would you know, girl? We go out every Saturday, bust our ass, so you and a lot of other losers can have a good time."

"And you get a scholarship in return."

Raymon looked pissed now. He'd had enough.

"You wanna know why I don't like white motherfuckers comin' here? Cause it pisses me off seein' sisters like you sellin' out their race."

"You what?"

"You heard me!" Raymon exclaimed, pointing a finger at Keysha's face. "You sell your own kind out for whitey. You even tryin' to act like 'em. At least I care about my brothers."

Keysha's eyes flashed fire, "You know Raymon, the only brother you care about is yourself."

With that she walked away leaving Raymon glaring at her.

***

About the time Jack made his grand entrance, Juleel had timidly made his way into the lobby. Maybe being around people would cheer him up, he thought. Besides, anything was better than being alone in the dark. Juleel was too gregarious for that.

He watched as other students gravitated to different cliques, where he surmised he wouldn't be welcome. Across the room he saw George, his one-time roommate, laughing with a group of new found friends. Maybe George was talking about Juleel's expulsion as his former roommate. That would account for the laughter.

Juleel sensed defeat.

Being in this crowd only made his loneliness more profound. He didn't want to feel sorry for himself, but he did. Juleel saw his fellow residents give him fleeting glances and quickly dismiss him as not cool enough to know. Could they immediately see he was gay? Did they think it was fun being Juleel Washington?

He realized he was just being petty and perhaps jealous of other people's happiness. Social skills were something he wished he possessed, but didn't. His mother had told him that people wanted to know him as much as he wanted to know them. His mother was a sweet lady, but in so many ways, naive. She also didn't know what it was like to be gay and black all at the same time. Walnutburg had taught him those painful lessons. He had tried so hard all his life to fit in. It just didn't happen.

With no warning, a huge strike of lightning exploded, nearly stopping his heart in the process. Was the world about to end? Catching his breath, he relaxed, only to abruptly hear frightened screams.

What now? Was something on fire?

Then from out of nature's fury, the gorgeous white boy he had seen on the lawn stood looking down on them from the front entrance. Everyone went silent. Juleel couldn't move or speak. He adored dramatics, and this was exquisite.

The white boy walked into the room with his suitcase. Lord was he a hunk. Up close he looked so...strong, so handsome. It was just too bad that his face was all scarred up.

Juleel's eyes followed the new boy across the room. He heard the cat calls and blanched at their audacity. When the newcomer reached the front desk, he said something Juleel couldn't make out to Robert Brent. A disgusted expression came to the Head Resident's face and that said it all. Brent could hardly tolerate the white boy. Juleel identified with the white boy. Brent had given him the same treatment this afternoon.

Juleel had to make the new boy's acquaintance, no matter what. If nothing else, they at least shared the same fate of being the ultimate outcasts.

CHAPTER 5

It seemed an eternity before Brent searched out a key and had Jack sign some official looking papers. Jack didn't even question what the documents might be. That was the beauty of having nothing and absolutely nothing to lose. Besides, Jack was tired and too wet to give a shit.

Behind him the boom box once more came alive and thankfully everyone started talking. Within a moment, a loud din of voices enveloped the room. He was now temporarily forgotten. At least they weren't staring at him, Jack noted with satisfaction.

Brent pointed to an entrance to his right and escorted him through a passage and down a hallway a short distance, warning him all the way about his do's and don'ts. Jack paid only half attention. Brent's rules meant nothing to him.

"There's no smoking, drinking, eating or drugs allowed in these rooms. If I catch you, you're out.

"There's a cleaning lady comes in once a week," continued Brent. "Don't have your room looking like a pig pen, understand?"

Jack grunted.

"You cause a problem, you're out of here," he again warned.

Brent reminded Jack of one of the older Institution guards named Melvin. He too had been pretentious in his authority, the pompous bluster. That was also why none of the inmates paid much attention to Melvin. They knew it pissed the bastard off.

Brent came to a door and fumbled in the dark with the key. At last, frustrated, he managed to fit it into the key hole, and the door swung open. The room was dimly visible with the last remnants of the evening's light coming through the one window. The storm was still doing its dismal best to blanket everything outside.

"One more thing," began Brent again. "I don't want to hear you don't like your roommate, got it? He's your problem. He and you better learn to live together and fit in."

"Fit in? What's wrong with him?"

A humorless smile came to Brent's face.

"Why nothing, Mulligan."

Jack sniffed and set his suitcase down. Brent put the key on the corner of the desk and turn to exit.

"You better know something," the Head Resident said in a low voice. "I'll be kicking your peckerwood ass if you even look at me the wrong way. So far, the Administration and I are the only ones who know about you, but that can change."

Jack wanted to laugh at the threat. He viewed Brent with disinterest. Who cared if the students knew about him or if this clown, Brent, liked him or not? Jack wasn't here to make friends.

"I have a question," Jack said.

"What's that?" said Brent sharply.

"Since you're such a profound expert on this...place," he said in a bored, deadpan voice, pointing around. "Where's the john? I gotta take a piss."

It was the kind of innocuous question that seemed innocent on the outside but through its vocal tone told Brent how little Jack gave a fuck about all he had just said.

The insidious question clearly pissed off Brent. He gritted his teeth, "Find it yourself, motherfucker."

Brent abruptly closed the door, leaving Jack in the dorm room with only the sound of the rain pouring outside.

Jack thought of Brent's answer and smiled. "Thanks for all your help," he whispered to himself.

Now Jack had a few moments of solitude. How sweet it was. Inside, you were never alone. There was always someone, an inmate, instructor or guard watching you.

Jack gathered in his surroundings—his new home. The room was good sized compared to the cell-like cubicle he had lived in at the Institution. There were two of everything needed, desks, dressers and beds. He noticed that someone had already claimed half the room. His new roommate, he presumed.

He saw a framed photo, but it was too dark to make out a face.

Crossing to the window, he viewed the downpour on the lush lawn and sidewalks of the campus. The wind was still tossing the trees and here and there a broken limb or a bunch of leaves littered the ground. The darkness fit his mood. He was now inside the dorm, and everyone he had met so far had made it clear how they felt about his presence.

His mind whirled in turmoil. Could he cope at Mt. Sidney College after so many years Inside? This asshole Brent didn't think so, but he was manageable. Jack didn't foresee a problem with the class work. But what about this roommate? Why had Brent spoken as if there would be a problem? Was the guy a raving racist or some kind of lunatic? Apparently, Brent saw a perverse humor in the housing arrangement.

His eyes drifted out of focus. Jack had to be careful. He'd play it smart and show these people what he could do. He imagined himself in classrooms and labs being praised and admired for his sterling intellect. Professors would be congratulating him for his constant scientific break-throughs. Perhaps a new species of plant or animal would be named after him. At graduation, shouts and cheers would go up when he accepted his diploma.

"Valedictorian of the class goes to Jack Mulligan. He's achieve the greatest honors this school has ever seen."

A sneeze brought him back. He felt a chill and realized his shirt was still damp. He'd show these fuckers, he thought. But he knew it would be difficult. How could he be an esteemed student in a black college, a white college or any college? These people hated and resented his existence. Deep inside he knew he'd better just get a degree if he could and learn to survive. He'd never been anything special or outstanding in his whole miserable life.

***

59

Moments after the new boy and Robert Brent went down the hallway next to the front desk, the Head Resident re-emerged from the darkness with a scowling face. Juleel wondered what the white boy had said or done. Maybe he'd stood up to Brent. That thought made Juleel smile.

A revelation dawned on him. The white boy must live on the ground floor, too. How wonderful. This gave him a greater opportunity to meet him and maybe become his friend...or more. Juleel didn't care if the boy was white. To have a true friend or lover, Juleel would accept anyone, even if they were purple.

He could go up and ask Brent what room the new boy was in, but Brent would probably tell him to piss off. Juleel knew the Head Resident hated him. Brent's disgust was palatable.

Juleel was pondering all the options when suddenly the electricity came back on and the lobby dazzled in the bright light. A relieved sigh came from the crowd as they clapped, cheered and slowly headed back to their rooms.

Perfect timing, Juleel thought. Excitedly, he dashed off to his room to make plans.

***

Tyrel and Danielle were sitting next to one another discussing the coming weekend, when the lights beamed on once more. They both squinted and laughed at their temporary blindness.

"Where's Keysha?" asked Danielle, looking around.

"I don't know," said Tyrel, "but there's Raymon, and he doesn't look too happy."

Raymon saw them at the same time and walked over. He looked as though his ego had been bruised, and now he was pouting like a small child.

"I'm goin' to the Delta house, Tyrel. I'll see you later."

"Do you know where Keysha went?" Danielle injected.

"She got all pissed off cause I said I didn't dig white people," frowned Raymon. "That girl better learn a few things about the real world. Fuckin' white people don't care about her or any other black person. Know what I'm sayin'."

"She said the same thing to me earlier," said Danielle.

"I was even gonna ask her out for the weekend," continued Raymon. "Then that ugly-ass, white motherfucker came wandering in here. What the hell's that sorry ass fucker doin' here?"

"I'll talk to her," said Danielle sympathetically. She could sense that Raymon might be more sensitive than first suspected.

"No don't! I got better things to do than educate her dumb, fucking ass."

"She really is a nice girl," said Danielle defensively. "Give her a chance."

"Shit! You give her a chance."

Danielle felt her face go hot. How could she have confused arrogance for sensitivity. Raymon, she realized, was quite incapable of having any caring thoughts of others. Mr. Big Deal football player, clearly only cared for himself.

"You're right, Raymon," Danielle said with her eyes flashing. "I won't say a word about you."

Tyrel looked impressed by Danielle's tough spirit.

Raymon didn't catch her tone but blundered on. "Ya'll don't worry about her or me. Keysha just got them ideas about white folk. Maybe she wishes she was one."

With that he stalked off to his room.

"I don't think Raymon and Keysha hit it off," said Tyrel.

"Yes and I can see why."

"Raymon isn't as bad as you might think," said Tyrel in defense.

"Well he certainly is full of himself."

Tyrel laughed, "He does have a good self-image."

"Sure, he's a sweetheart," she said sarcastically and laughed.

"Do you have to go back to your room right away?" Tyrel said speculatively.

"No not...yet. How about you?" She inquired sweetly.

"Not at all."

"You know it's early. Why don't we stay here awhile and you know...talk?" he stammered. "If it stops rainin' we could even...you know...take a walk. I'll show you around the campus."

"You're not trying to lure me somewhere?" She asked coyly.

Tyrel's face glowed, "No...no. I didn't mean..."

Danielle laughed brightly.

To Tyrel the idea of being with Danielle sounded delightful. He found her presence breath-taking and enchanting. He was definitely drawn to her, and frankly, couldn't remember when he'd felt this way before.

CHAPTER 6

When the power came back on, Jack noted the myriad sounds that went with it. First there was a solid sounding clunk from somewhere in the bowels of the old dormitory, and then the lights came on, air rushed out of the floor vents, followed by the distant voices of students heading back to their rooms. Jack considered how ironic it was that this ambient sound was around at all times, but the ears filtered it out as if it didn't exist.

He felt a tightness gathering in his chest muscles. Soon now, he thought, his new roommate would probably head back to the room and open the door. Closing his eyes, he took a deep breath. Try to get along, just fit in.

Abruptly, he felt for his wallet and worked it from his pocket. He slid out the creased photograph and gazed at it.

She must have been young when this was taken. Maybe only a few years older than Jack was now. He stared at the smiling face of his mother. Once again he reflected on the night he'd...he'd...Why had she stayed with his father? The abuse was incredible and unforgivable. His father had destroyed the person in the photo-the young girl with the smile.

After his trial, Jack had been whisked off to the Institution. His mother never came to visit, not once. He received a postcard from her some time later. It was postmarked St. Louis and indicated she'd moved there. She didn't ask how he was doing or what his life was like. She only cursed him and blamed him for making it impossible to stay in Steubenville.

That was not the last time he ever heard from her. Superintendent Brown had called him to his office two years ago and told him his mother had been arrested in St. Louis for vagrancy. The news seemed to please Brown, and his piggish eyes danced with amusement. When Jack asked him if he had an address so he could write back, he was knocked to his knees by a guard's baton. Then he was thrown in the stone cellar for two weeks isolation. His crime was wasting the Superintendent's precious time by being the spawn of low-life trash.

"It's scum like you that ruin it for the rest of us. Your mother obviously is garbage and deserves everything she gets," said Brown sternly.

Jack wished he could have grabbed Brown's throat, but the guards were too quick. At the door to the cellar, they bludgeoned him to the floor with their batons. Stabs of pain shot through his head and back. The world turned black and painful just before they threw him inside the isolation chamber. He awoke hours later in total darkness, stiff and bloody. His body throbbed in agony, his face was sticky with congealed blood. In addition, the clubbing had broken his collar bone and busted his knee cap.

Days passed before a doctor looked at him. Meanwhile he lay in his own excrement thinking he might die. Then, the guards unmercifully dragged him to the clinic, where he was cleaned up and his shoulder was set. Having not eaten in days, he was thin but he endured.

He always endured.

When he was put back in Population six weeks later, Jack was warned to keep his mouth shut about his treatment. No more needed to be said. Jack knew the rules. If a complaint was lodged, he would have had an unfortunate accident.

Two days later, Jack was summoned to Father Sanders office. He was the Institution's priest. An older, conservative type, the Father's dark suit was crisply pressed, his white collar tight, his sparse gray hair neatly combed. Heavy black-rimmed glasses added a wizened, pious appearance.

The priest spoke to Jack about the paradise that was heaven and the salvation through Jesus Christ that waited for some. God was selective. Since Jack and his mother had never seized upon God's grace, they were now paying the price.

For his part, Jack didn't believe in heaven or hell. When you died, the fucking story ended, period. No pain, no thoughts…nothing. Actually, it didn't sound that bad to Jack.

Jack slapped the wallet shut. To hell with Christian shit and his wayward mother. She'd ended up as just another broken drunk. He didn't need her. He didn't need anybody. He was playing this game alone and his way, and that's the way he liked it.

He heard a key slip into the door's lock and glanced across his shoulder. This must be his roommate.

***

"Say what!"

"I said, let's give the new white boy a big welcome."

Clarence Wonder or CQ to his friends couldn't believe what he'd just heard from Raymon. Was this jock crazy or what? Comin' in his room and talkin' some crazy shit.

CQ sat cross-legged on his bed facing Raymon who was sitting at his desk chair. CQ was of medium height and as thin as a stick. His face was kindly but pockmarked from severe acne.

Just before Raymon had popped in, CQ had been enjoying some hits from a particularly awesome joint. Some real good shit. So now he was mellow and wanted to stay that way.

"Man, you're a crazy motherfucker, Raymon. Whatcha' want to go messin' with that white boy for?"

Raymon smiled, "I ain't messin' with him, brother. I just want him to feel welcome and knowin' how I feel."

"Shit, Raymon."

"You're the man who can do one of those artistic things with paint," said Raymon with a sneer.

Raymon was referring to CQ's past record of being the premier graffiti artist in all of Newark, New Jersey.

He had painted overnight murals on public buildings until the local papers started reporting them as "Rembrandt-like." When the cops finally arrested him, the public outcry was tremendous. Several wealthy patrons of the arts held some fund raisers in his behalf and—viola—here he was, education paid for.

"What's you after?" asked CQ suspiciously.

"You know."

Suddenly things fell together in CQ's foggy mind.

"You mean you want me to do a little creative work outside that boy's room."

"You got it, man."

"What about Brent?"

"Fuck Brent," said Raymon dismissively.

"Sounds risky," CQ drawled.

"Just tell the white boy how much we love him," mused Raymon with a smile, "and how we definitely feel about him."

"Man, remind me never to cross you, motherfucker," said CQ, shaking his head. "When we going to do this?"

"Meet me on the first floor at two o'clock."

"Two fuckin' o'clock in the morning!" exclaimed CQ. "Fuck!"

Raymon reached into his shirt and pulled out thirty dollars. With a flick of the wrist, it landed on the bed next to CQ.

"I always believe in patronizin' the arts."

CQ grabbed the money.

"Motherfucker, for this much, I'll paint you a masterpiece."

"That's what I thought," said Raymon. "Be on the first floor, by the back entrance, two o'clock sharp."

"Wait till everyone gets a load of this."

Raymon erupted, grabbing CQ by the shirt and throwing him against the wall. "Not a word, motherfucker. This is between you and me. Nobody else. Understand?"

CQ was wide-eyed and breathing hard. "Yeah, yeah Raymon. You and me. Not a word."

Raymon released his grip, "Good. Anyone finds out we did this, we'll be packin' our bags before breakfast tomorrow."

CQ nodded in complete understanding.

"Sorry I wrinkled your shirt," said Raymon with a sneer.

CQ was now too frightened to tell Raymon he didn't want this job. Raymon would kill him. Whatever this white motherfucker had done to piss off Raymon must be good. CQ didn't want to be part of someone else's problem. But now, he was trapped.

***

Any apprehension Jack had about his new roommate evaporated instantly with his first observation of Juleel. There was something about the thin, black boy that conveyed a gentle but very bright spirit. No deceit or hidden agendas there.

"Hi, I'm Juleel Washington," his roommate said with a toothy smile. "We must be roomies."

Roomies? Something about the word sounded too intimate.

"Jack Mulligan."

They shook hands. Jack noted Juleel's rather limp grip.

"Are you a freshman or a transfer?" Juleel asked.

"A freshman."

"How lovely, so am I," Juleel said gleefully. "I'm an art major, but I did, at one time, consider drama. I just adore the stage. The lights and the applause are so exciting. Do you like the theater?"

"I don't know too…"

"Well Mt. Sidney has a fine drama group here on campus," interupted Juleel. "We'll have to see a play…together."

Jack grunted.

"Do you have a major?"

"Biology."

"Oh plants and animals."

"Just animals."

"What?"

"I'm going to be a veterinarian," said Jack, wondered why he was telling this to a total stranger.

"Oh I love animals, too," continued Juleel with an exaggerated wave of his hand. "My Mama and I have a cat named Brutus. Actually, he is really a she. But, you ought to see the gorgeous coat on this cat, Jack. Mama says it's the loveliest fur she has ever laid eyes on. Softer than those mink coats the models wear. Do you have any pets?"

"No."

"Well I understand. Many apartments and condos don't allow them," speculated Juleel.

"Yeah."

Not many prisons allow cats either, Jack thought.

He watched as Juleel started carefully rearranging each item on his desk. He seemed completely out of character for a college student. Meticulous and prissy, he never sat still for a moment.

"Can you believe that storm?" Juleel said nervously.

"Yeah, nasty," mumbled Jack.

"I noticed you got wet before you came inside."

Jack nodded. So Juleel had seen him in the lobby.

"I'm so glad I didn't get caught out in it. That lightning and thunder could give a soul a heart attack."

"I guess," said Jack, looking out at the dark campus.

Juleel babbled on about one thing or another for about twenty minutes with Jack occasionally making a reply. This guy, Juleel, was a talker. Just wind him up. Maybe Brent thought Jack would have an objection to the guy. He couldn't care less. The guy seemed harmless.

Thankfully, Juleel did wind down after a while and told Jack he had to write his mother a letter.

Make it two letters, Jack thought, and take your time.

"I wish Mama would think about getting a computer. Then we could e-mail each other. It's so much easier. But, for now, it's snail mail," said Juleel, getting a pad of paper from his desk. "I'm going to tell Mama all about you, Jack."

"Sure," Jack replied absently. He was already learning to tune Juleel out.

Jack reached into the top drawer of his desk and pulled out a crossword puzzle book and started working on a puzzle he'd been doing since last week. He derived great pleasure from word games and crossword puzzles. He'd started doing them Inside to pass the long hours. They provided mental stimulation to help prevent insanity.

Jack had guessed that Juleel was gay almost from the moment he stepped through the door. This was why Brent relished giving him Juleel as a roommate. Probably no one wanted to room with Juleel, and they certainly didn't want an ex-con white boy for a roommate either. How perfect. Get all the rejects together in one room.

As far as Juleel being gay, who cared. After being Inside for seven years, it was easy to spot homosexuals. Jack didn't feel uncomfortable around them anymore. As long as they didn't bother him with their preference, they were cool with him. People were all the same. Everyone was just trying to get by.

Juleel looked over at Jack who was still working on a puzzle.

"My Mama likes crossword puzzles," he said. "She says they build word power."

Jack shrugged, not looking up.

"Jack."

What now?

Jack peered over his puzzle at Juleel, who was studying him intently. He looked apprehensive and vulnerable.

"Do you think we'll become friends?" he whispered.

The question hung heavily in the air between them.

Jack hardly knew how to react. He wasn't the kind of guy who made friends easily. The Institution had a built-in atmosphere of mistrust that pervaded even the most innocuous microcosms. All you could hope for was to have someone watch your back. Friends were a luxury no one could afford.

Observing Juleel, he could sense his desperation. Juleel had probably been through uncountable disappointments. Being gay and black, he'd most likely suffered knocks and degradations that would make others cringe. Admirably, however, Juleel seemed to possess an inherent dignity and not a prepossessing self-pity. He was simply nervous about having Jack as a roommate. He probably thought Jack would bolt for the door when he found out what he was. Jack however liked Juleel.

"Sure," said Jack a moment later. "We'll be friends."

This seemed to please Juleel, who smiled tiredly and turned back to his letter writing.

Jack shook his head and resumed work on his puzzle.

CHAPTER 7

Paperwork was piled high on Robert Brent's desk. It never ended. It seemed as though the mountain of paper grew with every passing second. There were financial status reports for every student in Lincoln Hall, special request forms for students, such as music majors in need of rehearsal space; medical notification and dietary requests for kids who suffered from everything from asthma to diabetes. The pile was overwhelming.

Robert had a headache just looking at it. He surveyed the work that would take several days to keyboard into the computer and digest. He'd then would have to return all the files to the Dean of Admission's Office in a timely fashion. Unfortunately, Brent's only help in this task was a part time girl who was still learning to type.

Robert shook out some aspirin from a bottle on the desk and chewed two. He grimaced at the taste. His headache pounded on. He knew the daunting amount of work wasn't the reason for his headache. It was the white boy, Jack Mulligan.

Now that he had met Mulligan, he realized his worse nightmares weren't even close to being as tangible as the reality. Mulligan was trouble, big trouble. Brent knew that none of his warnings had meant a thing to the boy. Mulligan was probably laughing right now.

What could he do?

If he made an appointment to see Dean Jans tomorrow, the kindly Dean would view him as being prematurely rash and incompetent. On the other hand, if he did nothing and something catastrophic occurred, the less kindly Dean would want to know why he hadn't been kept apprised. Either way, Brent was fucked. There was no way he could win.

Dean Jans and the Board of Trustees were sitting back on their collective asses with their new found money, while he was doing all the work. Fuck it! Jans was treating him like a house nigger, not a colleague or a trained graduate student in a position of authority.

Brent didn't like babysitting for some white, jerk-off convict with a scarred face and an attitude. If this Mulligan guy wasn't going to play by the rules, he could leave. The sooner, the better. Hell, he probably was freebasing coke and plotting homicide this very moment with that detestable, little faggot roommate of his.

Brent smiled. At least both his problem children were in the same room. What a pair they would be: a fag and a convict or more likely, a pussy and a lion. How much better could it get?

Brent knew how to isolate problems to efficiently take care of them. After all, he had worked in college dorms before.

***

Keysha changed into a comfortable sweatsuit that was baggy and loose. Picking up the phone, she thought about calling her mother but then chose not to. Putting the phone down, she couldn't help feeling a wave of frustration. Why had she let Raymon Jackson push her buttons? She had heard bigoted crap before from far more expansive racists than he. Try her Uncle George, for instance.

Every holiday when the family got together, Uncle George would start in, after a few drinks, about those "white devils." It angered her father, who didn't possess a hateful bone in his body. Uncle George, for his part, enjoyed the confrontation with his brother. Maybe somewhere deep inside he thought he could convert Keysha's father into a hate-filled bigot like himself.

"Randall, they've kept the black man suppressed for four hundred years, and the sonuvabitches don't intend to stop," Uncle George would proclaim loudly. "If you can't see it, you must be blind. Or, have those bastards brainwashed you?"

"I know there are problems," Keysha's father would assure him patiently. "There's hate and bigotry in many places, but George, becoming part of that problem won't solve anything."

"As I said, brainwashed," George would reply flatly.

"Into what?"

"Into becoming their kind of nigger," he'd exclaim angrily. "You run and fetch at their command. The

Oreo cookie. Doin' their bidding. Yas massa! No massa!"

Keysha's father would frown, "You're so full of it, George."

"Am I now?"

"You sure are."

"Well let me tell you little brother, if I hadn't been passed over for promotion a half dozen times cause of my skin color, I'd be a vice president in my company," he'd yell bitterly. "You know what it's like to train those white sonuvabitches; then watch them become your boss?"

Uncle George had somewhat of a point. He had trained several white employees in the copy machine company where he worked. It was also true that many of them had gone on to get promotions. What he failed to always say to Keysha's father was that he also trained many black employees who also passed him by.

Keysha's father told her that he had a patient one time who had known George for years. This patient informed him that his brother would probably have been a top executive if it wasn't for his caustic attitude. It seems that Uncle George had a reputation as a hot head who's hatred and jealousy weren't undetected. Although extremely competent in business machines, his racial biases kept him at a lower station in the company.

Keysha felt sorry for Uncle George, the same way she felt sorry for Raymon Jackson.

Maybe she expected too much. Raymon was physically so attractive and that smile—it could melt your heart. But, Raymon's smile somehow belied a deceptive ugliness. His racial hatred and arrogance resided just below the surface.

Anger flushed her face. Why did she even care? Perhaps in a romantic notion, she thought she could change Raymon; make him into a kinder, gentler individual. What a daunting task that would be. Maybe, it was worth a try or maybe not.

Keysha sighed. When she had a chance, she would grudgingly apologize to Raymon and at least try to be civil. Her father had always said the hand of friendship was sometimes the hardest to give.

She would at least try.

***

When Jack opened his eyes later that night he thought he was still Inside. The darkness of the room was unfamiliar. The shadowed shapes of the furniture were different. And then consciousness took over, and he realized he was in the dorm room. The sleeping mound in the other bed was Juleel. He picked up his watch beside the bed and squinted at the luminous face. It was three o'clock.

Why was he awake? Something was wrong.

Call it a sixth sense, cultivated from years of survival, but something wasn't right.

Subtle noises such as hissing and rapid footsteps alerted him. Then he heard something softly touching the door and a flickering streak of light showed at the bottom.

Jack got out of bed clad only in boxers and a tee-shirt. He stood for a moment getting oriented and listening. Then he heard the footsteps running away.

The flickering light beneath the door became brighter; then he smelled smoke.

Fire!

Jack pulled the door open and a trash can full of water, which had been leaned against it fell in, soaking his feet and the carpet. Another trash can was outside the door with flames leaping out of it. Smoke was filling the hallway. Suddenly the smoke alarms went off with an ear splitting shriek.

Was the arsonist someone trying to burn the dorm down?

Jack turned back into the room as Juleel ran past him with a towel. He quickly threw it over the blazing trash can to extinguish the flames.

"Good thinking, Juleel," praised Jack.

Juleel seemed to grow three inches in height as he accepted the compliment.

Now the hallway was filled with sleepy students, all headed in varying degrees of dress, toward the exit. Most were grumbling and wore scowls on their faces, especially when they saw the source of the fire.

A door at the end of the hallway burst open. It seemed to make a loud gasping sound as it hit the wall. Robert Brent leaped forward, cursing as he ran. "What the fuck is going on?"

Before Jack could say anything, the big Head Resident stopped dead in his tracks and broke into another string of curses.

"Shit, what have you done?"

It was then that Jack looked at the wall on his side of the hall. Even he was shocked. It was covered from ceiling to floor with graffiti. A detailed depiction showed Jack sodomizing Juleel in the ass. The facial likenesses were astonishingly accurate.

Juleel gasped with a hand to his face. Anything to hide his shame. A tear slowly rolled down his cheek. How could they?

Above the drawing were the words, "Whites and faggots, perfect together."

Brent came striding up.

"This is what I get for having you two idiots around here!" he yelled through clenched teeth.

Jack bristled instantly.

"You can stow that, chief," said Jack coldly.

"Don't get smart with me, boy," warned Brent.

"We didn't do anything," Juleel murmured.

"Fuck! Just bein' here is enough," Brent growled in a quietly, dangerous voice.

"This isn't our work," Jack asserted. "This came from one of those decent students you talked about."

"Don't go there, Mulligan."

"I am there, boy," Jack exclaimed, instantly regretting his words.

Brent snapped around and marched up to Jack.

"You can bet that Dean Jans will hear about this!" Brent shouted. "I want you two out of my dorm and out of Mt. Sidney. I want that now."

Jack bristled.

"We're not going anywhere," Jack said evenly.

Brent looked at Jack with assassin's eyes. "We'll see about that, my man. Now you and your sweet, young roommate can clean up this mess."

One of the other students had wisely opened the exit door at the end of the hallway and placed a fan so the smoke was soon sucked out of the corridor.

However, a rank acrid smell still lingered in the air. It would be there for several days.

Brent began barking orders and soon the hall was visibly clean once more. Jack and Juleel put on their pants and did their share, but hard looks came from everyone. They too, blamed Jack and Juleel for this trouble and disruption of their sleep.

The carpet in their room was soaked, so Jack used the towel Juleel had thrown over the flames to sponge up as much water as possible. Robert Brent finally cooled down enough to direct them to a dehumidifier located in the basement. Jack brought it up and had it running in no time.

It was nearly four o'clock when Jack and Juleel finally finished cleaning up the mess. They were both beat. The rest of their neighbors had all gone back to bed. Brent seemed satisfied except for the graffiti. He steamed and stammered every time he looked at it. Robert Brent hated graffiti. To him, it represented the ghetto and the seamier side of poverty.

"Now we have to get this wall painted," he sneered. "Maintenance isn't going to like this."

Jack stood by sleepily, while Brent talked to himself. Jack was not interested in what the big man liked or didn't like. Sniffing, he watched Brent, his face impassive.

"Well, well, what have we here?" said a voice behind them.

All three turned to see Raymon and CQ smiling like two Cheshire cats with a trapped mouse. Jack realized, something was real wrong about both of them. They looked too entertained for some odd reason.

"Looks like someone has captured a scene of true love, Robert," said Raymon looking at the graffiti.

"Move along, Raymon," warned Brent. "We don't need you here."

"Oh, I can see that, Robert. I just heard there was an art exhibit goin' on here, and CQ and myself, being connoisseurs of art, didn't want to miss it. Isn't that right, CQ?"

"Yeah," chanted CQ nervously, his eyes dancing. "We just be checkin' it out."

Brent's eyes narrowed suspiciously, "You two don't know anything about this?"

Raymon smiled sheepishly, "No, don't know nothin', but I'll keep my ears open."

"Me too," added CQ.

"Yeah, I bet you will," said Robert sarcastically.

"Anything to help you, Robert."

Brent's face was bleak, "Yeah, you can help right now. Go to your rooms. This isn't your affair. Move!"

Then Raymon turned to CQ as he looked at the graffiti and then back in an exaggerated way at Jack and Juleel. "Bro, check it out, don't their faces look familiar?"

"Yeah man, they sure do," said a less enthusiastic CQ.

"Yes sir, I believe they look like these two gentlemen," Raymon said pointing at Jack and Juleel.

Brent frowned, "I'm going to ask you one more time Raymon, do you know anything about this mess?"

"No man," said Raymon staring at Jack. "I told you I didn't."

"Then get out!" shouted Brent.

Raymon held his hands up defensively and again smiled large.

"You know, you let white boys and faggots in your hood, Robert, pretty soon everything goes to shit."

"Move!" shouted Brent.

Jack and Raymon's eyes connected for a split second before Raymon turned on his heel and stalked away. That was all it took. Jack now knew who had set the fire and spray painted the wall. From what he could gather, so did Robert Brent.

CHAPTER 8

The morning sun brought the sound of loud, raucous voices as Jack opened his eyes to his first day as a student. The sound was similar to the racket in the Institution, but subtly quite different. Inside, there was no life in the voices, just the sound of each person fighting for his own share of food, space and air. Here there was an exuberance, an optimism that portrayed the day as having possibilities. To Jack, it was strangely frightening. Now he'd have to get up and really prove himself.

Juleel's arms came up from beneath his covers for a quick stretch. He glanced at Jack through puffy eyes. He looked tired. "I'd better get a shower. I've got an eight o'clock class."

Jack said nothing. He felt groggy from lack of sleep.

Juleel grabbed a clean towel from his closet. The one from the night before had been discarded, ruined by the fire. Then, he headed toward the bathroom.

Jack followed a few moments later. As he entered the hallway, he saw several guys examining the graffiti. They turned and walked away when they spotted him, but Jack detected some snickers. Jack glanced at the graffiti one more time then headed to the bathroom. Maybe the painters from maintenance would cover the obscene drawing before evening.

Anger rose in his throat. That guy Raymon thought of himself as pretty cute. If he wanted to stay healthy, he'd best drop the cute routine real quick.

The bathroom was filled with black guys shaving, going to the toilet and taking showers. Their loud talk was teasing and light, mostly about sports and girls. Jack felt like the anomaly. He was the lone white spot in the domino. He didn't care about sports and didn't know anything about women. Everyone fell silent when he entered. They were probably still sore about last night.

When Jack got back to the room, Juleel was dressed and had his backpack ready. He frantically checked his watch and headed for the door.

"Gotta' run. It's a good thing I don't eat breakfast."

Jack nodded. He was hungry.

"I'll see you later."

"Yeah."

Jack got dressed and headed for the cafeteria. Although it was crowded, at all the tables, when he sat down near the window, he soon found himself alone. Everyone moved away. So this was how it was going to be, he realized.

Jack smirked. This was rich. Kind of like having leprosy. Some would call it a curse; others would consider it a blessing. In his assessment, he didn't need these clowns for anything. Screw their rudeness. He could do without their friendship, too.

Jack ate quickly, drank two cups of black coffee and headed out the door. The September day greeted him like a old friend when he emerged from Lincoln Hall. It was a clear, warm and beautiful day.

Mt. Sidney College resided as a large cluster of structures perched on a plateau overlooking a large lake. The view was exceptionally peaceful with wooded hills bordering the school on three sides and the town of Mt. Sidney on the fourth. The far away lake seemed large and blue with scattered cottages and beyond, rolling, tree covered hills.

Armed with a map of the campus, Jack made his first foray into the unknown. Luckily, he'd spotted a stack of campus maps on the front desk. Brent must have forgotten to mention their existence. Since his travels had always been limited, it was quite possible he could get lost here at Mt. Sidney College. One thing he knew was not to ask other students for directions— not if he wanted to get a straight answer.

Soon he was at the Registrar's Office and after much standing around and endless waiting, he was able to sign up for his classes. One of the ladies behind the front desk, a plump woman with a red mole on her nose, told him he'd have to have his classes approved by his advisor.

"I don't have an advisor," he said.

"Yes you do."

"Where would he or she be?"

"You received a letter about this, Mr. Mulligan." she insisted.

"I didn't get a letter."

Superintendent Brown probably threw away any mail from Mt. Sidney College as fast as it came into

85

his office. The fucking prick. Jack couldn't inform this lady of that, but maybe he could pry a name out of her.

"Listen, could you humor me a little and tell me who my advisor is?" he said politely. "I'd appreciate it."

The big lady breathed hard and stomped off. Jack heard her say under her breath, "White people, always wanting something."

While Jack waited, he noticed other students giving him odd sideways glances. Hadn't they ever seen a white person? He felt conspicuous and out of place. His first day of real freedom was already starting to suck.

He looked up when the lady returned.

"Your advisor is Mrs. Clayton, on the third floor."

Jack started to say thanks but the lady looked over his shoulder and shouted, "Next!" So he picked up his papers and headed for the third floor.

Today was the first day of actual classes, and Jack was getting registered late. Most of the students in the crowded hallways and offices were there to make last minute changes in their schedules. This was why Jack had to endure long lines until the school's personnel could help him. Mrs. Clayton's office was the last stop in the slow process.

Jack waited patiently for over an hour in a crowded outer office until his name was at last called. He entered Mrs. Clayton's well organized world and closed the door behind him. In an instant, everything changed. Gone were the sounds of dozens of shoving people trying to talk over everyone else; gone were the constant pounding and screaming of rap music. Instead, soft classical music embraced him like a lover's hands and comfortable, oversized furniture beckoned.

Mrs. Clayton, a forty something woman, motioned, without looking up, for him to sit down, while she finished writing on some forms.

When she finally glanced up at Jack's scarred facade, her breath came short. Jack blushed with self consciousness. Was he that scary to look at? He realized then that his ruined face would probably have frightened his own mother.

Mrs. Clayton regained her composure, acting embarrassed about her reaction and readjusted her no-nonsense self. She was a short woman with kindly eyes and a silver Afro coiffure. After shifting some papers on her desk to buy time, she spoke in a resonant, finely enunciated tone. No eubonics here.

"Hello, I'm Helen Clayton, and I'm your freshman advisor."

"Jack Mulligan."

"I'm glad to meet you, Jack," she said formally.

Jack thought about her previous reaction, "Yeah."

She didn't seem to notice his sarcasm.

"I hope you'll have an enriching academic experience here at Mt. Sidney College. We want every one of our student to grow with us and fulfill their own individual destiny."

So far the experience had been everything but.

"Have you chosen a major?"

"Yes ma'am, biology."

"Wonderful, we need more scientists."

"I want to be a veterinarian."

"Oh, a doctor, lovely."

Jack nodded. It was lovely. He liked the sound of the word doctor. There was a built-in respect that came with the title, doctor. Being a vet also meant serving a better species.

Mrs. Clayton turned her attention to a computer beside her desk and started typing rapidly. "Is there a reason you are registering late?"

"Yeah, I only just arrived here last night."

"I see. Where are you from?"

This was a hard question. Should he tell her, the State Institution for Juveniles or just say his hometown from years before. Since she didn't have any record of him in her computer, it was probably best to tell her the latter. Why stir the pot?

"Steubenville."

"Where are you staying now, Jack?"

"Lincoln Hall."

"I see."

Suddenly, she frowned.

"That's strange," she muttered almost to herself. "You're records are here, but I don't see any bio information or much beyond your exceptional SAT scores."

Thank god, thought Jack. The Board of Trustees was indeed careful to keep his secret.

"Are you on scholarship?"

Jack started feeling uncomfortable. There was a empty sensation in his stomach. Fear wound him tighter and tighter like a clenched fist inside his chest. "Something like that."

"Well are you or aren't you?"

Jack stared out the window.

"What is it, Mr. Mulligan?" she insisted, viewing him strangely.

"I'm not at liberty to say."

"I beg your pardon."

The feeling in his stomach got worse. What was this woman's problem? Was she always this nosey? Couldn't she just let it go?

"You'll have to check with this guy, Jans—Dean Jans," Jack said, passing the buck. He'd never met Jans but he remembered the name from a few pieces of paper he'd seen with the Dean's pre-printed signature.

Mrs. Clayton gave him a troubled look. Jack could tell she'd probably be on the phone with Jans the moment he left her office. Being white and evasive was not something Mrs. Clayton was used to dealing with or would tolerate. Let Jans, whoever he was, tell her whatever he desired. Jack wasn't saying anything.

"I will be talking to him, Jack."

He nodded. Let's move on lady, he thought.

She gave another glance at the computer screen, then turned to Jack. "At any rate, you are signed up for a full schedule of classes and they are now approved. If you hurry, you may be able to attend one or two of them this afternoon."

Then she stood and held out her well manicured hand for Jack to shake. Her grip was firm. "Mr. Mulligan, good luck. I realize this may be different for you. Especially being such a man of mystery," She smiled. "I hope you have a wonderful year with us."

"So do I," he said, glad the interview was over.

As he left Mrs. Clayton's sanctuary, the noise outside struck his ears again. He took a step forward just as a girl cut in front of him. They crashed. She was stunned as if she'd hit an unseen wall. He grabbed her arm to keep her from falling over.

The girl gasped.

"Sorry," he apologized.

"No, I…"

Their eyes met, and for a brief moment, each held the other's gaze. Her breath caught. Jack knew that something like electric shocks ran through his body. This girl was so incredibly attractive. Her large brown eyes were wide-set, warm and intelligent. They drew you in and touched you.

She looked away embarrassed. The contact was broken. "Excuse me," she whispered huskily.

Jack mumbled an unintelligible answer and moved aside. The girl went inside and closed the door, but her sweet scent lingered. Jack breathed it in and then turned to go.

Maybe someday, with luck, he could run into her again.

His next stop was the bookstore, where he stocked up with three big shopping bags of supplies, plus a rented laptop computer. This was a must for his classes. The voucher, they'd given him before leaving the Institution, seemed to do the trick for money. So far, so good.

Jack raced back to his dorm room, dropped his supplies and then ran to catch what would normally have been his last class of the day, chemistry.

He was just in time to get a seat in the back of a cavernous hall before the professor started his lecture. Several students glared him. None spoke.

After the hour was over, Jack wandered around the campus, mapping its layout in his mind and then finally headed back to Lincoln Hall.

His first day was done.

He suddenly felt a sense of freedom he'd never had before. No guards, no dogs and no barked orders. It told him how dehumanizing incarceration was. Prison was a place where you became a mindless robot or maybe a highly trained dog. When the bells rang, you salivated for a meal or went to the john or prepared to sleep. Outside the walls and razor wire was this heaven. Now if he could just blend in to the background of Mt. Sidney. He could sort of disappear and no one would notice he was there. Then everything might work out.

***

This was insane. Keysha couldn't believe she was still thinking about the white boy who had bumped into her at the Registrar's Office. Mrs. Clayton had told her his name was Jack Mulligan when she asked. There had been a knowing look on the older woman's face when she told Keysha the name. Surely she hadn't suspected Keysha's interest.

Keysha blushed. Did Mrs. Clayton think she had anything but a mild curiousity.

Maybe it was those devastating blue eyes that had affected her. She had found herself staring into his cold, blue eyes, mesmerized by the deep reflection of herself. Together with his scarred, hardened looks, Jack Mulligan was quite a package. Something told Keysha that he was someone who had known a lot of hard times. She wondered if he was as rugged as he appeared. She hoped he wasn't all edges and no soft round places.

But who was Jack Mulligan? Why was he here?

She had had such a busy day. Her morning schedule was completely jammed with back to back classes from eight o'clock until noon. She realized immediately the schedule wouldn't work. Without some kind of break to gather her senses, she'd start to lose track of assignments or mix them up. Keysha knew she had to change at least one of those morning classes to another time.

Looking over her schedule, she had decided that French would be more manageable at three o'clock. She had then gone to the Registrar's Office for an approval slip from her advisor, Mrs. Clayton.

Little did she know she'd run into Jack Mulligan on her way into the office. She was stunned to see him, especially after his grand entrance into Lincoln Hall the night before. Gazing up into his ravaged face, Keysha had felt her legs grow weak and rubbery, her throat go dry and her breath shorten. She couldn't stop the uneasy feeling that swelled inside her. Up close, there was unbridled power in his wide shoulders and heavily muscled chest. She had the crazy desire to reach out and touch his body and...

Stop, she told herself.

Was she losing it?

What manner of being was Jack Mulligan? Did he have hypnotic powers? His presence was surrounded in questions. Of all the white people out there, why had he chosen to come to Mt Sidney?

Keysha had to know.

When she had asked him to be excused, he had stepped aside wordlessly. A gentleman, perhaps. She was so used to having guys come on to her and mouth their mindless pick-up lines. He had gotten further by saying nothing. He'd merely stepped aside.

Maybe he hadn't felt what she had. This angered Keysha somewhat. Didn't he see her interest or know…?

Keysha surmised that Jack Mulligan was dangerous in the best way—very dangerous.

CHAPTER 9

The hot, dusty practice field baked in the late afternoon sun as sixty young athletes and six coaches put the final touches on their collective game plan. Football practice had been extended by one hour by Coach Lawrence Dunn. Sweat and sometimes blood poured from the exhausted players, but the team needed the work. Dunn saw lack of focus, too much talking and too little physical contact. The Mt. Sidney Wildcats were contenders for the Conference Title and weren't acting like it. The game this Saturday—the first of the year—was crucial.

The opponent, Wesleyan College, was one of Mt. Sidney's biggest rivals. The year before, Wesleyan had knocked the Wildcats out of contention with a last minute field goal. Dunn was taking no chances on a repeat performance. Consequently, the plays for Saturday's game were repeated over and over, and the coaches screamed at mistakes or lack of all-out effort.

Raymon knew he was Coach Dunn's star player and the key man on the team. The success of this squad lay squarely on his shoulders. Dunn had said as much to the press. Being a star was a responsibility Raymon craved like an addictive drug. The down side was a pathos he experienced when he failed, which wasn't often.

Losses made him despondent as he replayed his own mistakes over and over. When it came to football, Raymon had been taught by his father to excel and to win at all costs. Nothing else was accepted. If a man had to play extra tough, use dirty tactics or even cheat, it didn't matter, as long as he won.

Raymon followed his father's advice, unquestioningly. The ol' man, like God, was always right. On the field, Raymon was brilliant, but his quest for victory was completely subjective. His personal performance and stats always took precedence over how the team fared. With all the publicity from the press, the fans never knew this. They perceived Raymon Jackson as a humble, unselfish gladiator sadly lamenting any losses with an heroic stoicism.

The self effacing attitude, Raymon knew, played well to reporters, scouts and most importantly to potential agents.

Raymon lived to bask in personal victory and hide in defeat. Losing was a dark purgatory he hated, but a win brought rewards. When Raymon won, everyone wanted to be his friend, girls wanted him in every way and life was well worth living. Even his academic performance or lack of it was conveniently overlooked.

Coach Dunn made sure that Raymon had no worries about grades. The fix was in. Raymon only had to attend his classes to pass. He never studied, wrote papers or did homework. In his estimation, why should he? A superior player shouldn't have to divert his attention away from his true destiny, gridiron glory.

Raymon and Tyrel left the field at the end of the day covered with sweat, dust and blood. Both were exhausted and hungry.

"Man, I thought the coach would never let us leave," said Tyrel breathlessly.

"You ain't lyin'," Raymon agreed, wiping sweat from his forehead. "Man, I'm whipped."

They both passed into the locker room, pulled off their gear and were soon in the showers. The blasting hot water offered some measure of relief to their sore, exhausted muscles. As they relaxed, the noise of the other player's voices echoed off the porcelain walls. The din was marked by laughter and jokes as they physically unwound.

Tyrel soaped up his huge chest and shook his head. "We'd best win this game on Saturday, or Dunn will have our asses."

"I'm just hopin' I have a big day. Get my name in the papers; attract those pro scouts," Raymon replied.

"You still dreamin' pro?" said Tyrel in dismay.

Raymon nodded, "You bet. I'm headed for the store, home. Know what I'm sayin'? I can see myself in a Dallas Cowboy or New York Giants uniform."

"Raymon, you already writin' your speach for the Hall of Fame."

"You right, Tyrel. I want those big dollars, cars and women. I want it all."

"Yeah, but what if you get hurt? Know what I'm sayin'. It can happen, Raymon."

"Not to me. I gots that charmed thing goin'. Understand?"

Tyrel raised his eyebrows and decided to change the subject. He didn't want to always talk about Raymon and how great he was. Raymon, in his estimation, was a good player, but in some ways he was too self confident to learn new techniques and skills. Perhaps he felt he'd be showing his weaknesses to his teammates. However, working on problem areas was what separated great players from merely good players.

"I'm takin' that girl, Danielle out to the Anaconda Club this Saturday. You want to come with us?" Tyrel mused.

"Isn't she the roommate of that big mouthed girl, Keysha?"

"That's the one."

"Now she's a good lookin' bitch, but that mouth be goin' too much," said Raymon boldly.

"She's alright," Tyrel countered. "She's just outspoken."

"Outspoken!" Raymon retorted. "She's just bitchin', Tyrel. Bitch, bitch, bitch. You hear what she say the other night about that white motherfucker livin' in the dorm?"

"She's just not prejudiced," Tyrel said, shaking his head knowledgeably. "I think she's tryin' to see both sides of the story."

"The story! The story is that the white man's been fuckin' the black man way too long," exclaimed Raymon, pointing a finger at Tyrel. "It's up to the brothers to keep what we can and get it over on the white man."

Tyrel shook his head. He'd heard Raymon go on about the white man stuff before. He didn't see the big deal. What was the harm in white people coming to Mt. Sidney College?

"Shit Raymon, you be thinkin' too much about that white boy. Shit he ain't nothin'.'"

"Damn straight," Raymon said adamantly. "I ain't no one's nigger. And that white boy…I want that pale-ass motherfucker outta' here."

Tyrel frowned and lowered his voice, "Raymon, you'd better cool it. You're on scholarship. Word is you and that skinny dude CQ did that shit outside the white boy's room."

Raymon smiled knowingly, "Man, I don't know nothin'.'"

"I'm tellin' you, Raymon, if they catch you, you'll be in deep shit," Tyrel said with worry in his voice.

"No one's gonna catch anything, Tyrel."

"Oh yeah."

"That's right," announced Raymon assuredly. "I'm too smart for that ugly white boy or his faggot roommate."

Tyrel couldn't believe this new revelation. "You don't like the brother either?"

"That little faggot's no brother of mine," Raymon said. "I can't stand sissy motherfuckers. If it was up to me, I'd kick the little fucker's teeth out."

Tyrel grunted his disapproval, "He botherin' you, Raymon?"

"Naw.'"

"Then what?"

"Just him bein' in the same dorm bothers me," Raymon replied. "What I think I'll do is make a package deal out of both of them motherfuckers."

"What you mean?"

"I mean, I'm goin' to fuck 'em up. The nightmare has just begun for those two. No what I'm sayin'."

Tyrel frowned, "I don't think that's a good idea."

Raymon sighed, "You're just too open-minded, Tyrel. It's a good thing I'm here to look after you and everyone else."

"I don't think I need your help," Tyrel said flatly, turning off the shower.

Raymon did the same, and they walked back across the cool, tile floor to the locker room.

"So you didn't answer my question, Raymon. You want to go to the Anaconda, Saturday?"

Raymon looked away and considered the invitation. The Anaconda was a local club and about the only decent student hangout around. Raymon knew he'd probably end up there dancing and celebrating Saturday's victory anyway. And, it would be a victory. Being the star, he needed to receive his public's adoration. Besides, he might get lucky and find some new and deserving female talent.

"I guess we could do that," he said haughtily.

Tyrel nodded and waited a moment. "Why don't you ask that girl, Keysha, to go with you?"

Raymon guffawed, "Man whatchu' think I am, a brother who's into pain? I go to the Anaconda to dance and have fun."

Tyrel persisted, "Hey, she's new around here, and besides she's suppose to be a good dancer. Danielle told me so."

Tyrel didn't really know this, but he figured it might help convince Raymon. Dancing was one of Raymon's specialties.

"So what?"

"You have to admit, she's fine," Tyrel added.

"She's okay," Raymon said raising his eyebrows. Secretly, he thought she was very hot. She'd be so sweet between his sheets.

"And?"

"And what, motherfucker?"

Tyrel smiled, "And you'll ask her out?"

Raymon immediately saw through Tyrel's insistence. The big guy probably felt that Danielle would be more comfortable if Keysha came along. Then, Danielle would have someone to talk to if the conversation lagged. Raymon quickly saw he could turn this to his advantage. He'd make it seem like he was doing Tyrel a big favor—an act of charity, so to speak. Tyrel would then owe him.

"Okay," he said at last. "If you want, I'll ask her out, but I don't think she'll go. She didn't seem to dig my cool, beautiful self."

"What?"

"She really gave me a ration of shit last night," Raymon said.

Tyrel eagerly assured him, "I'll get Danielle workin' on it. Keysha will go out with you this Saturday."

"Man you be just like an ol' lady. Fixin' people up. Shit, you gettin' too close to that girl, Danielle."

Tyrel buttoned up his shirt as a mental picture of her came to him. "She's alright."

"I can tell you're gettin' all serious. Talkin' that shit to her," Raymon said playfully. "You be drivin' babies around soon."

"No, no," Tyrel replied.

"Yeah, I know," teased Raymon. "I've seen it all before."

"Nothin' like that, Raymon."

They both finally finished dressing and walked out of the locker room. The September evening was warm and moist. This was heavenly after the hot day on the practice field.

Raymon turned to Tyrel, "I see you later, man, I'm goin' to the Delta house. Got me somethin' real fine goin' there."

"Okay, but don't forget to call Keysha."

"Alright, alright," Raymon said shaking his head. "But I ain't beggin' the bitch."

"I'll take care of that," assured Tyrel.

They parted with Tyrel pondering how Danielle would handle this. She was the one who had, at first, thought Raymon and Keysha would make a nice couple. Now, she didn't think so. Maybe somewhere opposites did attract but not Keysha and Raymon. They were both too stubborn. Tyrel saw nothing but oil and water, but having them on a group date might be fun.

Then a chilling thought came to him. What if the date became a nightmare? What if they argued? Both were opinionated and extremely headstrong. There was that potential.

Tyrel shook his head wishing these kind of plans were simpler.

***

Juleel finished wrapping the thick flat package on his desk. He could hardly wait for Jack to open it.

Three hours had been spent that afternoon picking it out—a crossword puzzle dictionary. Hopefully, there would be more. He just adored surprises, and he knew Jack would too.

He placed the gift on Jack's desk and decided he'd better get to work on his history and English. Juleel was a meticulous student, not brilliant, but a hard worker. He'd have to be too, his English professor, Dr. Potter, was very tough and demanding.

Today, the professor had assigned a two thousand word paper for the end of the week. Juleel and the rest of the class would have to give their analysis of their favorite poem by one of the romantic English poets, Shelley, Wordsworth, Keats or Byron. Juleel loved poetry, but writing two thousand words about one poem was difficult and, in his estimation, overkill.

Working steadily, Juleel almost didn't hear the door open when Jack returned from classes. Juleel's heart began to race as noticed Jack's wide shoulder pass by. Lord, was he hot.

"Hi, Jack."

Jack nodded and put his books down on his desk. His hand went involuntarily to the brightly wrapped gift, then withdrew as if it had burned his fingers. His eyes narrowed. He then plucked the card attached and read it.

Juleel could hardly contain his excitement.

"What's this?" Jack said, unsmiling.

"Just a little something for you."

"Did I ask for this?" he said in a stony tone.

"No, but…"

Jack's eyes drilled into Juleel and stopped him mid-sentence. He then held the package in his hands, not moving. Jack walked over to Juleel's desk and placed it in front of him. Juleel gazed up at Jack in disbelief. Didn't Jack like the gift?

"We have to talk," said Jack flatly.

"Aren't you going to open it?" asked Juleel in clear disappointment.

"Yeah, in a minute," said Jack. "Right now, we have to talk."

"What about?"

"We just have to talk."

Juleel blanched. What was wrong? Didn't Jack see how much he liked him? It was just a gift.

Jack pulled a chair around and sat down. He glanced at the floor and then looked directly at Juleel.

"Juleel, I only just met you. Understand? You are the only person, so far, who has so much as said hello to me in a civil voice. I think you can guess why. If you want to be my friend, we'll be friends. But Juleel…nothing more."

"What?"

"Do you know what I'm saying?"

Juleel felt the words sink in as Jack paused.

"I know you're gay, Juleel," Jack continued. "I don't mind. I'm cool with that. But, you've got to understand, I'm not gay."

Tears welled up in Juleel's eyes. Were there never any answers to his prayers? Surely, some day someone would respond with the love he so desperately needed. Why couldn't it be someone as good looking as Jack?

A tear rolled down Juleel's cheek. Jack saw a box of tissues on Juleel's desk and handed them to him. "Hey man, don't cry. I'm still your friend, and as far as I can tell, you're my best friend around here."

103

Juleel brightened a bit as he dabbed his cheeks with a tissue. "I guess I just...I mean I had hoped," he blubbered.

"I know Juleel," Jack said with understanding. "But it won't happen."

Juleel felt foolish and heartsick.

"Do you understand what I'm saying?"

Juleel nodded his head. "I know."

He felt as though the bottom had dropped out of something. He was so lonely. Momma was a hundred miles away, and he was already being spurned by most of the students at Mt. Sidney. He had just hoped that Jack might be really different...even romantic. He sighed, at least Jack wasn't a self-righteous, homophobic bigot like George had been.

Jack reached out his hand.

"Can we just be friends?" he whispered.

Juleel slowly and tenuously took Jack's hand.

"I think I'd like that," he said softly.

"Good."

They both smiled.

Juleel felt foolish but he sensed the sincerity in Jack's offer of friendship. Some things just couldn't be, especially in affairs of the heart. But all was not lost. Jack could be like a big brother he'd never had. That wasn't such a bad deal, he guessed.

"Now," said Jack, "let's see what you got me at the store."

CHAPTER 10

For six months, Thaddeus Brown panhandled through six states. He ate in soup kitchens and homeless shelters, occasionally found day work, but most of the time, just wandered the streets as a vagrant. His solitary journey seemed one of spiritual evaluation as he observed the human struggle for life and happiness—however fleeting—all around him. He sought, like so many before him, to find some meaning to his own existence but stumbled in his own failure to grasp any shred of truth in the illusory rationale of the universe.

He finally arrived in East St. Louis on a freight train just as winter was starting to extend its cold, steely talons. During the nights, he slept in community shelters but soon found them to be quite dangerous.

On one particularly chilly night, an older, gray haired man stumbled into a bed not ten feet away. The next morning, he was found with his throat cut and his pockets rifled. Whoever had murdered him must have thought the old guy had some change.

Would the same murderers think he had money next time?

By contrast, as bad as the nights were, the days were thankfully more pleasant. Most times, Thaddeus could be found hanging out in the public library, reading. His thirst for knowledge never ceased. The world of books gave him great comfort and hope. Besides, the library was warm and dry.

His table beside the window looked out onto the street and except for occasional cold glances from the librarians, he was left alone. The books and newspapers were companion enough. It was while checking the want ads in the local paper one day, he found an ad requesting resumes for teachers in East St. Louis.

Tearing the number out, he made a call and set up an appointment.

Clothes for the interview were going to be a problem. Fortunately, a church worker at the shelter overheard Thaddeus talking to another man about borrowing the man's shoes. Sympathetic to Thaddeus' situation, she took action. It had only been a few months since her late husband had passed away, his clothes were still hanging in the closet doing no one any good, especially herself. Why not give them to someone who could use them?

Approaching Thaddeus, she shyly offered the clothes. He could have kissed her. This was the break he'd been praying for. He thanked her for her incredible generosity with tears runing from his eyes.

So with a hot shower, a shave, a hair cut and a dead man's suit, Thaddeus made his way to the interview. His sterling credentials both pleased and impressed the board, and he was hired on the spot.

Soon he secured a small apartment above a laundromat and that autumn began teaching. All was going well. Thaddeus could think of no more rewarding career than teaching. He would be one of the many who molded young minds.

The bubble of fortune, however, soon burst.

The students in his classes were poor for the most part and completely uninterested in learning English literature and grammar. Although he didn't have any major problems with discipline, he could tell from his student's papers and tests that he was not connecting with them.

Remarks from some of the more taciturn pupils ranged from, "Mr. Brown, I just want to get a job, not read books all damn day," to "Why do I want to read a bunch of stories by a gang of dead white people."

He discussed this with several of his fellow teachers, but they had little interest either and were no more inspired than his students. As a whole, these purveyors of knowledge just put in time, collected their pay checks and went home. Marking time was the norm. The whole education system of East St. Louis had no focus upon goals or excellence. This, coupled with crippling urban blight, seemed to work like a large tumor that had eaten into everyone's spirits from top to bottom.

For several months, Thaddeus did his level best to utilize every educational technique he could think of to revive the children's sagging intellects. But alas, nothing worked.

Defeated, Thaddeus sank into depression and had to admit that the children of the inner city not only suffered from broken homes but also shattered souls. Many came from homes run by a single parent, traveled through dangerous, drug-infested streets to poorly run grade schools and were the products of under-funded pre-school programs. The number one impediment to a successful future for these kids was their own deaths, usually by gunshot at an early age. By the time Thaddeus got them in high school, they were so jaded and numbed into indifference, there was no way to teach them anything.

Going home at night to his small, dark apartment, depressed and deflated, Thaddeus started drinking. He found solace in the bottle. He could at least anesthetize himself to all the indifference and cruelty found outside his door. Soon, however, his consumption expanded until almost every day he walked into classroom with a hangover.

The principal of the school, Mr. Manning, noticed Thaddeus calling in sick way too often. This cost the school a fortune for substitute teachers. He spoke to Thaddeus about his absenteeism, and was told he suffered from a recurrent flu bug. Mr. Manning could smell booze, and he observed that inebriation was closer to the mark.

Weeks passed and the drinking became a larger and more important part of Thaddeus' life. He was now drinking morning, noon and night. He kept a bottle in his desk at work, one in his car and was now buying cheap Scotch by the case.

His students recognized the symptoms: the awkward walk, the thick-tongued speech. It was a point of fun to watch. It brought Thaddeus down to their level. The big shot teacher was now joining the rest of the sorry-ass world in the pit of ultimate failure.

Before long, Principal Manning had warned Thaddeus for the last time. The smell of booze permeated Thaddeus to the point he smelled like a distillery. Breath mints couldn't hide the odor. Manning called him into his office one rain-soaked March day and summarily fired him. His last words of advise to Thaddeus were to seek help.

With his little nest egg of savings, Thaddeus managed to keep drinking. Why stop? The world sucked. Everyone needed a little help here and there to get by. The pain of living would get you down otherwise. The bottle helped. It was a friend, his only reliable friend.

One year later, after being thrown out of his apartment and completely losing his dignity to the bottle, Thaddeus hit bottom in a filthy alley in St. Louis. Days had passed since he'd bathed or eaten. He was intermittently vomiting blood between spells of delirium and unconsciousness.

Holding on to an empty bottle of cheap port, his mind finally told him that worms were eating his insides. He had to get them out. Screaming loudly, his long dirty nails began gouging large gashes all over his body as he tried to extract the worms. The wounds bled profusely, and his clothes became red with its saturation.

A policeman saw him lying on the ground and thought he was a murder victim. He checked Thaddeus for a pulse and found one, weak and thread-like.

An ambulance was called and once he was in the hospital, it was touch and go for several days. Thaddeus, fought hard, however, and survived. When he emerged from the hospital, he was pale and thin but fortunately no longer interested in a bottle. His main problem was having no prospects and nowhere to go.

It was while in this state of mind, he happened upon a recruitment poster for the Marine Corps. A stern, steel-jawed young man stared at him, speaking of pride and patriotism. Thaddeus was sold in an instant. The Marines apparently needed, "a few good men." Thaddeus figured he might have a chance to turn his life around in the service. So, that afternoon he joined.

Three days later, he was sent to boot camp in Torence, Georgia. Camp Roman was spread out over two thousand acres next to a pest-filled swamp. It was run by a group of sadistic Drill Instructors who considered all recruits a bunch of worthless shit-bags who didn't deserve the air they breathed. Their idea of training was punishing recruits for having invaded their world.

Gunnery Sergeant Warren Whitaker was Thaddeus's Drill Instructor. He was a solidly built man of medium height with a small head, and beady unintelligent eyes. His two points of reference in the world were inflicting physical punishment on recruits and his unflinching love for the Corps. Sergeant Whitaker only knew one way to express either of these lofty goals and that was to scream orders at the top of his lungs.

On their first day at Camp Roman, Whitaker surveyed the platoon of new recruits, and his eye came to rest on Thaddeus who stood stick-like and drawn. Whitaker considered him a pencil-necked nigger, and he hated niggers—especially weak ones. On top of it all, Thaddeus was old. The Sergeant was used to having young boys just out of high school come into camp. They were full of enthusiasm and never questioned anything. Boys were easy to break down too and remold into soldiers. This old guy was not cut from the same cloth. Washed up physically from drugs, alcohol or something, he looked like trouble.

Standing at attention, Thaddeus, now twenty-nine years old, was a year older than Whitaker, thin from his stay in the hospital and obviously too intelligent for his own good. He looked different and acted different.

Sergeant Whitaker spotted Thaddeus, and a smile came to him. As a technique, Whitaker had found out early on that it was a good idea to pick one man out of the platoon to humiliate and ride night and day. Such an individual might be fat or thin, ugly or too good looking or like this one, black and frail. The criteria changed from group to group. What didn't change was that when mistakes were made, this chosen recruit became the scapegoat for all the platoon's fuck-ups. As human nature worked, the rest of the men centered their aggression on the poor bastard and not on him. A DI had to appear invulnerable and perfect. Whitaker's candidate for this platoon was going to be Thaddeus Brown.

The abuse started right away. When the platoon went out for a morning run the next day, Whitaker made a point of tacking on an extra mile because Thaddeus had not kept up. When inspection was held a week later, the whole platoon was punished with extra details because Thaddeus and his equipment weren't squared away.

Soon the young men, both black and white, began to hate Thaddeus for his constant fuck-ups. Thaddeus realized their anger in bitter remarks and disapproving glares. He had no friends among the group. Fortunately, because he was over ten years older than any of the rest of the men, they didn't commit any physical reprisals. It would have been like fighting one of their own fathers.

This didn't stop Sergeant Whitaker, however. He kept up the pressure. As time went by, he continued cursing Thaddeus for every infraction. Sooner or later, he knew Thaddeus would crack.

He did.

One rainy evening, the Gunny held a spot inspection. He wanted to see everyone's dress shoes. Thaddeus was sure that Whitaker wouldn't say anything about his shoes. He had always prided himself on his ability to put a perfect spit shine on the glassy leather.

But when Whitaker saw the foot wear, his voice hit an all time new decibel level. Holding the shoes aloft, he yelled, "You call this shined, boy? These shoes looks like SHIT! DO YOU HEAR ME, NIGGER!"

The last straw snapped in Thaddeus. He had done the best he could. He now had finally taken the last of Whitaker's bullshit.

"Maybe they're reflecting off you," Thaddeus said coldly.

Sergeant Whitaker couldn't believe his ears. At last, he had Thaddeus. Now he was really going to punish this punk nigger. Insolence would not be tolerated. Control was needed.

With one swift move, he smashed Thaddeus to his knees. Whitaker then pushed Thaddeus' head to the floor next to his shoes. "See these shoes you nigger sonuvabitch? See 'em?"

"Fuck you!" screamed Thaddeus defiantly, not able to move.

The enraged DI suddenly went wild, kicking Thaddeus in the ribs and ass. With the air knocked out of him, Thaddeus could hardly breath. Whitaker kept screaming about smart-ass niggers.

When he finally took a break from beating Thaddeus, the rest of the platoon was still standing at attention—frozen in fright. They were all too scared to even care. Their blank faces were those of little boys, trembling before an abusive parent.

Thaddeus was hurting all over. Blood was trickling from his nose and mouth. His breathing was raspy too, maybe from broken ribs.

Whitaker bent over, and put his face an inch from Thaddeus's bloodied countenance, "Get your gear, nigger. I got a real special job for you."

Ten minutes later, the DI and Thaddeus stood in a dark clearing beside the swamp. Rain was pouring down, and night sounds could be heard in the dark bowels of the swamp.

Whitaker smiled, "Well boy, you're goin' to dig a hole here. Get out your entrenching tool. I want that hole to be eight feet deep, two feet wide and six feet long. You know nigger, like a grave."

Thaddeus stood in a stupor. He was still hurting from the Gunny's boots. His ribs were making it hard to breath.

"MOVE!" Whitaker shouted.

Hours passed as Thaddeus labored in the rain. Soaked and covered with mud, he gritted his teeth and kept going. The rain came intermittently to drench him, and he began to shiver from exposure. Periods of the rain caused Whitaker to curse, and when Thaddeus slowed up, he'd start beating and screaming at him.

Finally, the big DI called a halt, and pulled Thaddeus out of the hole.

With the rain pouring, Thaddeus watched as a pistol materialized in Whitaker's hand. So he was going to get shot. Thaddeus was now too tired and beaten to even react.

"Do you know what I'm going to do to you, nigger boy?" asked the Sergeant with a deadly gleam in his eye.

"What?"

"I'm goin' to blow your fuckin' head off, nigger and then bury you in that hole."

"You won't get away with it," spat Thaddeus defiantly.

"Sure I will. You aren't the first."

Thaddeus saw no reason not to believe the Sergeant. The guy had spent two years in Viet Nam and had probably killed hundreds of people. He was a maniac and proud of his track record. If Thaddeus didn't do something, this would be it. The end.

He realized then that he still had the entrenching tool in his hand. Whitaker was too well trained to be vulnerable to a frontal attack. But, maybe just maybe, he'd get sloppy or distracted. The tool was his only chance. The right moment came a second later.

A bolt of lightning flashed nearby, illuminating the field and the swamp beyond.

In that split second, Whitaker's eyes blinked. Thaddeus struck. He swung the shovel with all the might he could muster. The tool buried itself in Whitaker's neck, making a sickening thud.

The impact was just right, crushing Whitaker's vocal cords so that no sounds were heard. Only a gasping gurgle emanated from his severed neck along with copious amounts of blood.

Sergeant Whitaker struggled to raise his service revolver, but Thaddeus was on him like a wild animal. The gun splashed into the mud. With a furious scream, Thaddeus kicked Whitaker in the groin. The Sergeant sank to his knees in the mud, still clawing at his throat. When he fell to his side Thaddeus hit him with the tool and then swung it over and over to finish him. Minutes went by and he kept the shovel going until exhaustion wouldn't allow his arms to work.

Falling to his knees, he analyzed his grisly work. Warren Whitaker looked like a pile of raw hamburger with a uniform on it. Thaddeus in a bizarre moment of irony, thought it humorous. He started laughing maniacally. He laughed and laughed, until his broken ribs sent him into spasms of pain and tears ran from his eyes.

Thaddeus Brown's sanity was completely gone. He had snapped.

The rain picked up to a downpour.

Still he laughed—laughed till he hurt. Fifteen minutes passed and he shook with convulsions. Then his stomach flexed and he vomited on the chopped-up body of the late Gunnery Sergeant. This mess at last served to clear his head.

The thought of escape finally dawned on him. He had to get out of there. Morning would soon reveal the grisly scene. Unless Thaddeus wanted to spend the rest of his life in prison, he had to escape from the camp.

Grabbing Whitaker's body, he tossed it into the hole, and as fast as he could, he filled it with dirt and mud. Time was wasting and his weary arms and shoulders ached with exhaustion.

He needed some new clothes. His were covered with mud and blood. Going back to the barracks was out of the question. Someone would spot him for sure. Then it hit him. When the rains came to Camp Roman, some of the officer's wives were permitted to hang clothes under the large outdoor pavilions. Clothes lines were strung up and hundreds of shirts, pants, etc. were there for the taking.

He sprinted to the pavilion, keeping a sharp eye out for guards. Sure enough, there were the clothes hanging and many of them civilian. He selected a pair of jeans and a shirt and quickly dressed. The dry comfortable clothes made him feel better.

A nagging sensation came to him that Whitaker might have been bluffing. Fuck that. That was like saying the rednecks who had castrated him were bluffing. Whitaker had threatened him with a gun. He wasn't going to die thinking the bastard was joking. When a man aimed a gun at you, he meant to kill you.

Once again he ran through the dark to the front gates, keeping to the shadows of the buildings. Kneeling behind a jeep, he observed the two guards smoking cigarettes just outside the door of the gate house. Thaddeus waited hoping they'd become distracted with something and wouldn't pay attention to the shadows.

A large truck came lumbering up a few minutes later, and the guards went into action. They checked the driver's papers and looked in the back of the truck. After chatting with the driver, a guard gave him directions. Thaddeus moved smoothly, keeping to the darkness. No one saw him as he silently slipped behind the guard shack and out the gate. Quickly he became one with the night.

He felt the cool, moist wind in his face as he ran. Thaddeus never looked back.

CHAPTER 11

Dean of Admissions, Maurice Jans was the quintessential college administrator. Short, impeccably dressed in an expensive three-piece Brooks Brothers suit, he was distinguished in a regal, aristocratic way. His dark hair had that touch of gray just at the temples. His tastes were discreet and subtle. His car was a Mercedes, which fit his well-honed image. He was fifty-five, a black conservative, Ivy League educated and comfortable—a man who lived in quiet satisfaction, secure in his position and with himself.

Jans never burdened himself with detail, but rather dealt with a broader scholarly spectrum. He was an idea man, a self-styled visionary. This was why he was oblivious to any potential difficulties that might arise from admitting a white, convicted murderer into Mt. Sidney College. Besides, integration was long overdue, and if money could be made doing it, what was the harm?

Not once did he think to phone Robert Brent, the Head Resident at Lincoln Hall, to discuss any problems concerning Jack Mulligan. If there were difficulties from the decision, surely it could be solved by subordinates. Implementation was something to be worked out by underlings and not fretted over by a thinker such as himself.

After making a lucrative deal with the state two months before to admit Mulligan, Jans had almost forgotten about his agreement. He had written down a memo to make sure that at the end of the semester he reminded the press of his glowing record of social ground breaking. At that time, he would call a news conference and let the world know how Doctor Maurice Jans had made a difference in one young man's life.

Mr. Mulligan would be humble and grateful, of course, as he thanked Jans and shook hands with the good Dean who had made it all possible for a ner-do-well to turn his life around. Everyone at the photo op would smile, and the pictures would find their way into all the dailies. Everyone would make out, the school would get extra funding, Jack Mulligan an excellent education, and Jans would bask in the kind of undeserved glory he loved.

Laboring over a proposal to a foundation, Dean Jans was annoyed when his secretary buzzed him.

"What?" he asked impatiently.

"Sir, Robert Brent from Lincoln Hall would like a moment of your time."

Now what?

He exhaled a breath, "Send him in, Theresa."

Brent came through the door dressed in a sports jacket and casual slacks. The younger man's face spelled trouble. Jans was an expert at reading people's faces. He could nearly always tell whether a visitor was bringing bad or good news. Today, this fellow Brent was bringing bad news. Brent shook hands and took a seat in front of Jans' desk.

"What can I do for you today, Robert?"

No pleasantries, this was business.

"May I be frank, Dean Jans?"

"Of course."

"Do you recall a white boy named Jack Mulligan who you sent to Lincoln Hall?"

Jans put on a show of being stymied, then brightened. "Mulligan, Mulligan...yes. He's the individual from the Justice Department. How is he doing?"

"I don't know if it's going to work out with him being at Lincoln Hall, sir."

Jans frowned. Now for the problem. "Why is that, Robert?"

He started rolling a pencil between his fingers.

"Well sir, two nights ago, we had an incident outside his room. Some...individual spray painted graffiti on the walls and started a fire in a trash can."

Jans dropped the pencil, "Vandalism? Dammit!"

"Yes sir."

"Did Mulligan do it?"

"No sir."

"Who did?"

"I don't know," Brent sputtered, now thinking that coming here was a bad idea. Why did he think bothering Jans would solve anything? "I've asked around but so far I haven't pinpointed the person responsible."

The Dean's face hardened. He hated incompetence.

Robert used the moment to take a new tact.

120

"Sir, the students in Lincoln Hall don't like this guy Mulligan."

"They don't?"

"No sir. He came to the dorm the other night and I..."

"Has he assaulted anyone?" asked Jans in a clipped tone.

"No sir."

"Did he spray the graffiti in the hallway?"

"No sir."

Deep lines creased a V between Jans' brows. "Is it because of his skin color?"

"Well, I..."

"Is it?"

"Dean Jans, don't you think we could diffuse the situation by getting Jack Mulligan out of this school? The other students don't want a white boy around. I just think..."

"You think!" shouted Jans, slamming his hand on the desk. "No you don't think, Robert. If you thought, you wouldn't be here. Do you have any idea what the press would do to this school if Jack Mulligan was expelled?"

Robert sat silently, while Jans stared at him.

"They'd crucify all of us," he continued. "This white boy is here two days, ends up being harassed, and we react by throwing him out. Does that sound correct, Robert?"

"I...no."

"Think of the stories in the news about reverse discrimination. Our funding for him, plus many other financial resources would dry up in a heartbeat. This isn't going to happen. Jack Mulligan is staying, Robert.

Work with him and work with his fellow students. Do I make myself abundantly clear?"

"But…"

"No buts."

The room grew bleak as Jans eyes stayed fixed on Brent.

"Yes sir," said Brent in defeat.

"This does not mean we are going to tolerate vandalism," Jans said with determination. "I want the perpetrator of the vandalism found. Is that clear?"

"Yes sir."

Brent didn't have to be told the meeting was over. He knew that all his well formed arguments had just gone up in smoke. For better or worse, he was stuck with Jack Mulligan.

Jans smiled but kept a hint of doom in his voice. "If you don't think you can handle this, Robert."

A threat? Brent was apprehensive now. He needed this job. "I'll see to everything. There won't be any more problems."

"Excellent."

Dean Jans rose and quickly escorted Brent to the door. The matter was resolved; now more pressing business needed his attention. Perhaps a round of golf. He shook the young Head Resident's hand and smiled. "It was so nice of you to come," he said in a dismissive tone. "I appreciate you keeping me informed."

Brent's mouth tightened with embarrassment. He knew the bum's rush when he saw it. "Yeah, sure," he mumbled. "Thanks so much, sir."

It was over in seconds.

When the door closed, Jans marched to his desk and pulled out the paperwork for Jack Mulligan's release. He wanted to know exactly what would happen in a worse-case scenario. That's why he was Dean of Admissions, he was always ahead of the game.

***

The dining hall, on the first floor of Lincoln Hall was crowded and noisy at the end of the day. More students seemed to show up for dinner than breakfast. It was six o'clock, and Jack and Juleel carried their trays out and looked for seats.

Six o'clock was significant for Jack. That was the time he had always eaten Inside. After years of eating at the same time, showering at the same time, going to bed at the same time, Jack was conditioned into a mental discipline tied to the clock. Every day, he awoke at the same minute and even went to the bathroom right on time.

He had once read about Pavlov's dogs in a science magazine, and he knew he was just like those trained dogs. The conditioned responses pissed him off. Ingrained habits were hard to break, though. He eventually would have to try. It was way too dangerous to be predictable.

Because it was now evening, the lights were dimmed in the cafeteria to give some semblance of atmosphere for dinner. There were numerous long and short tables scattered about and covered with white table clothes. A sideboard with extra dinnerware, forks and knives, plus condiments stood against one wall beside a tall dispenser for milk, juice and soda.

Jack spotted a long table with a couple of empty chairs and led Juleel to it. He dropped into his seat, and placed his napkin in his lap. It was then he noticed three other students at the end of the table immediately stand up and gather their trays. Disgust was written on their faces, as they carried their dinner trays to another area.

"Did we say something?" Juleel asked.

"Don't have to," Jack replied.

If these assholes wanted to give attitude, Jack could return it in kind.

Nearby Jack saw a group of guys, mostly athletes dressed in football jerseys, laughing and talking loud. It was apparent they were making comments about Jack and Juleel. Jack noticed that the leader was the big mouthed, idiot Raymon, who had been in the hallway the night before.

Then in a too loud voice Jack heard, "I wonder if they'll wait till they get back to their room to suck each other's dicks?"

This brought gales of laughter.

Another piped in, "I bet the motherfuckers want some of that peanut butter on their dicks for flavor."

Even more laughter erupted.

Jack noticed that Juleel's head was lowered in humiliation.

"Sit up straight," ordered Jack.

"What?"

"I said, sit up straight."

Juleel's head popped up, "They're talking about us."

"Yeah, I know what they're doing. So do you."

Juleel seemed to digest this and straightened his posture.

Jack nodded.

"Good. Don't ever let the bastards win."

Juleel started eating his dinner.

The guys at the table, led by Raymon, were hunting trouble. The type and the pattern were familiar. Jack had seen this at the Institution. There were idiots like these guys everywhere, always trying to intimidate and prove how tough they were. Rarely were they hard cases, just followers of a sort. Dangerous lemmings.

"Hey Raymon," one of them said, "why don't you clue them in on some basic facts."

So Raymon was going to stir up some action.

Jack understood what was going on and accepted it. He would, however keep his cool, and if Raymon wanted to push trouble he must do it on his own. Jack would do nothing unless Raymon got physical. Then…oh well.

More loud jokes followed about white boys and faggots. This was attracting attention. Some people were expectant and chuckled at the remarks, while others looked away or left the hall. These last individuals were few in number. Most sensed what was going on and stayed for the fun. The laughter was growing—louder and louder.

Jack was afraid that Juleel would crack. They ate silently not looking at the athletes. Maybe they would tire of this banal harassment and leave.

Finally, three of them walked over to their table. Raymon in the lead moved opposite Jack.

"Hey white boy, you think you're some kind of bad motherfucker?" he asked smiling. "I know you be an ugly one."

Laughter erupted, then died.

"Why, do you want to find out?" Jack replied mildly.

Raymon smile left his face, "Maybe I do."

Jack grunted.

"Looks like someone else cut your redneck ass up, boy. How'd you get so fuckin' ugly?"

Jack's eyes narrowed. One of his hands was hidden below the tablecloth with a serrated steak knife in it. He figured when they grew tired of the banter, things would get physical. The first thing he was going to do was cut Raymon.

"I don't like you, motherfucker," Raymon sneered.

"Is that a fact?" Jack spoke in such a gentle voice that it took a moment for Raymon to comprehend.

"Are you dissing me, motherfucker?"

"Damn," smiled Jack. "I knew I couldn't fool you."

For a moment, Raymon stood stunned, then with an oath started forward. A voice stopped him.

"Stop where you are, Raymon. Then, leave the hall. I want to see you in my office in one hour."

Jack glanced around. There stood Robert Brent, a cold glare on his face.

Raymon paused then turned to Jack. "I've got your number, white boy. You and this faggot motherfucker are history. Understand?"

"Raymon!" Brent growled.

"Yeah man, we be leavin'."

Raymon caught Jack's stare. Jack didn't waver an inch.

The athletes followed Raymon as he weaved through the tables to the door.

Brent eyed Jack and Juleel suspiciously, started to announce something, thought better of it and moved off to a far table.

"Did he have something to say?" asked Juleel.

"Guess not," said Jack getting back to his dinner.

Anger crossed Juleel's face, "I never liked confrontations, Jack."

Jack's eyes narrowed, "Nobody does."

CHAPTER 12

Dr. Nathan Ramapo awoke to the sound of his clock radio buzzing an insistent alarm. Seven a.m. Shit, another day. Without his clock radio, he would probably have slept until ten or eleven.

He clumsily reached to turn the radio off and knocked an empty Scotch bottle from his night stand to the floor. It crashed loudly making him wince. His head was splitting. Hammers of pain pounded inside his forehead. Staggering to his feet, he made it to the bathroom and relieved himself; then caught his reflection in the mirror. Damn, he felt and looked like shit. He vowed to immediately to give up drinking. Shooting pains punctuated his resolution—one he knew he probably couldn't keep.

Nathan Ramapo had sunk into alcoholism in a slow, gradual grind down, like drowning in quick sand. Middle age had not been pretty. He was a bachelor who at one time treasured his solitude but now found it to be a self-imposed prison. His life was steeped in loneliness with few choices available. The lack of viable alternatives was his living hell.

Drinking, he found, at least gave him a source of comfort, however fleeting. When the amber liquid flowed in a hot river to his stomach, he could bask in forgetful, sublime dreams. Anesthetized to the pain of his unending existence, he could blissfully not see, not hear or feel. He could forget his life of constant hell and his never ending call to misplaced stoic duty.

This morning, was the start of a new semester at Mt. Sidney College. He had received his schedule weeks ago, which included teaching an eight o'clock class on Monday, Wednesday and Friday. These were the hours that usually went to younger Associate Professors, not Full Professors such as himself. But a month ago, a tenured professor, Doctor Fleming, had suddenly developed a heart problem, announced his retirement and immediate departed. This had shaken up the English department, and, for at least this semester, Ramapo was stuck teaching an early class.

Stumbing around, he found a clean towel and after a long shower and two cups of instant coffee, he finally checked his tie in the mirror. The drinking was taking its toll. His face—once handsome—was puffy and slack. He was still tall and distinguished but was now getting thinner in the wrong places such as his arms and legs and thicker in his hips and waist. Nathan Ramapo was sixty-three and it showed.

Nathan rented a furnished, two story frame house on the edge of the campus. He needed to be close to work for he no longer drove a car. A progressive retinal disfunction gave him problems judging distance.

Rushing along as fast as he could, he made it to class just as the last of thirty students were being seated. Setting his briefcase on the desk, he extracted a text book and adjusted some notes on the lectern.

On the blackboard, he wrote his name in large script and turned to the class. "My name is Dr. Ramapo, and this is English Literature 20—an introduction to late nineteenth century writing from James to Dreiser."

Nathan scanned the faces in a clean sweep and at once felt his heart nearly stop and his chest tighten. Shock took the breath from his lungs. There, several rows away he saw a large white boy staring back at him.

What the…

There must be a mistake. This was Mt. Sidney College, an all black school. What was this young white devil doing here?

Who allowed this…this…this…sin?

No it couldn't be.

Ramapo looked again. Maybe his eyes were fooling him, but no…the young man was older in appearance, with deep scars on his face. He was brutal looking. The muscles in his arms and chest were over-developed from obvious hours of exercise. He had that aura…like the ones who…

Checking his notes, Ramapo could see his hands start to shake. Desperately, he tried to breathe to recover his composure but failed. Rage filled him. Fighting for control, he gripped the podium until his fingers hurt. Sweat popped on his forehead.

Whites! Why?

Sweat was now running into his eyes as he tried to start the lecture. Words wouldn't come forth.

Move, he told himself. Just move. Get the hell out!

Was the air getting thicker? Why couldn't he breathe?

The class was now beginning to notice his distress. They looked around at one another, uneasily, exchanging questioning glances.

"Excuse me!" Ramapo stammered at last and raced out the door.

Down the hallway he ran, bumping into a bewildered janitor who stood aside in alarm.

Nathan made it to a stall in the closest men's room and threw up. His head was spinning, but he felt slightly better. His mind whirled. Who's idea was this to bring a white boy here? It was one thing to pass them casually on the street, maybe even exchange a cordial word, but this institution was sacred. Mt. Sidney College was a sanctuary against the evil white world. How dare they bring a white devil in here.

Ramapo's fist struck the wall of the bathroom stall. Over and over he hit the metal divider until his hands were bloody.

Something would have to be done. No white bastard was going to ruin Mt. Sidney, his last bastion, his sanctuary.

***

Checking his class schedule, Jack couldn't help but feel an exhilaration. This was it, the beginning of his climb from incarceration to a better life. All he had to do was focus, work hard and soon he'd graduate and be out of here—degree in hand.

He could still remember when he'd decided to be a veterinarian. It was his path. The right path. He loved animals. The Institution kept a large number of animals on an adjacent farm and from time to time he had been bused there to work. Although most of the jobs were in the large fields, once in a while, he was assigned to the barns where he cleaned stalls and tended the chickens, cows and hogs.

There were dozens of cats in the barn to keep the rats under control. One of them was an old gray tom named, Targy. His fur was course and patchy from lack of grooming, part of one ear was torn and he was blind in one eye. There was also a scar on his cheek that no longer grew fur. That was probably what attracted Jack to him. Targy was scarred just like he was. His imperfections were there for everyone to see.

Soon they became good friends and Targy knew that Jack would always have a treat for him. He'd rub his old beat-up head against Jack's leg, waiting for Jack to pick him up and pet him.

It was a sad day when one of the guards told him that the farm supervisor had chosen three cats that didn't look healthy to be put down. Targy had been one of them. A terrible sense of loss swept through him. It was as if an old and good friend had died.

That night, in his bunk, Jack thought of the old gray cat and swore that if he ever got out, he'd work with animals. Animals he knew, didn't deceive, cheat, lie and abuse. Only humans did that.

His first class was English Literature, a subject he found fascinating. He had read all the poetry in the Institution's library but he had always sought more. There was something so satisfying to him about poetry. The beauty of the words and phrases, something…The great writers knew how to connect spiritually with the fragile soul and its place in nature and the inevitable mortality of all humananity. The last was a subject Jack intimately knew something about.

The first person he spotted upon entering the classroom was the girl he had bumped into at the Registrar's Office. She was seated to his right and Jack saw her glance over at him. She didn't look away. He could feel his heart rate increase. She was stunning. He blushed at her attention. She must have realized he was staring, for she abruptly turned away to her books.

Jack had never had a girlfriend. He had read about great love affairs and certainly he felt an instinctual attraction to females but that's as far as it went. There, of course, weren't any girls Inside. So unlike every male in this school, Jack knew he had no experience with girls either sexually or as a innocent flirtation. He was probably the one and only true virgin on campus.

Ironically, he'd killed two human beings but had never made love once. Hell, he'd never even kissed a girl.

Jack could never tell anyone, including Juleel, the biographical facts. They'd think he was weird or an idiot. It was far easier to indicate you were experienced in carnal pursuits. No one asked for any details. They were too busy dreaming of their own conquests.

Jack found a seat with a view of the girl. Her every detail filled his eyes with wonder. The first thing he noticed were her long, nicely shaped legs. Her skin was olive and blemish free. Her raven hair was braided long and thick. Her eyes were a deep, sensuous brown under high cheek bones.

He wondered what it would be like to take her clothes off; touch her. He felt a stirring in his groin. Maybe it would be worth some effort to find out.

Jack scolded himself. What would a girl as beautiful as this one see in a scar-face like himself? He had nothing. He was nothing. Nothing but a convicted murderer out on a bizarre parole program. Everything he owned came from the State. Imagine if she knew he had killed two people and one of them his own father. Besides, none of these black girls at Mt. Sidney would ever be caught dead in the presence of a white boy.

The Professor, a tall black man, walked in finally and wrote his name, Dr. Ramapo, on the blackboard. He turned and immediately did an awkward double-take when he saw Jack. Then he looked like he was choking. His face turn pale. This Dr. Ramapo then turned away as if he'd seen a ghost. Jack wondered if the guy had been looking right at him. There was panic written on the Professor's face.

What could be wrong with the guy? He looked like he was shaking. Was he sick or something? Then, to everyone's astonishment, he ran from the room, leaving everyone aghast.

Twenty minutes later, he returned.

Could this Dr. Ramapo have been reacting to him, asked Jack to himself? Was it his imagination that the guy had been looking directly at him?

Ramapo smiled wanly and apologized to the class and claimed he wasn't feeling well. "I think I ate something this morning that didn't agree with me," he said.

Maybe something big and white, thought Jack.

Ramapo shot Jack a severe glance as if he could hear his thoughts. "Let's begin today's lecture with some background on the Victorian age."

Jack took copious notes. He wasn't about to miss a thing. His job was to get an education despite this guy Ramapo or the distraction of the beautiful girl across the room.

***

After his first two classes of the morning, CQ headed back to Lincoln Hall. Time to get high and chill. He had a fat joint of some real good Jamaican shit waiting for him in his closet and afterwards his main man, John Coltrane, would take him far away with his seductive saxophone.

CQ's dorm room was perfectly situated for a pot smoker. A large exhaust vent was located in the ceiling of the closet. All he had to do was close the closet door and light up. Even someone a few feet away in the room couldn't smell the marijuana. For a very cool person like himself, this was perfect.

His thin legs propelled him up the steps and into the lobby. Suddenly a vice-like hand stopped him, and Robert Brent's gigantic frame loomed in front of him.

"Hey CQ, I've been waiting for you. I'd like to see you in my office."

Startled, CQ sputtered, "Yeah Robert, but like I got this…"

"Now!"

CQ glanced around with edgy eyes. What was this? Every instinct, honed from the streets of Newark, warned him to be careful or run. Brent's face looked strained.

"Yeah man. Okay."

Once in his office, Brent tried to put the thin street artist at ease. "Relax CQ. I'm not going to bite you." He sat down behind his desk, picked up a pen and rolled it between his thick fingers before he spoke again. "I just want to know if you know anything more about that mess in the hallway outside the white boy's room?"

Sweat started down CQ's face.

"No man, nothin'. You know?"

"No, I don't know," Brent said flatly. "Tell me?"

"I don't know nothin'."

"The painters were here this morning, CQ. Before they came, I had a look at that wall. You know, I don't think the average brother could spray paint that good. Know what I'm sayin'?"

CQ shrugged.

"I'd say an expert graffiti artist would have to have done that work," Brent mused. "What do you think?"

"You think it was good?"

Brent knew he'd hit on something—CQ's pride as an artist.

"Yeah, I think it took someone with a lot of skill."

CQ grinned, "It was probably done too quickly, though."

"What do you mean?"

"I mean, whoever did it was in too big a hurry. They could have worked with shadow to get more detail if they'd had time."

"You don't know anyone with that much skill around here?"

"Other than me," CQ drooled, "I don't know anyone that good."

"Then you see why I wanted to talk to you."

CQ's ego had almost sprung a trap. He knew Brent was trying to pin him to the drawing. The Head Resident would have him on a bus back to Newark before sundown if he didn't keep his stupid mouth shut. Now was the time to do some major back peddling.

"Come to think about it, Robert," he said smartly. "Maybe a lot of brothers could do that job. You know what I'm sayin'? Kind of looks rough on the edges, like doodling."

Brent surprised CQ by slamming his big hand on the desk and glaring at CQ. "Listen you little bastard, you know you're the only one who could do that shit in the hallway. Aren't you?"

CQ's eyes widened, "No man…"

"Don't insult my intelligence!" Brent shouted. "Who put you up to it? Was it Raymon? Tell me now, and I'll make sure they don't expel you from Mt. Sidney. If you don't…"

Now CQ was scared. He was on scholarship and didn't want to lose his one opportunity for an education. What were the alternatives? On one hand he had Brent who could probably shit-can him and on the other, Raymon Jackson, a bad motherfucker, who could tear his head off…maybe even kill him. He hated athletes and ex-athletes. These assholes always wanted to fuck with someone.

"I don't know nothin'. Nothin'!"

"Was it Raymon Jackson put you up to it?" screamed Brent.

137

"No man!"

"Then who?"

"Nobody put me up to nothin'."

CQ was getting flustered. This was harassment.

"You're lying." shouted Brent.

"No," whimpered CQ.

Brent now whispered, looking directly into CQ's eyes. "Yes you are. I can see it in your eyes."

CQ turned away, a trembling started in his body. "I don't know nothin', Robert. I swear."

Brent stood in fury, "Get out of here. NOW!"

CQ shaking, bolted for the door.

"Wait!" yelled Brent.

CQ froze.

"If I find out you're the brother did that shit, I'm going to personally kick your scrawny, little ass. Do you hear me?"

CQ nodded, too nervous to speak.

"Get the fuck out of here."

CQ jumped through the door.

Robert Brent collapsed in his chair. Why did he have to be the heavy—the policeman? Why had Dean Jans put him in this position? All this to protect Mulligan—a damn white boy.

CHAPTER 13

The telephone started ringing at seven o'clock in Keysha's room. She had just opened her books and was trying to concentrate on her homework. The classes she had signed up for were incredibly demanding. To do well, she would have to prioritize her studies, especially in psychology and math.

When the first ring sounded, she was recopying notes. Irritated by the distraction, she picked up, "Hello."

"Hey, good-lookin', it's me."

"Who?" she snapped irritably.

There was a short silence.

"It's me, Raymon. Raymon Jackson," the voice said defensively. "We met during the black out."

"Oh, hi," she said in a nicer tone.

"I just thought I'd see whatch you be doin'."

"Studying," Keysha said flatly.

"That sounds like a drag," he said smartly.

"Not if you're a serious student," said Keysha.

"Hey, do your thing, baby," laughed Raymon.

Baby! She was nobody's baby except her parents. Enough of this mindless chatter. "So what can I do for you, Raymon?"

"Baby, there's lots of things you could do for me," he said laughing.

Keysha blushed. She disliked the sexual innuendo. It made her feel like an object to be used. Did Raymon think this line of shit was a turn-on?

"I was thinkin' maybe you and me could get somethin' goin' this weekend. You dig? How 'bout Saturday after the game in which, by the way, I will be the star?"

"What did you have in mind?" Keysha said coolly.

Raymon played his trump card. "Well Tyrel and Danielle was sayin' they'd like to go to the Anaconda. So I thought you might wanna go too."

"Isn't that a snake?"

"Naw baby…it's a dance place in town."

"Let me think about it."

A pause ensued.

"Think about it?" questioned Raymon incredulously.

"Yes."

"Baby, this is Raymon Jackson you be talkin' to. I don't ask twice," he said in disbelief.

"Okay then. The answer is no."

Anger surged over the line. "Fuck you!" he yelled. "I can get a hundred bitches like you to go dancin'."

"Then do so," she said calmly.

"Shee-it!" he exclaimed.

"Goodbye, Raymon," Keysha said as she hung up.

What an asshole. She tried to get back to work but couldn't stop thinking about his words—bitch and fuck you and baby. Who did he think he was talking to? Just because he was an athlete, popular and blessed with good looks didn't mean she was going to fall all over herself to be seen with him.

Then her thoughts reverted to Jack Mulligan. He was in her calculus and English lit classes. She hoped he hadn't noticed her watching him today. She was afraid he had. How embarrassing.

The phone rang again. Was there no end to these interruptions.

"Hello," she said sharply.

"Don't hang up."

"Raymon?"

"Please, don't hang up."

"Alright, but make it quick," she said in a non-committal way.

Keysha could hear Raymon's breath exhale, "I'm sorry, okay. You're real touchy about nothin'."

"Nothing?"

"I didn't mean it that way," he blurted. This apology must be killing him, she thought.

"Will you please go out with me to the Anaconda Saturday night?" He asked slowly and clearly.

"After what you called me?" she asked incredulously.

"I said I was sorry," he said contritely.

"Is sorry suppose to cover all those obscenities?"

"No but it's all I can say."

He wasn't going to get away from this that easy. Keysha decided to toy with him.

"Well I don't like being referred to as a bitch."

"Sorry, okay, it won't happen again."

Keysha's voice hardened, "See that it doesn't."

"About Saturday night at the Anaconda, you'll have a good time, Keysha," he said, sounding as though he might start to beg.

"Do you think you can act like a gentleman?" she inquired.

"A what?"

"A gentleman," she repeated. "You know what one is?"

"Yeah, yeah, I can do that," he said desperately.

His voice didn't sound convincing to Keysha.

"Why couldn't you have spoken to me this way to begin with?" she admonished.

"I was pissed…angry," he answered quickly. "Forgive me."

Raymon was a strange guy. He seemed to run hot and cold. When he was nice, he could be engaging, but there was a wildness and a mean streak in him that she couldn't quite understand.

"You say Tyrel and Danielle will be there?" she asked.

"Yeah."

Keysha sat silent for a moment and let Raymon stew.

"Well okay," she finally spoke. "It does sound like fun. I haven't been dancing in a long time."

"Hey, solid," he said enthusiastically. "You won't regret it."

Funny, Keysha thought, she already was.

***

Tyrel waited for Danielle outside the library that evening. The air was soft and warm, and the huge old oaks swayed rhythmically in the light breeze. Squirrels played in the acorns, and here and there couples sat on the lawn talking and laughing. Somewhere in the distance someone was playing a cello. Its sad, beautiful tones floated through the air as if it were paying tribute to the pity of another day gone.

Tyrel was terribly exhausted. Practices, such as today's, physically and mentally drained him. It was hard to concentrate or study for exams when you were this tired. Danielle said she would help him, and that's why he was outside the library.

When he saw her coming, however, he noticed that all signs of his exhaustion seemed to instantly vanish. Could a woman do this? Tyrel observed how Danielle walked, striding with cat-like grace. No matter how old he became, Tyrel would remember Danielle at that moment. He'd see her in his mind walking as a lovely vision through the soft, dappled, late evening light.

Danielle was dressed in a red blouse with tight jeans forming over her hips and legs. Her sensual body fit into the clothes without making her look like a tramp or obvious about her startling good looks.

"Hey, Tyrel," she said with a dazzling smile.

"Hey yourself."

Her kiss was warm and seductive. Tyrel wanted to linger, but Danielle playfully pushed him back.

"We have to study," she scolded. "I don't want to be seen hangin' around some dummy."

"Okay, Einstein," he laughed. "Lead the way."

The library was a solid, two-story brick building constructed at the turn-of-the-last-century. Inside, heavy oak dominated the huge book-filled rooms, giving an atmosphere of quiet meditation.

Tyrel led Danielle to the second floor and back to a table in the corner. From there, a window looked out on the expansive campus. For two hours they studied, only occasionally stopping to teasingly gaze into one another's eyes. Twilight, then darkness came to the campus, before Danielle finally called a break and said she'd like to go for a soda.

"Is there some place close by?"

"Downstairs in the basement there's some machines," Tyrel said. "Let's see what they have."

Tyrel needed a snack desperately. With all the energy he expended, he stayed constantly hungry. Meals at the dorm were not great, and only hit the spot for a while. The problem was that Tyrel loved fast, high fat foods. He knew they weren't nutritionally the best food, but they satisfied his need for replenishing lost energy.

The vending machines in the basement had every kind of junk food known to humankind. Danielle selected a diet soda, while Tyrel got a regular soda, a bag of chips and two candy bars.

"Do you eat that stuff all the time?" asked Danielle.

"Yeah, I'm really hungry."

"We gotta get you something better," sighed Danielle. "That junk food will kill you."

Tyrel grunted as he wolfed down the chips. Danielle shook her head. "My mother would have a fit if she saw you eat that."

"Oh."

"She's a nutritionist and believes in eating a healthy diet. Tomorrow I'll get you something better, like carrot sticks," Danielle said, while batting her dark eyes. "I don't want any fat guy hangin' around me."

Tyrel laughed as he kissed her. He couldn't believe he'd just met her. She was so incredible and so beautiful. He wasn't sure about love at first sight, but he could believe that love might gain strength in a very short time.

"Did Keysha tell you about going to the Anaconda, Saturday night with Raymon and her?" he asked.

"No," she said in surprise. "But I haven't seen her."

"Raymon was going to call her."

"Are you kidding?" questioned Danielle with a frown.

"No, really," Tyrel said slyly. "What do you think?"

"Well I guess opposites could attract," she said, skeptically. "But isn't he kind of aggressive? You know, a lady's man?"

"He's had his share of girls for sure," Tyrel mused.

"I hope Keysha can handle this situation," said Danielle in a worried tone.

"Hey, come on," Tyrel said brightly. "Raymon's okay. Besides we'll be right there."

"Tyrel, your friend Raymon may think he's god's gift to women, but there are girls who don't necessarily want to be his doormat or live in his shadow."

Tyrel appeared guilty, "I kind of thought they'd make a good couple. You know…"

"You thought what?" she questioned in astonishment.

"That they might be good for each other."

Danielle laughed. "Let me get something straight," she said. "Did you set this up for Saturday night?"

"Yeah well," Tyrel mumbled, "sort of."

Danielle laughed again, "You're a match maker. I can't believe it. What a romantic."

"Naw."

"Yes you are. I had an aunt just like you, and now I'm hangin' with another one," she said shaking her head.

"Naw," Tyrel repeated sheepishly as he remembered Raymon saying the same thing.

"Oh but you are," Danielle said teasingly. "What a romantic. I'm just afraid you've missed your mark this time, Cupid."

"They'll get along, just wait," said Tyrel confidently.

Danielle shook her head, "This ought to be very interesting."

CHAPTER 14

News of the murder of Sergeant Warren Whitaker didn't surface for almost a week. All anyone knew was that he and Thaddeus Brown had disappeared. Four days of torrential rain hampered any search. Finally, dogs were called in and his unmarked grave was ultimately discovered.

Navy Intelligence and the FBI took over, and Thaddeus Brown became their prime suspect. Photos were circulated at post offices and to local police stations in a three hundred mile radius. Law enforcement especially concentrated in the eastern Kentucky area and East St. Louis where they thought he might go.

Thaddeus, however, was by then sleeping and living under a railroad bridge in Minneapolis. He had joined the legions of homeless who peopled America's underclass and now lived in nearly animal-like conditions. Knowing, as he did, that the search would take law enforcement into all his old haunts, Thaddeus decided to play the part of a vagabond, but not just any vagabond, a crazed individual.

To hide his features, he grew his beard and hair long and shaggy. The scruffy beard was no problem, since he had thick black whiskers, but the hair would take months to extend to a desirable length. To disguise his head in the meantime, he found a ratty fur hat in a land fill in Memphis. It looked funky, but no matter, he was now in the role of a deranged, homeless hobo.

After he had escaped Camp Roman, Thaddeus caught several freights over the next week until he had arrived in Minneapolis. As well as he could, he kept his eye on the newspapers, but it was a while before he scanned a small story about the "DI Murder." Logically, the FBI concentrated their search in the south. Thaddeus realized this was fortunate, but he also realized he'd better not get sloppy and get arrested anywhere. The police hassled the homeless unmercifully, but seldom arrested them unless it was truly warranted.

It sickened Thaddeus to watch the poor and wretched of the earth being humiliated and taken advantage of by those in authority and by the very wealthiest. The homeless were the people who needed help the most. They were the ones who had seen their dreams crushed and now begged and sold the last morsels of their dignity to a society that wished they'd simply disappear.

Being homeless in America was dangerous, too. As in all levels of society, Thaddeus found he had to cope with the realities of basic economics. Only so much food, shelter and necessary materials existed for a changing and large number of people. Supply and demand were the order of the day; survival of the fittest was the law of daily existence. To survive, one had to obtain necessities, especially food and then fight off others who would take them away.

Thaddeus learned from observing others how to find food in garbage cans and dumpsters. His wardrobe came from tossed out clothing. Begging became his new profession. He even became observant enough to spot easy marks for cigarettes.

Patience was the key, he found. He would wait till local restaurants dumped their garbage and fight the rats and other human predators for every ounce of it. Some of the kinder cooks and busboys would occasionally give fresh food to the homeless, but that was extremely rare. Most restaurant owners didn't want the unwashed masses hanging around their establishments. Ragged people were not good for business.

Months passed and Thaddeus became a homeless veteran. One cold night in November, however, Thaddeus awoke from his sleep to find his bag being pilfered by an out of work laborer from Florida. The rangy-looking white man had just arrived that afternoon and had complained all evening about not having gloves.

Thaddeus kept a foot long bar of steel in his hand while he slept. It came in handy for such occasions. Upon seeing the thief, he jumped to his feet screaming at the redneck who immediately dropped the bag but pulled a knife. Brandishing the steel bar, Thaddeus kept his eyes on the man as they circled.

"I'll rip you up, nigger," warned the thief.

"Bring it on, redneck."

149

Thaddeus waited for the man's onslaught. It came a moment later, when the white man lunged at him. Thaddeus whacked him in the face with the steel bar. The big laborer dropped the knife, hit the dirt and groaned loudly. Thaddeus came in for the kill hitting him two times more on the head. The last blow made a popping sound as the man's skull came apart. Blood and brain tissue sprayed on his pants.

His breath came hard as he drew in big gulps of cold air. Shit, he'd just killed a man! What was he going to do? What if the police came? He had to leave quickly.

That morning, he was on a freight headed for Canada. Anywhere but Minneapolis would do. A week later, having not eaten in days, he staggered into Montreal.

Winter was coming on. This was the season that usually killed a large number of homeless. There was no pity for those sleeping on heating grates or in doorways. The haves were quite content to see the herd of have-nots culled so to speak. It decreased the "excess population" Thaddeus considered in disgust.

Canadian winters were brutal. Thaddeus had to do something and quickly or freeze to death on the street. The shelters were filled with the same kind of perverts, mental cases and ex-criminals as those in the States.

Help came from a Catholic Church shelter and kitchen run by Father Charles D'Vesso. He was a short, hunchback Italian in his late fifties, who, despite a deformed spine, was blessed with a warm, bright smile and a sharp mind. Father D'Vesso was able to raise money for the homeless as no one else could. Even the most hard boiled businessman could not withstand the soft, pitiful eyes of D'Vesso. His face shined each time he helped a fellow human being, and it shined extra bright when he collected money for the needy.

Thaddeus, whose hair and beard were now long and wild looking, knew he couldn't possibly be recognized as a Marine deserter. When he showed up at a Catholic shelter to eat a treasured bowl of soup, he was pleasantly surprised at the kindness of the staff and their caring attitudes. Somehow he hoped he could show his appreciation for their kindness. He asked one of the staff members if he could help in the kitchen and was put to work washing dishes. The hot water and dirty dishes gave him a new and needed purpose and was quite satisfying.

After two weeks of washing dishes, Father D'Vesso approached him to say thanks. "You are a hard worker, young man."

"Thank you, Father. I can't tell you how great it is to wash dishes for you."

"Your charity is so appreciated. The needs of the people are great and everyone's hands can help."

Thaddeus introduced himself to the kindly priest as Joe. Father D' Vesso didn't ask for a last name and didn't make any further inquiries. D'Vesso seemed to respect privacy. After another week of washing dishes, peeling vegetables and mopping floors, D'Vesso again came to him, and this time offered him a job as a cook and maintenance man. Thaddeus was thrilled, and in the next months, tried to impress Father D'Vesso with his hard work and diligence. Thaddeus became indispensable at solving all-sorts of problems from plumbing and carpentry to cooking.

Five years passed uneventfully with Thaddeus working long hours. These were satisfying years in which Thaddeus immersed himself into the rigors of daily routine. No job was beneath him. He cooked, cleaned, ran errands and made himself available all hours of the day and night.

Father D'Vesso couldn't help but recognize his employee's intellect and always complimented him for his fine work. He could tell there was a dark, more than likely, criminal past haunting Joe and that the past kept him at the shelter hidden away from society and the probing eyes of the police. The soup kitchen was a safe haven, and Thaddeus clung to it like a drowning man to a life raft.

When D'Vesso tried to broach the subject of his past, Thaddeus always withdrew. He'd change the subject or walk away. The priest was a patient man and knew his cook would confess eventually.

Then one day, D'Vesso called Thaddeus into his office and introduced him to a wiry little man with a quiet manner but very shifty eyes. Thaddeus didn't like the look of the man and was cautious. Could he be from the police or was he a con man?

"Joe, I'd like you to meet, Mr. Talbot. He is an old friend of mine and a very skilled individual."

Thaddeus shook hands with the man and sat down in a chair that faced D'Vesso and Talbot.

"Joe, I called you here today to have a conversation about your future. As you know, you have never opened up about where you came from, or about your family or your education, although I think it must have been considerable.

"Yes but…"

"Never mind, Joe," injected D'Vesso with a soothing manner. "I'm not asking you to divulge your past. However, many in this world seek salvation and change. I know you as Joe, and you have become a friend and have worked extremely hard to change yourself into a truly charitable Christian."

"Thank you, Father."

"That brings me to Mr. Talbot. In the past, I have used his services on rare occasions to help a handful of people reclaim their lives. God has given Mr. Talbot an artistic gift. He can duplicate credentials and various other papers to give a person a new identity.

Thaddeus was shocked, "He's a forger?"

"Hey, watch it," warned the little man.

"Sorry," apologized Thaddeus.

"Mr. Talbot is more than that, Joe. He can create a viable background, so that if anyone gives a cursory check into a background, there will be depth to the credentials.

"Joe I know you are educated. Somewhere in your background you have probably gone to college, and maybe you were a professional man. It would be selfish of me to keep you working here when you could be contributing so much more. To make this possible, you will need a new identity. Mr. Talbot can give you one."

"But Father, I've enjoyed my work here."

"I know, but it is time to take a step in another direction."

Thaddeus started to protest but D'Vesso calmed him with a touch on the knee.

153

"Joe you are wasting God's gifts to you. I have already been remiss in my dependance upon your hard work."

"But."

"No buts, Joe. Let me help you get a real life back."

And so D'Vesso and Talbot started to work.

Thaddeus made dramatic changes over the next month. First, he cleaned up his physical appearance. He shaved the beard and cut his hair conservatively short. Mr. Talbot then shot some photos and started to work on the new identity papers.

D'Vesso, for his part, had him outfitted with a wardrobe from a tailor he knew. The two suits, sports jacket and casual clothes fit him like a glove.

Two weeks later on a cold and rainy day in March, Father D'Vesso sent for him. Mr. Talbot had arrived back at the shelter with Thaddeus' new papers. They were beautifully done. He now had a U.S. Passport, a New York State drivers license, Social Security card and two major credit cards.

"Don't get arrested," warned Talbot whose wandering eyes couldn't stay still for any length of time. "One thing false papers won't do is hide fingerprints. If anyone ever checks those fingers, they'll soon know who you really are."

Thaddeus Brown opened the passport and glanced at his photo and his new name. It was the name he'd have for the rest of his life, Dr. Nathan Ramapo.

CHAPTER 15

Achieving the right look on Saturday night was always a challenge for Raymon. He had to look sharper than the rest of the common chumps around campus. His fans expected style and class. After all, he was a star athlete, a student leader and, most importantly, very cool. He couldn't be seen wearing just any threads.

Raymon carefully inspected his closet and chose a gray collarless jacket with a matching black shirt. Cool. Only the best for today—his day. Raymon had played an excellent game earlier that day, and now he was going to show his new woman, Keysha, why he was considered stud material on this campus. All day he had felt lucky. Maybe she was the source of his luck. He hoped so.

Smiling at his image in the mirror, he re-ran the football game through his mind. It had been one of his finest performances so far. Raymon had scored three touchdowns, ran for two hundred eighty one yards and caught five passes as the Wildcats had rolled over

Wesleyan 32 to O. Coach Dunn had awarded him the game ball and had named him player of the week.

The students and alumni had chanted his name and cheered as he left the field. They loved him. He gave them the thrill they so desired. It was like a drug. The people in the stadium identified with the brave hero below. Fans had a vicarious relationship with their movie idols, rock stars and blue chip athletes, and Raymon Jackson was indeed the bluest of blue chip.

Raymon checked the time. It was a quarter to eight. Keysha and Danielle were going to meet he and Tyrel in the lobby at eight. That girl Keysha had better look gorgeous. If a woman was going to be seen with Raymon Jackson, she'd better be dressed in her best. After all, she was in the presence of a minor god, and she had better know she was one of the spoils.

Another quick look in the mirror and he was ready.

He found Tyrel waiting in the lobby reading a newspaper. Raymon frowned and shook his head. Why couldn't the big man dress with a little more flare? Did Tyrel care at all for his image? Attitude and "the look" were everything. The perception of success had to be honed and constantly upheld.

"Man, I gotta' get you to a good clothing store," Raymon said as a greeting.

"What?" answered Tyrel peering up from his paper.

"Look at chu," Raymon continued, shaking his head. "Man you're a bad ass, defensive football player. A star. Dress like one."

"What's wrong with what I've got on?"

Tyrel had on a pair of casual tan Dockers with a blue dress shirt. A darker tan sports jacket completed the ensemble.

"Tyrel you look too...too conservative. You know...white."

Tyrel waved off the remark, "Get outta here."

"No, I'm serious," Raymon said. "You look like one of those white business types from the suburbs. The kind that goes out on Saturdays and mows the lawn; takes his plump little wife and two kids to the movies and church on Sunday. Then come Monday morning fucks over a brother."

Tyrel laughed, "Get back, Raymon."

"Keep laughing, motherfucker."

"Raymon you somethin'."

"Alright, alright, don't pay attention to me," Raymon said, throwing his hands up in frustration. "I'll keep tryin' to get you dressed for success."

At that moment Raymon and Tyrel spotted Keysha and Danielle as they came down the staircase and into the lobby. Every male turned to stare. Most swallowed hard. The two girls were devastatingly gorgeous. Raymon felt the breath freeze in his chest just looking at Keysha, and Tyrel had a grin that a tire iron couldn't have dislodged.

Keysha was dressed in a chic black dress that made the most of her long legs. Her hair was down to her waist, and she had a mischievous smile on her glowing face as she strode confidently toward Raymon.

Danielle looked equally exquisite in a clinging red dress that plunged low in front to reveal ample cleavage. Her eyes were emphasized with dark mascara on her long lashes. The effect was startling.

"My Lord," whispered Raymon to himself.

Tyrel stepped forward, "You two look beautiful. Wow."

Both girls blushed.

"Let's do some dancing," Keysha said brightly to redirect their attention.

Raymon, however, let his eyes roam over Keysha. "Girl, you got it goin' on. You be drivin' me crazy. You look so fine."

"Well thanks," replied Keysha uneasy with the compliment. Raymon was sizing her up much as a farmer might judge a prize heifer.

Tyrel and Danielle started ahead walking hand in hand to the parking lot where Raymon kept his three year old BMW. The car had been purchased at a special, one-time-only price by Raymon at a dealership owned by a prominent alumni. Technically, maybe some of the NCAA rules had been bent, but Raymon was special. However, no other student could have bought such a car at such a low and undisclosed price.

As they walked along slowly on the way to the parking lot, Raymon kept up his torrent of killer lines. These were his tried and true favorites. "Baby, I'm hearing a song, no—a symphony—as you be walkin' beside me. There's no one who ever caused my heart to hear this kind of music."

Oh spare me, thought Keysha.

Raymon continued, "I'm seein' you baby, but I can't..." Then he stopped in mid-sentence. A frown hardened his face.

Out of the shadows in front of them came a large, solitary figure. It was the white boy, Jack Mulligan, who was on his way back to Lincoln Hall from most likely the library carrying his book bag. He'd probably been studying all afternoon and evening, even though it was Saturday. As he passed under the light of one of the street lamps, Keysha could see his ravaged face. Raymon stiffened as he watched Jack approach them.

When only ten feet separated them, Raymon seized the moment to impress Keysha. "Hey, check it out, look who we got comin' here," said Raymon with a loud sneer. "Do you always study on Saturday night, Mulligan?"

The mention of his name stopped Jack.

"Yeah, I heard that's your name, motherfucker."

Jack said nothing.

"Oh shit, I forgot," Raymon continued with a laugh, "when you're as ugly as ya'll, you don't have much else to do."

Raymon chuckled at his own humor. Keysha stood, mortified.

Jack slipped the book bag from his shoulder in silence. His stoic stare was somehow disturbing.

Keysha turned away, uneasy, while Raymon kept talking. "Aren't you going to say hello to my woman, Keysha, here. After all, this may be as close as you ever get to a genuine female at Mt. Sidney."

Jack's expression didn't change, his face was etched like hardened steel and not a muscle moved. Raymon moved closer to him, "Cat got your tongue, white bread?"

Raymon smiled and took Jack's actions for fear and bore in. He was the school yard bully now. "You like all them white motherfuckers, aren't you Mulligan? You're chickenshit."

No reply.

"Stop this." interrupted Keysha in disgust.

"What!" Raymon shrieked, not turning from Jack.

"I said stop it. He hasn't done anything to you. Leave him alone."

Raymon shook his head, "Well there you have it, Mulligan. I guess Keysha has given you a temporary reprieve, but I got some advice for you. Don't be makin' a habit of crossin' my path too often around here. Understand? I don't like white motherfuckers, and I especially don't like you."

Keysha diverted her attention in embarrassment. She was blanching in humiliation. Raymon's trash talk was childish.

"If we don't go now, Raymon," she said coldly, "I'm going back to my room."

"You ain't goin' nowhere," ordered Raymon.

"If you don't stop this now," she shot back. "I'm leaving."

Raymon frowned. Damn bitches. He sneered and turned from Jack. "I'll be seein' you later, Mulligan," he said stepping within a foot of Jack. "What kind of fuckin' name is that, motherfucker? Irish or somethin'. Is that what you are? Shee-it."

Jack made no reply.

Keysha grabbed Raymon's arm. She could see real trouble if they didn't go now.

In a low voice she said, "Let's go."

Raymon smiled, "Later, motherfucker. I know where you live."

As Keysha and Raymon walked away, Keysha glanced back. Jack's eyes caught hers. She knew then that she'd definitely made a mistake going out with

Raymon. She watched Jack pick up his book bag and move off alone into the darkness.

Tyrel and Danielle were waiting beside the gleaming silver BMW when Raymon and Keysha arrived. Danielle could see a tense, distressed look in Keysha's features. What had happened? Did Raymon act like a pig on the way to the car?

Raymon laughed extra loud as he approached Tyrel for a high five. "Hey brother, you shoulda' seen what just went down."

"What's that?"

"You know that white dude? We saw him goin' into the dorm," Raymon said excitedly. "I couldn't resist. I had to trip on the dumb motherfucker. He looked like he was about ready to cry."

"It was embarrassing," disagreed Keysha. "You made a complete ass out of yourself."

Raymon's temper flared, "Lighten up, Keysha. I was just havin' some fun with the white boy. Brent told me his name is Mulligan. What the fuck kind of name is that?"

"Did he do anything?" asked Tyrel.

"Naw, he's too scared. He's white. I just wanted him to know who the boss is around here."

Keysha was furious. She debated whether to walk back to Lincoln Hall and leave Raymon and his ego here in the parking lot. She knew, however, that she'd probably appear as the self-centered bitch. Better to ride the evening out. Besides, Tyrel and Danielle would be disappointed if she left now.

"Let's get going," declared Danielle who sensed Keysha's anger. She grabbed Tyrel's arm and practically pulled him into the back seat.

161

Keysha slipped into the front seat determined not to ruin it for everyone. How could she have agreed to go out with Raymon? She must be crazy.

Raymon started the BMW and slowly pulled out of the parking lot. He drove slowly and carefully not out of concern for his passengers, but because he didn't want anything to happen to his oh-so-precious car.

"Raymon you really ought to leave that white boy alone," said Tyrel a moment later. "I don't like the way he looks. He kinda' gives me the creeps."

Raymon, still chuckled and dismissed Tyrel's words with a gesture. "Not you too, Tyrel. Come on, shee-it. That white boy's probably changing his underwear after I goofed on him."

Keysha couldn't believe how arrogant and stupid Raymon was. He might be the best football player in the college, but he was also a self-centered idiot.

There was an unfocused thought that played with her consciousness in a fleeting way. Something—half forgotten—it kept bugging Keysha. Something about Jack Mulligan, the way he stood on the side walk his eyes riveted to Raymon.

Then she remembered.

When Keysha was in high school, she had taken a basic self-defense course from one of her father's friends, Mr. Morris, who was a former marine. One of the points made by Mr. Morris was how to position your body if someone was threatening. If the body was placed almost perpendicular to an opponent, it naturally presented less targets against an assault. Tonight Keysha had watched as quite undetected, Jack Mulligan had lowered his book bag and positioned his body. She had also taken note, that he relaxed his body to go into action if attacked. Only someone who had been in many confrontations would know how to do that without alerting an assailant.

Raymon, of course, was running his big mouth and hadn't seen a thing. Little did he know, but her timely intervention had probably saved him from a beating. Thinking back, Keysha realized that Jack Mulligan was not the least bit frightened of Raymon. If Raymon wasn't a moron, he'd have noticed, too.

Keysha was now uneasy about Jack Mulligan and the dark mystery surrounding him.

***

Jack entered Lincoln Hall and went directly to his room. Juleel was gone, but a note taped to the door told him that his roommate had found a male friend named Bernie and had gone to the movies.

Saturday night meant nothing to Jack. Having been imprisoned most of his life, one day was pretty much like any other. He had not gone to the football game that day, for sports weren't something that held any interest for him. He couldn't see the point of expending all that energy for momentary glory or alma mater. He lumped notions such as God and country, nationalistic pride or even gang turf as a weak-minded game. His only salvation lay within himself. Instead of wasting time, he had gone to the library and worked all afternoon and evening.

Jack's view of organized sports didn't mean he didn't make an effort to stay in top physical condition. Earlier in the week, he had discovered that Mt. Sidney had a workout facility that was open twenty-four hours a day for faculty and students. During daylight hours the place was packed but at night and early morning it was deserted. Jack had gone there two days before at four a.m. No one was there but an attendant. It was perfect.

The early hour didn't bother Jack, since he still couldn't shake his body's time clock which woke him every morning. He didn't want to sleep late. There were too many things to do. He had worked out hard Inside to get to his present condition. There wasn't much else to do in jail. He was just glad this school had a good facility to keep in shape.

Jack laid down on his bed and stared up at the ceiling. His mind filled with visions of what had previously happened outside. He had come close to taking out that football player, Raymon. He couldn't imagine what was wrong with the guy. Raymon had that beautiful girl, Keysha, so why show off? Could Raymon hate white people so much, he'd risk a severe beating?

If he had a girl such as Keysha, he certainly wouldn't be fighting.

Keysha. What a nice name.

Jack had to keep control around people such as Raymon Jackson. He couldn't fight every person on campus. He sensed his vulnerability and hated it. Too much was at stake for him. But, there were limits.

Jack's face became grim. The prophetic words of Superintendent Brown haunted him, "One incident and you will be back here. Then, you're mine." A chill ran up his spine.

Suddenly, he was swept with anger. Step lightly. It was a cold control that had brought him here to this time and this place. If Raymon Jackson kept up his act, however, he'd have to find a way to handle the fool. The very thought made him smile.

His glee was short lived as he once again pondered the girl, Keysha, who was apparently Raymon's woman. He recalled bumping into her at the Registrar's Office. Her smell made him dizzy. Oh well, she was way too pretty to be just anyone's girl. Raymon was a popular athlete and a logical choice for her. The attraction was understandable.

Jack sat at his desk and started to work on English literature. He shifted uneasily in his chair. Dr. Ramapo had assigned six chapters and a page-long paper to be written about the writer's point of view. Jack felt restless, though. Maybe it was something Raymon had said. Perhaps the mention of his name by the idiot.

The dorm was so very quiet. Most of the students were in town or at fraternity houses celebrating the Wildcat's victory today.

A new pang of hunger cramped his stomach. He shouldn't have skipped dinner to stay at the library. Maybe he could pick up a candy bar or something in the lobby.

He left the room and walked down the silent hallway. When he got to the lobby, he approached the machines, which were in a corner. Jack could see that half the selections were gone. Swell. He put his change in the machine and selected a bag of peanuts.

The lobby was completely empty. Were there any students remaining in the building? He was struck again that he had no clue to the significance of a social life and Saturday night. The students here needed recreation; he did not. They made plans for the weekend; he did not. Even Juleel was conditioned to getting out and having fun on the weekend. He had practically pleaded for Jack to go to the football game, but Jack had begged off. Now Juleel was at the movies, and he was standing in an empty dorm lobby snacking on a meal of peanuts.

Jack had to admit he envied these kids. He was the one who couldn't seem to have fun, laugh or enjoy life. He was always on guard ready for the house of cards, which was his life, to collapse. Maybe that was why he found such comfort in solitude.

Jack had been forced to live in crowded prison conditions most of his life. The quiet, empty lobby gave him a feeling of owning a space of his own. He was king of the lobby. Something about not sharing his whole existence with a mob was really enjoyable. Sure the notion was selfish, but Jack knew of only one person he could trust, one person he could count on—himself.

Back in his room, he once again dug into his studies. But at the end of one hour, he glanced at his clock. It was 10:15 p.m. His legs were stiff and his mind was losing focus.

A walk around the campus or the town might revive him. Besides, he was curious about where all the students went and what they did.

Grabbing his room key and wallet, Jack locked the door behind him. The smell of paint hit his nostrils in the hallway where a maintenance crew had covered the graffiti. They might cover up the message, Jack thought, but the ugly problem wasn't gone.

CHAPTER 16

The glass of Scotch shook in Nathan Ramapo's hand. Three days had passed since his panic attack in front of the morning class, and the tremors were getting perceptively worse. Since he had spied the white boy, whose name he now knew was Jack Mulligan, he had had more to drink than ever before. More was needed. He had to think and a drink helped him gain the control he needed. It was a necessary illusion he wholeheartedly embraced. That's why the drinking had gone on, unabated. Now his whole house smelled like a distillery. Books and papers lay everywhere, dirty dishes were piled in the sink, and Nathan sat disheveled in his favorite chair unable or unwilling to move.

His bleary mind swayed through unrelated thoughts.

Thaddeus—no—Nathan you are a drunk.

Absolutely not, I'm just thinking.

Goddamn white people have done this to you and to all black people. They never let you have anything of your own. That's why you drink.

167

But I can quit when I want.

Who are you kidding? The drinks help you focus, without the agonizing pain.

Tomorrow I'll stop.

He staggered into the bathroom just in time to throw up and convulse with dry heaves. Nathan hadn't eaten in over two days, and the booze was kicking his ass. He tried to remember the previous evening, but nothing came to mind.

Why had they ruined paradise? Why had those money-hungry fools in the Administration spoiled Mt. Sidney College? Now they had white people here. The doors were wide open—probably forever. This white boy, Jack Mulligan, would only be the first. Soon, there would by hundreds of white devils on the campus, in the hallways and, worst of all, in the classrooms.

Nathan Ramapo wandered into the kitchen and viewed his bleak future, one that held no promise. Tears stained his face. He wasn't a kid anymore. And, he was hitting the bottle much too hard.

Twelve years had passed in a heart beat since he left Father D'Vesso and had come back to the states to restart his life. But what kind of life? The years had passed prosperous but empty. His academic credentials had somehow passed muster when he was hired by Mt. Sidney and since that time he had distinguished himself admirably as an excellent teacher and writer. His three books on European literature of the 16th and 17th centuries were renowned. But, in spite of academic success, his life was sentenced to solitary emptiness; his work rang hollow and was forever unfulfilling.

The castration by the gang of rednecks when he was young had left him incapable of any kind of physical relationship with a woman. So he lived alone and apart. His hatred and distrust of whites had grown deeper with each passing year. However, he was wise enough to conceal his bitter feelings from his colleagues. The festering hatred inside combined with the booze was a dangerous mix, one that Nathan accepted but had no control of.

Dr. Nathan Ramapo. The name still didn't fit him. He was Thaddeus Brown. From time to time he had seen the FBI poster with his picture in the post office. The Feds never gave up. Fortunately the photo now didn't resemble his middle-aged appearance at all. Still, it was him in the photo. He was still wanted in connection with the murder of Gunnery Sergeant Warren Whitaker and was considered armed and dangerous.

Damn right he was dangerous.

In the dining room, Nathan saw his computer with the screen displaying its map-of-Africa screen saver. Time to chat.

He had managed to hook up with several interesting chat rooms where hatred of white people was the universal topic. Nathan loved these groups. The anonymous people of cyber space felt and thought just as he did. They held nothing back.

Ramapo selected one of the now familar web sites and soon typed in a hypothetical challenge: what if a white boy was admitted to an all-black college? What should be done?

The responses came quickly. Most said that student groups should hold demonstrations in front of the

Administration's offices, but others had a more militant turn. They advocated forcing the white boy out. If a few threats worked, fine, but if all else failed, have someone kick his lily-white ass. Put the fear of God into him. To hell with philosophy, an old fashion "whuping" would do the trick.

Nathan hated violence but maybe one couldn't always avoid it. He'd been the victim of violence and bigotry. He understood its impact, but this was different.

Nathan poured another drink and swallowed the fiery liquid.

He wasn't a common thug. Unlike those ignorant white racists in the Ku-Klux-Klan, he was a revolutionary. Being a college professor, his knowledge and education had led him to this point. His hatred of whites came from both personal suffering as well as seeing it in others. Blacks had lived through slavery, had endured the abuses of prejudice with no voting rights, little job opportunity, inferior schools and, of course, there were the beatings and lynchings. This white boy couldn't possibly know of that kind of suffering.

Suddenly a thought came to him in an instant of clarity. Of course...

A smile edged his bloated features. There was indeed an easier way to rid the school of this white scourge. It might just work.

Nathan could deceive Jack Mulligan. First, he would mentor him and even pretend to sympathize with his situation. He would help him in every way. Then at the end of the semester, he'd flunk him. Perhaps Jack Mulligan, being a serious student, would take offense at his failing grade. He might even become violent. All it would take would be a simple threat, and he'd be expelled. Voila! Mission accomplished.

Nathan looked around his house. It was time to clean up the mess of the past few days and ready himself for the battle. First though, he'd have another drink...one more to celebrate.

***

Keysha had to admit that Raymon Jackson did have some saving graces. From a state of fury upon entering his car, she had gradually and grudgingly become better company as the evening wore on. Raymon admittedly was charming and fun to be with.

The foursome's first stop was a quaint Italian restaurant for a wonderful dinner, then off to the Anaconda Club. It was located in an older part of Mt. Sidney and was reached by traversing a series of winding streets. Raymon expertly squeezed the BMW between two large American cars and turned the engine off.

"Well here we are, and I'm ready to burn off some of that dinner," he said.

They climbed out of the car, and Raymon took Keysha's hand and led her to an old brick building where a blue neon sign with striking snake's head pointed to a dark narrow staircase. A distant pounding beat could be heard emanating from below. Several couples stood outside on the sidewalk smoking cigarettes and talking.

Raymon leaned over to Keysha, "This is the best club in town."

The whole building, a former warehouse, looked in need of repair, but as they entered a cavernous expanse, the music hit them like a hammer. A dance floor in the center was filled with couples gyrating to heavy hip-hop and rap music accentuated by an impressive laser lighting exhibit. Raymon seemed to know everyone in the place. They managed to get a choice table next to the dance floor and everyone's eyes seemed to be on them. They were special—the beautiful people. Keysha felt momentarily like a princess. People seemed to hold Raymon in a kind of deference. He was what cool was all about.

Immediately, Raymon pulled Keysha out onto the dance floor. Keysha was a fine dancer but Raymon was an expert. Being an athlete, he had moves that rivaled Michael Jackson and had a sort of expressiveness that was more than just a feeling for the beat. Soon Keysha was laughing and having the best time she had had in a long time.

Tyrel and Danielle were close by on the dance floor and were moving rhythmically to the beat. For a very large man, Tyrel was surprising graceful. He very much had an inner sense of the music that flowed to his limbs when he danced. Danielle, who had studied dance for years was amazed, but her graceful moves with her hands and legs were sensual and innovative.

After thirty minutes or so, Raymon was feigning exhaustion and led Keysha from the floor. Keysha laughed as Raymon ordered drinks and acted as though he would pass out.

"Girl you are one good dancer. I'm plumb wore out," he said breathlessly.

"Yes, but how many people played football today?"

Raymon smiled at her defense of him. "Well we can't all be supermen."

Keysha giggled lightly and sipped her drink. Tyrel and Danielle joined them and soon other friends of Raymon and Tyrel stopped by. Keysha found herself being the envy of other girls in the club because she was with Raymon. She would probably have enjoyed the sensation even more if it wasn't for the nagging thought of Raymon having given Jack Mulligan a tough time.

The evening ended back at Lincoln Hall at one o'clock. Keysha and Raymon lingered behind Tyrel and Danielle as they said goodnight. Raymon was the perfect gentleman, and Keysha couldn't help but be impressed by his manners. A simple kiss goodnight sweetly sealed the evening.

She could feel his hard muscular chest beneath his shirt. Keysha was not immune to Raymon's charms and found herself looking forward to seeing him again.

***

Jack walked by himself for hours in the town of Mt. Sidney checking out various student hangouts and walking past fraternity row where the Greek houses were rocking in celebration of the Wildcats' victory. He observed from a distance but didn't get too close. There would be no welcome for him in any of these places. The music was loud and so was the talk and laughter. Jack wearily smiled and kept moving.

Mt. Sidney had a small downtown surrounded by residential neighborhoods. The stores were all closed, but at least the tree lined streets were beautiful and the evening warm and pleasant. After years behind walls, a simple walk was entertainment enough. After an hour, Jack ended up in an industrial section and spotted a small corner bar by the rail yard. He was thirsty, and the name Sparkies reminded him of a ginger ale he drank as a kid.

The inside was dimly lit and cramped with a row of booths on one side of a long, narrow room and a facing bar on the other side. A television was tuned to a baseball game, which several people were watching. In one of the booths, a card game for quarters was being played, and people here and there were conversing in low tones. No one gave Jack much notice, which he found comforting. He sat down at the bar and the bartender, who was talking sports to a gray haired man, slid down for his order.

"Yeah pal, can I help you?"

"A cola, please."

"You old enough?" the bartender said with a chuckle.

"Yeah," Jack responded dryly to the humor.

That seemed to satisfy the man. So he put ice in a glass and brought out a can of cola and sat it down in front of Jack. With free pretzels in a bowl on the counter, Jack started feeling at home with the crowd at Sparkies. At least among the predominantly white patrons, he didn't feel so different. He watched the ball game listlessly, sipped his drink and kept his ears open.

The cola was cold and refreshing after his walk. He watched the older men with their beer. Although he couldn't imagine himself as much of a drinker, Jack remembered when his mother had given him a sip of her beer when he was small. The taste hadn't appealed to him as he recalled.

Jack listened to the card players who were directly behind him. They were four middle aged guys: three white and one black, all beefy looking working men. They joked and talked while playing cards, and Jack envied their good natured comradery.

In the Institution, Jack had never made any real friends. You either had allies or enemies. If anyone knew you had a close friend, they could use that relationship against you. They could even kill your friend to get to you.

"Hey Stu," said one of the men, "did you ever get someone to replace Ronnie?"

"Nah," replied a big, florid looking man. "I'm still tryin' to find someone who knows what a day's work is. That last guy, Deupchak, wanted to show up on Saturdays at noon. What a pretty boy. His girlfriends were more important to him than the job."

The group laughed.

"So are you going to put an ad in the help wanted section?" one of them asked.

"Yeah, I guess. Unless you guys know someone."

There was silence for an answer; then a series of grunts.

Jack could use a weekend job. The little money the state sent didn't come close to any of his extraneous needs. He wondered what kind of work this man Stu

175

was talking about. Whatever it was, he figured he could handle it.

Jack slid from the stool and edged up to the booth. The four men looked up from their cards at the same time.

"Help you, son?" said the man named Stu.

"I heard you say you needed someone to work."

Stu looked Jack over, "You applying?"

"Yeah, I guess so."

"You from around here?"

"No."

"Where you from?" Stu inquired.

Jack considered it better not to tell him he was an ex-con.

"I go to school at Mt. Sidney."

All four men stared in disbelief; then began to laugh. "You look a might pale," said the black man with a wink.

"I'm there on a special scholarship," Jack said uneasily.

"Since when?" said the black man skeptically.

"Just this year."

The black man rolled his eyes.

"You know what hard work is about, son?" Stu asked.

"Yeah."

"You're sure?"

"Yeah."

"Where have you worked before?"

"Here and there."

Stu looked up, "What kind of work have you done, here and there?"

"Farm work."

"A farm boy," said Stu, laying his cards aside.

"Yeah."

"You ever worked in a brick yard?"

"No."

"Well it's not the kind of job that a PhD would do. It's back-breaking work. You strong enough to do that kind of work?"

"Yes."

Stu again seemed to size Jack up. Jack knew about proving one's worth. It was the unwritten code of all prisons and had been forced on him most of his life.

"I'm stronger than you or any of your men."

This brought hoots from everyone of the men, except Stu. He looked grim and dismayed. "Son, if there's one kind of man I don't like, it's a bragging one. I am the strongest man at my brick yard and that's not bragging. I doubt if a college boy the likes of you can keep up with me."

Jack knew it was time to put up or shut up. He had hit upon this man Stu's pride. "I'll tell you what," Jack said, "If I can beat you in an arm wrestling contest, will you at least give me a chance to work at your brick yard?"

Stu chewed on this and didn't reply. Jack came back, "If I win, you hire me, and if I don't work out, get rid of me."

Stu glanced around the table and a knowing smile came to his big red face. "Okay son, let's see what you've got."

Before anyone could back out, a table was set up at the end of the bar, and the regular patrons gathered expectantly to see Stu put this brash kid in his place. It was apparent to Jack that Stu had a local reputation and probably deserved it for being a strong guy. Jack was maybe over his head but he also needed a job.

They sat down opposite one another, and Stu sized Jack up. "What's your name?"

"Jack Mulligan."

"Well that's a good Irish name. I'm Stu Ableson. So let's see your arm up here, Jack Mulligan."

A crowd formed around them as they sat down at a table. Jack had seen enough arm wrestling to know that one of the strategies used by experienced guys was to try to slam the opponent's arm down at the get go. He figured Stu Ableson to be experienced at most things or at least at this and he was correct.

When one of the men yelled go, Stu jumped the start, but Jack countered quickly and foiled the older man's initial attempt for a quick victory. Stu's face registered new respect. Jack, however, realized he was in for a struggle.

For the first twenty minutes, their arms swayed slowly back and forth an inch at time. Sweat poured from both men, with Stu's chameleon face changing from red to scarlet.

The onlookers started a betting pool with Stu leading the money two to one. When the contestants made any slight move, money would change hands as the bar patrons yelled encouragement at the action.

Jack had to admit that Stu Ableson was blessed with tremendous strength. A life time of hard work in a brick yard could do that to a man. All Jack could hope for was that his youth would prevail and allow him to edge the older man out.

Another half hour went by and the strain was starting to take its toll on Stu. The crowd had grown in size and in their enthusiasm. Being competitive by nature, Stu then decided to take a chance and put forth a last big effort to beat Jack. He was aware that his strength was running out. He wasn't young anymore. With steel determination written on his face, he started moving Jack's arm down.

The crowd's cheers drove him on.

Jack strained to stop him. Stu poured it on—his arm bending. Jack grimaced. If he could just hang on another minute...then Stu's barrage intensified. Two minutes passed with Jack's arm locked at a forty-five degree angle. His heart was pounding. The muscles in his arm were screaming, hot and tight. Sweat poured in rivers down his face.

Then, Jack felt Stu's strength failing. Inch by inch, their arms went back to vertical. He could see the telltale signs of exhaustion in the older man's face. His arms were shaking now, but his will was made of iron.

Jack knew that Stu hoped for a moment to recover, but he wasn't going to get it. Jack now launched his own assault, taking Stu's arm half way down. Now he concentrated as Stu struggled. Jack increased the pressure with each passing second. Their faces turned crimson and their sweat ran in streams.

Suddenly—little by little—Stu's arm lowered. Then as if a plug was pulled, the older man's arm gave out and Jack with gritted teeth touched it to the table.

A hush fell over the crowd. How could this be? Their local hero had fallen. Stu Ableson didn't let them mourn too long, however. In the spirit of true sportsmanship, he yelled at the bartender, "Two beers here! I got a new yard man."

A cheer went up. Hands started clapping Jack on the back, and Stu shook his hand heartily in congratulation.

At last, Jack was one of them. He was fitting in, even if it was only in a small redneck bar in Mt. Sidney, Ohio.

CHAPTER 17

Excitement flowed through Juleel like a swift mountain spring as he rushed back to the dorm to tell Jack about his evening. And, what an evening! It couldn't have been more perfect. Now he had a close friend in Jack and now a possible companion in Bernie, a humanities major from Columbus. What could be better?

Juleel had met Bernie in his history class, and the two had hit it off right away. Jack had been correct in saying he would know when someone was interested in him. Juleel thrilled at the moment he and Bernie had made meaningful eye contact and both of them had known. Bernie was so sweet.

Now they met for lunch every day, studied together and were practically inseparable. Bernie lived in Martin Luther King, Jr. Hall not too far away. They both enjoyed movies, music and the theater. Juleel was even thinking of taking Bernie back to Walnutburg to meet Mama. He was sure she'd be thrilled.

Juleel wondered if Jack would be happy about his new found ecstasy. He doubted it. The long silences his roommate fell into seemed more and more ponderous. Jack never talked about his family or his past. Juleel surmised that Jack's childhood was less than idyllic. However, he couldn't imagine not having one or two good memories. Jack, however, didn't mention any.

Although they had only been at Mt. Sidney for a little over a week, Jack hadn't received a single letter, e-mail or a phone call from anyone. This seemed strange to Juleel. Didn't Jack's parents care enough to inquire how he was doing?

Jack's isolation from the student body was understandable. Juleel knew the feeling of being an outsider. He'd experienced the same fear and loneliness in Walnutburg.

Just two days before, Juleel had been shocked when he returned from the showers, and Jack was changing his shirt. He caught a glimpse of Jack's broad muscular back before he pulled his shirt down. There were deep scars lacing his skin as if Jack had been lashed like the slaves before the Civil War.

Scars such as those came from a severe beating. Who could have done it? His father? What could Jack have possibly done to deserve it?

Juleel had hurriedly looked away and had asked no questions. Whoever had inflicted the scars on Jack's back was part of Jack's background, a past he didn't want to discuss. Jack, for his part, had given him an inquiring glance, but seemed satisfied that Juleel had seen nothing.

Juleel had a feeling that Jack would tell him everything in his own sweet time.

As he entered the corridor on the first floor, he spotted something green on the floor ahead. Was it money? A fifty dollar bill was lying on the shiny linoleum as if it had slipped from someone's pocket. The owner would surely miss it. It was fortunate that an honest person, such as himself, had come upon it. Most people would stick it in their pockets.

Tomorrow Juleel would take the money to the office so the poor soul who had dropped it could enjoy its return. He bent to pick it up.

Suddenly, there was a whisper of movement. Juleel started to turn. Something was thrown over his head, and a hand clamped hard over his mouth so he couldn't scream. Then, a hard object smashed against his skull and his knees buckled. There were footsteps and an oath and Juleel thoughts turned to mud as he slipped into darkness.

***

"He is fun, Danielle. I'll admit it," Keysha announced when she entered her dorm room and saw Danielle ready for information.

Danielle clapped her hands in delight. "I had my doubts, but I'm so glad. Tyrel's said you two would get along."

"I thought you were the one who set this up," exclaimed Keysha in surprise.

"No! Tyrel did it, himself."

"Well, he was right. I think Mr. Jackson is so fine. I've never seen anyone dance better, and he seems to have lots of friends."

They both giggled.

"For the life of me," said Danielle, "I don't know why these guys came to us."

"I do, girl," said Keysha with her hands on her hips. "Cause we are the two hottest sisters in town."

Now they both laughed.

Both girls talked of the evening's events and relived the high points. Danielle related how Tyrel was so sweet and old-fashioned. Keysha was touched by Danielle's feelings for Tyrel. They were so good together.

"By the time we got back to the dorm," said Danielle coyly, "I was sort of hoping Tyrel would want more than a night's kiss."

"Now you watch it, girl," Keysha warned.

"I know, I know. But he is so cute."

"Yeah, but make him work for it."

"Hey, this is the new millennium," challenged Danielle. "We have more freedom."

"Human nature's still the same."

"Well, I don't want to wait too long."

"Waiting isn't that bad," exclaimed Keysha. "When one's in the oven, you'll wish you'd waited. I've had so many girlfriends end up pregnant and alone. None of these guys want to be fathers. They just want to have fun."

"Tyrel would be a great father, but you're right, not now."

Keysha grabbed Danielle's hand, "Think smart. If you two stick together, then it was meant to be."

"How about you and Raymon?"

"Hey girl, he's fun but…"

"I thought you liked him."

"I do, but I just met him," said Keysha. "All I know is that he's a terrific dancer, a lot of fun to be with and a confirmed bigot. Maybe if he straightens that out."

"Wow…you are tough, girl," laughed Danielle.

"Yeah I know, but you should have seen him with that white boy, Mulligan. It was so embarrassing."

"That bad?"

"Worse," she said, resolutely. "All I can say is he'd better change his behavior fast. My mama didn't raise me to be a hate filled bigot."

"Amen," shouted Danielle.

It was late, so both girls yawned and started getting ready for bed. Keysha thought about meeting Raymon the next evening, and although she had had a really good time this evening, she still had one big lasting doubt about him. This hatred he had for white people was a stumbling block. How different she would feel right now if the confrontation with the white boy, earlier that evening, hadn't taken place.

It was now two-thirty in the morning. Danielle and Keysha said goodnight and turned the lights out, but Keysha remembered that she'd better set her alarm. Maybe she could get up by nine and go to church before heading to the library.

She never kept her alarm clock within reach. Her mother had taught her that if she kept it at a distance, she would be forced to get up to turn if off. This little trick had worked more than once to get her on her feet and moving.

Crossing to her desk, Keysha peered out the window at the now peaceful but deserted campus. There was a full moon spilling its blue light over the lawn, and the trees on the horizon appeared as delicate, black lace against the night sky. From the shadows the cicadas sang their autumn song, and in the distance, a train could be heard wailing its departure from town. It was an incredibly romantic night, and Keysha was alive and young.

A movement on the sidewalk below caught her attention. At first she thought it might be a campus security man walking his beat, but then a lone figure appeared under one of the lamp posts. It was Jack Mulligan. He was by himself, a solitary figure in the moonlight.

He paused to look out—longingly—at the same moon she had just admired. His gaze swept the campus. Keysha wondered if he felt the same poetry in the moon or heard the same symphony of the dying cicadas.

She watched, her eyes tried to penetrate the ambient light. How alone he seemed. What circumstances motivated this strange, scar-faced white boy? Keysha whimsically wanted to join him outside; to feel him beside her, he who was wild and lonely.

***

A feeling of elation held Jack Mulligan as he stood under the lamp post and breathed in the fresh air, which was just becoming aromatic with autumn's blend of organic scents. He was a bit drunk as he had celebrated with Stu Ableson and his friends. Little did they know he was too young to legally drink. He didn't want to tell them, and they hadn't asked. What fun it had been, drinking beer and laughing.

Jack was free and now he had a job. It was a paying job, with people who accepted him. The extra money would be nice, too.

A brief fantasy infected him as he thought of the girl, Keysha. She was probably asleep and dreaming somewhere up in the dorm. It was late. Imagine having enough money to ask her out. Sort of a date. He'd, of course, know what to say and when to say it to charm her off her feet. She'd laugh at all his funny lines, and he'd adore everything about her.

The truth was, he had never held any conversation with a girl. He had no idea what girls liked or didn't like. He had no funny lines that could be repeated. She'd probably have a terrible time and hate him by the time the evening was over. His face fell. In that case, maybe it was better if he just forgot her.

It was best not to dream, especially about girls. Too many expectations were dangerous. Besides, thoughts of that proportion could drive a man crazy. No, it was best to keep one's eyes straight ahead and keep walking. He was an ex-con. Only so many good things could possibly happen for him.

Solemn once more, he climbed the steps to Lincoln Hall. It was time to go to bed. The lobby was deserted, and Jack's footsteps were the only sound to break the silence. Down the hallway, Jack could sense the sleeping students behind their doors.

Then he froze. The door to his room ajar by an inch.

Why?

Where was Juleel? Who was inside?

All of Jack's senses came alive. He was immediately back Inside, ready for war. Something was wrong—real wrong.

Carefully, he pushed the door open and flipped on the light switch. Every muscle was ready if anyone tried to jump him.

It was then he saw Juleel bound to a desk chair. Duct tape covered him from head to toe, and a black hood was pulled over his head. A sign was hung around his neck with the words, "Die Faggot" written on it.

Jack rushed to Juleel and tore the hood off. Juleel's eyes were wild with terror. Jack pulled the gag from his mouth and Juleel started coughing and talking all at once.

"I thought…you'd…," he coughed, "never get here."

"Just be quiet till I get you free."

Jack worked hurriedly and tore the tape off Juleel who was shaking all over. A egg-sized lump was protruding from the back of Juleel's head, and one of his eyes was swollen and discolored.

"Bastards!" Juleel spat angrily. "I wish I was big enough to kick their asses."

Jack marveled at the bravado of his shy roommate. "Whoa, chief. Let's get that eye taken care of before you go to war."

Juleel gradually calmed down. The skinny, black kid was much tougher than he looked. He had a temper, too.

Jack went to the lobby and got a cold can of soda from a vending machine. He then made Juleel place it on his swollen eye.

"How'd this happen?" Jack asked for the first time.

Juleel related the story of the fifty dollar bill and how he had been jumped.

"So you never saw who hit you?"

"No, but I have a good idea who it was and so do you, Jack."

"Yeah," Jack said wearily. "I think we'll have to take care of our favorite football player."

Juleel glanced up at Jack who had a far away look in his eyes.

"Could you tell how many there were?"

"At least two."

Jack started for the door, then turned, "Keep that can on your eye. I'll be right back."

"Be careful."

Jack nodded. He knew the athletes all lived on the third floor, so he took the steps up. The hallway was deserted and quiet. It was now three forty-five, and even athletes went to sleep eventually. He was hoping, however, that the two who jumped Juleel would still be awake and talking.

Lincoln Hall was constructed in an L shape with two long hallways. On a hunch, Jack started down the first long hallway listening for voices. He was rewarded when he turned the corner at the intersection. Four doors down, he heard laughter, and a light was shining under the doorway. Jack paused outside and listened. The first voice he heard was Raymon Jackson.

"Wait till that white motherfucker finds him," he said gleefully.

"You think he'll go to Brent?" came an unknown voice.

"Fuck no. Brent's cool. He doesn't like him either."

Jack's blood did a slow boil. So they wanted to play games. He instinctively reached for the door knob; then froze. In his mind he heard the distant voice of Superintendent Brown, "You come back and you're mine."

He gritted his teeth in frustration and pent-up hatred. He knew that a direct assault would get him thrown out of Mt. Sidney and see him back behind bars. That was too high a price to pay for these idiots. Nothing could be gained by being a hot-headed fool.

Laughter continued to echo in Jack's ears as Raymon and his friend recalled their fun with Juleel. He backed away from the door and walked back to the stairwell. Already he was formulating a future plan for Raymon Jackson. Mr. Athlete and school hero had some payback coming. Since part of every athlete's celebrity was tied to the public, Raymon would have to be given a new image—a sort of make-over. Humiliation was going to be a whole new concept for Raymon.

A game plan started taking shape in Jack's head—a very pleasing one.

CHAPTER 18

"Was there any damage to the room?" Robert Brent questioned angrily. "Shit, here we go again!"

Jack and a swollen-faced Juleel had just sat down in Brent's office before breakfast to tell the Head Resident what had transpired the night before. Jack knew it was a waste of time, but Juleel had insisted on informing Brent, saying it was the right thing to do. Brent, he realized, couldn't have cared less if Juleel had died as long as it was done in a tidy manner with no damage to Lincoln Hall.

"We're wasting our breath," said Jack in disgust.

"Hey, I'm not talkin' to you, Mulligan," Brent said in an acidic tone.

"Have you ever heard of a crime called, assault?" Jack asked incredulously. "Juleel here was mugged."

"Don't talk to me about crime, Mulligan."

"He was ambushed in the hallway." said Jack in disgust.

Brent looked at Juleel as if he were an insect on display. "What were you doing to provoke it?"

191

"Nothing!" exclaimed Juleel. "I was walking to my room."

Detest shadowed Brent's face. "You people prance around like little fairies and expect real men to respect you. Why do you have to flaunt your way of life?"

"I wasn't flaunting anything," Juleel's voice wavered.

"Are you trying to defend his attackers?" Jack inserted.

"I'm trying to say that if he didn't act the way he does, these guys would leave him alone."

Jack's temper flared, "Well maybe some of those red-blooded boys would like to step forward and object to my behavior."

"Don't get things stirred up, Mulligan," Brent warned, "or, you'll be out of this school right now."

This discussion was getting nowhere, Jack observed.

"Let's split, Juleel. This idiot's wasting our time."

Brent bolted to his feet as if to go after Jack. His face was red with rage. To his surprise, Juleel stepped between the two large men. "You're right, Jack. I think we'd better go to the police and the newspapers."

That froze Brent, whose eyes widened in horror. Jack saw fear and knew exposure of gaybashing at Mt. Sidney would come home to roost directly on Robert Brent's shoulders. He'd be fired within hours of such a news story by an Administration trying to cover up.

"Wait, wait!" Brent yelled, his hands held open in defense. "I'll look into this. I didn't say I wouldn't. Okay! Let's not get the press and outsiders in here. Maybe a mistake was made."

"You bet there was a mistake," Jack said. "A big one."

"I'll talk to the campus police."

"You'd better talk to that cretin, Raymon Jackson. I'm pretty sure he was one of the guys who attacked me," Juleel said.

"Did you see him attack you?"

"No, but…"

"Then you aren't sure?"

"I heard his voice," said Juleel positively.

"But you didn't see him?"

"No. They threw a blanket over my head."

Brent frowned. "Well I can't accuse him without witnesses. Was this after you were hit on the head?"

"Yes, but I know what I heard," said Juleel who was getting more and more upset every minute.

Jack had not said anything to Juleel about hearing Raymon laughing and boasting of last night's incident. He now had his own plans, and he wasn't sharing them. He had learned long ago that most crimes the police closed on were not solved because of brilliant investigative or forensic technique or deductive logic such as Sherlock Holmes supposedly used. Rather, the police relied on informants who listened as criminals ran their arrogant mouths. Most of the guys he knew in the Institution had talked themselves into incarceration.

Brent looked disdainfully at Jack. "I'm going to tell Dean Jans about this, and then we'll investigate further. In the meantime, Washington, stay in public places, and quit acting the way you do."

"Yeah, Juleel. Start acting like Raymon Jackson," Jack said sarcastically.

Brent bristled at the remark.

"I've had enough of you, Mulligan!" Brent shouted, while pointing at Juleel. "He knows what I mean."

"And that is?"

"It means quit baiting people."

"Juleel's not baiting anyone. He's the one being harassed."

Brent rolled his eyes, "Sure."

Jack didn't care for the big Head Resident. Brent had his prejudices which seem to rule his intellect. He was serious about his duties, but beneath the veneer of bluster was shallowness.

Jack and Juleel started to leave. Juleel was upset and seemed pensive. Brent stopped them as they reached the door. "Oh Mulligan, I'm going to speak to Jans again about you, too."

"Be my guest, chief," snarled Jack, whose dread was growing. "I hope you have a wonderful time discussing me."

***

The cafeteria in Lincoln Hall was usually not crowded on Sunday mornings as students took the opportunity to sleep late. Only those going to church or the library were up at this time. Keysha yawned as she picked up her tray of eggs, toast and juice and headed for a table.

She was extremely tired. It had been a late night, and she had not slept well. Too much partying had taken its toll, and a day in the library lay ahead. She had to dust away the cobwebs and focus on her studies, especially in math where a test was coming up.

She had left Danielle sleeping soundly ten minutes before. After slipping into a pair of worn jeans, she had carefully closed the door behind her.

Now sitting down at a nearby table, she sipped her coffee and ran back the events of last night. She was certainly confused about how she felt about Raymon. Sure, she enjoyed going dancing with him but that was all? As far as she could tell, he just wanted one thing from her and made no apologies pronouncing it. Now was the time to use a little logic before anything regretful happened. As her mother would say, "Think with your head and not your heart."

The sticking point about Raymon was that it was so easy to be impressed by him. He was good looking, had money, was an outstanding athlete with a bright future and everyone seemed to admire him. To be with him was to be the envy of everyone on campus. His bright light would illuminate any girl. The problem was that Keysha didn't want to exist in his or any man's radiance. She wanted to earn her own credentials and fully explore her own potential.

At the other end of the cafeteria, she observed Jack Mulligan and Juleel Washington enter the dining area carrying their trays of food. They were an odd-looking pair, Juleel being short, slight of build and black and Jack being tall, muscular and white. At the moment, both appeared grim. Keysha wondered if Jack was upset about last night's encounter with Raymon. She couldn't blame him if he was.

She studied Jack's face. Despite the scars, he was still disturbingly attractive in a rugged way. His body spoke of great power. His arms, shoulders and chest

195

literally rippled with solidly packed muscles. Keysha couldn't help but be captivated.

As she observed him from afar, he suddenly stood up with his coffee cup in hand and started toward the big coffee urn close by. Halfway there he noticed her and fixed her with his cobalt eyes. It was effective.

Her mouth moved involuntarily, "Good morning," she said huskily.

He swallowed hard, "Hi."

Both fell into awkwardness as they looked at one another. Jack broke the ice, "I…I'm having breakfast over there but."

"Oh that's alright," Keysha broke in. "I have to go to the library anyway. I'm sorry about last night. You know,…Raymon can behave poorly."

"Yeah."

"I don't know him well," she said in apology, hoping he'd understand.

He shook his head. "That's okay. I don't know him either."

Keysha looked away. "Well, I'd better go."

Jack nodded and moved off to get his coffee.

Keysha couldn't believe how tongue-tied she had become in front of him. She must have appeared a fool. One thing Keysha prided herself in was her ability to meet and talk to new people.

Keysha put her tray on the rack and walked to the front of the cafeteria. This brought her close to Jack and Juleel. Jack looked up as she came by and in a rare instant, smiled. Not a big smile, but definitely a smile. It magically transformed his harsh angular face making his features softer, younger.

She returned his smile and shyly waved, and then her glance caught the swollen face of Juleel Washington. The dark skin on his face was discolored, and his right eye was just a slit. What could have happened? This had to have come from a beating.

Jack…?

No. She could tell he and Jack were friends. Then who? It disturbed her that someone on this campus would assault an inoffensive person such as Juleel. Keysha guessed he was gay, and maybe that had something to do with it. Gaybashing was so unforgivable. It was stupid and terrible. Gay people didn't deserve the wrath of the mob.

Then her mind flooded with dark thoughts of Raymon. No. No never. He had been with her last night. Surely Raymon couldn't do such a thing. He couldn't be that cruel. Still as Keysha strolled along the tree lined lanes to the library, the nagging question of Raymon Jackson troubled her.

CHAPTER 19

"You need additional information, Nathan?" Dean Jans asked, as he pointed to a thick file on his desk. "Is Mr. Mulligan becoming a problem of some sort?"

"No, no. It's just that his being a lone white person...that is, at least in my class, I think I could better serve him as his teacher, if I knew something about him," Nathan said hesitantly.

Jans gazed uneasily across his desk at Nathan. "Let me explain the situation we have here as concerns Mr. Mulligan, Nathan. The file here is quite confidential. As you've probably guessed, Mulligan's our first white student at Mt. Sidney. The Board of Trustees has been under immense pressure from the State for quite some time to admit students of all races. But, be that as it may, Mr. Mulligan is even more special."

"In what way?" Nathan sensed a problem, an exploitable situation. Was the Administration hiding something?

"Well that's a sensitive area, Nathan," Jans said holding the file. "For me to tell you even a little about this file, I would have to know exactly why you need to know?"

Nathan was prepared for this. He projected his most concerned look. "I've been noticing, Maurice, that Jack Mulligan doesn't seem to be connecting with other students in my class. He is a loner, who is lagging in his academic performance. Perhaps because he's white, or he feels uncomfortable culturally with a—let's say—mixed situation. I don't know. However, if I can reach him now, I think I can really save his academic career and help him to adjust."

Jans seemed touched.

"Nathan, you are a truly wonderful teacher," Jans said smiling. "On the college level, it is seldom that any of our colleagues have time to notice the distress of one student, but you have. I really must commend you."

"Thank you, Maurice," Nathan said in his most sincere voice.

"Let me then quickly go over Jack Mulligan's file with you. But first, I must swear you to total secrecy concerning its contents," Jans said in a whisper.

"Nothing will leave this office," Nathan said. "You have my word."

For the next fifteen minutes Jans laid out Jack Mulligan's whole biography. Even Nathan was shocked. He wanted to grab Maurice Jans and shake him like a leaf. Fury cascaded deep inside him but his mental and emotional discipline kept it in check. What had gone wrong here? How could the Board of Trustees have let this criminal into Mt. Sidney? Did anybody have any ethics or was money their only motivation? This Jack Mulligan was a murderer for Christ's sake.

Nathan fought for control of the revulsion he felt at Dean Jans' words. Rage boiled inside and continued as he acted out a pseudo-concern for Jack Mulligan.

"I knew his problems were deep seated," Nathan said shaking his head, "but Mr. Mulligan clearly needs my help."

"It is sad Nathan when any young man has this kind of past. But, let's hope we can turn him around."

Nathan smiled. "Yes, turn him around and head him in the right direction."

***

Juleel felt his sore, discolored eye as he examined himself in the mirror. The swelling was going down but his vision was slightly blurred. A school nurse had told him he should be able to see clearly in a week or two. Juleel still worried. Being a bit of a hypochondriac, Juleel thought about life as a blind person.

He imagined how people would pity him and how he would bravely march on while everyone proclaimed his bravery. Life would be dull with no challenges but also no expectations.

Juleel's initial anger at his attackers had passed. He now, however, wondered if he'd made a mistake coming to Mt. Sidney College. Gays apparently weren't welcome here anymore than in Walnutburg. He had apparently changed locales for the same old thing. How could he have thought that more educated, urbane people would be more tolerant?

Looking over at Jack, who was deep into his studies, he said, "Jack, maybe I ought to leave Mt. Sidney."

Jack turned, "Hey come on, it's just a black eye. I've had a dozen like that one. It'll go away."

"But will the reason for the black eye go away. Maybe, Robert is right, maybe I just send out repulsive, subliminal messages that no one can stand."

Jack shook his head, "That's bullshit, Juleel."

"Is it?" Juleel said resolutely. "In Walnutburg, I was known as fairy boy, nigger fairy and as the suck-ass nigger. My poor mother, she had to watch and endure those names, when it was all my fault."

"There are idiots and rednecks everywhere," said Jack as he tried to imagine the abuse Juleel had gone through and failed.

"Yeah, everywhere," Juleel said in a distant voice.

"You're feeling sorry for yourself."

Juleel considered this for a moment and asked, "Am I?"

"You know you are," admonished Jack.

"I can't stand most people in this school," he said bitterly. "I know what they think."

"Then this is your chance," Jack said resolutely. "You can turn it around, right here. For you to go back to Walnutburg would really crush your mother. It would make all those morons in your town and here validate all they said about you."

"Yes but…"

"No buts," said Jack pointing a finger at Juleel. "I know a little about how you feel here. Do you think I don't know what it's like to be an outsider?"

"Yeah, but…," muttered Juleel.

"Do you think I'm immune to fear? I'm in a strange place, among black people. They don't like me, Juleel. So I've got a choice, run or stay."

Juleel could only think that it was easy for Jack who was so large, to say and do brave things. Juleel Washington was not large or fearsome. He'd been running all his life.

"Fuck'em if they don't like you," Jack continued with a hardened stare. "Life isn't easy. You have to do some things for yourself."

"But getting beat up…"

"Look at my face," Jack exclaimed, gesturing to his scars. "I know what it's like to get an ass kicking."

Once more, Juleel felt like pressing Jack for more details of his past. It might solve the mystery of how Jack had gotten here.

"What happened to you, Jack? Your face."

Jack froze in his chair. A darkness came over him and a wall came down. "Let's just say that a long time ago, I paid for a mistake."

CHAPTER 20

Late summer passed into autumn, and the old oaks, poplars and maples on Mt. Sidney's campus turned from deep green to hues of orange, yellow and red. A colorful carpet of leaves spread out, and an unseasonable chill in the mid-October air made the students groan as they braced for an early winter. No one seemed ready to part with summer's comforting warmth—not even the professors.

Jack dug deeper into his studies as the weeks passed by. He found the work satisfying, and the routine of the classroom and the library a stabilizing force. As his exam grades indicated, he was doing well in all his classes except Dr. Ramapo's literature class. No amount of hard work seemed to impress the professor. This was disturbing to Jack since he was budgeting more out-of-class time for that one class than all the others.

Jack's daily routine started at four-thirty in the morning when he would go to the weight room. He'd do an hour of grueling exercise, his muscles straining under heavy dumb bells and barbells. Then, the rest of his day was dedicated to study, which he approached in the same manner as his exercise workout. His focus on academics was razor sharp.

Jack saw Keysha every day but the two only glanced at one another or exchanged an occasional awkward hello. He also saw her with Raymon Jackson. As a couple they looked more than chummy. Jack figured she'd made a wise choice. Jackson was a big guy on campus and he had a car. Fun and transportation. It sounded good to Jack who walked everywhere.

As far as Raymon was concerned, Jack knew it was prudent to keep a distance from Raymon. Not that he feared the football player in any way, but for the past several weeks, Raymon had left Juleel alone. Maybe Brent had spoken to him. Jack hoped so, but he wouldn't count it.

The job at Stu Ableson's brick yard was working out well. Jack had called his parole officer and told him everything about the job. Two days a week, plus Saturday Jack reported to the yard. The parole board was pleased. They considered his job a positive step towards his rehabilitation. In addition to their support, they even helped Jack secure a State driver's license.

Being a new driver, operating trucks on busy streets was challenging at first, but Jack was a quick study. Within a few weeks he was a competant and safe driver. In fact, several of the older hands at Ableson's thought he drove too slow, but Stu told them maybe they should take a lesson from Jack and slow down.

Jack decided to be up front with Stu about his situation at Mt. Sidney. He correctly figured that the

State parole people would eventually call Stu. It was better to level with a straight-shooter such as Stu than to hide information.

Stu, as it turned out, had been in trouble as a teenager, too and had spent time behind bars for stealing cars. He understood how a person could take a wrong path and end up on the wrong side of the law. He also knew the importance of rehabilitating one's self. If anything, he rallied behind Jack and his efforts.

"Just keep your nose clean and work hard," he told Jack. "You won't have any problem with me."

"Don't worry," Jack said appreciatively, "You'll get a good day's work from me."

Jack didn't disappoint either. He drove himself hard loading trucks with pallets of brick, concrete block and aggregates. Stu supplied all the local contractors and was busy six days a week. The other laborers in the yard called him, "The Machine" for Jack was unstoppable.

On work days, he returned to Lincoln Hall through a back door. He would be exhausted, his clothes stiff with dirt and sweat. The grit from the brick yard seemed to clog his nose, throat and eyes. The great compensation, of course, was his pay check. Money earned for the first time in his life gave Jack an incredible sense of satisfaction. He opened a savings account upon Juleel's urging and watched as his money accumulated.

Juleel laughed and called Jack the "Silas Marner of Mt. Sidney College." Juleel knew that Jack took great pride in saving the money from his job. It appeared to raise his self-esteem several notches.

Juleel's eye had healed and like Jack, he fell into a solid habit of study as the weeks passed from September into October. He and Bernie were now becoming inseparable. They were together every weekend, going to the movies, to plays and even to the Wildcat football games, which Bernie hated. Now that Juleel had a significant other in Bernie and a great friend in Jack, he felt as though his life had balance and a chance of normalcy.

He still fretted over Jack. Juleel realized that his roommate had erected an emotional barrier around himself for some sort of protection. But, protection from what? That was an interesting question. No amount of prodding could get Jack to talk. He seemed to work night and day without taking a breath. He didn't even smile. He worked in the brick yard to exhaustion and had no friends or even female interests at all.

Juleel couldn't figure the last. Jack wasn't gay. Juleel had caught the way in which Keysha Jordan and Jack had looked at one another in the cafeteria. Juleel tried to encourage Jack to act upon it but to no avail. It was as though he'd never been out with a girl before.

"I'm telling you, Jack," he said one evening, "Keysha is very interested in you."

Jack smiled, "Yeah, she probably can't believe what a sorry sight I am."

"I don't think so," Juleel said coyly.

"I do," mumbled Jack, stone faced again. "Besides she's Raymon's girl.

The last was true.

Keysha was being wined and dined every weekend by Raymon. He was having his best year ever as an athlete, and there was talk of him being voted All-American. With this in mind, he needed to be seen with one of the prettiest girls on campus. Keysha obliged but was growing steadily more weary of playing the role of trophy girl friend.

Keysha longed for a relationship in which she could share her feelings, her interests and her dreams. With Raymon, she just sat and smiled at his now stale jokes and his boisterous arrogance. Fortunately, Raymon had acted like a gentleman so far. Keysha found him attractive but shallow. What you saw was what you got.

One person who kept intriguing her was Jack Mulligan. Besides seeing him every day in class and at the dorm, she had noticed him deep into his books at the library. He was a hard worker. She could tell he was bright and motivated. She also noticed how isolated and alone he was.

Figuring that he was shy, she found Jack's humility most appealing, especially after listening to Raymon talk about himself for hours. She could feel a definite connection when their eyes met, but Keysha could tell that Jack was hesitant to act upon it. She wondered if it was because of their differing races or maybe because he saw her with Raymon. She still remembered Jack standing on the sidewalk below her window gazing at the moon just as she did.

Keysha pondered whether it was time for her to make a move. If she at least started talking to him, maybe her friendliness would break the ice.

Danielle had told her that she had twice seen Jack in soiled work clothes coming into the dorm. He must have a job, Keysha surmised. It must be something physical and dirty. Hard physical work would fit him.

Danielle recognized Keysha's interest in Jack but considered it foolish. What could her roommate possibility see in a scar-faced, ragged-ass white boy? Jack Mulligan was a loner and everyone knew what those guys were capable of. Danielle realized, however, that Keysha was bored with Raymon. But the white boy.? Why couldn't she find a brother as loving and nice as Tyrel?

The love Danielle had for Tyrel was well established. They spent every spare moment together. She couldn't believe how fortunate she was to have found true love so quickly. Tyrel was sensitive, funny, a gentle lover and good looking.

They had quietly gone off in early October to an apartment belonging to a friend of Tyrel's. For a whole day they made love, drank wine and talked. Their hunger for each other had grown feverish. Their passion surprised even themselves. Both Tyrel and Danielle now used their love to focus on their school work at Mt. Sidney. They studied every night together, hitting the books intensely. They were not going to be like so many other couples who saw their love disappear into ruined futures.

As the brisk autumn wind stirred the remaining leaves of the ancient oaks foretelling a change in the air, transitions were about to happen inside Mt. Sidney College to the best and worst of people.

Part II

The runaway slave came to my house and stopt outside
I heard his motions cracking the twigs of the woodpile

Walt Whitman
Song of Myself

CHAPTER 21

Nathan Ramapo slid the bottle from his desk drawer, poured himself a straight Scotch and carried it to the window. The soggy drizzle of early afternoon had turned into a cold, driving rain. It hurled down from a black, heavy sky, hitting the puddles in the gutter below his office like buckshot. A cold north wind swept down the street between the buildings of the college causing the few brave students abroad to lean against it. They clutched their books and hunched over as they headed for the nearest shelter.

Ramapo took a deep swallow from his glass and wiped his mouth with the back of his hand. The liquor failed to comfort him. This was the first drink he'd had in six weeks, and it wasn't meant for celebration. Since his meeting weeks ago with Dean Jans, no further progress had been made in removing Jack Mulligan from Mt. Sidney. Although he possessed enough lethal information about the boy's criminal past to cause a scandal, he also knew he'd be releasing it at his own peril. Dean Jans would fire him on the spot if news of the leak led back to his door.

To his dismay, Nathan had observed that most students were no longer distressed by Jack Mulligan's presence. They had grown used to him, and his existence was no longer shocking. Now he was part of the landscape and not an anomaly.

Ramapo had bitterly realized soon after seeing Jans that his plan to flunk Jack Mulligan and bait him into a confrontation wouldn't work. Jans would, under pressure, want to see some of Mulligan's work, and after analyzing it, he'd know of Ramapo's perfidious plan. Nathan knew that being labelled a racist would spell complete ruin for him in liberal-minded intellectual circles.

He had initially held out some hope that Jack Mulligan might be an underachiever, but the contrary seemed to be true. He was decidedly hard working and an excellent writer. His essays showed a complete understanding of subject and many times were written with a creative slant that even Nathan hadn't thought of.

Under normal circumstances, Ramapo would encourage a student such as Jack Mulligan, but Nathan's racial hatred was too finely focused. Sometimes his rage seemed to choke out his own breath. Jack Mulligan had to go. There was no other way. A new plan had to be made and implemented soon.

Fortunately, a new possibility had shown itself two days before. It was probably a long shot, but Ramapo had been turning it over in his mind. He had been in the student union, seated at his usual booth beside the large, double kitchen doors. This was a perfect place for observation, since several strategically placed plants practically hid his presence. Few students sat in this locale. Young adults preferred being seen. Ramapo, on the other hand, found the booth's seclusion a comfort and as an added bonus a good listening post.

For some peculiar engineering reason, the unique acoustics of the room worked to the advantage of anyone seated there. Nathan could clearly hear conversations at other far away tables without being spotted as an eavesdropper.

Ramapo often smiled at his auditory advantage. Because of it, last year he had overheard three students, one a graduate student working for him, discuss how a copy of his final exam was being circulated. Apparently, it had been stolen from his office by the graduate student who was at that time lining his pocket by selling copies.

Ramapo smiled as he thought back to the shocked expressions on several student's faces when he passed out a completely different test. Most of the offending scholars had failed, which pleased Ramapo, but his greatest pleasure came when he and Dean Jans had fired, in disgrace, the graduate student responsible for the theft of his test. Cheating was something Nathan Ramapo detested.

Nathan now thought of the two students he had overheard talking about Jack Mulligan. Both were obviously athletes. He had recognized one as Raymon Jackson, the current star of the football team. The other, a rather large fellow, had been in one of his classes the year before. His name, Nathan recalled, was Friday—Tyrel Friday.

It seemed that Jackson wanted the white boy Mulligan immediately tossed out of Mt. Sidney. He was all for racial cleansing even if it warranted violence. Friday, however, wore a grim expression and shook his head. Obviously he had heard the Jackson boy's discourse about Jack Mulligan before. He calmly expressed his opposition to Jackson's racial slurs and obviously thought he was the more mature voice of reason. Nathan seethed. He hated such brainwashed rubbish.

"Raymon why don't you give it a rest," Friday had said. "You're obsessed with that white boy. He ain't nothin'."

"You don't get it, do you, Tyrel? The black man, he got to take care of business once in a while. We don't have everything like whitey has. We got to protect what's ours."

Hallelujah, smiled Ramapo.

"What you think, you own Mt. Sidney, Raymon?"

"Yeah, in a way I do," Raymon spoke sharply. "And the block I live on, too. This is my hood. I don't want no white man near me."

Ramapo smiled.

"You gotta deal with white man, sometime," Tyrel pleaded.

"Yeah, but not in my back yard."

"Raymon, I wouldn't do somethin' stupid," Tyrel warned.

"You keep tellin' me that," laughed Raymon, "but I'm gonna keep rattlin' that white boy's cage. As a matter of fact, I'm not leavin' out that faggot motherfucker he rooms with either. Fucker's probably suckin' that peckerwood's cock as we speak."

214

Nathan looked at the bottle on his desk as he thought back to the conversation. He took another drink and sat down. Exhaling a deep breath, he pondered. Should he involve another individual, especially a student, in his plans? It was risky.

Raymon Jackson was a high profile student, a great athlete, obviously popular and to Ramapo's advantage, a voice that students listened to. If he were to be fed certain information, he could be very effective in exposing Jack Mulligan and securing his ultimate removal.

Nathan Ramapo recalled a maxim his father repeated frequently when he was a young boy, "Fish or cut bait." It was meant to invoke the sentiment that at times when one came to a crossroad in life, a decision had to be made—do something or don't. Nathan Ramapo was now at such a crossroad and was desperate.

Should he risk his academic career? Was the removal of Mulligan worth the effort or was it just a postponement of the inevitable. Nathan stewed in his own twisted emotions. Was this the right way to proceed? Raymon Jackson did seem to share a similar viewpoint as his own. The decision had to be made—now. Risk it all or stand pat and silent.

Ramapo poured another drink and swallowed the amber liquid in a quick gulp. Then, he reached for the student phone directory.

***

The weather report on the radio told Raymon Jackson a story he didn't want to hear. For the next several days, the weather would feature cold winds and rain. Raymon hated football practice under such conditions. He sat down on the edge of his bed and absently brought the tip of a pen to the corner of his mouth and chewed on the plastic nervously.

The telephone suddenly rang at his elbow, startling him. He absently lifted the receiver off the cradle and carried it lazily to his ear. "Yeah?"

There was a momentary pause of silence, and he almost hung up when a reluctant male voice came back. "Is this Raymon Jackson?"

"Yeah, that's me," challenged Raymon irritably.

"This is Dr. Nathan Ramapo, Raymon, over in the English Department. I'd like to have you come by my office sometime tomorrow to discuss some business."

A frown creased deep in Raymon's face. He stared at the phone, fearfully. "Business?"

"Yes."

"What's this about?"

There was an odd tone in Ramapo's voice. "We can talk about that when you get here."

Raymon licked at his lips, shook his head, "I don't have any classes of yours."

"This isn't about academics," interrupted Ramapo, "but it is important."

Raymon was confused. Should he hang up?

As if to placate him, Ramapo continued in a low, suggestive voice, "I'd like to talk to you, if I may, about a fellow student named, Jack Mulligan."

"I don't know him," Raymon shot back too quickly.

"Sure you do, and I think we'll have much to talk about."

216

Raymon licked his lips sensing a trap. Was he being sucked into something? "Hey man, I don't really know the dude. I've never even talked to him."

"I'm sure," came the flat reply. "Let's meet tomorrow afternoon. Say, one o'clock at my office?"

"Is this for real?"

"Oh I assure you this is for real, Mr. Jackson."

"Yeah, but…"

"One o'clock, Raymon. Be there," ordered Ramapo and broke the connection.

Raymon's hand shook as he dropped the receiver onto the hook. A frown now corrugated his forehead. How could an English professor know anything about his hatred of Jack Mulligan? He didn't like it. Tiny beads of perspiration began glistening along his hairline.

He had been so careful not to let anyone, he didn't trust, know his thoughts and plans. Raymon's life was one of personal achievement, and he didn't want to share any spotlight. When Jack Mulligan left Mt. Sidney, he'd take full credit. He'd be the man. As far as he was concerned, Mulligan was his personal project.

Now a wrench was being thrown into the gears of his plan. This Dr. Ramapo—what did he want? How could he know anything? And, if he did know something, who had told him?

Could it be Tyrel? No, he was a brother, and although they didn't always agree, Tyrel wouldn't rat on him. That left only one other person—that motherfucker, CQ.

***

Whistling a tune CQ was thinking of a painting he was working on. He never saw it coming. It being Raymon Jackson.

He had just left his room and turned the corner to the stairwell, when he was caught by his shirt and lifted bodily from his feet. He hit the wall hard. The blow to his back forced the air from his lungs. Pain seared him. Stunned he stared ahead blankly, the pain now came in waves from everywhere.

His eyes lost focus, but they returned when he found himself chin to chin with an angry Raymon Jackson. "You been runnin' your mouth, motherfucker. Haven't you?"

"What?"

"Don't act innocent, motherfucker," hissed Raymon.

"No man…I ain't talked to no one."

"Yeah you have, motherfucker," Raymon spat, his eyes hopscotching across the graffiti artist's face. "Who you been talkin' to about the white boy and the faggot?"

"You be trippin' man!" CQ shrilled. "I ain't talked to no one. I swear!"

Raymon brought his knee up savagely and CQ doubled in pain. "You're lyin', bitch."

CQ struggled to talk, "No…no."

"Then how come I got a call from this dude, Professor Ramapo in the English Department? He wants to talk to me about Mulligan."

CQ's eyes rolled wildly, like a trapped animal. "I don't know, man. I don't even know the dude."

Raymon's right hand descended in a short vicious arc, connected with CQ's face knocking him to his knees. "You better be right, motherfucker, or I'm takin' you out. You understand?"

The little man was whimpering as he collapsed in a heap at Raymon's feet. Why had he ever gotten involved with Raymon? He had nothing against the white boy. He'd spray painted the hallway that first night as a joke. Just for fun. Now this crazy motherfucker, Raymon, was threatening to kill him. The sonuvabitch was sick.

Raymon pulled CQ roughly to his feet.

"You better pray when I see the man tomorrow, he don't mention your name," Raymon growled, pointing a finger in his face. "Or, I'm comin' after you, boy."

Raymon let go of CQ, spun on his heel and stomped down the stairwell leaving the shaken graffiti artist leaning against the wall crying in rage.

CHAPTER 22

The English Department offices were located in historic Davis Hall, one of the oldest and most revered buildings on campus. Its three story, brick exterior had welcomed black students for over one hundred-fifty years as they developed their skills as writers and journalists. It possessed an intimidating but dignified character from its ten Doric columns along the front side to its heavy double oak doors guarding the entrance. Davis Hall was the home for the academic elite who both taught and carried on a constant vigil as arbitors of the English language and its awsome power. The punishment for entering this temple with a lack of discipline was being labeled as nothing less than a literary dilettante.

The day after Professor Ramapo's phone call, Raymon approached Davis Hall with leaden feet and a bowed head. One would have been hard put to think this was one of America's most outstanding athletes. Raymon's mind was in turmoil, as he tried to consider—back and forth—who had exposed him. Who was his Judas? Who could possibly want to ruin him? If it was CQ, the little bastard would pay, big time.

Raymon Jackson was a celebrity but here he was—out of his element—in a place where neither the coaches nor the press could help him. He didn't have to be told that exposure as a racist or a trouble maker, would mean never seeing a professional football uniform. The thought of that completely humbled Raymon.

Professor Ramapo was an authority figure on campus and a gate keeper to his future. One derogatory word from him and Raymon Jackson would be destroyed.

Raymon stood outside the main doors frightened and unable to move. He didn't want to see or talk to Dr. Ramapo. He knew what the man would say. Tyrel had been right. He should have kept his mouth shut. Now it was too late. Maybe he could beg for forgiveness or grovel at the Professor's feet for a second chance.

He glanced up trying to decide, when he saw Ramapo from a second floor window glaring down at him. His eyes were piercing. The older man's finger pointed at him and crooked a chilly greeting.

Raymon swallowed hard and with shaky legs walked up the steps.

***

Keysha had been studying a scar on the top of Jack Mulligan's forearm for five minutes. It was shaped in an irregular oval and must have come from a very nasty puncture wound. She caught herself staring and redirected her attention back to the calculus class where both she and Jack were seated. Luckily, this was material Keysha was quite familiar with, and she could momentarily indulge in a bit of daydreaming.

Feeling intrusive, Keysha's scrutiny next went to Jack's face. She was continually fascinated by his face. She put together his features, minus the scars, especially the long one down his forehead and cheek. The scar ran deep and made him look savage. She involuntarily licked her lips and thought how seductive and seemingly inaccessible he was. The scars helped this illusion.

She had asked herself a thousand times why she couldn't connect with him. Was it because he was white or was she afraid of some sort of peer rejection? Would her friends abandon her for dating a white man? Keysha had always been popular in school. What if she did something, however, that suddenly changed all that? Could she withstand the social recrimination?

Keysha knew she was attracted to Jack. She'd felt it the first time their eyes met outside the Registrar's Office. He was so strong and quiet. Despite a dark, almost scary side, she could tell he was painfully shy. She was sure he felt what she felt but he would never approach her. If a move was to be made, she'd have to initiate it.

A mild deception had been forming in her head for some time. What if after a class, she approached Jack for help in math? She could make up some academic distress and bat her big brown eyes. A true damsel in distress, without, of course, insulting his intelligence. Maybe he'd feel gallant and come to her aid.

The class ended with Professor Banes in mid-sentence. He excused them, and Keysha gathered her books and moved out into the hallway. Her supple body was tingling with anticipation as she decided to try her scheme. Would he think she was too brazen? Would he coldly say, no? She shivered at the thought that she might have misread him. How embarrassing that would be if he rejected her plea.

Jack was one of the last students to depart the classroom. He came into view with his notebook and text under his arm. He had a fluid way of walking with his small tight hips and large shoulders. Keysha closed her eyes for a second and gathered herself; then fell into step next to him.

"Hi," she said shyly.

Her voice seemed to almost startle him.

"Hello," he whispered hoarsely, his blue eyes penetrating into her. Those eyes—deep, expressive, intelligent.

Keysha's heart was pounding. "I...I was wondering...I mean...I've been having a hard time in calculus. You know, those derivatives. They give me fits."

He studied her for a second which seemed to linger forever. Could he see into her mind and through her innocent deception?

"Have you spoken to Professor Banes?" he asked in concern.

"No," she replied quickly. "I'm kind of intimidated by him."

Was he buying this, or was her plan falling apart like a house of cards? She must sound like an idiot.

"He is a frightening man," he said with a tinge of humor.

Keysha knew Professor Banes was a slight, soft spoken man and a gentle soul. Jack must be teasing her.

"I meant intellectually," She blurted, once again feeling foolish.

He seemed to consider this, "Would you like some help?"

Keysha's heart leaped with joy. She didn't even notice the incredulous stares from the students passing by.

"Would you? Could you?" she exclaimed in honest relief. "I mean you're in my class, and we live in the same dorm."

Her arm brushed his and she felt his warmth. Those muscles moved like sinewy snakes under the skin.

"What's giving you problems?" he asked.

As Keysha made up difficulties for Jack to solve, she found herself giddy just walking beside him. He was the most rugged male she'd ever seen. Most importantly, he gave her an unspoken respect as an intellectual peer, unlike Raymon who expected Keysha to be a mindless ornament for his glory.

"Do you have time to go to the library?" Jack asked.

"Yes, if you have time to help."

Jack smiled warmly. It was a nice smile. His face was transformed, losing much of its sinister demeanor. "I think for you, I have time."

They then walked side by side out of the building and into a bright, late autumn morning. The crisp air refreshed their spirits. The leaves had fallen, and the bare branches of the trees stood starkly against the sky and swayed slowly back and forth.

Keysha couldn't believe how easy it was to talk to Jack. It was delightfully different from Raymon and his mindless jive. Raymon always seemed to need an audience to adore him. It was funny how strolling with Jack Mulligan was more exciting than all the lavish evenings she'd spent with Raymon and his beloved BMW.

Then out of nowhere, a voice shattered it all.

"What the fuck you doin' with him?"

They both turned at once.

Raymon was standing not ten feet away with one of his worshiping followers, a guy named, Samuel. He was now focusing a venomous glare of betrayal on both Keysha and Jack. Keysha could tell trouble was ahead. Thoughts from the encounter on her first date with Raymon came to mind. This was all she needed.

It was time to diffuse the situation.

Anger flashed in Keysha, "It's none of your business Raymon what I'm doing with Jack."

"My ass!"

"Let's go, Jack," she said, grabbing his arm.

"So it's Jack now," said Raymon stepping directly in front of Jack. His eyes drilled into Jack as a direct challenge. "I'll determine who she talks to," he sneered.

"You'll determine nothing, Raymon," said Keysha from the side. "So leave us alone—we're goin' to the library. Jack's helping me with math."

"Helping you!"

Raymon's shout came as a signal, and a crowd of onlookers began to gather around them.

Jack then responded, "Maybe you'd like to help us both with calculus. I'm sure that someone as brilliant as yourself would have a whole new twist on the subject."

"Don't dis me, motherfucker. If she needs help, I'll give it to her," Raymon sputtered angrily. "You understand. She doesn't need anything from a criminal motherfucker like you."

Keysha turned to Jack, who looked as though he'd been struck with a hammer.

"What?" muttered Keysha.

"Ask him, Keysha," Raymon said twisting the corner of his mouth into a smile that failed to reach his eyes. "Didn't you know? The white boy here murdered his own father. Ask him!"

Shock registered on Jack's battered face. Keysha was confused.

"Tell her, motherfucker!" shouted Raymon so that the growing crowd could hear. "Tell her how you murdered two people. One of them a brother."

Keysha couldn't believe such a thing could be true. She stared at Jack's pain stricken face hoping for a rebuttal. Instead, his eyes instantly grew dark and old, as if they had been in too many corners of hell and had seen too much.

He stoically gathered himself, lifted his head and silently pushed his way through the crowd.

Raymon laughed loudly, "That's right, white bread," he shouted at Jack's retreating figure, "you go run to your room or wherever you fuckin' go. Maybe that faggot roommate of yours can give you something you haven't had in a while."

Keysha spun to Raymon. Her slap caught him hard, causing him to step backwards. A gasp came from the crowd.

"Damn!" he screamed. "What's that for?"

"You make me sick." Her eyes bore into him mercilessly. "That was cruel and mean."

"Well bitch, someone had to inform your dumb ass and let you know who the dude be."

"Go to hell."

Keysha stomped away shaking her head in anger. Don't cry, her mind screamed. Then, she stopped and turned. "Don't ever call me or talk to me again."

Raymon frowned, "Who you think you're talkin' to girl. I'm the man, Keysha. Hear me, bitch?"

***

It was two o'clock in the afternoon when Nathan Ramapo started drinking. A smile of relief came to him. He had already called a graduate assistant to cover his afternoon classes, so he could now savor a long awaited victory. Raymon Jackson who had been by earlier was now armed with all the facts he needed to destroy Jack Mulligan. Nathan could hardly wait to see what would happen. News of Mulligan's crimes would quickly awaken the whole campus. Think what the alumni would say when they heard.

His meeting with Raymon Jackson had been short but productive. Jackson proved a receptive vessel for the information from Ramapo. In fact, Nathan found the young man's hatred even more intense than his own. This was delightfully refreshing.

227

Sipping his drink, Nathan recalled part of the conversation with Raymon. The running back had, at first, been nervous and extremely worried about incriminating himself. He had squirmed in his seat, much as a trapped animal. Sweat had beaded on his forehead, and he had wrung his hands and played nervously with a large ring on his finger.

"What is your opinion of the white student, Jack Mulligan?" Ramapo had said without fanfare.

Raymon answered hesitantly, "Told you, I don't know him. I've just seen him around. You know—he's alright."

"Come, come, Mr. Jackson. I know for a fact, you can't stand him and that you'd like to see him expelled."

"Who told you that?"

"I know everything," smiled Ramapo under his heavy lidded eyes.

Raymon eye's danced suspiciously. He tried to sputter a rebuttal, but Ramapo's gaze silenced him. "Relax, Mr. Jackson, I fully agree with your assessment," he said in a low voice. "Mulligan is in one of my morning classes. You have no idea how it galls me to see him there."

Raymon slumped in disbelief. What was this? "Have you got a tape recorder or somethin' goin'?" he said suspiciously.

"No, Mr. Jackson. You may be assured of my complete discretion. If you'd like to look around, be my guest."

For five minutes, Raymon searched the room for bugs. Nathan patiently stood back and waited. He was impressed by the young man's caution. At last, Raymon seemed satisfied and sat down.

Nathan then continued, "You, Mr. Jackson, can help me banish this caucasian menace."

"This what?"

"Mulligan," he said resolutely.

"You mean it?" Raymon quizzed.

"I do," Ramapo said. "White people have no business being in this school. Their presence will destroy everything that a good number of exemplary black people worked hard for."

"Damn," Raymon said smiling in relief. "I thought you were tryin' to trap me."

"Not at all. I recognize in you a bright, motivated young man and a valuable ally."

Ramapo shoved a file across his desk at Raymon. "It's all in there, Mr. Jackson. This file will tell you all you need to know about Jack Mulligan."

Ramapo figured correctly that Raymon wasn't a reader, so he verbalized the salient points to him. The running back's eyes widened with each new revelation. Twenty minutes later, Ramapo sat back, "So what do you think, Mr. Jackson?"

"Let's take it to Dean Jans."

Ramapo laughed. This kid was slow on the uptake. "That's where the information came from, Mr. Jackson. The Administration doesn't want you or your peers to know about Mulligan. Come, you can do better than that."

Ramapo then knew he'd have to spell it out. "You, Mr. Jackson, are a prominent, man-about-campus and you're looked up to. You may even one day become a pro athlete."

Raymon frowned, "I will be in the NFL."

"Certainly," Ramapo restated thoughtfully. "What I'm trying to say is that your thoughts and deeds carry weight. People want to know what you espouse…say. If students could learn what's in that file from someone as influential as yourself, well…"

Raymon's eyes brightened with comprehension. "I see."

"Good," said Ramapo.

"Wait till I tell them what you found."

Shocked, Ramapo's voice grew cold, "No, no, Mr. Jackson. If you are to work with me, you must never divulge where you received your information. I'm in a precarious position. This folder is highly confidential."

Raymon nodded, "You'd be in trouble."

"That correct, Mr. Jackson."

Raymon whistled silently.

Nathan continued, "But, if word circulated quickly and enough people found out, neither one of us could possibly be implicated in the fall-out. When every student knows, fingers will point in so many directions, and no one will know who started talking first."

"Solid!" exclaimed Raymon, who seemed to at last fully understand. His beady eyes brightened.

Ramapo's heart leaped. He could tell the boy would get the ball rolling in a big way. Raymon's exuberance showed. He'd save the day for Mt. Sidney. Nathan laughed to himself. He had chosen his consort well. Now he could sit back and watch.

CHAPTER 23

Word of Jack's criminal record spread around campus like wildfire. Outrage and fear soon ignited the flames of ignorance like gasoline and fire to eradicate any intelligent rationale. Suddenly, every student seemed to have an opinion about ex-cons being allowed on campus. Some demanded Jack's instant expulsion, while others thought rehabilitation might work but not at Mt. Sidney College. It seemed the consensus opinion, however, that being a criminal and white on the campus of Mt. Sidney College was not an acceptable combination.

A petition soon made its rounds on campus and rumor had it that two-thirds of the students had already signed it. Jack Mulligan became the unknowing rallying point for every racially motivated frustration and hatred. Students felt betrayed. They questioned why they had not been informed about the Jack's past.

A beleaguered Dean Jans was drowning in phone calls from angry parents who were concerned for their children's safety. No amount of assurance seemed to placate them. They were appalled at Jans and the

Board of Trustees and as a result were now hunting for new and "better" schools for their children. Some parents were even threatening Jans himself with lawsuits.

A protest march was supposedly planned, and the newspapers were starting to get wind of the controversy. He shivered to think what would happen if this incident went national. Mt. Sidney College, an academic beacon during the Civil War and the civil rights movement, would be ruined as black students denounced the school as having sold out to white America.

Jans hadn't slept for more than a few hours per night in a week. He sucked down antacid tablets with black coffee and tried to find out who had leaked the damaging information. Blame, however, seemed to emanate from a hundred different directions. The futility of pursuing a culprit soon became apparent.

Damage control became the new order of the day. Jans, who was an expert, had to find a way to shift responsibility for the Jack Mulligan fiasco to other individuals or groups. Covering his ass, he told himself, would serve the greater good than acting in any overtly heroic way.

How he wished he had never heard of Jack Mulligan or agreed to admit him in exchange for extra State funding. He shook his head. This should have been his finest hour; not some inescapable nightmare.

***

Jack Mulligan kept pretty much to his usual routine. He simply ignored the firestorm around him.

Since he hadn't made any friends, except Juleel, while at Mt. Sidney, he wasn't affected by anyone's hostility. The wide berth the students gave him in the cafeteria grew progressively larger, of course, but it really didn't matter. In fact, the cat calls of "murdering motherfucker," and "chickenshit white motherfucker," didn't even faze him. Jack Mulligan was here to get an education—nothing less would do.

Still, the verbal abuse in the dorm, the classroom and walking between buildings grew daily. Soon, Jack figured, they'd get physical and when they did, an example would have to be made. No one put their hands on Jack Mulligan. No one.

Out of frustration, Jack felt the word "nigger" come back bitterly into his throat. He just as quickly admonished himself. He simply wouldn't go that route.

The evening after Raymon had told everyone about Jack, he'd finally confided his past to Juleel. He figured Juleel should at least hear his side of the story. Although stunned, Juleel said he understood. Jack thought that strange, since he really didn't understand, himself. All he really knew was how to survive.

"What will the school do to you, Jack?"

"Who knows. Probably throw me out."

Juleel frowned, "That's terrible. You've worked so hard."

Jack shrugged, "Hey, shit happens."

"It's not right, though," Juleel said in outrage.

Jack looked at the floor, paused, then looked at Juleel. "You're a good friend, Juleel. I couldn't ask for a better roommate, but," he paused, once more dropping his gaze, "if you want to leave...as my roommate, I'll understand. It could get rough around here. You may not want to be near me."

Juleel could feel an angry tear forming in the corner of his eye. His voice was bitter. "Do you think anyone wants to room with me, Jack? Get serious. I'm a faggot, a queer. I'm considered a leper. Like you, Jack, I've always been an outsider."

Jack nodded his complete understanding.

Juleel then surprised him. "Since you've come to Mt. Sidney, I've grown by your example. I'm not bending my head in shame, anymore. To hell with them, Jack. I am what I am. I'll look them or anyone, straight in the eye."

***

Keysha and Danielle grew quiet around each other. Danielle, of course, had heard what had happened in front of the library with the white boy and Raymon but kept her silence. Keysha seemed pensive and withdrawn since that day. That worried Danielle. What could Keysha be thinking? Danielle hated to see someone as nice as Keysha hurt by a pig like Raymon.

Both were taking a break from homework. The room was quiet and it seemed time to talk.

"I heard what happened the other day," said Danielle with a look of genuine concern.

"I don't want to talk about it," said Keysha, who was sitting cross-legged in the middle of her bed. She wore her favorite tattered, grey sweatshirt and pants and a petulant expression. Her trademark hair hung down on the patchwork quilt she had brought from home, and her face, devoid of make-up, looked melancholy, especially around her puffy eyes.

"You're sure?" Danielle said. "Cause you seem upset."

"What good would it do to talk about it?" asked Keysha. "It was all over before it even got started."

Danielle looked confused, "What's that?"

Keysha looked up at her friend. "Being with Jack Mulligan."

"The murderer!"

The words struck hard, causing Keysha to pause. "Yes."

"I thought you were crying about your break-up with Raymon," Danielle said, sitting down on the bed next to Keysha.

Keysha's eyes rolled to the ceiling. "No way, girl! I couldn't care less about him."

"You mean you been seein' that white boy?"

"No, but I would have, though."

"He's a murderer!" exclaimed Danielle in surprise.

"I don't believe that."

Danielle eyes narrowed, "The courts did, girl."

"He's different now. I know he is."

"Don't be blind, Keysha. Since day before yesterday, you've been sittin' in this room cryin' and carryin' on, and I thought you were upset about Raymon. Now you tell me you got this murderer on your mind. Are you crazy?"

"I guess I am," whispered Keysha. "For the first time in my life, I think I might be in love."

"Love!" Danielle exclaimed, throwing her hands in the air.

Keysha put a hand on Danielle's arm. "He's not what you think. He's sensitive, shy and alone."

"Remember how you warned me to be careful around Tyrel? Make him work for it, you said."

Keysha smiled, "I didn't say I was ready to go to bed with him."

"But, he murdered his own father, Keysha?"

"Did anyone on this campus bother to ask the circumstances?" asked Keysha with a steely voice. "Apparently, the authorities decided he was worth taking a chance on, even with his record. We don't even know why he acted violently. But, will one person at Mt. Sidney College at least give him a chance?"

"Are you saying you will?"

"Yes, I will." Keysha declared.

Danielle looked stunned, "But Keysha…"

"No buts!" interupted Keysha. "He's been here for two months, and as far as I can tell, he hasn't hurt a soul. All he wants is to be left alone. He works ten times harder than anybody else on campus, minds his own business and for all that, the students here treat him like he has a disease. He eats alone, walks alone, studies alone. He might as well be in prison."

Danielle stared at her friend, "You feel sorry for him, Keysha. That's not love."

"That afternoon—a few days ago," began Keysha, looking off as if seeing Jack Mulligan in her mind, "we were walking together, enjoying each others company. We laughed and talked—really talked. There was definitely a connection. He's so incredible and smart."

Danielle rolled her eyes in disbelief. "What would your parents say if they knew what you were thinking?"

"My parents would understand, Danielle. My Uncle Robert is white. He's married to my father's sister, Denise. My parents would understand."

"Even with this guy's criminal record?"

That gave Keysha reason to pause. Her parents were not bigots, but they were straight-laced. They had many white friends, but their friends were never in trouble with the law.

"I think they would understand."

Danielle shook her head skeptically, "If you say so."

Keysha's face brightened, "Jack is a lovely person."

"Lovely," laughed Danielle, "after being around Raymon, you think the white boy is good looking?"

"Raymon is ugly inside, Danielle. He's a pig," said Keysha, bitterly. "I never want to see him again."

"Whoa girl…"

"No I'm serious, Danielle. He took such delight in hurting Jack in front of that crowd that day. What kind of person would do that?"

"He is self-centered."

"More than that, Danielle. Raymon Jackson is like a lot of boys I knew in high school. They were always trying to impress."

"I know he's trying to drag Tyrel into this," said Danielle with new concern.

"Don't let him do it. Tyrel is sweet. He doesn't need Raymon."

"You got that right, girl."

James Ankrom

The telephone then rang, interrupting them.

Keysha lifted the receiver on the second ring. "Hello."

"Hey baby, it's me," spoke the smooth but elated voice of Raymon Jackson. "Think we could get together and talk?"

Keysha gripped the phone in revulsion, her knuckles white with a mixture of anger and dread.

***

Raymon Jackson had been waiting for a few day to pass before he called Keysha and offer his most insincere apology. She just had to cool down. Women were way too emotional and didn't know their own minds. That's why they needed the strong hand of a man. He had a way of calming them down. Just give them a little sugar, turn on the Jackson homeboy charm and wait for their forgiveness.

He knew Keysha was one hard bitch, but so what. He wanted her, period. She could bitch and complain all she wanted. Her body was too incredible to pass up. It made him reel with desire.

Raymon was presently feeling quite satisfied. He had had one of his best weeks at Mt. Sidney. For two days, he had basked in the pleasure of spreading the word about Jack Mulligan. It was great, especially since the student's practically thanked him for setting them straight. There was a commaraderie, however hateful, in having a common enemy. Raymon wanted to be at the doorway when the cops escorted Mulligan back to jail. He couldn't wait to laugh in the white motherfucker's face.

238

Now, however, he had to mend a few fences and get back what belonged to him.

When he made the call to Keysha and heard her voice, there was the expected long silence, then she spoke. "Raymon, please don't call me again," came the stony reply.

"Aw, come on, baby," Raymon said gently. "I'm sorry I caused such a fuss."

"No you're not, Raymon. You enjoyed it. In fact, you loved it. Humiliating others probably helps build your perverted ego."

"You're right, you're right," said Raymon humbly. "I've been so bad. I know it. I'm just asking for you to find it within yourself to forgive me."

This was always one of Raymon's most successful lines. What it did was put the value of redemption squarely in the woman's hands. He knew they all wanted to forgive him. Maybe they thought they could change him for the better, too.

"This isn't a joke," warned Keysha coldly. "You're little routine may work on other girls you've dated but not me. You've crossed a line. In fact, the only person I want to talk to is Jack Mulligan."

"What?"

"That's right, Raymon. He doesn't play games, and he doesn't patronize me as if I'm an idiot."

"Well he sure didn't tell you he was a murderer, either."

Keysha's breath caught, "Why should he? Maybe he considers his own past, his business. Did you ever think that?"

Raymon gritted his teeth in anger, fighting for control. "When the motherfucker starts messin' with what's mine, it's my business!"

"What'd he messed with that was yours?"

"You."

The shoe had fallen. A silence hung like a precarious weight over the phone.

"Raymon, I have some sad news for you," said Keysha in a low, clear voice. "You never possessed me, owned me or even influenced me. How did you ever get such a moronic idea?"

Raymon's temper broke, "Listen bitch, don't be givin' me your shit. You mine, till I tell you you're not."

"Don't ever call me again, Raymon. Whatever you imagined or thought you imagined about me, didn't happen. It's over."

CHAPTER 24

The late afternoon sun slanted through the windows in Robert Brent's office revealing the last vestiges of a cool autumn day. The Head Resident sat tilted back in his desk chair, his heels hooked in the open bottom drawer of his desk. He studied some pages of a paper he held in his hand incuriously.

The proverbial shit had hit the fan, he brooded as a bit of a smile lifted the corner of his mouth. Now everyone knew about Mulligan. How it had happened, he didn't know and, quite honestly, didn't want to know, but Dean Jans' memo, which he held in his big hands, emphasized the seriousness of the situation. Jack Mulligan's days as a student were definitely numbered.

Whatever had thankfully happened, Mulligan was no longer his problem and Jans was off his back.

Brent had to admit that the white boy had not really caused him that much trouble. Mulligan was quiet, didn't drink or get into any fights. He actually minded his own business. Too bad he was white.

Being white and having a criminal record was lethal. Brent and Dean Jans confidentially knew of many students at Mt. Sidney who had juvenile records. It was not unusual, and as long as they kept their noses clean, no problem. But, Mulligan was different, he was white and a murderer. America had long chastised the black man for wrong doing, well now it was payback time.

A soft knock made him glance up at the door. "Come in," he said mechanically.

The door opened and Juleel Washington peeked in. "Can I talk to you?" he asked with a swallow that made his Adam's apple bob.

This was all Brent needed.

"Yeah, come in."

Juleel sat down as if dropped into the chair and wasted no time. "What are you going to do to help Jack Mulligan?"

This had to be a joke.

"What?" laughed Brent incredulously.

"He needs your help, and you know a lot of people."

Brent's smile faded, "I had a feeling it was only a matter of time before someone found out about his past. Just today, I received a memo from Dean Jans about Mulligan. The Dean is getting hammered. Pressure's coming from alumni and parents to resolve the situation and expel Mulligan. If the Board of Trustees agrees, that's it."

"Do you know what will happen to Jack?"

"He'll probably go right back where he belongs—a jail cell," Brent said flatly.

"Maybe you could talk to the Board?" Juleel pleaded.

"Me!" exclaimed Brent in disbelief. "I'm nobody, kid. I'm an employee of Mt. Sidney College. I get room, board and tuition, plus a chump salary for wiping the noses and tucking into bed a hundred and twenty six freshmen and sophomores. Besides, I don't even like Mulligan."

Juleel appeared shattered, "We've been getting threatening calls, letters; even notes taped to the door."

Brent was suddenly uneasy. Would someone dare try to injure or kill him? "I'll call campus police then."

It was Juleel's turn to laugh. "They can't do anything. You know that."

"That's the best I can do."

"No it isn't," said Juleel in a strong, clear voice. "You could call a meeting of everyone in the dorm. You could explain to everyone that Jack's paid his debt to society. Tell them how hard he works."

Brent frowned, "If I did that, Dean Jans would have my job before I finished the first sentence. His memo, in fact, instructs me not to do anything. As I said, I'm an employee, I do what I'm told."

"Do you also call Jans massa, too?" shouted Juleel. "Have you ever once had a single thought of your own?"

Brent slammed his fist, "That's enough, Washington! You can leave, now."

Juleel continued, "I know you don't like me because I'm gay, and I know you don't like Jack because he's white, but we've been model students. You could intervene, you could educate, you could even act like a human being."

Robert Brent knew that Juleel was appealing to a part of him he kept well disguised. Yes, he could do all

243

the things Juleel mentioned, but to what end? Why take a chance? Brent had always been a team player and perhaps that was his greatest strength and weakness. Why be a rebel? There was no way he was going to ruin his future for a white ex-con.

"I told you, no, Juleel. Is there some part of that word you don't understand?"

Juleel rose from his seat and walked stiffly to the door. He stopped when he reached for the knob. Fixing Brent's face with his eyes, he whispered, "Coward."

Then he was gone.

***

Tyrel and Danielle left the Mt. Sidney Triplex at ten-fifteen and although the movie was billed as a comedy, their spirits were decidedly flat. They walked the short distance back to the campus, and Tyrel tried to make small talk about the movie and football. Anything to lighten the mood. Danielle said yes or grunted at the appropriate times but seemed to be in her own world. Tyrel guessed she was thinking about Keysha.

Tyrel had, like the rest of the school, heard about the Jack Mulligan's criminal record and had endured Raymon's bigoted, twisted version of that record for several days. Frankly, Tyrel was tired of the whole thing. The way he looked at it, Keysha and Raymon didn't get along. Raymon hated the white boy and the white boy hated Raymon, and Keysha and the white boy, for better or worse, did get along. How the white boy saw this whole thing was anyone's guess.

"Danielle, you still thinkin' about Keysha's problems?"

"Yeah," she said absently. "I think she's going to make a mistake meeting and talking to Jack Mulligan."

"She's what?"

"She told me this evening just before we went out that she's going to talk to him the first chance she gets."

Tyrel nodded in disbelief, "I guess that means Raymon is out of the picture."

"Yes and for that, I can't blame her," Danielle said bitterly.

Tyrel would go along with that. Just today Raymon had tried to get several other guys on the team to help him burn an effigy of Jack Mulligan on the steps of the Administration building. Anything to show off. No one seemed to want to go along with it, and Raymon berated them as chickenshits.

"I know Raymon's pissed at Keysha," he stated.

"Well it's his own damn fault," shot back Danielle angrily.

"I know, baby. I know," said Tyrel defensively. "I'm just tellin' you what's goin' on."

A tear showed in Danielle's eye. "Why can't he just back off?"

Tyrel thought about that and shrugged his massive shoulders. "You know Danielle, Raymon's a really good football player cause he's got this aggressive kind of thing goin'. What's the word…?"

"Tenacity." she said.

"Yeah, he has tenacity. He has to win all the time. Now he's lost Keysha, and even though now, I don't think they would ever have gotten along anyway,

245

James Ankrom

Raymon can't stand the fact that he's lost something. What burns him worse, of course, is that he's lost to a white boy."

Danielle's eyes rolled, "Raymon needs help."

Tyrel regarded Danielle warily as they entered the stone gates to the campus. She looked upset, but was breathtakingly beautiful.

Some shouting off to their right caught their attention. In the distance, two big trucks were parked on a service road leading to the football stadium. A mass of students and college employees were busy unloading lumber and construction supplies.

"What's going on over there?" asked Danielle.

"They're getting ready for Homecoming weekend," observed Tyrel dryly. "This year, Coach Bob Morgan is coming to visit. Remember last year he became coach of the Buccaneers. He used to go to this school, so he's this year's honored guest."

"So what are they doing with that stuff?" pointed Danielle at the lumber and scaffolds.

"Building a speaker's podium and some kind of big paper mache statue thing in his likeness with his old jersey number. The school is retiring his number at half-time."

"How nice," Danielle said absently.

Tyrel moved in front of Danielle and looked intently into her eyes. "Danielle, I think it's a bad idea to get as involved as you are with Keysha's problems."

Danielle stared back, "I'm just helping a friend, Tyrel."

"Are you?" questioned Tyrel in a deep baritone. "Or are you starting to meddle."

"No I…"

"Don't Danielle," warned Tyrel, putting his hand gently against her face. "They will work it out. Raymon's got his stage, but something tells me he'll eventually run out of steam. Keysha will either hook-up with Jack Mulligan or she won't. But Danielle, let her decide. Just be there as a friend."

"Well…"

"Uh…uh! You know I'm right." he said, putting his arms around her.

"I hate it when you make sense," she said stubbornly.

"I know you do," Tyrel laughed. "You get that little twitchy thing goin' with your nose."

"What?"

"Yeah," smiled Tyrel playfully. "I seen it before. That little nose just be goin' back and forth."

Danielle jokingly poked Tyrel and giggled.

"No I don't."

"Yeah, I know it's tough not knowin' everything."

Danielle hugged and kissed Tyrel, "You are so rude."

***

Not too far away, in the shadows of a doorway, Jack watched the same group of students unloading trucks, too. He had read in the school newspaper about the big time coach coming back to Mt. Sidney for Homecoming. There would be lots of reporters covering the event. It would be perfect.

A picture of Raymon Jackson began to form in his head.

CHAPTER 25

After calculus class the next day, Jack found himself wandering aimlessly around the campus. It was an overcast day with an insistent breeze making it seem colder than it really was. A few days earlier, he had bought a winter jacket and was now glad he had. Pulling it close, he zipped it high and raised the collar.

Kicking leaves as he walked, Jack realized how much he needed to think. So much was happening and he needed direction. He soon found a secluded spot with a seldom-used bench under a shag-bark hickory. Jack sat motionless, listening to the sounds of the campus in the distance. Crews of men were blowing leaves and the muffled voices of students could be heard far off from time to time.

Jack had not slept well the night before. His body felt heavy with fatigue, and his mind was dulled from lack of sleep. He had hoped to see Keysha today and try to explain his past, but she hadn't been in any of his classes.

What did it matter? She probably wouldn't listen anyway. How do you justify murder to another person, especially when the victim is your very own father? How do you tell someone about the kind of rage it takes to kill, and then expect the listener to understand the desperate fear behind the final act?

Jack recalled one of the rare times he and his father had been together. It had been on a spring day about two years before he killed him. Jack had been watching television in the living room, while his mother slept off a hangover. His father had come into the house after working on his car. He must have been feeling triumphant after getting his ancient Dodge to start, for he told Jack to get in and they'd go for a beer.

Jack remembered how he had looked forward to just being with his Dad, who usually shunned him as the son of someone his mother had probably slept with. He had gleefully climbed into the passenger seat, while his father turned over the ignition and listened as the engine coughed, rattled, then sputtered to life.

They drove no more than a mile, while Jack studied his father's unshaven, bleary-eyed face. It was warm that day so his father wore a pair of filthy Bermudas that showed his milk-white calves and blue veined ankles.

His father parked in front of a small bar not far from one of the mills. Inside it was dark, cool and musty. He sat on a bar stool sipping a coke, while his father talked sports with the bartender and a big guy with a gigantic, swastika tattooed on his beefy arm. Jack guessed the big man belonged to the Harley parked outside. He'd heard about bikers before and how they were mean when they got drunk. This guy with the swastika looked like he might fit the bill. Definitely bad news.

At some point in the conversation, a well dressed black man walked in and asked to use the phone to call a tow truck for his car. The bartender sneered coldly and pointed to a pay phone on the wall. Jack's father eyed the black man; then clamped his fingers painfully on the back of Jack's neck and said, "Watch this boy." The words were slurred, and his sour breath made Jack want to throw-up.

"Hey Herman," his father said in a too loud voice to the bartender. "Do you usually let spooks waltz right in here?"

The bartender seemed to pick up on his father's question and snickered, "Once in a while, even a roach will get into the best of places. Course if it stays, you get an exterminator."

The biker took a big swallow of beer and swung around. "If it's one thing I can't stand, it's the smell of a fucking nigger."

The black man, dialing the pay phone, began to fidget nervously. He was a short, thin man with a bone colored jacket and bright red tie.

"I haven't stomped a nigger's ass in at least a week," mused the big guy in a gruff voice. "It's like a habit with me. Kinda' relaxes me."

Jack's father laughed, then peered over at the black man.

"I didn't know niggers could afford fancy such fancy clothes. Maybe when they dress like that, they're tryin' to get a white woman or somethin'. Fuckin' spear-chuckers are always after white women."

The dapper, black man completed his call and nervously went out the door. The biker leisurely finished his beer, belched and, as if on cue, got up from his stool and started for the door.

"Come on boy," his father said gleefully, "this ought to be fun."

He and his father followed the black man and the biker into the street. It was nearly dark and the gray neighborhood looked even shabbier than usual. A vagrant was searching through a nearby dumpster, looked up, dismissed all of them and went on with his work. In a nearby yard, a dog started barking. The black man walked to his car, a burgundy Cadillac, which sat—hood up—fifty yards down the street. He turned as he heard the steps of the biker behind him. A frown furrowed his dark features.

"May I help you?" he asked in a low voice.

"Yeah," said the biker, "I'm wondering how an ugly lookin' little nigger like you can afford a car like that. You some kind of drug dealer?"

The black man seemed unfazed by the insult. "I'm not a drug dealer, sir. My name is Reverend Cecil Williams. I'm Pastor at Calvary Baptist over on Shoreham Street. I was on my way to visit a very ill parishioner when my car broke down."

The biker snickered, "Well I don't care who you are, nigger. I don't let fancy-assed coons like you walk into my neighborhood. You fuckin' understand that?"

"Please sir," the Minister said calmly, "I don't want trouble. I'll be gone as soon as the tow truck gets here."

Jack's father then stepped forward. "You know nigger, I don't have much use for dick-head preachers, myself. You go around stirring up the rest of the niggers; thinkin' you're better than the rest of us."

"No sir," said Reverend Williams. "We are all God's children and brothers."

"Fuck!" said the biker. "I think you consider yourself better. And don't call me brother. I'm no brother to a fuckin' nigger."

Fear now imprinted itself in the preacher's eyes.

Jack could see what was going to happen next. His legs shook, and he wanted to run away, but he seemed riveted to the sidewalk. Besides, his father would give him a beating if he ran.

"Please, I want no trouble," Reverend Williams said.

"Too late for that, nigger," the biker sneered.

Jack's father laughed, "I think we could fix this nigger's car ourselves, don't you?"

The big man laughed, too. "Yeah, he needs it customized."

With that the biker and Jack's father started kicking out the headlights. Pastor Williams attempted to place himself in front of them but was given a backhand slap that sent him into the gutter with a broken nose. Blood spattered onto his white shirt until it matched his red tie. The big guy grabbed a piece of two-by-four from the dumpster where the bum sat placidly, watching them. With his huge tattooed arms working double time, the biker smashed out the Caddy's windshield; then started denting in the hood and sides of the car. Jack's father took out his pocket knife, opened the passenger door and proceeded to rip the leather seats apart.

Reverend Williams pleaded with them. "Please...please stop."

After ten minutes, the once fine Cadillac was transformed into a crumpled, cut-up piece of irretrievable junk. The tires were punctured, and not one panel on the car was left undented.

The biker strutted proudly up to the prone figure of the preacher and suddenly kicked him in the face with his size sixteen Doc Martins. Jack's father added his help with another jolting kick to the preacher's ribs as they began to beat Cecil Williams senseless. The biker then spit into the now unconscious man's face as a final insult.

He spotted Jack standing to the side in shock. Jack was frightened at the ferocity of the whole display. The biker laughed so loud, it echoed off the nearby houses. "Hey boy, you want to help kick this sorry piece of shit?"

Jack couldn't answer. He was too stunned to move.

"Come on, boy," his father implored. "Show the man whatcha' got."

Still he stood unmoving.

"You ain't scared of this nigger?" asked the biker.

"No, he ain't scared," assured his father. He gave Jack a bleary assessment. "Get your ass over here, boy, and show this man what you can do."

Jack still didn't move. He was terrified and feeling queasy. The bloody figure of the preacher lay in the gutter, not moving. Could he be dead?

His father's face reddened with anger and embarrassment. "Boy, you'd best get your little ass over here now and kick this nigger's behind before I take off my belt."

Jack knew about his father's love for using the belt. He'd been at the receiving end before. He took a few tentative steps forward, until he stood over Cecil Williams. Looking down at the prone figure, he could see the battered face and smell the coppery odor of the preacher's blood. He knew he had to kick the man or he'd be in big trouble.

Gathering his resolve, he gave a small, half-hearted kick to the black man's chest. The preacher didn't react.

"Shit, boy," chuckled the biker, "is that all you got? You kick like a little girl."

"Kick him like a man, boy," chimed in his father.

This time he gathered himself and let loose a big kick. "That's it, boy!" yelled the biker. "Kick him again."

He kicked again with all his might.

"That's my boy," his father screamed proudly. "Keep it up! Kick that nigger!"

Jack continued kicking until his legs felt weak. He could feel the scalding tears of disgust roll down his cheeks as he heard his father's braying laughter. A bitter taste came into his mouth and he felt suddenly sick.

Still he kept kicking. Over and over and over. Harder and harder. Again and again and AGAIN!

He'd make his father proud. He'd show him. The sonuvabitch!

Jack no longer saw Reverend Cecil William's poor bloody face in the gutter. He instead imagined his father's drunken, laughing features and hatred boiled up inside him.

Finally the biker and his father grabbed him with a laugh.

"You got an ass-kicker in this one, friend," the biker said.

"Yeah, he's quite a boy," His father said proudly. "Don't like them niggers either."

They both laughed as comrades.

Jack stood, catatonically looking down at the Reverand Cecil Williams, a man of God.

"We better split," said his father gazing down the street as if someone were watching.

"You got it, buddy," said the biker as he and Jack's father shook hands on a job well done. The biker roared away on his Harley, and Jack and his father headed home in the Dodge.

For many days afterward, Jack couldn't eat or sleep as his mind relived Cecil Williams' beating. Nightmares haunted him. How could he have participated in such a terrible thing? Reverand Williams hadn't insulted anyone or harmed anyone in any way.

When his father found out Jack had gone to his mother and tearfully related the incident, he beat him with his belt. For once, he felt he deserved the pain inflicted by the leather.

Jack re-focused his eyes and stared coldly at the withering trees and bushes. Now he wished he hadn't cried all those times. He hated himself for showing his father how he hurt. Well he'd killed the drunken prick, and he would never regret it. Never.

***

When Jack returned to the dorm that afternoon, there was a piece of paper taped to his door. It was a

255

message from Robert Brent telling him to drop by his office.

Jack knocked on Brent's door, heard him reply and with a sinking sensation walked in. Brent seemed happy to see Jack, which naturally could only mean Brent had bad news for him.

Brent wasted no time, "Got a message for you, Mulligan. Dean Jans wants you in his office ASAP. If this is what I think it is, you'd better pack your bags, boy."

"Yeah, sure."

"You think I'm kidding?"

"I don't give a damn what you think."

Jack felt his temper rise, but he kept control. There was no sense in talking in a civil way to someone as idiotic as Brent.

Ten minutes later, Jack was let into Jans' office by his secretary. Jans was reading over some papers and didn't even glance up but mumbled for him to sit down. Jack sprawled into a chair and waited. Twenty minutes passed, with Jack cooling his heals. Finally, he had had enough.

Jack stood up, "Hey pal, I'm leavin'."

"You can't!" said Jans calmly. "I need to talk to you."

"Then make it quick," ordered Jack sternly, glancing down at his watch. "I'm busy and you're wasting my time."

"Your time?"

"That's right."

Jans smiled in a lifeless manner. "You arrogant…"

"You're still wasting my time." Jack interrupted coldly.

Jans slammed his pen on the desk. "This won't take long."

"Good."

Dean Jans picked up some stapled papers that he had been studying and slid them across the desk to Jack. Jack picked them up in a leisurely way, leafed through them and indignantly tossed the document back onto Jan's desk.

"Do you know what that is?" asked Jans.

"No, and I don't care."

"Over two-thirds of students signed that petition. It calls for your immediate expulsion."

"Assholes."

Jans' eyes narrowed, "What did you say?"

"You heard me. This school is full of racist assholes."

"How dare you?"

"I don't like racists, do you understand?" Jack snapped.

Jans exploded, "Son, maybe you don't understand the precarious situation you're in. I'm the only person standing between you and a prison cell! The students, alumni and board want you out of here."

"Don't act like you're doing me a favor," said Jack. "You let everyone on this campus know my background, so it's your problem. If anything happens, I'm calling a press conference and letting everyone know what you did."

"Don't threaten me!" Jans shouted.

"Then don't threaten me. I've pretty much had it."

"Then quit."

"Never. I'll leave when I want."

"You what?"

James Ankrom

Jack laughed as he stood up and walked to the door, "Don't fuck with me, Dean. I have nothing to lose. Do you understand?"

The world inside the office became silent as the if the universe was holding its breath.

Jans turned pale. Jack knew then, he had gotten through.

***

Jack awoke with an anguished cry as his mind came struggling out of a nightmare. He came awake and looked over at Juleel. Good, he hadn't awakened his roommate. Eyes slitted, he looked out the window and noted a hard, cold rain coming down. The rain matched his spirit perfectly. Cold, dreary and hard.

He started to sit down at his desk, but knew he had to urinate. Silently, he padded to the bathroom wavering tiredly on the cold tile floor. When he finished, he went back to his room and to bed. He sneezed. Damn he was coming down with a cold. Wrapping his covers tighter, he leaned back and closed his eyes. Far off he could hear thunder.

He couldn't quite sleep. He was now in a nether world between conscious thought and dreams— somewhere on the edge. He felt apart and disconnected, trapped in incomprehensible circumstances, an order beyond purpose or meaning. It was a place where atonement was forever impossible.

CHAPTER 26

Danielle got back to the dorm just after three o'clock the next day. She spotted Raymon Jackson waiting in the lobby looking like a little boy who had lost his puppy. He nervously waved her over as if he needed her in a hurry.

"We've got to talk," he said without fanfare.

"Okay," she said. "About what?"

"About Keysha. This shit she's pullin' has gotten way out of hand. She thinks she can dis me by hangin' with Mulligan?"

Danielle breathed a sigh and frowned, "Sit down Raymon and let me explain a few things to you."

They took two seats in worn, overstuffed lounge chairs with patches of duct tape to keep the stuffing in. Students walked past them without so much as a glance.

"Raymon, as hard as it might be for you to understand, Keysha isn't that interested in you. Yeah, she went out with you a few times, dancing and such, but she's not going to do it anymore."

"Shit!" he said, shaking his head. "What's wrong with her?"

"Raymon be honest with yourself. You want a trophy girl to be seen with. Keysha ain't no trophy. She's too smart for that."

"But a white boy.

Danielle knew how hard it was for Raymon to accept defeat and sympathized, "I know, but she hasn't talked to him since you made that scene outside the library."

"So she's not going out with him?"

Danielle instantly realized her tactical error giving Raymon a certain amount of hope, "No, not at the moment."

"Good, then I can still save her," he said in a brighter tone. "I'll make her see."

Danielle shook her head in disbelief, "Raymon did you hear me at all? Keysha isn't the girl for you. You're wasting your time."

Raymon fixed on something far away, "She'll come around. Is she up in your room?"

"No. She's in class."

"When will she be back?"

"I don't know, Raymon. Later. But, you're not going to like what she tells you."

Raymon frowned, "I'll decide that. Could you give her a message?"

Danielle gave up. This guy was bull-headed and hopeless. "Sure, what is it?"

"Tell her I'd like to see her one more time, so we can talk. Tell her I'll meet her after practice outside the locker room at the stadium at seven-thirty."

Danielle nodded laconically. His excitment only made her sense further dread. He was such a self-centered fool.

"If I see her, I'll let her know," she said in defeat.

"Good," he said with a confident smile. "I'll straighten her out. You'll see. She'll know who her man is."

Then, he stood and walked away without so much as a goodbye.

***

When Raymon returned to his room, the phone was ringing insistently. He picked it up quickly. "Yeah."

"Hello Raymon, this is Professor Ramapo."

"Hey, what's shakin'?"

"I've got some excellent news about Mr. Mulligan, I thought you'd might like to hear," Ramapo said in a slow drawl.

"What's that?"

"The board is meeting this week. They're under a lot of pressure from parents and alumni, they're going to go for a full expulsion of the white boy."

"Solid!" shouted Raymon happily. "When can I help him pack?"

"It shouldn't be long," Ramapo said. "I knew you'd be as pleased as I am."

"You got that right."

"Well Raymon, you can be proud of the fact that you were the one who precipitated this whole chain of events. If it wasn't for you, and you, alone, Jack Mulligan would have marched right on to graduation."

Raymon preened with pride. He had accomplished what others couldn't have. Just ask Professor Ramapo. Too bad Keysha—the bitch—didn't think so.

Ramapo paused to let the words sink in. "I've got a little something for you, to show my gratitude, and I was wondering if you'd stop by about seven-thirty tonight and pick it up."

Raymon sighed, "Man, I'm real sorry. I can't do it tonight. I'm suppose to meet a girl at the stadium around then."

"Oh I see," Ramapo said in a deflated tone.

"I could stop at your office tomorrow."

"That's bad for me. I'll be at a conference the next few days," Ramapo said in a disappointed tone. "I was very much hoping to give this to you before hand."

"Hey, that's alright," Raymon said. "There's no hurry. I'll see you when you get back."

"Yes I suppose so," Ramapo said, clearly resigned.

"I only wish this girl I'm meeting was as anxious to see me," Raymon said. "Her name is Keysha Jordan, and she says she doesn't want to go out with me anymore because I rattled Mulligan's cage."

"Get a new girl!" exploded Ramapo. "You deserve better. How could any upstanding black girl sympathize with a beast?"

"That's not all. The bitch now wants to date Mulligan."

"Oh sweet Jesus," crowed Ramapo in disgust. "Dump her, get rid of her! She's a traitor to her own race—the trash!"

Even Raymon was shocked at the Professor's passion. This guy must hate whites worse than he did.

"Anyway, I'm going to have a talk with her."

"Forget her, I'm telling you."

"I got to try," said Raymon truthfully. "She doesn't know what she's doing."

"That's assured," said Ramapo once again composed. "But I guess I can't talk you out of it. It's foolish, however."

Raymon was now growing weary of the bossy professor.

"Listen, I'll see you after you get back," Raymon assured.

"Okay then," Ramapo said. "Please make it soon. You truly deserve this reward for your good work."

***

Nathan Ramapo put the receiver back in the phone's cradle and stared off into space. In front of him was a small vial containing potassium cyanide, a syringe and a bottle of wine. Ramapo had a pair of tight plastic gloves pulled on his hands and had been preparing to draw the deadly liquid from the vile and place it in the wine. It was a vintage meant especially for Raymon Jackson.

Covering one's tracks was something Nathan considered prudent. He couldn't allow a big mouth such as Raymon Jackson to continue his mindless preening all over campus. The football player had served his ultimate purpose. Nathan knew that sooner or later the gossip could implicate himself and bring trouble to his door.

Now, however, Raymon had unwittingly brought forth a new and better sacrificial candidate. She was a traitorous bitch who truly deserved death. It was perfect—made to order. A scummy bitch who loved white boys. This Keysha Jordan would taste death, and the more brutal the means, the better.

Ramapo picked up the cyanide vile and took it over to his wall safe and carefully placed it inside. Returning to his desk, he considered how he should accomplish the death of Keysha Jordan. She would be waiting at seven-thirty near the end of the stadium where the dressing room was located. He also knew that at that time of day, the stadium was usually deserted. He quickly reached into his desk and withdrew the oversized envelope with Jack Mulligan's prison records. A few moments of study told him how he'd kill her. Every criminal had a favored *motus operandi*, and Jack Mulligan's, it seemed, was murdering with a knife.

Perfect.

CHAPTER 27

By five-thirty, Danielle wondered if she'd see Keysha in time to give her Raymon's message. She glanced at the clock with trepidation. What could such a meeting possibly accomplish? Raymon was being completely unrealistic and Keysha despised him. Danielle also knew Keysha well enough to know that her roommate would probably ignore the invitation completely. Tyrel had been absolutely right to advise Danielle to stay out of it.

She studied for another forty-five minutes, grabbed a quick bite to eat in the cafeteria and found herself back in her room at seven-fifteen. Still no Keysha. Danielle figured her roommate must still be working at the library.

Maybe she should take a quick walk to the stadium dressing room and let Raymon know that Keysha wasn't coming. There really wasn't any reason he couldn't just meet Keysha here at the dorm. Raymon, she knew, didn't want anyone around in case Keysha verbally dumped on him. He probably feared his reputation might get tarnished.

As a far flung favor to him, she grudgingly decided to walk down to the stadium and tell him the bad news. After all, he was Tyrel's best friend. Maybe this time, the pig-headed fool would listen.

Danielle slipped her jacket on and then paused. Crossing to her desk, she scribbled a short note to Keysha and placed it conspicuously on her roommate's desk. This wouldn't take long, she thought. Then, no more involvement. This was the end.

***

Jack reported to work at two o'clock in the afternoon at Ableson's Brick Yard. Although Stu Ableson's business was always brisk, today was total chaos. A delivery truck had broken down on the way back from a construction site, leaving only two other trucks to cover.

Stu was standing in the center of the yard barking orders at everyone. Jack hurried to the big fork lift he usually drove and quickly started moving pallets of brick and concrete block onto the trucks. Soon he had one truck loaded as tightly as he could get it. Stu was pleased with Jack's work. He had noticed early on that Jack had a natural knack for packing trucks compactly. This made the loads more stable and unloading smoother when the trucks arrived at the construction sites.

"Jack you're riding with me," Stu yelled. "We're taking this to the estate job north of town; then we have to get back and load again. Old man Parson's waiting for a load of concrete block at that new discount mart he's building."

Jack had been told that Tom Parson's was one of Stu's oldest and best customers and that the contractor wasn't a patient man. He and Stu had known each other for thirty years, and although not friends, they worked together well and respected each other.

Stu drove the truck to its extreme, streaking to the north side of town as fast as it would move. Jack sat in silence, contemplating his shaky future at Mt. Sidney College. Dean Jans and the Board would most likely end his academic career this week. Then it would be back to the Institution.

"You sure are quiet, today," commented Ableson.

Jack, startled from his reverie, glanced over at the big man and attempted a smile. "Just thinkin'."

"About what?" Stu said. "Some girl givin' you a hard time?"

"No, just the Dean of Admissions."

"Why? What's going on?"

"The whole school knows about my record."

Stu raised his bushy eyebrows in surprise. "How the hell did they find that out?"

"Don't know, but they did. All it takes is one person."

Stu shook his head, distastefully, "So what're they gonna do?"

"Probably kick me out. Dean Jans same as told me so. There's a petition and parents are putting pressure on the Administration."

"Shit."

"Yeah," said Jack sadly. "If I don't show up one afternoon, it might mean I'm back Inside."

"Oh hell."

"Yeah," agreed Jack.

"Maybe I could go talk to them," offered Stu as he down-shifted into a lower gear.

"Don't think that would do much good. You're white, and I don't think they'll listen. Thanks, though."

"Well, when we get done tonight, we'll go to Sparkies and figure something out. I'll call my lawyer, too. See if he can help. He might as well earn some of that retainer I pay him."

The rest of the afternoon, Stu and Jack hustled from one job to another. By the time they were done, it was dark, and they were both exhausted.

Stu parked the truck in the yard, and he and Jack walked the few blocks to Sparkies. A brisk, freezing wind was blowing debris around the street. Jack shivered, and dreaded the eventual walk home.

Sparkies was crowded with all the regulars, but Jack and Stu slipped into their usual booth and drinks soon appeared. Overhead a pall of smoke stirred restlessly in the breeze from the door being opened and closed.

"My attorney should be here soon, Jack," Stu said, between a deep swallow of beer. "In the meantime, relax. What an afternoon, huh? I'm whipped. Man, I'll sleep like a baby tonight."

"I wish I could."

"Myron will help, Jack. You'll see."

Stu had called his lawyer, Myron Porter, earlier. The attorney told Stu he'd meet him at Sparkies that evening. Stu seemed to have a lot of confidence in Porter. The lawyer had gotten him out of jams before, and Stu figured Porter would think of something.

But deep inside, Jack had his doubts. He could hear the cell door banging shut. Would he die behind bars? Alone—always alone.

***

Raymon Jackson went to his room after practice. He was so exhausted from running play after play he laid on his bed staring at the ceiling. Why couldn't Coach Dunn get off this punishment pace all the practices seemed to have anymore? The man was obsessed with winning the Conference title.

He decided to close his eyes for just a second, then he'd go to dinner and afterwards meet Keysha at the stadium. Soon however, his mind drifted and all he could think of was a tall, leggy girl he'd seen in the lobby of Lincoln Hall. She was one fine looking bitch. But, she kept eluding him everytime he wanted to talk to her.

Suddenly he came awake.

His eye caught the time on his clock, 7:25 p.m. Damn, he was late! Keysha wouldn't hang out for long. He ran out the door in a mixture of panic and frustration leaving his jacket on the bed.

CHAPTER 28

Planning a murder in such a short time wasn't easy. Nathan had to hustle to get everything in place. This included the right weapon, clothing and a clear workable plan.

He had gone to the rendezvous point outside the stadium earlier in the day and hurriedly checked out the lay of the land. His mind took in the location of every bump in the landscape, every obstacle such as fences and concrete barriers in one photographic sweep. If he was going to be there after sunset, he didn't want to be stumbling around in the dark.

After his surveillance, he left before someone could later recall his presense.

Timing was going to be a decisive factor. According to rumors he'd heard, Raymon had in addition to other bad habits the distasteful trait of being chronically late. He was late for classes, dates, football practices and even game day preparations. If it wasn't for the fact that Raymon Jackson was a football star, he'd never get away with such behavior. Ramapo's only worry was that this would be the one time Raymon was prompt.

On his coffee table, Nathan spied the shining, razor-sharp hunting knife with its ten-inch blade glistening like a jewel. Nathan had earlier honed its edge to make sure it was ready. He now picked it up and placed it in its leather scabbard.

Nathan considered Keysha Jordan. Although he was sure he'd never met her, he built up a solid hatred for her for betraying her race. What kind of low-life bitch would trade a fine black man such as Raymon for an ugly bastard such as Jack Mulligan? Stupid, stupid, girl. It would be a pleasure to rip her apart. He'd actually be doing her a favor.

In Nathan's mind he'd not only save Keysha from shaming herself with an interracial affair but also he'd consecrate her as a heroine and martyr to her fellow black students. She'd become an example to all African-Americans of the pitfalls that lay in wait for those who contemplated the evils of interracial involvement.

With everything ready, Nathan slipped out the back door and stopped in the dark to orient himself. His ears soon adjusted to the usual night sounds, and then his eyes opened to the detail in the shadows. He started off across the yard, leaning into the wind sweeping by him. His dark clothing nearly made him invisible.

Nathan was glad the stadium was not too far away. It was cold out here. He arrived minutes later and found a place of concealment behind a narrow copse of trees. His eyes and ears were open to every movement or person who might approach.

271

Nathan pulled the knife out of the scabbard, leaned it against a tree and waited. Where was she…the fucking bitch?

"Come on!" he whispered nervously.

Then, finally, his ears picked up footsteps. They were faint at first; then grew louder and louder. Then, as if in a vision, the figure of a girl emerged from the darkness and onto the paved tarmac outside the deserted Wildcat locker room. A street light bathed her figure in an orange halo of light.

Nathan's eyes narrowed their focus.

She was beautiful, a fallen black angel ready to be purified. Nathan picked up the knife and started forward. It was time for her redemption.

***

"Another beer, Jack?" Stu Ableson inquired.

Jack held his hand up—enough. "I gotta go, Stu." Then he glanced at the short, balding man in the expensive suit who sat beside Stu. "Mr. Porter, I appreciate your help."

Myron Porter looked up and held out his hand. "No problem, Jack. We'll see if we can put a new wrinkle in the college's plans for you."

Jack nodded, shaking the lawyer's hand, trying to feel optimistic and failing.

"Take it easy kid and don't worry so much," Stu assured.

The cold night air was bracing as Jack stepped out of the bar. The wind was still ripping down the dirty street, tossing litter everywhere. Jack suddenly realized he had to pee. He ducked in the alley next to the bar.

He didn't want to go back inside and end up drinking more and being there the rest of the evening.

Jack felt a little better about his legal prospects after talking to Myron Porter. But, there was no sense in getting too overjoyed. The chubby barrister had apprised Jack that since he had lived up to his end of the parole agreement, as set by the State of Ohio, Mt. Sidney College was bound to live up to their end of it, too. Myron said he'd give Dean Jans a call tomorrow and explain this to him.

So now Jack had an attorney. The notion gave him a feeling of empowerment and importance. My attorney—Myron Porter.

He could just see Dean Jans' face when he received the phone call tomorrow. The good Dean would shit. Conditional parolees weren't supposed to have personal lawyers, just lame public defenders.

Jack zipped up his pants and started back to the dorm. Bleakly, he knew he was walking into more trouble than he'd ever had in his life, and he had no friends except Juleel and Stu Ableson. He was alone, as he had always been alone. He just didn't want to die alone, looking through the bars of a prison.

Seven long years inside had taken away a chunk of his life. They were precious years when most teens dated, went to senior proms, saw movies with friends and flirted with girls at football games. Jack, instead, had passed those years fighting for his life and soul.

Keysha Jordan came to mind and a rush of sublime calm enveloped him. He recalled their walk the day Raymon Jackson interrupted them. She was special, a gem he could...Jack shook his head at the thought. Keysha Jordan now wanted nothing to do with him.

She deserved better than an association with a loser like him.

***

Keysha swept into her dorm room at seven-thirty bringing in a wave of the cold wind from outdoors. The autumn chill gave her cheeks a color that only enhanced her beauty. She missed summer's warmth, but loved the quiet solitude of the late autumn.

Setting her books down, she spied a note on the corner of her desk. Picking it up, she read:

Keysha,

I'll be back in a short while. I have something important to tell you. Have gone to the library.

Danielle

Keysha's eyebrows pinched in confusion. She'd just come from the library and hadn't seen Danielle. She had been there nearly all day researching a paper. She even skipped a few classes to get the work done. It seemed as though she would have seen her roommate if she'd been there.

Oh well, she thought, returning the note to the desk, maybe she'd been too pre-occupied. Keysha smiled, maybe it was like one of those old black and white, silent movies where all the characters miss each other as they walked in and out of doors in a long hallway.

Keysha had hoped she'd run into Jack Mulligan at the library, and they could talk. She'd wanted to tell him that she was willing to give him a chance as a human being instead of immediately judging his past and summarily condemning him. To her disappointment, however, he had failed to show.

She'd see him soon she figured and when she did...A sweet warmth spread through her. Her legs felt shaky just thinking about him.

CHAPTER 29

"Where the hell is Raymon?" Danielle cursed herself. "Damn, I must be crazy! It's freezing out here."

Danielle found the dark, isolated area outside the locker room eerie and forebodding. The wind had picked up to forceful gusts, blowing dust in swirling spirals between the parked service vehicles at the side of the stadium. The oppressive darkness seemed to squeeze the illumination of the lone street light into a tight circle which battled against the nocturnal elements.

Glancing at her watch, Danielle decided one more minute was enough. This place gave her the creeps. Tyrel could give Raymon the bad news about Keysha. She didn't care, and she wasn't going to freeze her ass off much longer.

A titanic blast of cold air suddenly hit her in the side causing her hair to fly wildly about her face. Danielle reached up and pushed the tendrils out of her eyes.

It was then she saw a movement to her left.

A shadow moved, coming alive. Fast! Too fast. The darkness came at her.

Suddenly, she felt something plung into her with incredible force. Air rushed from her lungs. She at once had no breath. Then she saw the red stained blade above her. Blood...her blood? Her feet came off the ground on the next thrust. She was lifted up and hit the ground hard. The shadow was over her. Then the pain came again—so much pain. It was blinding!

Then Danielle sank into darkness. It happened so fast.

There was no time for thought. Her last dreamy vision was of Tyrel. He was smiling as he waved a long and very lonely goodbye.

***

Nathan's muscles sprung forward—exploding and fluid—the blade in his hand held low.

The girl's head turned and froze at his onslaught. Her eyes widened instantly in terror.

Nathan swung the blade from low-down, catching Danielle in the abdomen. The force stunned her. She fought to scream but Nathan's knife was already out and onto another slash cutting cleanly across her throat.

Blood gushed outward onto his shirt.

His free hand slapped viciously across her terrified face. His temples were now pounding as adrenalin whipped him into a frenzy.

"Bitch!" he snarled.

Danielle fell in a heap. Spasms racked her as blood poured from her throat. Her legs kicked out of control.

"Whore!" Nathan yelled in her dying face. "Do you want the white sonuvabitch now?"

Nathan then went wild—slashing over and over—with demonic force. With each strike, he felt a release and began laughing insanely.

Danielle's body finally stopped moving. Her face could only register surprise in its death.

Tears fell from Nathan's eyes. Sobs racked him violently.

Keysha Jordan, he justified, had at last been redeemed. Saved by this simple act of purification.

A giant blast of cold air startled him. He assessed his precarious location. Danielle's body was in plain sight. Campus security could spot him easily or, God forbid, the police. He had to move the body. NOW—quickly before someone saw him.

Nathan grabbed an ankle and pulled Danielle's body behind one of the Ford pickups. His eyes nervously moved back and forth, probing the darkness. Could someone have seen him?

The knife still lay on the pavement where he had stabbed her. The blade dripped with her blood. He ran to the spot and picked it up. The blood was still sticky and warm. His legs felt rubbery and his stomach boiled. Shit! He had to get away.

Staggering and stumbling, he headed off into the darkness. His route had been pre-planned—a good thing—for now he had trouble thinking rationally.

The girl had been the perfect sacrifice. But despite her death, racial purity would never be restored until Jack Mulligan was also cleansed from Mt. Sidney College.

***

As Raymon trudged toward the stadium locker room, he tried to think of what to say to cool Keysha's unreasonable anger. He had to win her back at any cost now that she was ostensibly unattainable.

Raymon wasn't used to ups and downs in a relationship. Women were supposed to be passive and subservient—like his mother. His father gave the orders; she obeyed him and she never, never questioned. It was as simple as that.

He refused to think of Jack Mulligan as anything but white scum. Keysha would eventually think of him same way. Why? Because a man's woman had to assimilate the very thoughts of her man. His philosophy became her philosophy. Raymon would teach her. He was the all-knowing boss, the alpha male.

The strong wind tossed the tops of the trees and bushes back and forth violently. Raymon thought of his warm team jacket back in his room and cursed himself for not wearing it.

He rounded the corner of the stadium and stopped short as he noticed a figure in the distance running along the retaining wall. Joggers. Man, those motherfuckers were crazy. Why couldn't they exercise during the day time like normal human beings?

In the parking area outside the locker room he stood, studying the emptiness made more desolate by the hard gusts of cold wind.

No Keysha. Shit!

He should have known she wouldn't show up. Bitch! His anger grew bitter with her absence. The least she could do—after all he'd sacrificed—was to meet him. He'd spent a fortune wining and dining her; making her feel like a real woman, his queen.

Didn't she know that without him to guide her and give her an esteemed status, she was nothing?

Striding away, he felt his shoe stick. Then he spotted a large dark spot beside one of the maintenance trucks. A reflection from the light told him it was wet. Did somebody spill some paint—red paint? He squinted. Funny, red wasn't one of the school's colors.

Bending down to scrutinize the fresh paint, Raymon suddenly froze. This wasn't paint. Paint had a smell. With a morbid fascination, he slowly touched the red spot with his fingers. It was warm and sticky.

The hair on his neck raised.

Blood!

Whose blood? This wasn't from a small cut on someone's hand. The spot was too large. It was also warm and fresh. Too fresh!

Raymon's eyes traveled to the corner of the red pool where it seemed to be smeared around the corner of a truck. Three short steps away, he spotted two legs and feet. He froze. Terror tunneled into his eyes. His heart began to pound.

Raymon shot to his feet, straightened and turned abruptly. Was someone watching him? He recalled the jogger he seen.

He slowly stepped between the trucks and looked down. It took a moment for his eyes to adjust to the deep shadows. A female body was lying face down. Was it Keysha? Nausea and fear gripped him like a vise. He had to look. He had to.

Fear touched its icy finger to his spine.

Squatting, he lifted a limp shoulder for a closer look. Blood was thick on the face. Who...? Horror froze his heart as he stared into the slashed face. Then his breath caught! He stared, his eyes transfixed in recognition. He couldn't look away.

"Danielle, Mother of God, Danielle," he whispered.

CHAPTER 30

As Jack got closer to campus, he could hear sirens wailing from what seemed like a dozen different directions. "Someone must've really fucked up," he thought with a laugh. Wonder who died? The cool air had magically combined with the alcohol in his system to make Jack feel giddy. It was a pleasant sensation.

Whatever was happening was someone else's problem. He had his own crosses to bear.

At last Lincoln Hall appeared, and Jack saw a large group of students milling around the entrance. Two police cars were parked outside, their lights spiraling lazily. Cop cars made Jack uneasy. He glanced warily at them and mounted the steps. Inside, more students were gathered in groups, talking in low voices. Two uniformed cops had their notebooks out asking questions and pointing. Some of the girls were outwardly crying.

What the hell was going on?

His eyes then locked on Keysha, who was in the center of one of the larger groups of girls. Her eyes were swollen and red. She was crying in convulsions and being consoled by the others. He hated seeing her cry. Something really horrible must have occurred, but what?

Nobody noticed as Jack slid through the crowd and went back to his room. Pushing the door open, he saw Juleel reading a book at his desk. Juleel registered surprise as he assessed Jack's inebriation.

"I might have had too much to drink," Jack volunteered.

"A shower sometimes helps," Juleel replied, slightly amused.

"I think you're absolutely right," Jack said thickly.

Jack took off his soiled work clothes and placed them in a laundry bag in his closet. Then dressed in just a tee shirt and boxers, he headed to the shower room. The spray of the warm water immediately soothed his aching back and shoulders. His head also started clearing.

He thought of Keysha crying, and the police presence. Had someone been mugged or robbed? Maybe, but would Keysha be concerned to the point of tears? No, something more serious must have gone down. Jack felt uneasy. Superintendent Brown's voice came back, "If there's one incident, you are back here."

How he wished he could comfort Keysha, but he knew she didn't need him at the moment. He'd do her a favor and steer clear.

Back in the room, Juleel greeted him with a shocked expression. "Jack, I just heard the most awful thing. You're not going to believe it."

Jack pictured the scene he'd witnessed in the lobby.

"What?"

"Danielle Myers was murdered tonight, down by the stadium."

Jack's stared in disbelief, "Murdered!"

"That's right," Juleel said, tears welling in his eyes. "Stabbed to death by a maniac. It's terrible."

Jack's heart sank. The effect of Juleel's information was sobering. Juleel kept talking, but Jack couldn't hear him. Now he knew why Keysha was crying. Murder. But, who would do it and why? Superintendent Brown's warning echoed now with more clarity.

Jack's legs felt weak as he sat down at his desk. Juleel noted the change in his roommate. "What's the matter, Jack?"

Jack's eyes looked unfocused. "Guess who's going to be the number one suspect?"

Juleel paused in comprehension, and then spoke in a low voice, "No, you're wrong…not without reason. They couldn't."

Jack shook his head, "The cops will be here shortly. I guarantee it. When they talk to campus security or any of the students, my name will go right to the top of the suspect list."

"You were at work."

Jack nodded, "I worked late and then had some beers with Stu and his lawyer. The lawyer was going to help me out."

"You have an alibi then," Juleel stated in relief.

"It's not that easy," Jack replied. "I might have been walking home at the same time the murder happened. This is bad. I was by myself, so only I can account for that time."

284

Juleel's eyes clouded, "That's conjecture, Jack. You have no reason to kill Danielle."

"You and I know that, but the kids on campus will provide the cops with a motive," said Jack bitterly. "In case you haven't noticed, I'm not too popular."

An oppressive foreboding descended on both of them. The walls in the room suddenly shrank to the size of a cell.

Jack sensed a long night ahead.

***

Nathan Ramapo's trip back to his house seemed to take hours but in reality was only a ten minute journey. His leg muscles cramped in the cold making the trip painful. He wasn't in the best of condition. Too many nights of drinking and not enough exercise had done its damage. Nathan wanted to walk slowly. But, it was imperative he hurry to complete his plan.

In a tight crouch, his breath came in gasps, as he stumbled up the alley. Finally, he made it to the wooden gate of his back yard. The worn gate creaked on its hinges, and a neighbor's dog started barking. Nathan froze, and then in a panic ran for the back door, fumbling for the key.

Why were his hands shaking for God's sake? The door's lock popped at last, and Nathan entered the house and safety.

When the door closed, Nathan sank to his knees, his heart pounding. Then, in sudden horror, he saw the copious amounts of blood still on his hands and the large spattered areas on his shirt and pants. It looked as though he'd taken a bath in blood.

Wide-eyed, he frantically tore at his clothes, ripping them from his body. Then he kicked them into a pile, grabbed a garbage bag from beneath the sink and quickly stuffed them in. They had to be disposed of.

Blood was everywhere. Nathan panicked. Blood...the girl's blood. He had to get it off! Why was it so sticky?

DAMN, just get it OFF!

Nathan ran for the shower.

He fumbled frantically with the faucet handles until the water came on—full and scalding—as hot as he could stand. Nathan scrubbed his skin to the point of pain. The blood mixed with the water and ran in a red stream into the drain, but finally and thankfully, it cleared.

Nathan's panic also gradually subsided. He breathed easier.

Once he dried off and redressed, he went back to the kitchen and grabbed the bag with the bloody clothes. Patience, he told himself. Have patience. Now was the time to think rationally. He could dispose of the bloody clothes tomorrow.

His main focus now had to be the knife. If Jack Mulligan was to be accused of murder, the weapon had to be found in close proximity to him. Nathan wiped the handle with a paper towel and then placed the knife in a clean cloth he found under the sink.

There was no time to hesitate, he had to get to Lincoln Hall. Placing the knife under his corduroy jacket, Nathan headed into the night once more. Fifteen minutes later he was standing beside a tree scanning the open area he'd have to cross to get to the side of the dorm. Could he get there without being seen? At least he knew from his research at the Registrar's Office where Jack Mulligan's room was located.

Mulligan's file had told him everything he needed to know to frame the white boy. Nathan Ramapo was, if anything, meticulous.

Assured that he wasn't being watched, Nathan crossed the wind-swept yard and slipped behind the overgrown boxwoods under Mulligan's window. The bushes made a scraping noise against the brick wall as they were buffeted by the roaring wind.

Nathan carefully placed the knife at the foot of the foundation where the police would easily spot it. A smile came to him as he thought how hard it would be for Jack Mulligan to explain away the knife to the cops.

"Goodbye, white boy," Nathan softly whispered to himself, his voice lost in the breeze. Turning, he ducked and squirmed from behind the bushes—then froze! Sirens were sounding from three directions. The girl's body must have been found.

Crossing the yard in a stiff trot, he blended into the deep shadows of a line of tall bushes and ran along it until he came out onto a sidewalk near one of the frat houses. Just as he appeared on the walk, a deep voice sounded behind him, "Professor Ramapo."

Nathan jumped, "What?"

Tyrel Friday was no more than five feet in back of him.

"Sorry I scared you, sir," said Tyrel calmly. "I just thought I'd say hello."

Nathan had to settle his heart, which was beating like a bass drum in his chest. Gritting his teeth for control, he managed an edgy smile, "Good evening…Mr. Friday isn't it."

"Yeah, I had your course in American lit last year."

Nathan nodded.

"Well it's good to see you. I was just out for some air. It's good for one's health, you know."

Actually the brisk wind was bone-chilling. Tyrel raised his eyes in disbelief. "Well I'm heading indoors," Tyrel laughed. "I'm freezing."

"Then goodnight, Mr. Friday, he said nervously. "It was so nice seeing you again."

"Yeah, good night, Professor."

Suddenly a police car raced down a nearby street. Its lights swirled in the darkness, as its siren blared. More sirens could be heard coming from other directions.

"Someone must have died," mused Tyrel off-hand.

"What?" Nathan asked in alarm.

Tyrel caught the panicky alarm on Ramapo's face. "Just joking…but it must be somethin' bad with all these cops."

Nathan's breath eased, "Yes, I suppose. Well, goodnight."

He then turned and stiffly walked off.

Tyrel shook his head. Man, these professors were strange dudes.

***

Television trucks and a dozen state and local police cars blocked the street by the stadium. Bystanders huddled behind hastily constructed barricades trying to catch a ghoulish glimpse of the body. Murder in Mt. Sidney wasn't an every day event.

Standing by an unmarked police car, Raymon studied the ground at his feet, while a plain clothes detective asked him questions. "You say you were supposed to meet this girl here at seven-thirty?" repeated the stocky policeman pointing at the body.

Raymon let his breath out impatiently. Had these cops asked that same question twenty times? "No, not that girl. Keysha Jordon, my girlfriend. That girl is her roommate, Danielle."

Once again, Raymon Jackson impatiently repeated his story to the detective, Lieutenant Sam Bergman. Why couldn't this cop get it straight, so he could go home? He had to get out of here. The adverse publicity could possibly impact his football career.

Soon the newspapers would scream with headlines connecting him to the murder scene. The press loved scandal. A young woman murdered and a big-time athlete involved.

His mind recalled Danielle's butchered face and body. Raymon swallowed the bile in his throat. Dammit, he had to forget what he saw. He couldn't afford to get sick, too.

Sam Bergman rubbed the bridge of his nose. He was a short, heavy-set man with iron gray hair and deep furrows above his shaggy brows. He took voluminous notes and seemed to be directing many of the other police at the scene.

Raymon couldn't believe he was being interrogated with such fervor. You'd think he'd been accused of murdering Danielle. The thought was sobering. He'd told this cop everything he knew. He wasnt hiding anything. Maybe it was another case of a cop busting a brother. That's all he needed.

"Do you know anyone who might have had a problem with this young woman or with your girlfriend?" Bergman flipped through his notes to find the name.

"No," then Raymon caught himself. "Wait a minute—maybe one."

Bergman's head snapped up.

Raymon remembered the dark figure he had seen running from the stadium. The size of the person was close.

"There's a guy that goes to school here," Raymon said. "He's a white boy named Jack Mulligan. He's here on parole or something. He even murdered his own father. Sonuvabitch has a fuckin' bad attitude. I had a run-in with him a few days ago. Maybe this is his way of getting back. Besides he digs my girlfriend."

"What do you mean?"

"He's always tryin' to talk to her. You know what I'm sayin'."

Bergman looked confused, "Did she respond to him?"

"Naw," Raymon lied. "Keysha don't like no white boys."

Bergman raised his eyebrows in disgust, "Kind of like you."

"Yeah," said Raymon, unthinking, not catching the sarcasm. "She's like me. He's white. He probably thinks all black folk are alike. We're all niggers to them."

"I see," said Bergman curtly.

Bergman put his pen in his coat pocket and viewed the murder scene. "We'll need a formal statement, Mr. Jackson. One of the other men will see you tomorrow. Thank you for your cooperation."

Angrily, Raymon raised his hands in frustration. More questions tomorrow! Motherfucker.

Sam Bergman didn't seem to notice Raymon's body language and walked away without a backward glance. Then he stopped and turned. "Where can I find this, Jack Mulligan?"

"At the dorm...Lincoln Hall."

CHAPTER 31

Across the lobby, pushing his way through the front doors, Keysha saw Tyrel enter the dorm. She watched him as he first scanned one side of the room, then the other. The gathered students grew suddenly silent, and all eyes were fastened on him. Tyrel registered the stunned expressions and knew something was seriously wrong.

Keysha rose from where she was sitting, wiped her tear-stained cheeks and crossed the room. "Hey Tyrel. Where you been?"

"Up at Turner Hall. You know, the psych library," He said, his eyes still hopscotching around the room. "What's y'all doin'?"

"I need to talk to you, Tyrel."

Tyrel didn't like what he was seeing or hearing.

"About what, Keysha?" he asked, suspiciously.

"Let's go to your room," Keysha whispered.

Tyrel saw Keysha's furtive expression.

"What's goin' on here, Keysha?"

Keysha look stricken. "I'll tell you when we get to your room, Tyrel."

Tyrel didn't move.

"What's goin' on, Keysha?" His voice was more questioning.

Keysha was in a corner, "Tyrel, it's about Danielle."

"Danielle..." Tyrel's voice broke into an edgy rasp. "What?"

"Please Tyrel, let's leave here," Keysha repeated. She was now praying she could get Tyrel out of the lobby and away from the prying eyes and ears surrounding him.

"Keysha,...tell me," Tyrel demanded. "Where's Danielle?"

Tears rolled down Keysha's face. She fought for control but was losing. "Dead, Tyrel...Danielle's dead."

Tyrel's eyes widened in horror. He dropped his book bag, and looked out at the crowd as if he were hunting for Danielle. This couldn't be. Where was she?

"Dani..." he whispered and then shouted, "DANIELLE!"

Keysha backed up a step.

"DANIELLE!!" he screamed, edging Keysha to the side and bolting for the staircase. He covered the distance in three long strides, and bounded up the steps two at a time.

Keysha couldn't believe how fast he disappeared. Tyrel's screams echoed throughout the stairwell, "Danielle! Danielle!"

Keysha followed him knowing where he would go. Her heart felt heavy with anguish as she climbed the steps. On the second floor landing, she could see the door to her room ajar. Her steps grew progressively slower.

Inside, Tyrel was seated on the end of Danielle's bed, hugging her pillow and rocking back and forth. He didn't raise his head when she entered. His breath came in short gasps as if air was imprisoned in his large, powerful chest.

The faint sounds of the night and the dorm seeped into the room. He reached for her then, and she sat down beside him. Keysha could see disbelief in his every gesture. She grabbed his hand and held it.

Tyrel responded to the soft pressure of her fingers.

"Danielle, oh God no, not Danielle. Keysha…," he whispered.

Keysha wanted to cry but knew it wouldn't help Tyrel cope with his loss. Her voice came out low, "Tyrel, I'm so…so sorry."

"What happened to her, Keysha?"

The question had no soothing answer. The truth was cold and horrifying. But, she had to tell him.

"Danielle was murdered, Tyrel. Tonight. Her body was found by Raymon down at the stadium."

Tyrel's eyes flared wildly, "Murdered?"

Keysha nodded.

He fought for comprehension. How could…

"Who would want to murder her?" he asked.

Keysha didn't have an answer. She could only put her arm around his large shoulders and feel them sag.

"I told her…Keysha. I told her I loved her," His voice was choked in distress. Then something burst inside his huge body and he began to cry. It began as shudders—his body quaking. Danielle was gone and she would never come back. Deep racking sobs then tore through him as he fell apart in Keysha's arms.

***

Dean Jans was reading in his study when the police phoned at ten p.m. His wife Eve, dressed in her robe, answered it. She had just brushed her teeth and was preparing for bed. Eve Jans was a small woman with greying hair, but with a quick wit and a warm, caring disposition. When the police told her they urgently needed to talk to her husband, she rushed to his study.

Maurice Jans looked up from that day's *Wall Street Journal* and sighed. Now what, he thought? Jans hated late night calls, they always boded some horrible dilemma. What had happened now? Did some student get arrested for drunkenness?

"Hello," he said irritably into the receiver.

"Dean Jans," came a male voice. "This is Detective Sam Bergman of the Mt. Sidney Police. Sorry to be calling you so late, but there has been a homicide on your campus tonight."

Jans sat up straight.

"Murder!" Jans said in a startled voice.

"I'm afraid so, sir," Bergman continued. "A freshman co-ed named, Danielle Myers."

The name meant nothing to Jans. He couldn't be expected to remember the name of every student at Mt. Sidney. What galvanized him was the word, murder.

"What can I do for you, Detective?"

"Well sir, if you could meet me at the Registrar's Office, I'd like you to pull Miss Myers' records for our investigation."

"Certainly," said Jans. "I can be there in fifteen minutes."

Jans hung up said goodbye to his startled wife, who had been listening, and rushed off. Minutes later, he arrived at his office. Police cars were already in front awaiting his arrival.

He walked stiff-legged to the door, and greeted Sam Bergman formally. The stocky detective routinely showed him his ID.

Once inside, Jans logged into Danielle Myers' records at the computer and started printing them out.

Bergman stood outside, watching the Dean with some sympathy. This was bad news for the college. Parents, he knew, liked to think their children were isolated from criminal violence at college. It was as if they were in a protective cocoon. News of a homicide on campus shattered that illusion.

"Would you care to call the parents, Dean Jans, or should I?" said Bergman.

Jans stood poker-faced at the question. "I guess I should," he replied sadly. "Miss Myers' parents will be upset enough."

"Tell them they must come to Mt. Sidney to identify the body," Bergman said in an officious manner. "You understand?"

"Yes."

Dean Jans seemed sick, as he sat down behind his desk to make the call. A sickly pallor came to his dark features. He wasn't good at relating bad news. How he hated this.

Picking up the receiver, he punched in the numbers and waited. The phone rang and was picked up on the seventh ring by a woman with a sleepy voice. "Hello," she said.

"Mrs. Myers?" Jans blurted.

"Yes."

"This is Dean Maurice Jans at Mt. Sidney College. I'm calling tonight concerning Danielle."

"Is something wrong?" she said more clearly.

"I'm afraid so, Mrs. Myers. Is Mr. Myers with you?"

"Yes, Dean Jans. What's going on? Has something bad happened?" she asked with growing concern.

"Could I speak to him?"

Now her voice grew stone cold. "No you'll speak to me."

Jans swallowed hard.

"Are you sitting, Mrs. Myers?

"Will you please tell me what is going on?" she demanded.

Jans was desperate to find an easy way and was drawing a blank.

"There's been a tragedy, Mrs. Myers." he began softly. "Your daughter, Danielle, is dead."

He heard the phone drop and a woman's low wail. Then Doctor Myers grabbed the phone. Jans had to repeat himself. It wasn't easy.

For the next half hour, Jans rubbed his forehead, while he tried to inform and console Mr. and Mrs. Myers' about Danielle's death. As an aside, he filled them in on the actions of the police. Jans had never felt so inadequate to a task and was visibly subdued after he hung up.

Sam Bergman stood close by. His lined face seemed nearly immune to Jans' anguish. "What's the story, Dean?'

Jans shook his head, "In twenty-five years, that's the hardest phone call I've ever made."

"Did you tell them we need them here?"

"Yes, they'll be here tomorrow. It's such a waste."

"Murder always is, Dean Jans."

Jans caught the weary glint in Bergman's eyes. "I'll make sure they get to police headquarters as soon as they arrive here."

"I appreciate your cooperation."

"Detective Bergman," he said. "How do you explain the murder of a bright young woman to her parents."

Bergman sighed, "I'm afraid there is no explanation, sir. Murder is the ugliest part of police work. It's vile and it's brutal, and I'm afraid, the victim's family never gets over it."

From nowhere, a mental picture of Jack Mulligan came to Jans. Could he be the one responsible? The white boy was a convicted murderer, after all. Didn't that prove he was capable of such carnage.

Sam Bergman folded his notepad and started to rise from his chair. He was stopped by Dean Jans, "I may have the name of someone you will want to question."

"Who?" said Bergman, opening the pad once more.

"A white student, an ex-con named Jack Mulligan."

CHAPTER 32

"What if I told the police you'd been studying all evening right here in the room?" suggested Juleel, a glimmer of hope invading his eyes.

"No, too many people saw me in the bar," Jack said. "Besides, Stu won't lie for me. He's a friend, but he won't lie. I wouldn't want him to either."

"Well you can't just sit here."

"Sure I can," Jack said shifting his gaze from the floor to his roommate. "If they're going to arrest me, they will. Running won't do any good. I don't have the resources to get very far. Besides, if I run, I'll look even more guilty."

Juleel put his head in his hands and grimaced. Frustration, which should have been Jack's, overcame him. He could understand why the police would logically question Jack, but arresting him was insane and not fair.

"How long before they'll come?" Juleel muttered.

"Probably before midnight," Jack said as he walked to the window to see if they were already there. "They'll talk to Dean Jans, who doesn't like me; to

299

Brent, who doesn't like me. And probably a few others and then…they'll come calling."

"Yeah, but what evidence do they really have to arrest you?"

"None, but they'll detain me on suspicion. I'm on parole, remember, and the cops can do anything they want."

"This is America, Jack."

Jack turned with a knowing smile, "Not if you're on parole."

"Come on, Jack."

Jack smiled, "Let me give you a quick civics lesson, Juleel."

Juleel scooted his chair closer to Jack. Jack had a lifeless expression on his face. "Juleel, the police in this country are under siege. The public wants protection from cradle to grave. They won't tolerate anything less. When a crime is committed, a culprit has to be immediately found. If not, the powers above come down on the chiefs-of-police and they, in turn, come down on those below them. You've probably heard the expression, 'shit rolls downhill.'

"Well with all this pressure to always solve a crime—immediately—cops take short cuts. They have to. If a bird looks like a duck, flies like a duck, smells like a duck…well you get the picture."

Juleel sat spellbound as Jack took a breath and continued.

"The cops are going to arrest me tonight or tomorrow morning because it's the easiest thing to do. Case closed. The public, the students and alumni can then rest assure that justice was quickly served."

"Whatever happened to fair play?" Juleel croaked hoarsely.

"You're gay, Juleel," Jack said in surprise. "You grew up in Walnutburg. When you were harassed, did you think it was fair? When they beat you up, did you think that was fair? Have you ever really, deep inside, thought anything was fair?"

Juleel thought back to his past and knew Jack was right.

***

Sam Bergman left Dean Jans' office and went immediately to work. He scanned Jack Mulligan's file and called the boy's parole officer. The P.O. gave a glowing account of Mulligan and his progress. The boy sure didn't sound like a psycho. Before he pulled Mulligan in, he'd have to hear more than just a few people's opinions. Still the M.O. fit, so he'd have to talk to the boy.

Bergman's next stop was Lincoln Hall. He introduced himself to Robert Brent in the lobby and followed the big Head Resident to a small office. Once he was seated, he wasted no time.

"Tell me about a student named, Jack Mulligan?"

"The dude is trouble. No doubt about it," said Brent, who appeared too over-zealous in his assessment of Jack Mulligan.

"What's he done to cause trouble?" asked Bergman with his notebook open.

"He's white! What else does he have to do?"

"I need incidents, young man," said Bergman sternly, hoping that Brent wouldn't waste more of his time.

"We had to repaint the hallway outside his room when he first came here because of the graffiti," said Brent with indignation.

"He painted graffiti on the wall?"

"No," said Brent. "He caused other students to do that."

"I'm confused."

"These kids can't be expected to stay silent when a white criminal is placed in their dormitory. So they acted out. You know, they spray painted around Mulligan's door. They even set up trash cans of water at his door that spilled all over the floor."

"But Jack Mulligan didn't do this himself."

"No but…"

"Mr. Brent," interupted Bergman slowly and calmly, "I need to know what Jack Mulligan has done?"

"Nothing but…"

"So Jack Mulligan hasn't caused any trouble on his own."

"No, but his attitude really rubs everyone wrong."

Bergman's had now had enough of Brent. "Mr. Brent, it sounds to me like the students in this dorm had better grow up. Bigotry and racism are not inherent to just white people."

Bergman pushed himself out of the chair in front of Brent's desk and headed for the door.

"Thank you, Mr. Brent." he said coldly.

"He's a criminal. Don't trust him." Brent yelled after him.

Bergman let himself out of the office and called one of the uniformed cops over to go with him. Maybe the Head Resident was right. He'd soon find out.

He made his way down the hall in back of Brent's office and was soon outside Jack Mulligan's door. Bergman's knock brought a slim, baby-faced black kid who viewed him suspiciously.

"Yes?" the kid said in a soft voice.

"My name is Detective Sam Bergman," he said, showing his ID. "I'd like to speak to Jack Mulligan."

The black kid stepped back, letting Bergman in. The detective's eyes swept the room taking note of everything. It was a typical college dorm room. Across the way was a big, brutal looking young man he guessed was Jack Mulligan, sitting on the corner of a bed assessing him.

"Are you Jack Mulligan?" asked Bergman.

"Yeah, I'm Jack Mulligan."

Bergman smiled and noted Jack's scared face.

"I'm Sam Bergman. I'm a detective with the Mt. Sidney Police. I'd like to ask you a few questions."

"Okay," said Jack, "Have a seat."

Bergman noted the politeness and pulled a nearby chair close to Jack. "You know there was a murder of a young co-ed tonight on this campus?"

"Yeah, I heard."

"We noticed that you have a record and are currently on a parole program."

"Yeah."

"Can you tell me, Jack, where you were between six and eight o'clock this evening?"

Jack gave a fleeting glance at his roommate, which Bergman noted. Could there be a conspiracy going on between these two. He had seen people corroborate an alibi before.

"I worked this afternoon till five-thirty at Stu Ableson's brickyard. Then, I went with Stu to meet his lawyer at Sparkies on Second Avenue."

"I know the place," said Bergman scribbling a note.

"About seven-thirty, I started walking back to the dorm. I got here about eight o'clock and I've been here since."

"Did anyone see you walking home?"

"Not that I know of."

"Do you often walk home alone?"

"I work sometimes four days a week," Jack replied. "I walk home from work on those days. I don't have a car."

"But you walk alone?"

"Yeah."

"Was this particular trip tonight any different?" Bergman probed.

"Yeah. It was cold and the wind was terrible."

"Had you been drinking?"

"Drinking?" Jack said with chagrin. "That would violate my parole."

Bergman noticed the non-answer and decided not to pursue the truth since at the moment it had no relevance. "Jack, did you know Danielle Myers?"

"I knew who she was. That's all."

"Had you ever talked to her?"

"No."

"How about her roommate," Bergman leafed through his notes. "Keysha Jordan. Did you ever talk to her?"

"Yes."

"About what?"

Jack gave him an even look, "I have two classes with her and we've spoken after class before."

"I see," said Bergman. "Did you ever date?"

"No."

"There are other students who say you did."

"Is that right?"

Bergman saw a stiffening in Jack's neck muscles. "I've heard that you were sort of stalking Miss Jordan."

"That's a lie!" interrupted the black kid.

"Juleel," Jack warned.

Bergman turned, "Oh…tell me more, Juleel."

"Raymon Jackson, the football player, and Keysha broke up. Jack was just friendly to Keysha," blurted Juleel.

Bergman returned to Jack, "Is that true?"

"Yeah."

Bergman moved his arm in a small sweep, "You've been here a few months, Jack. How's it been being the only white student at this school?"

"It's okay."

"Just okay?" asked Bergman, skeptically. "I figured you must be real happy being here instead of Inside."

"That's just geography," dead-panned Jack.

"Ever get lonely?" said Bergman.

"No."

"Ever wish the girls here were more receptive to you?"

"No."

Bergman snickered, "That's not what a number of other students have told me. They say you've caused a lot of trouble. Deceived them. What's that all about?"

"They can think or do what they want," said Jack flatly.

A uniformed policeman entered the room with a grim frown on his face. He whispered something in Bergman's ear. Bergman glanced at Jack and nodded at the uniformed cop.

"Excuse me, fellas," Bergman said as he rose to his feet. "I'll be right back."

Sam Bergman walked out into the hall where Bob French a forensic tech from the county waited. French was a short, lean man of sixty who wore a perpetual sour expression. "I got something for you, Sam."

"What's that?"

French held out a clear evidence bag with a large hunting knife inside.

"Is that the weapon?" asked Bergman, examining the knife through the bag.

"We think so," said French. "Won't know till we get it back to the lab."

"Where'd you find it?"

French did his best to look unamused and failed. "One of the uniforms found it right outside this kid Mulligan's window."

Sam Bergman shook his head in disappointment. He had hoped Jack Mulligan would be a dead end. Being in the situation the kid was existing in had to be tough. Mulligan was an underdog, and Bergman liked underdogs.

Maybe Jack Mulligan had snapped. A jury would have to decide. For right now, he was bringing the kid into custody.

Bergman re-entered the dorm room with no fanfare.

"Jack Mulligan, please stand up. You are under arrest for the murder of Danielle Myers. You have the right to remain silent. You have the right to an attorney…"

As Sam Bergman read Jack his rights, the older man noted how the boy didn't resist being handcuffed or verbally protest his arrest. Jack Mulligan accepted his fate silently.

CHAPTER 33

Keysha was shocked when she heard that Jack Mulligan was being arrested for Danielle's murder. All her illusions crumbled like a house of cards. How could she have harbored even one romantic thought of him? He must be an animal. Had she misjudged his character that badly? His gentle demeanor now seemed monsterous.

Standing in the lobby of Lincoln Hall, the students talked of nothing but the horrible murder and of Jack Mulligan. Most thought it was the college's fault for ever allowing him on campus. Didn't the Administration see how dangerous he was? Mt. Sidney should be held at least partially responsible for the Danielle Myers' murder.

Then, a hush fell over them as they watched three policemen emerge from the hallway where Jack Mulligan's room was located. Then, immediately after them, four more policemen, two in plain clothes escorted Jack Mulligan in handcuffs.

The cat calls and racial slurs started as if they had been rehearsed. The student's remarks were ugly and showed their real thoughts of white people in general and Jack Mulligan in particular. Keysha felt embarrassed at the display. The police, who were outnumbered, looked nervous, especially a short, plain clothes cop whom Keysha guessed was in charge.

Jack Mulligan's impassive face seemed chiseled in stone. It showed nothing but resigned contempt. Keysha recognized his attitude and was confounded by it. Could he really have murdered Danielle and knew it? If so, he displayed no visible remorse.

Suddenly the crowd of young people parted as Tyrel raced toward Jack. His face hid none of his fury. He knocked one policemen down, but another very large officer caught him and with a brutal move of a baton brought Tyrel to his knees.

"I'm gonna take you out, motherfucker!" Tyrel screamed. "You hear me, motherfucker. You're mine!"

Two more cops jumped on Tyrel and handcuffed him. Tyrel strained at the cuffs but finally quit his struggle. One of the uniformed cops looked at the head detective as if to say, "Do you want me to arrest him?" The stocky detective spoke in low tones to him and must have said to hold Tyrel until they were gone.

Keysha watched Jack as he neared her. He stopped when he saw her. Their eyes burned into each other. People were yelling at him, yet he didn't seem to hear them or move. The moment felt like ages, but it was probably only a second. Keysha experienced a cold emptiness in her stomach, and her breath came in short gasps. The detective brushed by her to guide Jack onward. Someone shouted something next to her, but all Keysha could see were Jack Mulligan's blue, melancholy eyes.

James Ankrom

The police pulled him through the door and into a nearby squad car. The whole procession was performed quickly and efficiently, and Jack Mulligan was whisked away.

Was he really guilty of murder? Keysha didn't want to think about it. She had lost one friend this evening.

Keysha found an unoccupied couch, sat down and leaned back. She was dizzy, her knees trembled and there was a large ache in her heart. She thought of Jack and wondered if she would be dead now if she'd continued her interest in him. Ironically, Danielle had warned her to stay away from him. Had Danielle seen something she hadn't? Had she known? Now Danielle was dead.

Getting to her feet, Keysha slowly walked across the lobby. She just wanted to get to her room and away from everyone.

The police were talking to Tyrel who was now sitting in a chair, still cuffed. His head was lowered in pain, rage and shame. He was taking this hard. Everything around him was crushed, and all that kept him going was his hatred for Jack Mulligan.

Hate and more hate.

A tear came to Keysha's eye. She felt helpless, and more tears were bound to follow before this night was through.

***

Nathan Ramapo put down his binoculars after watching the police put Jack Mulligan in a squad car.

310

Good. His job was done. The white boy was history.

Ramapo stood on a wooded hillside nearby. His vantage point gave him a clear view of Lincoln Hall. He had taken up this position an hour before, knowing that the knife would be incriminating enough to lead to Mulligan's arrest.

As the police cars drove lazily off campus, Ramapo breathed a relaxed sigh and headed back to the house and his study. A burden had been lifted from his shoulders. He had restored order and purity to Mt. Sidney College. Now young men and women of color could once more come here to pursue their dreams without being forever blemished by white culture.

The white population in this country couldn't understand how much African-American's needed something of their own. The white devils were the ones who had enslaved them; had taken their dignity and had eliminated their inherent culture. No amount of reparations could ever mend that damage.

Did the United States government, who only represented whites, think that they could fix the wrongs against black people? Never. Too much had happened for that.

It was a shame that the school's administration couldn't see what he saw, and think with his focused kind of racial clarity. Then, and only then, could the hatred the school's leaders discouraged in black students, be instead nurtured and directed.

***

Robert Brent was now the voice of reason as he attempted to calm the raw nerves of a handful of firebrands he viewed as potentially dangerous. At this point, with Jack Mulligan under arrest, there was no sense in students getting rowdy and possibly destroying property.

One of the first rooms he visited was Raymon Jackson's. The running back had come back to the dorm without speaking to anyone. He'd gone directly into his room and closed the door.

Brent tapped twice on the door and waited. Raymon opened his door a few inches, saw who it was and waved the Head Resident in.

"Whatcha' want, Robert?" Raymon said emphatically.

"Just checkin' on you. How you doin'?"

"I'm alright."

Robert saw it differently, "Funny, you don't look so good."

"Yeah?"

Brent's eyes furrowed, "Yeah man."

He watched as Raymon started pacing back and forth. "I shouldn't have involved Danielle in my problems," Raymon said. "I only wanted her to tell Keysha to meet me at the stadium this evening. Why did she go instead?"

"Well that's not your fault. If you'd been there on time Raymon, you might also be lying on a slab in the county morgue."

"Or I might have saved her life," Raymon shot back.

"Maybe."

"Whatchu' think, I can't whup that pale motherfucker?"

Brent shifted the subject.

"Have you seen Tyrel?"

"Not yet."

"He could probably use a friend right now," Brent said.

"I don't know what I can tell him."

Brent shook his head, "Tyrel's a friend. And he's hurtin'. Go see him. He'd be there for you."

CHAPTER 34

Sam Bergman sat in a tiny interrogation room facing Jack Mulligan across a bare table. He took Jack through the time line of his alibi for the tenth time. Jack changed nothing. Bergman realized he wouldn't. The kid was a tough nut. Even if the boy was guilty, he'd never confess or break down. Bergman, like most good cops, however, was persistent.

"So you left Sparkies at seven-thirty and walked home?'

"Yeah."

"And you didn't see anyone?"

"No."

"You know, of course, that thirty minutes is a long time that can't be accounted for?"

"I did account for it."

Bergman shook his head, "You were walking but no one saw you?"

"Yeah."

"Well, maybe you took a detour and killed Danielle Myers."

"No."

Bergman pulled his chair closer to Jack. "Let's talk about that knife. You ever see it before?"

"No."

"Know how it got outside your window?"

"No."

"You think it was an accident that it ended up there?"

"No."

Bergman turned, "How so?"

"Someone put it there to point the finger at me," Jack said.

Bergman smiled skeptically, "Like who?"

"I don't know."

"Right."

"A lot of people at that school don't like me," Jack added.

"I've noticed."

Bergman sniffed, and pulled out a handkerchief. He blew his nose hard enough to sound like an out-of-tune trombone.

"According to your record, Jack, you killed your father with a knife and there was a boy at the State Institution you killed with a knife," he said putting his handkerchief back in his pocket. "You see why we are suspicious when we find the murder weapon—a knife—so close to where you live?"

"Yeah."

"According to Raymon Jackson, Keysha Jordan was going to meet him outside the dressing room at the stadium around seven-thirty. Do you know anything about that?"

"No."

"You weren't having any kind of relationship with Miss Jordan?" Bergman asked.

"No."

Bergman raised his thick brows, "That's strange. Raymon Jackson, Robert Brent and several other people say you were."

"Did you talk to Keysha Jordan?"

Bergman had heard that the Jordan girl was coming in the next day to make a statement. "No, but we will."

Mulligan grunted.

"Were you not sweet on her?"

Mulligan gave a blank stare, "No."

"Come on Jack, I hear she's a real pretty girl?"

Jack continued to stare.

Bergman shook his head, "You saying you don't find anything about her appealing? I find that hard to believe."

Jack didn't answer.

Bergman leaned closer and whispered, "Is it because she's black. Maybe that's what turns you on. You know she's different; sort of exotic."

A crooked smile came to Mulligan's face and then in a blink disappeared. Bergman wasn't getting anywhere. Mulligan obviously wasn't into bragging about his sex life or anything else.

"You really don't seem to know much or you're not cooperating, Jack. I hope for your sake it isn't the latter."

"I've told you all I know."

"Okay Jack, but, if I find out you're lying..." Bergman warned. "Well I can be as tough as nails. Don't you forget it."

Bergman's knees cracked as he opened the door and called for a deputy. A moment later, a large balding man materialized, checked Jack's handcuffs and led him out to his cell.

Sam Bergman slowly gathered his notes and ambled back to his office. His head was pounding from hours of questioning and re-questioning Jack Mulligan. The horrible coffee in the community pot didn't help his soured disposition either. The kid wouldn't budge from his story. Bergman suspected he never would.

Too many things seemed too pat for Bergman's satisfaction. First, there was the fact that no one, except Mulligan's roommate, seemed to like Mulligan. Second, Mulligan had no apparent motive to kill Danielle Myers. Sure, Mulligan might have had more than a passing interest in the dead girl's roommate, but murdering the Myers girl wouldn't help that. Besides showing an interest in a girl wasn't a crime.

Then there was the murder weapon, which was conveniently tossed outside Mulligan's window. The boy he had just interrogated wasn't a fool. He'd been around cops before. He'd know they'd find the weapon; the murderer would know that, too.

***

Jack Mulligan laid back on a lumpy cot in his four by eight cell and considered his options. There didn't seem to be many.

As it stood now, he was the prime suspect, and this Detective Bergman seemed bent on pinning the murder on him. Whoever had really murdered Danielle was still out there and was surely having a good laugh at how well his devious plan had gone. Knowing the police as he did, Jack realized that they would make the evidence fit whatever scenario they wished to invent. Motives were fabricated by smart prosecutors.

Since Bergman had mentioned Keysha, Jack guessed they'd try to say he had a rage of unrequited love. Farfetched, yes, but effective to a jury when coupled with his criminal record. Then they would fill in holes using character witnesses such as Raymon Jackson and Robert Brent to testify that he had a stalker's mentality and had pursued Keysha.

He figured the trial would be over within six months, and he'd be in the state pen shortly thereafter for the rest of his life. Hell, they might even execute him.

Jack fell asleep and awoke at eight o'clock with a dry mouth and stiff joints. Shortly after, a burly sheriff's employee brought him a plate of food. The powdered eggs and limp bacon were tasteless, but at least the food hit the spot.

It had occurred to Jack that he ought to try to figure out who hated him the most at Mt. Sidney College. Maybe he could then think of who would kill Danielle Myers. After all, the knife had been planted to implicate him.

Jack rolled through the possibilities over and over, but came up blank. There was Raymon Jackson, but he was too self-centered and stupid. No, the killer, if anything, was bright and clever.

Jack recalled a fellow inmate named Ken Morrison, who had been Inside before being transferred to Ohio State Prison. One evening, he had told Jack that the most dangerous kind of man wasn't the guy who went ballistic and later cooled down in remorse. No, the most dangerous man was one who laughed and smiled to your face but harbored unspeakable hatred for you. That person was cold and calculating. He would seek your destruction without leaving the slightest trace of his intentions.

Jack figured he may have run into such an individual. He'd be the kind of psycho who wouldn't stop till Jack was either in prison or dead.

CHAPTER 35

Raymon Jackson tapped on Tyrel's door at two o'clock in the morning and, without waiting for a response, pushed the door open and walked in. Tyrel was lying on his bed staring at the ceiling. The big man turned his head listlessly, noted Raymon's presence and returned his gaze upward.

"Whatcha' want, Raymon?"

"Hey, I just thought I'd see how you were," Raymon said uneasily. "Figured you'd be awake."

"I can't sleep. I just can't…"

"Yeah."

Several silent and uneasy moments passed. Then Tyrel rolled to a sitting position, "Was she dead when you found her, Raymon?" asked Tyrel in a small voice.

"Yeah, she was dead, brother, but let's not talk about that."

Tyrel snapped his head to Raymon, "What else is there to talk about—football, pro-scouts? Important stuff like that."

Tyrel's bitterness was palatable.

"I don't know," Raymon said increduously.

"Shee-it."

"She's dead, Tyrel. Danielle's dead," Raymon said. "They got that motherfucker Mulligan in jail. He killed her."

"You were so right about him," said Tyrel in a broken voice. "You were so damn right."

Raymon perked up, "Hey, I knew he was a criminal motherfucker. Shit, that motherfucker didn't fool me."

"I wish he hadn't fooled me," Tyrel said sadly. "I wish he hadn't fooled...Danielle."

"Yeah, I know."

"I just want to rip his heart out. If I could just have a few moments with him," whispered Tyrel, clenching his fists. "I just want..."

He cupped his hands to his face, as tears ran down his cheeks and his voice trailed off.

Raymon turned his head away. He hated seeing people cry. His mother had been big on crying. His father would smack her dumb ass when she started whimpering and getting teary-eyed. Raymon's father told him early on that faggots and pussy motherfuckers were the only kind of guys who cried.

"You got to get some sleep, Tyrel. People gonna want to ask you lots of things tomorrow. They'll want to ask me stuff, too."

"Yeah,...I guess," whispered Tyrel.

"All we can do is make sure the murderin' motherfucker gets what he deserves," said Raymon solidly.

"If it's the last thing I do," Tyrel proclaimed, "I want that white sonuvabitch dead."

321

***

The murder of Danielle unnerved Keysha more than she cared to admit. She tossed and turned in bed all night. It was three o'clock in morning, and sleep had eluded her for hours as she cursed herself for being unable to turn her mind off. The empty room was no help. It seemed dark and haunted. Danielle's presense spoke to her in every object she had touched and left behind.

The dead girl's books, her makeup, her papers with her written thoughts lay only feet away. But no Danielle. Now she had passed on, hopefully to another and maybe more beautiful world.

Keysha wiped her wet cheeks again and again. She dearly missed the warm presence of Danielle, her smile and her sense of humor. A morbid picture of Danielle lying on a cold refrigerated slab in the morgue didn't fit in. Keysha shivered at the thought.

To think, she had been taken in so thoroughly by Jack Mulligan. But, why had he chosen Danielle to murder? Why not her?

She hoped Danielle wasn't at the stadium on her account. Yet, Keysha had heard from a friend that Raymon Jackson had asked Danielle to relay a message to her about meeting him outside the dressing room. She was late getting home, or she would have told Danielle she would never meet Raymon anywhere, anytime.

Had Danielle gone in her stead? Lord, she hoped not.

Keysha shook her head. She had to stop. She couldn't keep battering herself this way.

Earlier, she had received two phone calls. One from the police asking her to come in for a statement and the other from Danielle's father. He and Danielle's mother would be coming by tomorrow to pick up Danielle's belongings. Keysha didn't want to think about it. Danielle and her mom had been so close. Unlike most mother-daughter relationships, they really liked each other.

One more glance at the clock convinced Keysha that she wasn't going to get any sleep. She turned the bedside lamp on and decided to get busy. Perhaps she could pack Danielle's belongings and make it a little easier for Mr. and Mrs. Myers.

Keysha slipped into a pair of jeans and sweatshirt and after brushing her teeth started the first of several trips to the basement for boxes. Finally satisfied that she had enough containers to pack Danielle's things, she started to work.

It struck her almost instantly that every item she picked up had last been touched by Danielle. It gave her an eerie feeling. These objects, these clothes, Keysha pondered were once a part of a living, breathing human being. Someone had ended her life. The life-essence which validated one's existence was now gone. The link to this world was forever broken.

By daybreak, Keysha had Danielle's belongings packed. No more tears dampened her face. Keysha had cried them all. Suddenly, the walls of the room seemed to squeeze in on her. She had to get out of the room. Grabbing a jacket, she left for a walk—a long walk.

As Keysha stepped out of Lincoln Hall, the morning was just dawning in subtle shades of gray and blue. The sidewalks of Mt. Sidney were deserted, which pleased Keysha for she didn't need more people and their questions.

Heading into town in the cool November air, she hardly acknowledged a light rain beginning to fall. The traffic on Main Street was heavy with people heading off to work. The tires of the passing cars made sticky sounds as they flashed past her. Keysha, however, was too insulated by her own thoughts to notice.

Two hours later, she found herself once again back at Lincoln Hall. Her hair now hung in dark wet strands, and although she was soaked and cold, Keysha's exotic beauty came through and made her mystery even more appealing. Any memory of where she had wandered was lost, but miraculously, she felt more centered.

Glancing at the clock above the main desk, Keysha saw it was eight-thirty. She had earlier decided not to go to classes. It would be impossible to concentrate, and she just couldn't face everyone's questioning eyes.

"How'd you get so wet?" a voice sounded behind her.

Startled, Keysha spun around.

She held her hand to her chest and looked to the side. There was Raymon Jackson. He stood balancing his weight on his right foot, posing in his cocky attitude.

The last thing Keysha wanted was to exchange banter with him, "I just took a walk."

Raymon assessed the clinging wet clothes that fit her body like a glove. He seemed to like what he saw. Keysha saw his gleaming eyes analyze her figure and was reviled. Couldn't this guy ever get carnal thoughts out of his mind?

"Baby, you shouldn't have to walk all by your sweet self in this weather," he said leering.

"I'll walk where I want and when I want. Thank you."

"Damn! Can't you ever be nice?" Raymon asked frowning.

"Listen Raymon," Keysha said in forced patience. "I really don't feel like exchanging flirtations with you. I've had a rough night. Two hours ago, I packed Danielle's stuff and later today, I'll be seeing her parents. Perhaps you'd like to join me."

Raymon's face paled, "Well, I…"

"I didn't think so," Keysha said turning. "Goodbye."

"Wait!"

Keysha stopped again to face Raymon.

"You know I found her last night," he said bitterly. "And, I'm the one who warned you and everyone else about Mulligan. But you wouldn't listen to me. How do you like your white boy now?"

"Did I ever say I liked him in the way you think?"

"Sure you did," Raymon accused. "You probably would have loved to jump into his crib."

"Enough," said Keysha furiously, turning away.

"You just need a real man to straighten you out, baby."

"Go to hell, Raymon."

"Why don't we go out, baby and talk this thing through?"

"You are an ass," said Keysha. "A girl is murdered and all you can think about is yourself."

Raymon's face mocked sympathy.

"Baby, I didn't mean it that way. I just meant that...well we all have to go sometime. You know what I mean? Life goes on."

Keysha couldn't have been more revolted. She despised callous indifference. She snapped, "Let's get something straight, Raymon. I have no intention of going out with you, anywhere ever again. I told you that a week ago, and I still mean it."

Keysha walked stiffly toward the staircase with Raymon angrily in pursuit. "Don't be dissing me, bitch. I'll tell you when and where we go, understand?"

"Leave me alone," shouted Keysha.

Raymon roughly grabbed her arm. His grip was painful.

"I've had enough of your fuckin'mouth and your fuckin' attitude, bitch."

"Don't call me that, and let go of my arm."

Raymon laughed, enjoying himself. Then, from behind, a voice interrupted his sadistic glee. "Let her go, Raymon."

Robert Brent stood six feet away with his arms folded. "Let the sister go, now."

Raymon released Keysha's arm. The spot where his hand had clamped ached. She was sure to have bruises.

Raymon remained cocky, "Hey motherfucker, who you think you're talkin' to?"

Robert, darkened with anger, stepped up and leaned into Raymon's face. "I'm talkin' to you, asshole. I'm talkin' to a brother who is about to lose an athletic scholarship and some teeth. Would you like for me to speak to the coach, today?"

Rage etched a hardness into Raymon's face, but he knew the battle was over. Suddenly, he changed gears, and in an instant, his smile reappeared, "Hey, that's cool, Robert, no need to get all heated up."

"Good."

Raymon smiled at Keysha but no humor was there, "I'll see you later, Keysha."

"Mind what I say, Raymon," warned Robert.

Raymon smiled knowingly at them, turned abruptly and strolled out the front door.

***

The local newspaper that morning had headlines in big bold letters, "CO-ED Murder at Mt. Sidney." A news photo of Jack Mulligan being led away from Lincoln Hall told the world who to blame for Danielle Myers' murder. Nathan Ramapo looked up from the newspaper and felt sick.

Who was Danielle Myers? Who the…He had killed Keysha Jordan.

Or had he?

Could that mindless idiot, Raymon Jackson, have misled him? Was Raymon's story about Keysha Jordan a fabrication? If the newspaper was correct, he had senselessly committed cold-blooded murder on an innocent person. It said, Danielle Myers was a freshman and was brutally murdered outside the stadium.

My God, no. No, no. Cold blooded murder. What had…

The only bright spot was Jack Mulligan's arrest. But, that didn't salve Nathan's guilt. He had murdered an innocent person. Danielle Myers had been in the wrong place at the wrong time, and Keysha Jordan, the white Devil's whore, still lived.

He opened a nearby cabinet and withdrew a bottle of Scotch. His hands shook as he poured a tall glass and drank half of it in one swallow.

Nathan knew that no matter what the outcome of this whole affair, he would have to live with the murder. The moral high ground was lost. Now the fragile purity he had so carefully nurtured was permanently ruined.

He took another swallow. The Scotch burned, but not enough. His hands still shook.

This was Raymon Jackson's fault. The fool had obviously lied to him. Nathan hated liars. They were the kind of people who truly kept the black man from rising. Look at the nation's black leaders—all liars.

Jack Mulligan, of course, would get his, but Raymon and this Keysha Jordan would pay, too.

Someone had to pay for Danielle Myers' murder.

CHAPTER 36

Sitting back on his bed, Tyrel Friday hardly believed a week had passed since the murder. It had been a long, painful week. All his efforts to deal with the loss of Danielle had been doomed to failure. He was marking time and hanging on. Fortunately, his friends and family were there for him. He had called his dad twenty times. Dad could be relied on, no matter what.

Danielle's parents had come to Mt. Sidney the day after the murder. Mr. Myers looked like he hadn't slept, and Mrs. Myers was obviously on some kind of strong medication. It kept her jaw slack and her eyes staring blankly into space. The Myers understood the kind of suffering Tyrel was enduring. Mrs. Myers gave him a hug, and Mr. Myers shook his hand. Danielle had written glowing letters telling them how incredible he was. For Tyrel, however, there seemed to be nothing but emptiness.

He and Keysha had taken two days to be with Danielle's parents. Keysha was a real trooper. She had talked with Mrs. Myers for hours and had been with

329

her when they visited police headquarters to identify the body. Tyrel didn't go with them. His absense made him sick with guilt. He felt like a coward, but he just couldn't look into Danielle's dead face knowing he hadn't been there for her.

Keysha said she understood and that it wasn't as bad as all that. But, Tyrel noted something in her strained face and eyes that betrayed her statement for a lie. He had a notion that the official identification of the body was horrifying. Mrs. Myers had been led back to her hotel afterwards, and a doctor had been called in to further sedate her.

Two days later, they left Mt. Sidney. Tyrel had said goodbye and waved as they left. He even promised to visit them the next time he was back in Philly, but deep inside, he knew he never would.

Keysha was there, too. What an angel she was. She seemed to always know the right words and the right gestures. She and Mrs. Myers held each other and cried. Tyrel could only look away and try not to get choked up himself.

When the Myers' car was out of sight, Tyrel saw Keysha's show of strength come to an end. It had been a brave act, one of total courage. Tyrel let her cry into his huge chest for nearly an hour. Keysha then went back to her room in emotional exhaustion. Tyrel wondered if she had slept for even an hour since Danielle had been found.

On Friday, a memorial service was held. The President of Mt. Sidney, all the Deans and the Board of Governors gave speeches. All classes at Mt. Sidney were canceled and as far as Tyrel could tell, everyone in the school was there. Speech after speech was made praising Danielle as an exemplary student and eulogizing her loss to her family and friends.

Professor Ramapo gave the most intense and emotional speech of the day. It was almost as though he had known Danielle on a personal level. He had compared her to Joan of Arc and had hinted that the gains of all black people could be traced to the kind of courage Danielle had shown. He finished by saying that all students of color in the nation could now thank Danielle Myers for keeping the hope of equality alive.

Tyrel's one consolation was the arrest of Jack Mulligan. The police had found their man quickly and efficiently. Tyrel could only hope they would execute the bastard. Jack Mulligan's scarred, white face should have been a warning. Raymon had seen through him. Mulligan was some kind of sick pervert.

Right then, Tyrel swore to himself that he'd never trust another white person again. Raymon had said that even Professor Ramapo was against white ex-cons coming to Mt. Sidney. The government was trying to shove whitey down every black man's throat. Well he'd had enough. No more. If they wanted murderers and white scum coming here, then they were going to hear about it from Tyrel Friday.

***

Juleel sat in the crowded cafeteria studying the plate of food in front of him. Spaghetti, his favorite, was being served. Somehow it didn't hold much interest for his taste-buds that day. It wasn't as appetizing as his mother's but whose pasta was? For the past few days since the murder and Jack's arrest, he had not heard one voice break the silence of his world. His fellow students were taking their hatred out on him. It was a form of guilt through association. Even his professors were treating him coldly.

Perhaps now was the time to contact his mother and quit school. Of course, it would devastate her. However, a new start, in a new school might be the very thing he needed, unless he desired years of virtual isolation. Even Bernie had abandoned him. His last several calls had been ignored. So much for love.

The day before, he had gone to see Jack Mulligan at the county jail, downtown. The two story, brick building was surrounded by a chain-link fence topped by razor-wire. Guards with automatic weapons sat in posts on either side of a small exercise yard. It was a scary place, but Juleel had considered the visit the least he could do for his best friend. Besides, Jack needed something to read and a few goodies.

Upon entering, he had been frisked and questioned about his purpose for visiting. Then, he had endured almost an hour waiting in two different locked rooms. Finally, he had been led by a rotund, florid-faced guard into a corner room where the only furniture was a wooden table with three chairs. Juleel guessed that prisoners and their lawyers met there.

"A guard will be present at all times," informed the fat deputy in a robotic voice. "Anything said between you and the prisoner can be used in a court of law. Do you understand this?"

Juleel said yes and nodded. He sat down on one of the chairs.

A few minutes later, Jack was escorted in, wearing the jail's day-glo orange coveralls. Shackles had been placed around his legs, and his hands were cuffed. The restraints made metallic sounds as he moved and sat down. Juleel could see the strain in Jack's face. There was a new tension to his worn and hardened features.

"Hi, Jack," said Juleel tentatively. "How have they been treating you?"

"Fine," said Jack. "You shouldn't have come, Juleel. This isn't a good place."

"I can tell," said Juleel rolling his eyes around the room. "I just thought I'd bring by some reading material. You know, to pass the time…"

"Juleel I'll be fine. They're processing me back to…There'll be a trial."

"When?"

"Soon."

"Have you got a good lawyer?"

"They sent over a public defender, but he was replaced by a guy that Stu Ableson knows."

"Is he good?"

Jack shrugged.

"I guess you know the students are holding meetings to pressure the police and courts to give you the maximum sentence," said Juleel looking at the floor.

"That's the death penalty. Lethal injection."

"I know," whispered Juleel. "Is there anything I can do?"

"One thing."

Juleel brightened, "What Jack? Anything."

"Will you somehow tell Keysha Jordan that I didn't kill Danielle Myers. I know I'm going down for the murder, but I want her to know."

Pain and desperation could be heard in Jack's voice.

Juleel could hardly look at him, "Sure. I'll tell her Jack."

Jack seemed relieved, "Thanks Juleel, you're a pal."

They talked for a few more minutes before the deputy told Juleel he'd have to go. Jack didn't say goodbye but turned and walked away. He didn't look back.

Juleel put another fork of food into his mouth. It was tasteless, and he wasn't hungry. He returned his tray to a portable rack near the kitchen and started to leave. The solitary confinement of his room awaited. Then he spotted Keysha Jordan eating dinner with another girl across the dining hall. Keysha appeared worn, as if she had not slept in a long time. He questioned whether he should bother her, especially since the murder had only been a little over a week before.

His promise to Jack came back to him, however. Now was probably as good a time as any to relay his friend's message. Taking a deep breath, Juleel crossed the hall to the table. As he walked, he could feel everyone's scowls and attitudes of disgust.

He saw Keysha catch his approach. She looked around to see if anyone else was watching. They were.

"May I speak with you, Keysha?" he said, then glanced at the other girl who was gazing back at him in shock. "Alone."

"Yes, but I'm…" Keysha started to say.

"Please. I'll only be a minute."

The other girl thankfully cooperated and rose to her feet. Juleel read her expression, she just wanted to get as far away as as possible. She grabbed her tray, told Keysha she'd see her later and quickly departed.

"May I sit down?" Juleel asked.

"Yes, sure Juleel."

Juleel drew his chair in, "First, I'd like to say how sorry I am about Danielle. You guys were so close."

"Thanks, Juleel."

"I have a message from Jack Mulligan," he whispered, stopping when he saw the shocked expression on Keysha's face.

"I don't know if I really want to hear it, Juleel."

"Please Keysha," Juleel pleaded, "He only wants you to know that he didn't kill Danielle."

Keysha's face went blank, "And you think I should believe him?"

"I can't tell you what to believe," said Juleel. "But I know he didn't murder anyone."

Keysha gazed at him incredulously, "I don't know everything about this case, Juleel. But, I do know the police have him behind bars, and they must have some evidence."

Juleel felt impatience mounting inside. If he couldn't make so much as a dent in Keysha's armor of disbelief, how could he ever expect anyone else to consider Jack's innocence. Bias against Jack was piled deep and intractably high.

"All I can do Keysha is relay the message. Jack figures he'll either be executed or spend the rest of his life behind bars. He just wanted you to know he didn't do it."

Abruptly, she rose to her feet, "Juleel, one of my best friends was just murdered. I can't forget her or how she died. Don't expect me to pity, Jack Mulligan. I can't do it."

With that she walked off, heels clicking and a moment later, he followed. Again heads turned as he headed for the door.

As Juleel emerged from the cafeteria into the hallway, Raymon Jackson was directly in front of him with some of his teammates. The running back saw him and immediately started his trash talk, "Hey check it out, look who's here. The sissy motherfucker who was gettin' dicked by the murderin' motherfucker."

Juleel's anger flared, "Well at least he's got a dick."

"What'd you say, motherfucker?" Jackson frowned.

Juleel knew he should get away from Raymon, but his hatred overcame his better judgement. "You know Jackson, I don't know which is smaller, your dick or your tiny little brain."

The players in back of Raymon all chimed at once, "Oooh!"

Raymon's smile left his face, "You've crossed a line, faggot. You're mouth just led you down a wrong path."

Juleel looked around helplessly. A crowd gathered anticipating blood. This was Walnutburg all over again. Juleel had seen the same hungry expressions; the same lust for violence.

With a last ounce of bravery, Juleel lifted his middle finger into Raymon's face, "Fuck you."

Raymon's fist connected twice to Juleel's chin and eye and he hit the floor. Then, two powerful kick's hit him in the ribs and drove the air from his lungs. Juleel was paralyzed by pain. He lay on the floor helpless trying desperately to get air back into his lungs.

Raymon bent over him, "Motherfucker, no one talks to me that way. Know what I'm sayin'?"

Juleel coughed through blood, "Go fuck yourself."

"Now there you go," Raymon proclaimed as if pleading for the bystanders to understand his dilemma. "This silly, faggot motherfucker just has to keep it goin'."

Juleel's hand was lying, palm down in front of his face. Suddenly, Raymon stomped on his fingers. Loud snaps could be heard as bones broke. Juleel screamed. Some in the crowd winced. The pain was blinding as Juleel writhed in agony.

Once again, Raymon bent down. "Let's see you give me the finger now, asshole."

Juleel's eyes were glazed in torment.

Raymon continued. This was his theater, "If I ever see you around, you'd better cross the street, motherfucker. And, if you ever dis me again, I'll break your fuckin' face.

Juleel realized that at least two of his fingers were broken. His hand was swelling fast. Somehow he had to make it to the infirmary. The pain was excruciating and seemed to roll through him in waves.

How he hated Raymon Jackson. If it was the last thing he ever did, he'd get that sonuvabitch. It was time to fight back, and the first step was proving Jack Mulligan was innocent.

CHAPTER 37

A soft tap sounded on Detective Sam Bergman's office door.

"Come in," grumbled Bergman as he stood looking out his window at a dark parking lot.

His cubbyhole office was located on the second floor of the police headquarters building. For twenty minutes, he had been gazing through the grimy glass, deep in thought, when he heard the knock. The door opened and Bob French, stepped into the room.

French was the Head Forensic Tech and one of the old timers. He had been here even before Bergman joined the department. Although small in stature, Bob was a giant intellectually. He was Harvard educated and a superb analytical scientist. His rumpled suit and lack of size must have fooled a lot of criminals. They couldn't know how he had put more of their number behind bars than all the most macho cops on the force. Bob never missed anything in the lab. He was extremely precise, and his work could always be defended in court. That's where it counted.

Bob presently had a manila folder in his lap as he brought out a pack of cigarettes and shook one loose. He held it for approval. Sam nodded and shoved a dirty ash tray at the forensic man. Bergman had given up the habit years ago, but understood the craving in others.

Bob lit the cigarette and watched the smoke curl to the ceiling. "We got a problem with that knife we found at the dorm," he said, exhaling.

Sam raised his eyebrows.

French continued, "We lifted one print from it, and it isn't the kid's."

"Are you sure?"

Bob gave him a crooked, maudlin smile.

Sam nodded, "Any ideas?"

"We sent the partial to the Feds," rasped French, tapping his ash into the ashtray. "We should know something tomorrow."

"Anything else you collected that I should know about?"

French opened the file folder. "Yeah, we found black, polyester blend fibers in two places on the dead girl's sweater and pants. These fibers must have been from the perp's clothing. They didn't match anything from the girl's clothes."

"How about Mulligan's clothes?" Sam asked.

"We looked in his closet. He doesn't own any black polyester clothes. His roommate," French said, pointing to the report, "Juleel Washington, says he's never seen Mulligan wear black."

"Are the fibers unique?"

"Not at all, I'm afraid."

French handed Bergman the report and stood up. "Sorry I don't have more, Sam. But I think we've got the wrong man."

"Yeah, back to square one," growled Bergman.

French put out his cigarette, and crossed to the door. "If I find anything else, Sam, I'll let you know."

"Thanks Bob."

After French left, Sam sat and studied the report. He'd have to let the prosecutor know what was going on. His name was Hal Ringwood, and he was an ambitious young man who was seeking re-election this year. That made him a gigantic pain-in-the-ass.

So Mulligan was the wrong man. Inside, Sam felt good about that piece of information. Jack Mulligan wasn't a punk. He was a tough cookie, but not a punk. Bergman glanced at the clock and shook his head. It was ten after nine; Ringwood would be relaxing at home and wouldn't want to be disturbed. He'd have to be told, however, and now was as good a time as any. Sam found the number and dialed the phone. Ringwood picked up on the third ring.

"Hello," he said in a raspy voice.

"Hi Hal, it's Sam Bergman. Sorry to be calling you this late, but I have some disturbing news."

"What's that, Sam?"

"It's about the murdered girl," Sam replied. "The boy we have in custody, Jack Mulligan…he isn't the murderer."

There was a long pause. Sam hated Ringwood's long pauses. They always portended the prosecutor's disapproval. Ringwood liked everything neat, tidy and stupidly simple. Unfortunately, crimes weren't always simple affairs.

"You're sure, he didn't do it?"

"Yes sir."

"Then who, Sam?"

"The way I see it, Hal," began Bergman, "the real murderer planted the knife outside the boy's dorm room to frame him. I suspect we have a racially motivated individual, a fanatic. Whoever he is, he must have some blinding hatred for Mulligan."

"Well hell," Hal replied. "So we have a frame up. Why didn't they just kill Mulligan instead of the girl?"

"Who knows? Murderers are strange," said Sam. "All I know is that Mulligan has been cleared."

Sam heard Ringwood sigh, "And you're convinced he was framed."

"That's the way I see it," Bergman replied. "If it wasn't for modern forensics, the killer's plan might have worked."

"Do you have any idea what the papers are going to say?" Ringwood snapped. Sam knew how Ringwood hated to let go of a pre-conceived notion, such as Mulligan's guilt.

"No and frankly Hal, I don't care," replied Sam caustically.

"This could cost me an election," grumbled Ringwood.

"That's unfortunate, Hal," declared Sam with justified indignation. "I'm not a politician, I'm a cop."

Bergman heard Ringwood exhale in frustration, "Well get something on this case—pronto!" ordered Ringwood. "The citizens of Mt. Sidney want action."

"We'll be on it," said Sam impatiently and hung up. He and his staff had been breaking their backs since Danielle Myers was killed. They had gathered forensic evidence, interviewed over seventy people on campus, researched the backgrounds on at least twenty of these people. Yes, they had been "on it."

Bergman fumed a few moments, and then called the jail, which was located behind police headquarters. He asked for the head Sheriff's deputy in charge and waited. Soon a voice came over the line, and Sam instructed the deputy to arrange the paperwork for Jack Mulligan's release. He also requested that someone bring Jack Mulligan to his office.

A half hour passed before an armed Sheriff's deputy knocked on Bergman's door and led a shackled Jack Mulligan into his office. Mulligan seemed passively icy. This was the kid's survival mode, Bergman thought. Don't think too much and certainly don't feel.

Bergman's eyes narrowed on the handcuffs. "Get those cuffs off his wrists, Deputy," he ordered sharply.

The deputy, a young thin man, obeyed at once, "It's procedure."

"Not when we're releasing someone," said Bergman irritably.

Jack Mulligan's face instantly transformed to one of confusion. He rubbed his wrists as soon as the cuffs came off.

The deputy had Sam sign two release forms then he departed. Once the door was closed, Sam pointed to a chair for Jack. "First, I want to tell you how sorry I am that we kept you for a week in our luxury suite."

"I've seen worse," said Jack, "and the food wasn't bad."

Sam smiled at Jack, "That's not what I've heard."

"Yeah, well…"

Bergman took a pad of paper and slid it in front of his desk blotter. "Jack can you think of anyone at Mt. Sidney College who could hate you enough to kill Danielle Myers and try to frame you for the murder?"

Jack rubbed his chin in thought.

"No-one and everyone."

"What?"

"There's just too many people who dislike me to even think of selecting one," Jack said solemnly.

"None stand out?"

"The last few days, I've had plenty of time to think about that," Jack continued. "I can think of a lot of people who hate me, but they all loved Danielle Myers."

Bergman could see that Jack was as stumped as he was, "Any loner types who hang out on the fringes that you've noticed? You know, some kind of odd-balls."

"No. I'm the only one like that," said Jack with a fleeting grin.

Bergman sat back and flipped his pen onto the desk, "What are you going to do now, son?"

"Go back."

Sam raised his eyebrows.

"There's someone at that school who wants you dead."

"Yeah."

"Doesn't that bother you?"

"I haven't got the luxury of being bothered," Jack said with a shrug. "If I don't go back, the state will reinstitutionalize me."

Bergman nodded agreement, then reached into his desk drawer and withdrew a card, "If you think of anything pertaining to this case, Jack, or observe anything strange, give me a call."

Jack took the card and put it into his shirt pocket.

"It's late," said Sam, "let me give you a ride back to your dorm."

"Thanks but I can walk."

"It's nasty out there, Jack and besides, it's on my way home."

Jack smiled, "Okay."

"Hell, after what we put you through kid, it's the least we can do."

CHAPTER 38

It was well after midnight before Bergman pulled up to the curb at Lincoln Hall. The ancient, three-story monolith sat snuggly in a ground fog which shrouded its first story and enhanced its Gothic mood. Here and there lights dotted the facade as a few nocturnal scholars burned the midnight oil.

Jack had been silent all the way from police headquarters. Only the squawking of the radio broke the quiet hum of the car's engine. Bergman respected Jack's solitude and said nothing. The kid had enough problems to face without his input.

Bergman turned to Jack when he put the car in park, "You want me to go in with you, kid?"

"No, I'll be okay."

"They could get rough," Bergman said, indicating the students.

Jack made an effort at a smile, "Yeah."

"Son, take a piece of advice," Bergman said in a low tone. "Stay clean, get an education and don't look back."

Jack nodded, the scars on his face danced giving him a grotesque menace, "Count on it."

Bergman smiled.

"You know, you're a decent guy," Jack said. "I won't forget."

Bergman smiled, "Good luck, kid."

Jack stepped out of the car and shut the door. Bergman gave him a last look, waved and drove away. He and the car disappeared a hundred feet later, swallowed by the soupy fog. Jack watched the receding tail lights and wished he could help Bergman, but unfortunately he knew no more about the murder than the detective.

Turning at once to Lincoln Hall, he suddenly felt cemented in his tracks. A healthy fear gripped him with dread. It screamed for him to leave—to flee before it was too late. A murderer was lurking somewhere nearby, a sick bastard who desperately wanted him dead.

Jack shook off the feeling. His destiny—for better or worse—was linked to this place and this time. He had to go in. Before he could ponder any alternatives, he bolted up the steps and through the front doors. The lobby greeted him with warm emptiness. A television was still on, tuned to an old black and white Bette Davis movie. Jack started immediately for his room, not wanting to be seen by the residents just yet.

As he headed towards his hall, Robert Brent came out of his office, saw him and froze in disbelief, "What the fuck are you doin' here?"

Jack stopped and twisted around, "The cops cleared me, Brent."

"Bullshit!" Brent said with a hard glare.

"Yeah, it's true," said Jack sarcastically, "Life's a bitch isn't it, Brent?"

Brent's shook his head and gestured, "These people are going to eat you alive."

"Don't bet on it," said Jack.

"Oh, more trouble…?"

"Not unless somebody wants some."

Brent continued, "They think you're guilty and so do I."

"You can think whatever you please, Brent."

"I will," said Brent with a cold glint in his eye.

"Yeah, the police told me you and that idiot, Jackson, were right at the top of the list of my critics."

"Like I said, I think you're guilty."

"You would."

Brent sighed, "It's too bad the College will have to run extra security for your sorry ass. As far as I'm concerned, the students could hang you tonight."

"You're a real sweetheart, pal."

Brent shot Jack a fierce expression, "You're just like my old man, worthless and no good. How many more lives will you destroy?"

Jack summed up Brent as a hate filled fool. The Head Resident was sadly too dull-witted to even recognize his own prejudices.

"You'd better talk to others about destruction," said Jack in a whisper. "I'm here to study and learn."

"Yeah, learn, motherfucker." Brent grumbled, moving back into his office.

Jack departed, too. He was bone tired, and it was late. On the way, he passed two other students who frowned in wide-eyed disbelief. They mumbled to themselves as they passed from sight.

Jack figured the word of his return would soon be everywhere.

He was relieved to see a light under the door to his room. Good, he didn't want to wake Juleel when he came in. He tapped on the door lightly, entered and saw Juleel look up in astonishment then relief.

"Jack!" he screamed in delight. "How…when?"

Juleel's hand was in a cast, and he had bandages on his face. He jumped from his bed and wrapped his arms around Jack.

"No kisses," grinned Jack.

"Oh!" waved Juleel at the rebuke, "This is so great. Did they find the real killer?"

"No, but forensic evidence, however, eliminated me."

Jack looked at the cast, "What happened to you?"

"Oh nothing, an accident," Juleel replied dismissively.

Jack knew he was lying. Someone had gotten rough with Juleel? His first guess would be Raymon Jackson. Jack sat down at his desk, "The cops now think the killer was trying to frame me."

Juleel's face slackened, "You mean whoever killed Danielle is still out there?"

"It's possible."

Jack could tell that Juleel was breathing funny, as if short gasps were his limit. "You seem breathless, Juleel," he said in a concerned voice, "You alright?"

"My accident," Juleel mumbled evasively, "I broke some ribs."

"What?"

"You know me, I'm a klutz," Juleel said, diverting his eyes.

Suddenly, they heard the sound of dozens of feet and loud voices. Jack stood up. They looked towards the hallway just in time to see the door to their room slammed open.

Tyrel Friday stood framed in the doorway; his face filled with white-hot rage. Behind him Raymon Jackson and a number of onlookers, all watched in predatory glee.

"You murderin' motherfucker!" shouted Tyrel.

Jack realized that reasoning wouldn't get him anywhere with Tyrel or any of the rest of this mob.

"I didn't murder anyone," Jack said in a low, threatening voice. "Now, get the fuck out of my room."

Tyrel's eyes bulged as he launched forward bent on tearing Jack's head off. His big hands clamped onto Jack's shirt, which tore loose, revealing Jack's upper body and the dozens of scars and deep wound marks.

Tyrel's intent was to drive Jack through the wall, but with a quick move, Jack side-stepped and neck-tied the big man as he went by. Tyrel flipped and crashed into a bed collapsing the frame. From years of football training, Tyrel jumped to his feet and, in an instant, was charging again.

Jack saw it coming and was ready. Now it was his turn. Enough of this big clown. With his work boots still on, Jack came down hard on Tyrel's shins. The big man faltered and screamed in pain. Then, Jack drove his fists in a powerful, three-punch combination to Tyrel's stomach, rib cage and head.

Tyrel bent forward and Jack hit him three more solid punches to the face. Tyrel collapsed to the floor and was out cold.

The crowd in the hallway was stunned. They couldn't believe their eyes. The whole action had taken no more six seconds.

Raymon Jackson didn't waste a moment. He wasn't letting this white boy get away with knocking his friend out. He leaped in for a sucker punch, but it never connected. Although quick, he wasn't quick enough. Jack, reflexively, spun away as if by magic, leaving Raymon to hit air and stumble. Jack's counterpunch, however, didn't miss. It connected with Raymon's nose sending an explosion of blood spattering into the crowd. They wanted blood, they now had it. Raymon hit the floor with a solid thump right next to Tyrel.

"You fuckin' broke my nose!" he screamed, writhing in pain. "Fuck...I'm bleedin'."

The other students were now mesmerized in disbelief. How could this be? Never had they seen such explosive savagery. What manner of man was this Jack Mulligan?

Suddenly, a shout came from the hallway, as Robert Brent shoved through the crowd. When he saw Tyrel and Brent on the floor in two pitiful, bloody heaps, he could hardly believe it. Standing over them, Jack Mulligan looked like a carved statue. His scarred, muscular torso exuded raw, primitive power.

Jack glared at Brent.

"Get these two idiots out of my room!" he ordered.

"What'd you say?" asked Brent.

"I said get'em out of here, or I'll call the cops," he said in low threatening tone.

"Who the fuck do you think you are..."

"I'm Jack Mulligan," he interrupted. "I didn't ask these two assholes to come here. Now get'm out of here."

Brent started to say more, but thought better of it. Instead, he told some of the onlookers to help Raymon and Tyrel back to their rooms.

CHAPTER 39

Keysha stared moodily at the paper she had just printed out for English class. She prayed it would get her an A, especially since she had practically lived in the library doing the research. Maybe Professor Ramapo would begin to take note of her work once he saw this paper. So far her work had not reached the highest plateau for his lit class.

Ramapo was an odd duck. Keysha recalled last Friday's class. She could have sworn he was staring right at her. His gaze was penetrating and cold. It made her feel uneasy. Keysha found Ramapo frightening. Yet, maybe his presentation mastery was what gave her the impression he was speaking directly to her. It was funny how practiced speakers, actors and rock stars could do that.

It was now one o'clock, and she had worked almost all morning without stopping. The one interruption had come from Ravina, her talkative neighbor. She had burst in that morning chattering about Jack Mulligan being back at the dorm.

Apparently, Ravina had been one of the crowd that had followed Raymon and Tyrel down to Jack Mulligan's room to "see the fun." The two had attacked Jack, expecting to extract revenge, but, to their surprise, had themselves received a thorough defeat. Jack had apparently knocked them both out without even raising a sweat. Raymon even had a broken nose. Ravina regaled Keysha about the white boy's big muscles, but said they were covered with scars just like his face."

Keysha had smiled when Ravina had left. So the police must not have had a real case against Jack Mulligan. Apparently, he had been telling the truth. Now she felt guilty at doubting his side of the story.

She couldn't help but sense that Tyrel had gotten what he deserved. He had unfortunately listened to Raymon. Tyrel was a sweet guy but was presently vulnerable, and Raymon was more than too willing to exploit Tyrel's grief, despair and loneliness.

But now, Jack was back. She wondered how he was going to survive here? As far as she was concerned, he was innocent, but what about the others? Jack would have to weather a hurricane of hatred for the time being.

Keysha again remembered her brief walk with Jack. He had been so engaging and appealing, and his touch so seductive. Damn, she had to get him off her mind. This was crazy. Her mother would have a fit. Being interested in an ex-con was not wise. In fact, Jack Mulligan might be abusive or even dangerous.

Keysha turned when she suddenly heard a knock at the door. Now what? Ravina again? She opened the door petulantly.

Jack Mulligan stood in front of her. His body filled the doorway, dwarfing her with his wide shoulders. Her legs turned to jelly, as she gazed up at him.

"Oh," she murmured.

"Did I catch you at a bad time?" he asked shyly.

"No…no," she whispered, her resolve completely gone.

"May I come in?"

"Yes…please," she said almost stuttering.

She admonished herself for her lack of will. A boy such as Jack should not be in her room. Too late now. But she couldn't help but think he was the sexiest man she'd ever seen.

When she closed the door behind him, she could see he was surveying the room.

"Is my room such a mess?" she inquired with a giggle.

"No. It's just that I realized, I've never been in anyone else's room but my own."

Keysha shook her head sadly, "I guess you haven't made too many friends."

"No, I guess not."

"So what brings you here?"

Jack faced her, "I just got out of jail, and I didn't have a chance to tell you how sorry I was about your friend, Danielle."

"I see. Thank you," said Keysha, who couldn't keep her eyes off Jack.

"I didn't harm her, you know."

There eyes met in a moment of intense clarity. His gaze held so much pain and truth. Without further words, he convinced her in that single moment— totally convinced her.

"May I get you something to drink?" she said softly.

"Sure."

"All I've got is bottled water."

"That's my favorite," he said teasingly.

Smiling, she opened the tiny apartment refrigerator in the corner and extracted two bottles. His eyes never left her, and she wondered if he was studying her every move. Perhaps he would memorize this moment in time, forever.

"I have a lime."

"That's alright."

She pointed to a chair and put the bottle of water in front of him. Then, taking a seat opposite, she looked out the window. A breeze stirred the oak trees moving them in a swaying rhythm. The silence between them was only broken by the sound of Keysha's digital clock.

"Is it true that you were attacked last night?"

Jack turned his face away and pursed his lips, "I don't want trouble."

She smiled, "I heard Raymon Jackson's nose is broken."

"He accidently caught one of my elbows."

"Accidently?"

"Yeah."

"I heard it improved his looks and his attitude," she said laughing. "I think he's needed that for quite some time."

Jack gave her an impish smile, "If you say so."

Keysha grew serious again, "A friend of mine said she had never seen someone move as fast as you did."

Jack considered this and replied, "When I was Inside, you either learned to fight or you didn't survive. It was that simple. The rest is just attitude."

"Attitude?"

"You know, sort of a focus." he said never having vocalized a methodology for violence. "When someone is going to harm you and you can't get out of it, then you have no choice. It's fight or run. If it's run you'd better be fast, and you'd better be prepared to pay another kind of price. Inside, you'd lose respect and dignity in quick order if you ran."

Something about the way Jack Mulligan spoke the last sentence told Keysha that loss of dignity was important to him. Perhaps the loss of dignity could get extremely ugly.

"I think it's terrible watching a person such as Raymon Jackson provoking a fight," Keysha said. "What he said in front of the library was unforgiveable."

"At least he's coming from the front," Jack said. "The enemies I dread come from the darkness. They are the same breed that probably murdered your roommate."

Keysha thought of Danielle. Had she known her attacker? Did she see him coming? Did she know the person's intent before the knife plunged into her? The thought sent a chill through her.

Jack swallowed some water, "That same person wants to kill me."

"What?"

"This police detective, Bergman, thinks so too," added Jack.

"Oh no," she gasped.

"Whoever he is, he hates me enough, to kill an innocent girl to frame me," Jack said with pent-up frustration. "He almost succeeded."

"Then you think he's still out there?" Keysha whispered.

"Yeah, I think so."

Keysha felt a tingle in her spine, "That's frightening, Jack. Do you have any idea who?"

Jack's face grew melancholy, "No, not really."

Keysha's eyes widened.

Jack finished the water, "Keysha, I wanted to warn you, keep a good distance from me. Don't be seen talking to me. I don't want you to be this guy's next victim."

"Do you think…"

"I don't know, but I think you should be careful."

Keysha felt a growing sense of forboding. Right now she only wanted to be near him, but she was touched by his concern. She wondered if he knew. Perhaps not. But, his eyes never seemed to leave her. She imagined his hard chest against her.

Jack whispered gently, "You know, I like you."

She felt as though her legs would give out beneath her.

"I know."

His hand lightly touched her cheek, and she closed her eyes. Would he kiss her?

"I don't want you to die because of me," he said. "Forget me."

The words froze her.

Like a ghost, he stood and, without another word, walked out the door. Keysha stared after him as the wind hammered the outside walls of the dorm.

A smile came to her.

"He likes me," she said gleefully.

No matter what happened, Keysha now knew that Jack Mulligan felt as deeply for her as she did for him. His touch still burned on her cheek, and his scent filled the room. He had said what he had to out of caring and that was all that really mattered.

***

"The motherfucker caught me by surprise. Know what I'm sayin'?" Raymon drawled through his smashed nose.

"Sure he did," Tyrel smirked.

"That's right," affirmed Raymon pacing back and forth in front of Tyrel who was seated at Raymon's desk. The running back looked like he'd been through the toughest game of his life. The left side of his face was swollen badly, his nose was taped where it was broken and his left eye was a painful slit.

"Damn, it's hard to breath with this nose," he said almost to himself.

"Yeah, the coach is going to be pissed when he sees you."

"Fuck the coach!" Raymon growled. "This thing with Mulligan is personal now."

Tyrel peered at his friend. "That guy is bad news, Raymon. He hit me so hard, I thought my heart would stop. Hell, I got two cracked ribs, and I think two of my teeth are going to fall out."

Raymon needed to get a macho spin to what had happened last night. He had an image to uphold. He couldn't let anyone think he wasn't the ultimate alpha male on campus.

"I'm taking that motherfucker out," he said.

"You better leave him alone." warned Tyrel.

"Shit Tyrel, you scared of the motherfucker?"

There was a pause, "Yeah."

"Damn Tyrel," said Raymon in disbelief, "you've faced men twice his size."

"This dude isn't just strong," Tyrel replied patiently. "He knows how to fight. He probably learned that shit in prison. You go fuckin' with him, he'll really hurt you."

Raymon stepped in front of Tyrel.

"I never thought I'd hear Tyrel Friday turn chickenshit on me."

Tyrel rose to his feet, "Watch your mouth, Raymon."

Raymon turned away, "Tyrel, you're psyching yourself out?"

"He's a bad motherfucker," said Tyrel with conviction. "Besides, Brent told me the police cleared him, completely."

"What!" exclaimed Raymon. "You believe that? The cops are white. Maybe you be forgettin', they found the knife outside his window."

Tyrel sat down once again at the desk. "Raymon, anyone could have planted that knife out there."

"But they didn't."

"How do you know?"

"Cause no brother or sister on this campus would kill Danielle," Raymon said. "The only motherfucker who would murder a black person and never blink an eye is that white sonuvabitch."

"Dammit, Raymon!" shouted Tyrel. "You don't know what's goin' on with every brother on this campus. Who you tryin' to kid?"

Raymon could see there was no convincing Tyrel. Brent must have turned him around. Fuckin' Brent. All he wanted was smooth sailing so his fat ass wouldn't have to do anything.

"Well maybe you won't do anything, but I am," Raymon declared.

Tyrel was out of the chair and headed to the door. "I'm tellin' you Raymon, Mulligan will do a lot more than mess with your face next time."

CHAPTER 40

The street that Nathan Ramapo lived on was quiet and shaded by majestic maple trees which sprouted giant limbs. The houses had all been built at the turn of the last century when quality and craftsmanship counted for something. Big porches predominated, along with shiny hardwood floors and warm, cozy fireplaces. Everyone on the block felt a kinship with his or her neighbor and that aura of neighborly friendliness pervaded. This congeniality, however, was lost on Nathan Ramapo who remained private and aloof.

His neighbors thought of him as the eccentric black man who lived alone and taught at the college. He wasn't friendly, and he didn't even convey civility. They warned their kids to stay away from him, not speak to him and certainly not to step one foot on his unkempt lawn.

The only exception was the paper boy who tossed the daily *Mt. Sidney News* onto Nathan's porch every morning and once a month collected the subscription money. The paper boy figured Nathan Ramapo to be an "uppity nigger" like his ol' man had told him. The boy's father was from Jersey and still lamented the fact that the niggers had ruined his hometown.

On the morning after Jack Mulligan was released from jail, Ramapo, clothed in robe and slippers, emerged from his house and picked up the morning paper which had been thrown on the porch. He slipped the rubber band that held it together and unfolded it to the front page. The headline at once struck him with a hammer-like blow, "Suspect Cleared In College Co-ed Murder."

"No," he whispered, a stunned frown furrowing his forehead.

Inside the house, he read and re-read the news article. This couldn't be. How could they say that there was insufficient evidence to hold Jack Mulligan? The police had the knife that he, Nathan Ramapo, had planted, and they had knowledge of Mulligan's past criminal record that he, Nathan Ramapo, had made public. Wasn't that enough? It was so logical; it added up.

Fools!

Ramapo slammed the paper across the room, the impact jarring a painting from the wall. The frame shattered as it hit the floor with a loud crash.

Now what was he going to do? Jack Mulligan had to go, one way or another. Sweat popped on Nathan's forehead and his hands shook. How many deaths would it take? As his father used to say, "If you want something done right, do it yourself."

It was time for Jack Mulligan to meet his maker, and Nathan was going to send him there. If the state didn't have the guts to kill him, then vigilante justice would have to prevail. Clearly and efficiently, the white boy was going to die.

Nathan needed time to think. His hands were shaking. He scanned the room in nervous desperation. First, he had to calm down and get a drink.

***

Keysha saw Jack sitting alone eating his breakfast in the cafeteria. He wasn't hard to spot. The quarantine line the other students had imposed around him had now widened another twenty feet in every direction.

It was disgusting. Did they think he suffered from the plague? Maybe they thought he should be caged like a wild animal and have food thrown to him through the steel bars.

Holding her head high, Keysha marched over to Jack's table and set her tray down. Heads turned as if on hinges as she walked by, but Keysha's eyes never veered from the table where Jack Mulligan sat drinking his coffee.

For his part, Jack kept an impassive facade. His ice-blue eyes swam into her deep brown ones and held.

"Good morning," she declared pleasantly and unfolded her napkin.

"Good morning."

"Could you pass the salt, please?"

Jack picked up the salt shaker and handed it to her. Their fingers touched and both of them felt the warmth.

Jack whispered, "Are you insane?"

"Absolutely," she whispered back.

Jack's smile betrayed his next words, "Do you know that there could be a killer watching us this very minute?"

"Are you frightened?" Keysha asked.

"Only for you."

"I've thought a lot about this," stated Keysha, while buttering her toast. "No matter what, you can't give in to fear. As of this moment, we are very good friends, and I'm not going to hide or sneak around when I want to talk to you."

Jack pondered Keysha's words and respected the sound of them, but he had learned long ago, not to tempt fate. His scarred face lost some of its grimness as he resigned himself to her presence.

"Is that okay with you?" Keysha inquired coyly.

"Yeah, I suppose it is."

Keysha's eyes sparkled with delight as she smiled. It was a big, beautiful smile. She could see over his shoulder that everyone in the cafeteria, including the staff, were watching and whispering to one another. Let them watch and let them whisper.

"We're being observed," she said.

"Yeah."

"What do you think they're saying?" she asked mischievously.

"I don't know, but I guarantee most of them won't want you as even an acquaintance by this afternoon."

"Oh well, that's their loss," Keysha said, placing her hand on top of his. "If kissing everyone's behind is what it takes to be friends, I don't need the friendship."

Jack raised his eyebrows, "Okay."

"Now eat your breakfast," she scolded playfully. "You're way too skinny."

Jack laughed and took a mouth full of food. They ate in silence for a few moments; then, Keysha spoke after a sip of coffee, "There is a symphony concert on the Friday of Homecoming week. Would you like to go?"

Jack nearly choked on his food, "You mean with me?"

"No, with your twin brother. Of course, with you," She said, her eyes full of amusement.

"You mean like a date."

Keysha was amazed at the way Jack addressed the word, which sounded terribly old fashioned.

"I…I've never been on a date," he blurted, looking away in embarrassment.

Keysha thought back to the hundreds of nights she'd enjoyed herself at the movies, dances and dinners. Jack had never been able to do that. It seemed so unfair.

"Well this will be your first…date," she whispered gently. "And Jack Mulligan, I'm going to make it the best."

"Then I guess my answer is yes," he said.

Little could they know how memorable it would be.

Part III

Vincit Omnia Veritas
(Truth Conquers All Things)

CHAPTER 41

The telephone on the night table next to Raymon Jackson's bed started ringing early in the morning. Raymon cursed softly, dug his head into the pillow, but the noise refused to go away. The rings kept coming. He opened his swollen eye experimentally and realized the sun was shining. His head felt sore and swollen, and the telephone wouldn't stop ringing, so he snaked one hand from under the covers and grabbed the receiver.

"Yeah."

"Mr. Jackson, Nathan Ramapo. Are you awake?"

"I am now," said Raymon, failing to disguise his annoyance.

"Get dressed and meet me at my office...It's important. Let's say twenty minutes."

Raymon frowned, "Dr. Ramapo, I...

"Twenty minutes," ordered Ramapo and hung up.

What did this crazy motherfucker want now, thought Raymon? He had done all that Ramapo had talked about. It hadn't worked. Who could have predicted that Mulligan would be as tough as he was?

369

He vowed, however, he'd soon avenge what the white boy had done.

Raymon's tender nose was a painful reminder of their encounter. Mulligan had thrown a few lucky punches. But, no one could best Raymon Jackson for long. It couldn't be done. Wait till everyone saw what he'd do to the motherfucker.

Raymon showered and dressed in record time, and walked the few blocks to Nathan Ramapo's office. When he entered the building, the hallway smelled musty. Raymon hated damp places. There was something unhealthy about such places.

On the second floor, he knocked on the professor's door, heard him shout to come in and entered. Ramapo sat behind his desk drinking Scotch from a filmy glass and cleaning a .357 magnum whose parts were scattered on a newspaper. He looked haggard and pasty like he'd been sick and hadn't slept for a week. There was a dangerous, crazed glint in his glassy eyes.

Raymon took a seat facing Ramapo and waited while the professor rebuilt the pistol with practiced precision. Where had he learned to do that, wondered Raynon? Did he have a background in weaponry?

Finally, Ramapo reattached the last piece of the magnum and spun the cylinder. The mechanical clicks whirred then stopped. Ramapo picked up a single bullet from the desk and carefully placed it in the chamber and then without hesitation aimed it at Raymon.

Raymon saw the gaping mouth of the barrel and paled.

"Hey, whatchu' doin'?"

"Mr. Jackson have you ever thought of your own death?" Ramapo asked in a soothing voice. "Have you ever thought of not hearing, touching, tasting, seeing or thinking? Have you ever considered the vastness of eternity?"

"No…I"

"Of course you haven't," Ramapo said with a chilling dispassion. "Your existence is all dazzle and bright lights. All you contemplate are football plays, girls, cars and parties."

Raymon couldn't take his eyes from the gun.

"I could kill you now, Mr. Jackson, and you wouldn't have to worry about your future or any of those things. You'd never have to contemplate a family, responsibility, retirement or old age, either."

An uneasy silence followed. Sweat beaded on Raymon's brow. Then as if he'd just made a decision, Ramapo put the gun down. "See what it's like to live with death?"

Raymon, now shaken, gulped a breath, "Yeah…yeah, man."

"Mr. Jackson, what should we do about Jack Mulligan?"

"I don't know."

"You have failed me, Mr. Jackson."

Raymon started to reply but Ramapo held up his hand to still him, "It's not your fault. It's mine. I thought that once the authorities had Mulligan in custody, that would be the end of it, but, unfortunately, I was wrong."

"I guess they didn't have enough evidence," said Raymon.

"Bullshit!" shouted Ramapo slamming his fist on his desk. Raymon jumped, "I...they had more than enough. I'll tell you why Jack Mulligan was let go. He's white! Plain and simple!"

Raymon nodded.

"He mustn't get away with this, Mr. Jackson. You and I are the only ones who can do anything about it."

"What can we do?"

"You tell me," said Ramapo. "What is it that Mulligan values more than anything else? The students hate him and feel he's guilty of Danielle Myers' murder. The school's administration, at this point, only wishes that he'd disappear. So we've won the PR battle.

"Now, we have to find out what he cares for more than anything else and then...then we'll have the key to his destruction. We'll take it all away from him."

A fleeting thought came to Raymon, "You know, Dr. Ramapo, I don't want to lose my scholarship."

Tyrel's unheeded warnings were now handy.

"What are you frightened of, Mr. Jackson? Is it Mulligan?"

"No."

Ramapo pointed to Raymon's swollen face and black eye, "Did he do that?"

Raymon set his jaw, "He got lucky."

Ramapo again picked up the gun and clicked the cylinder.

"Hey, wait a minute," Raymon said, wide eyed. "I ain't cappin' no one's ass."

"Then use your brains. Keep an eye on Jack Mulligan. He'll tell you what he values. He has a flaw, Mr. Jackson. Find it."

"Yeah, well…"

"Go!" shouted Ramapo. "Talk to me later when you find something."

***

"You're going out with Keysha!" exclaimed Juleel with joy. "This is so great. She's divine."

Jack grunted, "Yeah."

Divine wasn't a word Jack would use.

"Well you're excited aren't you?" asked Juleel.

"Yeah, I guess."

Juleel exhaled and shook his head, "Where will you go?"

"She wants to see some concert the week of Homecoming."

"Oh, the symphony concert on Friday."

"Yeah, that's the one."

Juleel jumped to his feet and grabbed Jack's shirt sleeve. "Well Jack you have to prepare," he said brightly.

"Huh!"

"Jack come here," said Juleel in a perplexed tone, pulling Jack to the closet the bigger man hardly used. "Look at this pitiful collection of clothes."

Jack didn't comprehend.

"Two work shirts and a pair of coveralls," stated Juleel for Jack's clarification. "You can't go to the symphony in coveralls."

Jack nodded absently. Juleel might have a point.

"We simply have to get you some clothes," laughed Juleel in anticipation. "Also it might be a nice touch to send her flowers."

"Flowers?"

"Yes, you know those colorful little plants that girls adore," said Juleel not believing how obtuse Jack suddenly appeared.

"You think she'd like flowers," said Jack in a confused tone.

"Everyone likes flowers."

Juleel, for a brief moment, felt a pang of jealousy. Why couldn't Jack have the same feelings for him as he did Keysha? He dismissed the notion in a millisecond. Jack, he grudgingly knew, wasn't gay and never would be, period.

"Don't despair, Jack," he said, "let's go shopping and get creative. It's such a good thing you have me to guide you."

"Yeah," Jack said in total disbelief.

Three hours later, they had been to several stores, and Juleel could tell that Jack would never be as excited about shopping as he was. Fortunately, they had managed to purchase two mix and match sets of conservative white and blue dress shirts with a pair of khaki pants and another pair of darker cords. Jack had also seen a tweed jacket that fit him in a Salvation Army used clothing store. Juleel had grimaced, but Jack had liked the jacket and also bought a dark red and blue tie.

"You look like a casual banker," teased Juleel. "If I could only talk you into something more contemporary."

"I don't feel comfortable in those baggy clothes."

"The brighter colors would highlight your eyes," Juleel said.

Jack shrugged in an uncomprehending fashion, "Yeah, I know…but I think I'll stick to something less flamboyant."

Juleel shook his head at his friend's decision.

"How will I ever instill a flare for fashion in you?"

Jack smiled, "I guess I'm just a lost cause."

Standing on the sidewalk on Main Street, Juleel put his finger to his forehead, "Jack, we almost forgot the flowers."

"Are you sure about this, Juleel?"

"Trust me, Jack."

They entered a florist shop two blocks away. It was warm and fragrant inside and the colors of the flowers were dazzling. Juleel loved flowers. He had worked one summer for two weeks with a florist in Walnutburg. But when word reached the owner that he was gay, he'd been immediately fired with the owner inventing a phony story about Juleel being incompetent.

Juleel, looked around at all the flowers and felt a consuming joy in the natural beauty of the blossoms.

"Which ones should I buy, Juleel?" asked Jack in confusion.

"For friendship, I'd say carnations, but for romance, it has to be roses."

Jack blushed and stood uncomfortably for a moment.

"What's it going to be, Jack?"

Jack stood with a far away, brooding expression.

"Roses."

"What's that?" Juleel said, purposely acting like he didn't hear.

Jack frowned, "Roses."

"A little louder."

Jack whispered, while smiling, "Roses."

"Good," said Juleel as he caught the proprietor's attention. "Sir, we need a dozen, long-stemmed roses."

CHAPTER 42

Tyrel Friday folded his newspaper and carefully laid it on the corner of his desk. He had just read the article concerning Jack Mulligan's release. The investigating officer, Detective Sam Bergman, had been quoted as saying there was no concrete evidence to link Jack Mulligan to the crime.

Tyrel shook his head, which still ached from Jack's fist. He felt like a fool. Why had he jumped so quickly to the wrong conclusion about Mulligan? He had capriciously gone off half-cocked. He remembered his primal need to strike out at something—anything—and Jack Mulligan was the convenient target? Now he was proven innocent.

Raymon had said...Raymon! Yeah, Raymon. His good friend and teammate, had fed him all the correct facts he needed about Mulligan. And to his own shame, he had listened. The brainwashing had worked. Was he so mindless and easily led that he couldn't formulate his own answers? Maybe like a lot of other people, he sought out easy answers–the kind of answers to solve all problems.

What would Danielle think now? Tyrel tried to conjure her voice and her face. Danielle's instincts had always been essentially correct and appropriate. First of all, she would probably have admonished him to apologize to Jack Mulligan. The attack on him had been unconscionable.

Tyrel looked out his dorm window at the bleak campus. His feelings matched the cold mood of the day. A cloud of darkness seemed to follow him everywhere he went. Whether he studied here at the dorm, walked across the campus or was at the library, the beautiful memories of Danielle haunted him and made her loss even more profound. She had been everywhere with her warm, delicate touch. Could he ever get over her death? Would the anguish inside him ever really heal?

Damn, how he missed that girl, now more than ever.

***

Robert Brent held the phone between his ear and shoulder, while typing on his computer. His call to the police had been put on hold as soon as he said he didn't have an emergency. The waiting was annoying, but he had to talk to Sam Bergman.

Finally he heard a click and voice came on the line, "Bergman, may I help you?"

"Detective Bergman, this is Robert Brent over at Lincoln Hall. I'd like to talk to you about Jack Mulligan."

"What's happened?" exclaimed Bergman in alarm.

"Nothing yet."

"Then, why are you calling?"

"Well, first of all, I'd like to know why you released him?"

Brent could hear an impatient exhalation on the other end of the line, "Did you read this morning's paper, Mr. Brent?"

"Yes and I find the words, 'insufficient evidence' baffling."

"Why's that?"

"Cause you found a knife outside his window," said Brent petulantly.

"We feel it was planted, Mr. Brent."

"Then who killed, Danielle Myers?"

"We're still working on that."

"Is the killer on this campus?" inquired Brent.

He could hear Bergman exhale again, this time louder. "Mr. Brent, I'm not at liberty to discuss this case any further."

"But..."

"I'm sorry, Brent," said Bergman in a patronizing tone. "Let me assure you the investigation is proceeding. However, Jack Mulligan has been cleared. I've got another call, Brent. You have a good day."

The line went dead. Brent hung the phone up and sat back studying the ceiling. If Mulligan didn't kill her, who did? Surely not Raymon Jackson. No, he was egotistical but not sadistic. Besides he had no motive. There must be someone.

Pulling a sheet of paper from a side drawer, Brent started compiling a list of people he wanted to talk to. Maybe he could uncover the truth where the cops couldn't. If he found the killer, then he'd be the hero of the day.

***

The library was packed when Raymon Jackson entered. Students jammed every desk. Books and papers were stacked high as final essays were prepared and tests were studied for. This was an alien world to Raymon. Books had always been boring to him. He just didn't understand people's fascination with them. A book wouldn't make someone run any faster or jump any higher.

Raymon wandered from room to room. He was looking for Tyrel, who, according to friends, was here studying. What a chump. Why did Tyrel waste his time studying? He should be establishing himself, on and off the field, as a player. Pro athletes didn't need this shit.

Wearing dark sunglasses to hide his black eye, Raymon still smarted from Jack Mulligan's handiwork. His only consolation was that Professor Ramapo, as crazy as he was, had a secret plan for the white boy. He was here to assure Tyrel that he was going to obtain retribution for Mulligan's assault.

Raymon's search led him to the second floor of the library, where he found Tyrel reading at a corner desk. Raymon plopped down across from Tyrel and pushed his sunglasses to the top of his head. "Tyrel, whatchu' doin' with all these books? You should be chasin' bitches and partyin'."

Tyrel twisted his face wryly, "I'm getting an education, Raymon. That's why I came here."

"You'll be a pro my friend," smiled Raymon picking up one of Tyrel's books. "What the hell is this?

Robert Burns' *Romantic Verses*? Fuckin' dead, white man shit."

Tyrel pulled the book from Tyrel's grip, "Did you come here to interrupt my work, Raymon, or is there something you need?"

Raymon held his hands up defensively, "Hey, don't let me take you away from all this. But, I do have some news. Check it out."

"What's that?"

"You know Professor Ramapo? He called me to his office this morning. He says he's got something in store for our white friend, Mulligan. That white motherfucker is going down."

Tyrel frowned, "Why don't you cool it, Raymon? The police have cleared him. Mulligan hasn't done anything to anybody."

Raymon put his shades on the table, "Look at my face, Tyrel."

"So he hit you, he was protecting himself."

"You gettin' soft, Tyrel," Raymon said in disgust.

Tyrel sat back in his chair. "Let it go, Raymon."

Raymon's face turned bleak, "No, not when he's movin' in on my woman."

"Keysha? Get back."

"I ain't lyin'," Raymon spat. "I heard it this afternoon. I couldn't believe it. Fuckin' bitch is a traitor."

"Shit, Raymon, you're just jealous," shot back Tyrel. "You know she doesn't want to go out with you."

"Hey motherfucker, she just needs to find out who her man is."

"She has," laughed Tyrel. "It's Jack Mulligan."

"Fuck you!" Raymon exclaimed.

Tyrel laughed and said in low voice, "Raymon, you never once tried to get to know Keysha as a person."

"Where you gettin' that shit?" asked Raymon frowning. "From Danielle?"

"Damn right," said Tyrel solidly. "I learned a lot about myself from that woman. She taught me to be a better man."

"Don't you know, women don't know shit," proclaimed Raymon.

"You really believe that?"

"It's true."

"Then I feel sorry for you, Raymon."

Raymon knew there was no sense wasting more time talking to Tyrel. He was so full of Danielle's bullshit. "You know it's useless comin' here," said Raymon. "You don't even listen."

"You be right there. I'm not listenin'."

"And, I was hopin' you'd join me and Professor Ramapo."

Tyrel shook his head, "No way, Raymon. Don't involve me in that shit. I don't need or want it."

"And I thought you had balls…shit," said Raymon coldly. "That white motherfucker must have hit you harder than I thought. He's made you into a coward."

Before Tyrel could react, Raymon stood up and marched out of the room. Tyrel Friday could forget his friendship from now on.

***

Tyrel mulled over Raymon's last words. He realized he didn't even care enough to get angry.

Instead, he felt a deep sorrow for Raymon. It had to be tough carrying around that much rage.

But what about the odd pairing of Dr. Ramapo and Raymon? What was that all about? Dr. Ramapo was a respected guy. Why would he want to get tangled up with Raymon in some crazy thing against Jack Mulligan?

Tyrel sighed, his concentration was broken for now. He knew he wouldn't get anymore work done today. Picking up his books, he prepared to leave. Then, without any prompting or warning, a misplaced thought edged into his mind. The shock of it made him sit down.

Tyrel thought back to the night Danielle was murdered, he had seen Dr. Ramapo. Tyrel remembered how he had startled the professor. Maybe Ramapo was, in fact, more than startled. Shocked would be a better work. Ramapo had said he was out for a walk. But was he really?

A cold feeling seeped through Tyrel. Could there have been another reason Professor Ramapo was outside Lincoln Hall that late at night?

CHAPTER 43

A light mist gave promise to another damp November day. Jack pulled the collar up on his jacket and studied the progress being made on the Homecoming statue. A handful of volunteers were securing a protective tarp over the structure so the plaster and paper-mache wouldn't melt like candle wax.

The reasoning behind the statue escaped Jack's logic. Why put in so much work for a has-been athlete such as Bob Morgan? All that work to honor a millionaire who wouldn't give anyone at Mt. Sidney the time of day. Oh well, it was someone else's effort and someone else's sweat. He should be glad they were doing it. He had his own purpose for the statue, and it wasn't school spirit. Homecoming, after this year, would never be the same again.

Next week, the guest of honor might be Bob Morgan, but the star of the show would be Raymon Jackson.

***

The Creative Arts Center sat cheek to jowl with the sports Coliseum. From its location, the CAC, as it was called, faced glumly the rest of the academic buildings located up the hill from it. No one seemed to remember who had decided to place the structure near the athletic buildings, but its occupants felt apart from the more serious disciplines such as English and mathematics. Perhaps CAC's location gave the artists inside a sort of rebel stance, a lone wolf separateness.

CQ was on his way down the hill to the Arts Center, when, without warning, Raymon Jackson fell into step beside him. CQ's stomach suddenly knotted. He had been purposely avoiding Raymon after the confrontation in the stairwell.

"Hey nigger, whatchu' doin'?" Raymon asked smartly.

"Who you callin' nigger?"

"You, motherfucker," Raymond chortled. "I haven't seen you around lately."

"Yeah, well."

"You ought to stay in touch," said Raymon slapping the thin artist on the back.

CQ grunted at the painful slap but kept walking. Since the day he'd been assaulted, CQ considered Raymon absolutely crazy.

"I got some news for you," Raymon said as if asked. "You're going to help me get some shit on the white boy."

"Raymon, I ain't doin' nothin' for you. Understand?"

"Hey bro, this ain't no big deal."

"Good, then whatever it is, keep it to yourself. Leave me out of it," CQ proclaimed boldly.

Raymon mocked a hurt expression, "Hey motherfucker, I cain't do that. We brothers."

"I ain't your damn brother."

"What! Are you still holdin' it over me cause of what happened on the stairs?"

CQ glared at Raymon. He had not enjoyed being humiliated. A decision had been made that day. No longer would he be Raymon's fetchin' nigger. CQ did have some pride.

"Just stay away from me, Raymon."

"Hey, who you think you're talkin' to, nigger?" frowned Raymon. "You're my bitch till I say different."

"Bullshit!"

Raymon grabbed CQ by the arm, "Don't dis me, motherfucker."

CQ suddenly shook the arm off with a surprising show of strength, "Get away from me you freak! You touch me again, I'll have you up on charges. You fuckin' understand?"

Raymon was taken back. This was unbelievable. A crowd of students, also on their way to the CAC, stopped to see what was going on. CQ saw safety in numbers.

"So you got some kind of shit goin' on for that white boy. Well guess what, I don't care. It's nothin' to me. Understand?"

Raymon's eyes became slits of cold fury. "You going to regret this, motherfucker. Know what I'm sayin'?"

CQ put his hands out toward Raymon and shouted, "Stay the fuck away from me! Leave me out!" Then spinning on his heel, he stalked into the building.

Once inside, CQ ran to the nearest restroom, dived into a stall and threw-up his breakfast. The confrontation with Raymon had taken all the courage he had. Now all he could do was try to stop his knees and hands from shaking.

***

Keysha couldn't help but stare at the roses that had just arrived for her. It had been ages since she had gotten flowers from a boy. Certainly Raymon never sent any. But now, Jack Mulligan had sent her these lovely, long-stemmed, red roses.

She snipped an inch from the bottom of the stems and put them in a vase that had served as a pencil holder. Once the roses were on her desk, Keysha delighted in how they brightened up the room.

Now it was time to read the card. She wondered what Jack would say to her. The note was simple but brought a warm glow.

Dear Keysha,
I think of you so often. I can only hope that with these flowers, you'll remember me from time to time.
Love,
Jack

Love...She smiled. How could she ever forget Jack Mulligan? He wasn't like anyone else. He had the ability to visit her soul with just a word or a glance from his blue, piercing eyes.

Her phone rang beside her and she picked it up absently, still thinking of Jack, "Hello."

"Hey baby, it's Raymon."

Immediately, her heart sank, "What do you want?"

"Just wantin' to know if you've forgiven me?"

"There's nothing to forgive, Raymon," she said coldly. "I'm seeing someone else, and I don't think we have…"

"Who's that?" Raymon interrupted.

"None of your business."

"Hey, I'd like to know who the competition is."

Raymon was playing a game. Word was now all over campus that she was more than friendly with Jack Mulligan.

"You know who it is, Raymon?"

"Would he be of the white persuasion?" asked Raymon, too cheerfully.

"Yes and much more gentlemanly than you."

"But not as cool."

"Well you'd certainly know," said Keysha sarcastically.

"No doubt," Raymon said, ignoring her sarcasm. "You know I was going to cut you a break, Keysha. Let you ease back to me, sort of like you were on probation. But, you're making it very hard."

"Raymon the only place I'm easing to is beside Jack. He's a hundred times the man you are or ever will be."

"We'll see, bitch." He said in a now acidic tone. "When I get done with your white bread boyfriend, you'll see who's the man. And you know what, you'll be beggin' me to take you back. I…"

Keysha slammed the receiver down. Anger made her clench her fists.

Damn Raymon!

CHAPTER 44

Stu Ableson had been doing paperwork all afternoon and cursing every ten seconds as he proceeded. This was the part of owning a business he hated the most. Sure, he had an accountant, but he still had to keep track of all the purchases and receipts, plus there was a mountain of state and local paperwork on employee withholdings. He also had to track the changing inventory of concrete block, twenty styles of brick and ten aggregates such as stone dust and various grades of sand. It was a big job.

He was just studying some purchase orders when he heard a tap on his door.

"Come in," he growled at the interruption.

Jack Mulligan pushed the door open and stepped in, "Have I caught you at a bad time, Stu?"

"Jack!" exclaimed Stu with a welcoming smile, his bad mood instantly dissipating. "Damn boy, it's good to see you. I needed a break anyway. Hey, I read in the paper how the cops let you go. That's great. So how you doin'?"

"Fine. I guess I'm completely off the suspect list."

"Thank God. I was beginning to wonder if you were coming back to us. What's it been three days of freedom now?"

"I had to take care of a few things before I came in," Jack said. "I guess I should have called."

"Don't worry about it, Jack. We're just happy to see you."

A corner of Jack's mouth lifted in a smile.

Stu indicated a seat, "Sit down, son. When can you come back to work?"

"That's what I'm here for. Can I start today?"

"Don't know why not," said Stu happily. "We can sure use you. I've got a load of sand needs to go to a site out on Route 46. Norm called in sick, so I'm short a driver."

"Okay, I'm ready," said Jack, getting to his feet.

"Swell, and when you get done," said Stu jovially, "go down to Sparkies and tell George your drinks and dinner are on me. I'll meet you there about six-thirty."

"Sounds good, Stu."

The two shook hands and Jack headed for the door.

"I want to thank you, Stu for everything. I appreciate it."

"Don't worry about it, kid," Stu said dismissing Jack's thanks. "Everyone needs a hand from time to time."

Stu could tell by Jack's expression, his help had meant a lot. He was touched by the younger man's humility, "Now get that sand out of here, and we'll talk later."

Jack waved and shut the door.

***

391

Juleel heard the knock on the door and flinched. What now? He rose and opened the door a crack, ready to slam it shut if it was trouble. Keysha Jordan stood there with a shy, playful look on her face. When she saw Juleel her face lit up.

"Hi Juleel. Is Jack in?"

Juleel opened the door wider, "Keysha, this is a surprise. No, he's at work, but he'll be back later this evening."

"Oh..." she blurted, her face falling in disappointment.

"Would you like to come in for a moment?" Juleel said.

She hesitated, then said yes and stepped in. Juleel had her sit at Jack's desk chair. Now he could play host. If his mother had taught him anything, it was how to be gracious.

"Could I get you some tea, Keysha?" he said formally. "This time of day, I like to have a cup."

"Is it herbal?"

"Mint."

"Oh I love mint tea, yes."

As Juleel fixed the tea on a small electric hot plate, he noticed Keysha eyeing everything on Jack's desk as if trying to learn more about him. Knowing how silent Jack could be, Juleel could understand her desire to know. She saw a picture, cut from a magazine, of a log cabin beside a stream, and beside it was his book of crossword puzzles. She leafed through it absently.

"Jack loves to do those puzzles," Juleel said, noting her interest.

"I used to do them in high school," she said.

"I get so frustrated with them," explained Juleel with a gesture of his hand. He placed the tea bags in the cups now and added the steaming water.

"There's no pictures of his family?" said Keysha.

"He never talks about his family," said Juleel quietly as if someone were listening. "You know about his father, of course?"

Keysha nodded.

"As far as his mother, he told me she moved somewhere out west, and he doesn't know exactly where. He has no brothers or sisters."

"He's alone," stated Keysha sadly.

"Yes, I'm afraid so," said Juleel. "Here's your tea."

"I saw him from my window one night at the start of the semester," recalled Keysha as if she could still picture him. "He was out on the walk, by himself. He stopped by that bunch of lilac bushes out front and stared up at the moon. I had been doing the same thing; so I guess, unbeknownst to him, we shared something together."

"Did you tell him about that?"

"No. He might think it was silly."

"Don't bet on it," said Juleel. "You'd be surprised."

She took a sip of tea and continued, "On that night, he seemed more solitary than anyone I've ever seen. I remember looking at the moon and feeling its attraction. Funny, how I wanted him to know I understood."

Juleel nodded and drank his tea. He knew the inner turmoil Jack endured, and the stoic strength which helped him survive.

"You know Keysha, he really likes you a lot."

James Ankrom

"He does?"

"Yes. He doesn't say much, but when he does, he's sincere."

Keysha's heart raced, "You know he sent me roses."

"I know, he spent an afternoon trying to decide what kind of flowers to send."

"I love roses," said Keysha. "They're such a thoughtful gift. When I received them, I couldn't wait to thank him."

"Then they've done their job," Juleel said.

Juleel set his cup of tea on the desk. "I'm glad it's you he adores. You're good people, and Jack needs good people."

"Well thank you," she said sipping the hot tea. She noticed the cast still on Juleel's hand. "How's your hand?"

Juleel blushed, "It itches. Momma told me that means it's healing."

"I heard how it happened," Keysha said frowning.

"It's okay. I've had worse."

"I don't know how you and Jack stand it," Keysha said angrily. "Raymon and his friends won't back off."

A sudden knock on the door caught their attention. Juleel raised his eyebrows to Keysha, "Wow, I haven't had this much company all semester."

He walked across the room and opened the door without pretext. It was a careless thing to do. Suddenly, his breath caught in his chest. There was Tyrel Friday, all two hundred and seventy pounds of him, unsmiling and grim-faced.

***

394

Dean Jans was leaning back in his overstuffed desk chair, thinking about the implications of Jack Mulligan's exoneration, when the phone buzzed and his secretary's voice announced, "Dean Jans, there's a call on two from Robert Brent."

"Thank you," said Jans and punched line two. "Hello Robert, what can I do for you?"

"Hello sir. I just wanted to talk to you about Jack Mulligan."

Jans' stomach churned into knots as he bolted straight up in his chair, "What now? Is something wrong?"

"No," said Brent thinking of Detective Bergman's similar reaction. "I just wanted to ask you a few questions. You know, just to clear up some things in my own mind."

"What's that?" said Jans stonily.

"Well, I was thinking about Mulligan's records. Weren't those records sealed? How could a student find that stuff out?"

Jans grimaced, "I'd like to find that out myself. Only a handful of people knew of his criminal past. You were told, naturally, because you would have direct contract with him."

"I see," mused Brent. "But no other student had access?"

"No," said Jans, an edge developing in his voice. "What are you getting at, Robert?"

"I just can't figure how everyone found out."

"I don't know, but there were no leaks from this office."

"Did any of the faculty know?" Brent continued.

"Hell no!" Jans spat angrily. "Why are you so interested?"

"I'm just running it through my mind, that's all," Brent said casually. "I just thought maybe someone on the faculty might have found out."

"Only Dr. Ramapo knew."

"What?"

"Dr. Nathan Ramapo knew," Jans said in a low voice. "Mulligan was doing poorly in his class, and he thought it would be useful to know more about his background."

"When did he look at the files?"

"A few weeks before…Hey, wait a minute. Don't you go getting any ideas in your head," Jans warned. "I've known Nathan Ramapo for over ten years. He's a noted and respected member of this college. He's frankly beyond reproach."

"He had the file, though?"

"Yes, but he said he locked it up, and I believe him."

"Well if you say so," replied Brent.

"I have no reason to doubt Dr. Ramapo's word."

"Well, thanks for the info, Dean Jans."

Beads of sweat were forming on Jans' forehead, "You're welcome, Robert. I have to go."

Jans' replaced the receiver. His hands were shaking. What was wrong with him? If he couldn't answer questions from one of his own people, how was he going to face the alumni during Homecoming?

***

Robert Brent sat at his desk with notes scrawled over a legal pad. A frown came to his face as he considered Dr. Ramapo.

Why would Nathan Ramapo want to help Jack Mulligan out? Had it occurred to anyone that students don't receive help in college unless they request it. College professors aren't like high school teachers. They never play the role of surrogate parent. They were way too busy. No, Dr. Ramapo must have had some other reason for wanting more information about Jack Mulligan.

CHAPTER 45

"How can this be?" whispered Sam Bergman to himself, while his eyes scrutinized the forensic report in front of him.

It was late afternoon and a slow day—crime wise—in Mt. Sidney. Some younger officers hated such days, but Sam was more introspective. He considered a day such as this a gift. The reprieve gave him more time to deal with his case backlog.

He had earlier been sitting at his desk typing reports when one of the Department secretaries had brought him a Fed-Ex package from the FBI's Washington labs. It lay on a desk corner for an hour before Sam finally took time to look at it.

When he pulled a manila folder out of the bright Fed-Ex Pak, Sam could tell by its heft that it was loaded with information. The first thing Bergman saw was a set of photos of a young black man in a Marine dress uniform. The man looked straight and proud as did most young Marines who had this same photo taken. On the borders of all the photos was written a name, Thaddeus Brown.

The partial fingerprint French had sent to Washington had raised a flag in the FBI's computer files. The soldier in this case, Private Thaddeus Brown, had deserted the Marine Corps thirty-four years before and was still wanted for questioning in the murder of a drill sergeant.

Sam studied the biography and the profile study. Brown was from a small town in Eastern Kentucky. He had been an honor student in college, had taught school in East St. Louis until he was fired in 1966. Strangely, he had joined the Marine Corp when he was in his late-twenties. Prior to his days in the Marines, Brown had had no previous criminal record.

Could the FBI lab have screwed up? Maybe the print match wasn't correct. If true, the murderer would be a middle-aged man.

Bergman shook his head. He had friends who were in the Corps during the Viet Nam war. They had told him stories of how tough the training was. The DI's were all combat veterans. Most hated being reassigned to train raw recruits and took it out on the new men. They worked them unmercifully and didn't tolerate mistakes.

Could a presumably sensitive man such as Thaddeus Brown have cracked? Perhaps the drill sergeant had pushed him too far.

Whomever Thaddeus Brown was, he must have either died or completely changed his identity. Most deserters were caught within hours or days. They'd go back to their hometowns and be arrested while sleeping with their girlfriends.

The difference in Private Thaddeus Brown's desertion was murder. The Marine Corps was not tolerant of those who killed their DI's. It made them look a tad less invincible.

There was a note attached to the file from an Agent Steve Bachmann. He apparently wanted Sam to give him a call as soon as he read the file. Bergman picked up the phone and dialed the number. Within moments a secretary came on the line, and Sam requested Agent Bachmann. She took his name and put him on hold, while classical music played in the background.

Sam then heard a series of far-away clicks and then a voice, "Agent Bachmann."

"Hello Agent, this is Lieutenant Sam Bergman with the Mt. Sidney P.D. I just got your cold file on Thaddeus Brown and read through it. You requested I call you."

"Thanks Lieutenant," said Bachmann in a youthful tenor voice. "When we saw the flag raise on this file, we naturally became very excited. The FBI likes to close all cases no matter how old. In fact, I always think it makes criminals nervous when they realize we never give up trying to find them."

"Well I hope we can be of some help," said Sam, liking this young man immediately. Bachmann's enthusiasm for the job was apparent. It was a trait all cops should have. "The partial print is from a knife used to murder a co-ed at Mt. Sidney College."

"Do you have any suspects?"

"We had one but he's been cleared," said Sam. "We think the weapon was planted to implicate him."

"Any reason for that?"

"He's white."

"What?"

"Mt. Sidney College is one of the oldest black colleges in the nation. It was founded by a group of emancipated slaves in the 1870s. The young man who was suspected is the first white student on campus. The weapon was found outside his window."

Bachmann sighed, "So you think there's a racial angle?"

"Yes I do," said Sam positively. "I think the girl was killed to frame this young man."

"Wow."

"This kid had a past criminal record. He's out on a special release program," informed Bergman.

"What was his original crime?"

"Murder."

"I see," Bachmann said with a whistle. "This is getting thicker by the minute. Do you think you'll need our help?"

"Not at the moment," Sam said dryly. "But if you have any more information on Thaddeus Brown maybe you could send it along."

"I'll do that," Bachmann assured. "Could you keep me posted."

"You got it."

After Sam hung up, he re-read the entire file, digested it and wrote some notes. Thaddeus Brown would now be sixty-three years old, extremely bright and would be very crafty. He could either be someone hiding out in a low-profile, low paying job, such as a maintenance man or he could be an administrator or professor. Sam's hunch was the latter.

***

Jack delivered the load of sand to the construction site and started back to the yard. He was exalted to be back on the job and doubly exalted to be out of jail. A few days before, he had considered his life essentially over. He'd thought he would be spending the next several decades in prison for a crime he hadn't committed. Now, however, there was hope once again.

A convenience store came up ahead on the right and reminded him of one of the items he needed for Raymon's surprise. He braked the rig in a side parking lot and let the engine idle, while he entered the store. An Asian man was alone behind the counter, and gave Jack an uneasy smile as he took in Jack's size and disfigured face.

Jack spotted the adult-sized fitted briefs for those who suffer from incontinence. When he brought them to the counter, the clerk raised an eyebrow. Jack noted the reaction and said, "My grandfather. He has a little problem."

The clerk smiled his understanding through a mouth full of cracked, discolored teeth. He rang up the purchase and handed Jack his change. Jack walked outside, tossed the bag into the truck and drove three blocks before pulling over once again. This time, he opened the bag and pulled out a single pad. Yes, one would be all he'd need. He jumped down from the cab and deposited the rest of the bag in a nearby dumpster.

By the time Jack got back to the yard, it was six-thirty and already dark. Most of the delivery trucks were parked in a row along the yard's fence, the drivers having gone home. Jack went into the employee's locker room. He dialed the combination to his locker and opened the metal door. There, neatly stacked, was everything he'd been collecting: the black pants, turtle neck, blanket and ski-mask. On top the stack was a roll of gray duct tape and a sewing kit. The adult pad was the last item necessary. Jack placed it on top the pile and closed the door.

Back outside, he maneuvered through the pallets of block and brick to the yard's front gates. When he passed the main office, his head came up. Outside the chain-link fence, a chrome-covered Harley thundered down the street, the bike's exhaust gave a growl which echoed off the nearby buildings. Jack wished he had a fancy bike like that. Then, he wouldn't be walking everywhere, and he'd have a new kind of freedom and mobility.

Jack saw a light in the office. Stu must still be working on paper work. Jack respected and admired his boss's hard work. He hoped someday, with the same kind of dedication, he could carve out a spot, such as Stu's, in his own place as a Vet.

He picked up his pace to Sparkies where a cold drink and a sandwich awaited him. The brisk air had brought out his appetite.

***

"Hello."

The tone over the phone was wary.

"Hi. Is this Dr. Ramapo?"

"Yes," came a cautious and questioning voice.

"This is Robert Brent. I'm the Head Resident over at Lincoln Hall. I was wondering if I could ask you a few questions about one of your students."

"Who?"

"A white boy named, Jack Mulligan."

There was a pause and Brent began to think Ramapo might hang up, "Are you still there, Dr. Ramapo?"

"Yes, I…" stuttered Ramapo, suspiciously, "What reason would you have for wanting to know about this particular student? I like to think my students' grades are strictly confidential."

"This isn't about Mulligan's grades."

"It isn't?"

"No, sir," said Brent. "I understand from talking with Dean Jans that you had Jack Mulligan's complete file just prior to his background being made public to the student body. I'm trying to find out who might have leaked that information."

"It didn't come from my office," said Ramapo defensively. "Do you understand?"

"Maybe an assistant or a visiting student saw it?"

"Nonsense," exclaimed Ramapo. "What do you think, I leave such information just lying around? It was locked in my safe."

"Oh," Brent said, unconvinced.

"Is there anything else, young man?"

"Would it be possible to get a list of names of students who visited your office during the time you had the files?"

"Impossible!" said Ramapo, sharply. "I won't give out such information for a witch hunt. That sort of thing is confidential."

"To whom?" asked Brent. "If I don't get a list, then the cops will. I'd like to check with these people, first."

"What?"

Brent let Ramapo hang a moment, "I feel that whoever leaked Mulligan's record could be involved in Danielle Myers' death."

This must have affected Ramapo deeply. He suddenly seemed calmer and more resigned, "Well okay, Mr. Brent. That's different. Come to my house this afternoon, and I'll have the list for you."

"Thanks Dr…"

The line went dead. Brent looked at the phone in his hand. Strange man, Dr. Ramapo, but at least he was cooperating. He'd have the list. Then maybe Brent could get to the bottom of this whole mess.

***

Jack stopped outside the door to Sparkies. He saw the lights inside and listened to the voices spilling out into the early evening. It was happy hour. Working men were gathering inside for a drink before going home. The outlying streets of the industrial district might be drab and deserted but inside all was cheerful.

Jack could hear a country song about lost love playing on the juke box, and as he entered the smoky opaqueness, twenty heads turned. Then there were shouts of welcome from all over. Overhead the familiar blue-grey pall moved sluggishly near the ceiling. He shook hands and greeted the regulars he knew and finally pulled up to the bar.

It was then he saw a large, bald man with a beer belly looking at him. The man, who was drinking shots, had an art gallery of tattoos on his beefy arms and was wearing a cutoff vest with a biker's insignia on the back. Jack summed him up as trouble.

405

He recalled again the day in Steubenville when his father had taken him to the bar. That biker, that day, had looked a lot like this one. Both were two-bit losers. Who else would kick the hell out of a peaceful little man such as Pastor Cecil Williams.

This guy had the same cocky demeanor. Jack noticed how the regulars were steering clear of him. Even George seemed nervous.

Jack had once feared men, such as this one, when he was ten. They were unpredictable and volatile. But Jack Mulligan wasn't ten anymore and didn't scare as easily.

George slid down to Jack, "How you been Jack? It hasn't been the same here without you."

"It's probably been a sight better," Jack joked.

George laughed and said, "I got a call from Stu, awhile ago. He says I'm to feed you our special—meatloaf and mashed potatoes—and fix you up with a drink. Sound good to you?"

"Absolutely, George," Jack said. "Could I have a cola?"

George shook his head, "That won't put hair on your chest, Jack."

"I guess I'll have to live with that," Jack smirked.

George drew the glass of soda and put some extra ice in it. "I'll have your dinner in a few minutes."

Jack nodded and picked up the drink. It tasted cold and was refreshing. That's when he saw the biker moving his way. A moment later, he stood beside Jack, "Hey buddy, aren't you the guy I read about in the papers who had trouble up at the college?"

Jack turned, "Yeah."

"Man, what a fuckin' mess," he said shaking his big bald head. "I saw it in the papers and couldn't believe how fast those spooks were into blaming you for that black bitch's murder."

Jack sipped his drink, "Yeah well."

The biker held out his hand, "I'm Ragin' Roy Smithers, kid. Can I buy you a drink?"

The man acted as if his name meant something. Jack ignored his hand and mumbled, "I've got one."

The biker withdrew his hand and frowned, "The cops ever figure who cut up that nigger?"

Jack eyed Roy coldly, "No."

Smithers lowered his voice, "You know, I know a group of guys that understands what you've been through, kid. They could help you."

"Oh."

"Yeah, we know what it's like for a white man in this world. You know with the niggers and Jews getting everything. The white man's got to start sticking together. Know what I'm sayin'?"

"Yeah."

"We call ourselves the Sons of Aryans and…"

"Nazis."

"Sort of," sputtered Smithers in a low voice. "I mean we're true patriots. None of that Hitler shit. But, we take care of our own, and we don't take shit from niggers, spics and Jews."

Jack picked up his drink, turned to Roy, "You know pal, I don't need your help, and I don't like you. How about staying the fuck away from me."

"What!"

"You heard me. I don't want you around me."

Smithers gave him a lethal glance, "What are you, some kind of faggot, nigger lover? I'm tryin' to be friendly, junior."

Jack grabbed his drink and started to walk away. Smithers grabbed his shoulder. "Hey, don't walk away from me, punk."

"Get you're hand off me," Jack said in a stone cold voice.

Smithers laughed and gripped his shoulder harder, "Fuck you, boy. Do I look like I take orders from a pussy like you?"

Jack grabbed his hand and squeezed. The biker's face turned purple as the pain of Jack's grip registered.

"Do you want me to kick your fat ass?" asked Jack.

A silence spread over the bar. Everyone was now aware of trouble. George, moved closer, "I don't want any trouble you two. Do you hear me, Jack?"

"Yeah," Jack said, letting go of Smither's hand.

"Hey bartender," interrupted Ragin' Roy, "Go fuck yourself."

"Hey pal, you can get the hell out of here!" shouted George.

Smithers face was flushed with rage. He was clearly used to being feared. Now he had to give these punks a lesson. Swiping the neck of his beer bottle from the bar in one movement, he took a swing at Jack's head. The movement was too telegraphed, however. To his surprise, the bottle never connected.

Jack easily ducked away, snapping a hard shot into the biker's solar plexus. Ragin' Roy's lungs deflated in a burst of sour air. Jack's arm then came up quickly and his fist connected with Smithers' jaw.

All Smithers would later remember were his teeth breaking and his brain going black. Stunned, he hit the floor hard. He lay there pondering why the ceiling fan blades weren't turning. Then, hands roughly snatched him under his arms and pulled him up. George yelled, "Get him out of here!"

Ragin' Roy Smithers was literally tossed across the sidewalk by three construction workers. He fell onto the hood of a '73 Buick, the cold surface stinging his face. He then rolled off and fell into the gutter.

He instinctively knew if he went back in, he'd only manage to get his ass stomped again. The Mulligan kid was way too fast and way too strong. Besides the kid apparently had a lot of friends in there. Fuckin' nigger lovers, all of them.

Couldn't these guys see what he was trying to do for them. Getting rid of niggers should be a priority. They didn't deserve Ragin' Roy's vision of a white man's world. How dare they, fuckin' ingrates.

Smithers got to his feet swaying uneasily. His eyes were still seeing stars. He staggered to his bike and managed to kick start it to life.

He was going back to his own kind. Guys who were real men and thought the right way about the damn minorities.

Fuck this place.

James Ankrom

CHAPTER 46

Tyrel was surprised to see Keysha in Jack's room. Then he remembered what Raymon had told him in the library. He guessed she must be friends with Jack's roommate, Juleel. He peered from the doorway into the room, painfully remembering his last visit.

"Hey Keysha, how you doin'?" he asked in a sheepish tone.

"Fine Tyrel. How are you?" answered Keysha, edginess registering in her voice.

Tyrel turned to Juleel. "Is the white...is Jack Mulligan here?" he asked awkwardly.

"No," replied Juleel tensely. "He's at work. Why do you want him?"

"Yes Tyrel," affirmed Keysha, suspiciously "why do you want him?"

"We don't want any trouble," warned Juleel, hoarsely.

Tyel then hung his head and shuffled his feet.

Juleel waited, looking confused and fearful, his hands trembling slightly.

Tyrel turned to the smaller man, shifting his eyes finally to look directly at him. "I think I owe the man an apology and actually you, too. I sort of went off the other night. I was wrong, and I shouldn't have."

Juleel looked up at Tyrel in disbelief as if he were expecting a punchline. "You're not kidding are you?"

"No, I'm dead serious. What I did wasn't right. I'm really sorry."

They stood staring at each other for a long moment, as Juleel assessed Tyrel's motive. Could someone as angry as Tyrel was really now be repentent. Should he trust the big man. Then, Juleel let out his breath, "I think I believe you."

Tyrel was truly humbled. He looked so uncomfortable with his eyes studying the floor.

"I'm proud of you, Tyrel," Keysha added. "It takes courage to admit you're wrong."

"Won't you come in and sit down, Tyrel?" Juleel implored, stepping aside and indicating one of the beds. "I'll fix you a cup of tea."

"Tea?"

"It's very good," said Keysha, making a gesture, which Juleel didn't see, for Tyrel to accept a cup.

"Sure," said Tyrel, sitting on the edge of Juleel's bed.

Juleel rushed around for a moment with a paper cup and finally gave Tyrel a steaming cup as if he were offering it to the President. Tyrel took a sip.

Juleel waited expectantly.

Tyrel smiled, "It's good."

Juleel sat down and appeared thoughtful, "What may I ask, made you change your mind about Jack?"

"I read the papers," said Tyrel. "I found out that the forensic evidence absolutely cleared Jack. Besides, once I thought about it, I realized that if the whi…if Jack had killed Danielle, he wouldn't have been stupid enough to put the murder weapon outside his own window."

Juleel nodded in agreement.

"He's been my roommate for a couple of months," he said, "and I can tell you, he's not stupid or cruel."

"Well I'm going to act differently toward him," Tyrel said lightly. "Besides, he's as about as tough a bastard as I've ever seen. He's one bad-ass sonuvabitch."

They all laughed.

Tyrel finished the tea and frowned at Juleel, "By the way, I'll give you a warning. Raymon, along with Professor Ramapo, are planning something bad for Jack."

"Dr. Ramapo?" Keysha exclaimed.

"Yeah, Dr. Ramapo doesn't want Jack to be here," Tyrel said. "Raymon came to the library trying to get me to join them."

"Do you know what they're planning?" Keysha asked.

"No, I didn't ask."

Keysha pulled a strand of hair away from her face. "That explains why Jack's barely passing Ramapo's lit class. I've seen Jack's papers. They come back with C's and D's on them. But, when I read them, they're excellent."

"This is all Jack needs," Juleel replied throwing his arms in the air. "More hate and more problems."

"It could be just talk," Tyrel said. "You know Raymon."

"I sure do," said Juleel.

***

An hour later, Jack was still being immortalized at Sparkies. Everyone wanted to buy him a drink. The older patrons and even George the bartender had never seen such power in a knockout punch. They couldn't believe the biker had been decked with one blow.

Jack tried to explain he'd only gotten lucky but no one believed him. They called him "Champ" and said he had a future in the ring. Comparisons were made to Joe Fraser and Rocky Marciano. He even heard phrases like, "great white hope."

Jack reddened at the last. He knew for a fact, he was nobody's hope.

Stu finally arrived and heard what had happened. Of course, with the retelling, the punch got harder and the biker larger. All this was embarrassing to Jack, who blushed over the incident.

"You're quite the hero," teased Stu.

"Oh come on!" said Jack. "Not you too?"

"Hey kid, these guys live for this stuff," Stu explained, sipping his beer. "You've now become a working class hero. They'll talk about this over beers for years to come."

Jack shook his head.

"What did that guy say that caused you to pop him?" Stu asked as he picked up some pretzels.

"You know that Nazi bigot crap," said Jack in disgust. "He said he knew some guys who'd back me up. I told him to get lost."

Stu grimaced, "I'm Jewish. I've met some of those guys. They look just like everyday guys, but they're full of hate. Most don't even know a single black man or a Jew. They just hate them because of the shit their daddies fed them."

"Well maybe he'll tell his friends to leave me alone," said Jack. "I just want to be left alone."

***

Across town, Nathan Ramapo was loading a nine-shot clip into his .45. The hardened steel felt cold in his hands, as he thought of what he must do.

"The goal of all life is death," he whispered Freud's words to himself.

All along he'd known he'd have to take care of Jack Mulligan, himself. It always came down to the motivated individual, the overman. Other ways had been tried and had failed. Mulligan was still here. His presence mocked him to near insanity. A bullet was the only answer left. He'd also have to silence Raymon Jackson and that little whore, Keysha Jordan.

He had found out a few days before who Keysha Jordan was. Up until then, he had considered her the bright, beautiful girl in the third row of his morning class. But now she had done the unthinkable. She had given herself to a white man. His stomach turned. Interracial relationships sickened him. She'd pay for her transgression.

But first things first. Another must die before even Mulligan, Raymon and Keysha.

The door bell rang.

His guest was right on time. A shadow moved on the other side of the curtained front door. Ramapo reached for the knob and opened it.

"Hello, Mr. Brent," said Nathan cheerfully. "I've been expecting you."

CHAPTER 47

It was late that evening when Jack finally made it back to Lincoln Hall. He had walked the last quarter mile in a cold misty rain, and his jacket hung damp and heavy. The temperature was dropping fast. He shivered, fighting back the chill, until he entered the warm lobby.

Stu had been kind enough to drive him as far as the gates of the college, and would have negotiated the winding lanes to the dorm had Jack not stopped him. It was too risky. Jack couldn't let a friend be recognized by the killer who could be anywhere. Whomever this maniac was, he was probably monitoring Jack's every move.

In the past few days, his senses had become alert to everything: shadows, movements and every noise. His life might hang in the balance of a split second of awareness and reaction.

Once in his room, Jack took off the wet jacket and hung it by the radiator to dry and then changed his shirt. Juleel was off somewhere. To be out this late was unusual for him. His absence made Jack feel uneasy. Could something have happened?

He cursed his caution. Damn, he was becoming an old lady.

He sat down at his desk and reached for his books. The week in jail had caused him to fall behind in all his classes. He had tests coming up in biology and math. Clearing his mind would be difficult. He still felt the adrenalin from earlier that evening.

Nazi's! Every fuckin' weirdo such as Roy Smithers wanted something. Now the Nazi's wanted him as a spokesperson for hate. Jack shook his head at the thought of these small minded men, who harbored such intolerance for those who were different.

Opening his bio notebook, he reviewed his class notes and slowly his mind began to focus on the work. A half hour passed and then, he heard voices and a key in the door. Jack looked up in time to see Juleel, Keysha and Tyrel Friday enter the room.

Juleel had a somewhat silly smile on his face. One would have thought he'd been drinking. "Jack you're home. We've been waiting all evening for you."

Jack's eyes stayed on Tyrel. What was he doing here? Would he attack again? Jack mentally prepared himself for the worst.

Tyrel, however, edged past Juleel and Keysha and slowly walked up to Jack and extended his hand, "I wanted to tell you how sorry I am about what happened the other day. I acted like a fool, and I shouldn't have."

Jack stared at his hand.

Could this be real. The others held their breathes.

"Do you mean that?" asked Jack in uncertainty.

417

"Yeah, I do," Tyrel mumbled in a remorseful tone. "I really am sorry."

Jack hesitated and then carefully grasped Tyrel's hand. Juleel and Keysha smiled.

"This calls for a celebration!" shouted Juleel. "Let's all have a cup of tea."

Everyone laughed. Without anything being said, the four felt a bond of friendship taking shape between them.

Tyrel put his big hand on Juleel's thin shoulders, "Juleel I'd love to have more tea, but I've got a test tomorrow."

Juleel's face dropped, "You're sure?"

"Yeah man, I'll take a rain check, though. It was great."

This brightened Juleel once again.

Tyrel waved to everyone and departed. Juleel began making tea and singing a Puff Daddy song to himself. Keysha crossed the room in two graceful strides and kissed Jack on his cheek.

"Thank you so much for the roses. They are lovely."

Jack blushed. Keysha's kiss lingered on his cheek.

"You're welcome," he said.

Juleel grinned knowingly to himself as his tea kettle sung on the hot plate. Jack and Keysha could hardly keep their eyes off each other.

"What took you so long to get here tonight?" asked Keysha.

"I had to work late, and Mr. Ableson treated me to dinner."

"Oh, too bad," sighed Keysha wagging her finger teasingly. "You missed having dinner with me."

Jack smiled, "That would have been better, I admit."

"Do you have more work this evening?" asked Keysha as if there was a more desirable option.

Jack considered his priorities. He did need to study.

"I have some time," he said to his own surprise.

"Good."

"Here's the tea," broke in Juleel as they all sat back and relaxed. "I hope it's hot enough."

The room smelled of mint, and the warmth gave Jack a mental glimpse of what the idea of home must be like. Here in this dorm room was a tiny slice of it. Home was more than a place, it was a state of mind. It was where all of life's great plans were launched; where you were always unconditionally loved, no matter what.

Keysha watched him over the tea cup. Jack met her eyes. He noticed everything about her as she sipped her tea. She sat opposite him with her legs crossed wearing a pair of tight jeans. The shape of her body with the soft curves of her breasts and hips fascinated him. When she moved, he wondered at her gracefulness. When she spoke, she brought forth words in gentle wisps of breathlessness that made him want to linger on every syllable.

"Let's take a walk," she suggested a few minutes later.

"It's cold and damp outside."

"Will you melt?" she teased.

"No."

"Then grab your coat and let's go," she said with a wink.

"Okay," he whispered, half mesmerized.

419

They had just finished their tea, and Jack grabbed his now dry jacket. His anticipation at being alone with Keysha was delightfully exciting.

"I'll meet you in the lobby," Keysha said. "I'll be just a minute."

When she left, he felt a wretched pang of loneliness. The room was suddenly drab and empty once more. The sensation wasn't new to him. He fought the depressing notion of isolation in almost every waking moment. It came from years of forced confinement.

All his life, Jack had only had himself to count on. He knew he could only look within himself for strength, skill and courage. Relying on others could get you killed Inside. The long nights in the Institution had been designed to break the individual spirit and crush it with fear.

Once in the lobby, the wait was longer than he anticipated. It felt like eternity. He fidgeted sitting on one of the over-stuffed couches. Where was she?

Jack had no idea that young women usually took longer to get ready than men. He began to think that maybe she had changed her mind. He could understand it. Keysha could certainly do better than him.

Then suddenly there she was breezing into the lobby. Keysha's bright smile and beauty froze him with joy. She wore a blue winter jacket with a bright red scarf, matching beret and gloves. Her physical presence made him light headed. Immediately she grabbed his hand, and guided him out into the night.

"I heard it might snow tonight," she stated in obvious delight. "I love snow."

"So do I," said Jack, a vision of the mountain cabin, he thought of from time to time came to him. It was layered in snow but was warm inside.

"My mother played with me once in the snow," he said.

That sounded stupid, he thought.

"Only once?"

"Yeah, I think."

Jack felt like an idiot mentioning his mother. She was long gone, and whatever memories he had were meaningless to this girl.

"When was that?" asked Keysha with great interest.

"I was small, maybe four years old," he replied trying to remember. "That was all before…you know."

Keysha heard his voice die and didn't pursue his thought.

"You know I really don't know anything about you," she said.

"There's not much to tell."

"Do you have brothers and sisters?"

"No."

"Cousins."

"No."

"My family is so large," she said incredulously. "I can't imagine, for instance, the holidays without a packed house."

"Yeah," said Jack, who couldn't imagine a holiday spent with anyone human.

"Where did you live, Jack?"

"Before the Institution?

"Yes."

"In Steubenville, Ohio," he said, now not enjoying recalling his past. "We lived in a run-down dump near a steel mill. I can remember things breaking down in that house all the time."

"What was she like, Jack? Your Mom."

"Oh, she was fun when I was real little but she changed."

"Changed?"

A cold blast of wind caught Keysha's words and carried them through the oaks and hemlocks. This walk might be cut short if it got colder. Jack, however, didn't want it to ever end. He could feel Keysha's warmth beside him and smell her fresh scent.

"How did she change?" repeated Keysha.

Jack tried to recall all those long ago events, "He, my father," stammered Jack. "He drove her crazy. He took what was precious about her and crushed it. He destroyed her."

Keysha's face clouded, "I'm sorry Jack."

"Nothing to be sorry about."

"Yes,…there is."

Jack fell silent.

"Where is she now?" Keysha asked.

"In St. Louis, the last I heard. Probably drunk or dead."

Keysha suddenly moved closer to Jack gripping his arm tightly.

For the next twenty minutes, Keysha told Jack about her family and friends. He reveled in her descriptions of each person and their idiosyncracies. Her life seemed so much more rich and wonderful than his.

Jack realized how different they were. He could never tell her about his life or about the dreadful monotony he'd endured. He couldn't make her comprehend those endless hours, days, months and years of hopelessness. Inside was about surviving on tiny bits of secret dreams that kept one's sanity intact.

Jack listened intently to Keysha's stories about her mother, father and brothers. He didn't have any family anecdotes, but hers were fascinating to him. Keysha's family sounded fun. A real family that gave unquestioningly to one another. If that kind of love could be multiplied to a whole community or to a nation, the thought of wars would end that day. Human cruelty would become a thing of the past.

Sometime later, they found themselves on a deserted sidewalk near the Creative Arts Center. A copse of blue spruce gave them temporary shelter from the chilly winter breeze. Jack could hear the soft song of the tree tops and feel their sonnet in his head. For all the world, there was only this one moment and Keysha. His eyes filled with her long, braided hair, her soft, olive-brown skin and her deep expressive eyes.

She touched his scarred cheek and the contact spread a magnificent warm radiance. Jack had waited all his life for her touch. Her sweet scent enveloped him and suddenly their lips touched ever so gently. He pulled her to him. The kiss was long and soft, and he gave himself to her at that moment for all eternity and beyond.

Neither of them wanted the moment to end. There would never be another like it. Never would their love be so new or so fresh.

Never.

Flakes of snow started coming down around them like bits of moonlight dropping from heaven. The brilliant flakes caught in Keysha's hair and glowed as if made of lace and silver.

She laughed with glee, looking up, "I told you it would snow."

Jack smiled with her, and they both held hands and danced around with the joy in falling snow. Jack sensed happiness he prayed would never end. Why couldn't the world just stop right then. They kissed once more holding each other desperately, never wanting to let go.

***

"Mr. Brent, have a seat," said Nathan Ramapo. "I think I may be able to help you with that list of students."

"Thanks Dr. Ramapo," said Brent. "I think we can narrow down the list of who spilled the info and get to the bottom of this."

Brent felt that a breakthrough was at hand. If the cops couldn't find the murderer, then he would. This was what the cops should have been doing. He could suddenly see the headlines in the paper hailing his investigative genius.

"Let me get you a brandy. It will cut the chill," said Ramapo amicably.

Ramapo left the study and Brent looked around the room. The professor was a untidy man. There were books and papers stacked on every surface and covered with thick dust. Stale cooking smells inundated the atmosphere with a rancidness. On top of it all, the heat was cranked to the moon, and Brent began to perspire.

A moment later, Ramapo returned with two glasses. He motioned for Robert to sit across from him and carefully put a glass with amber liquid in front of him.

"So what are you looking for, Mr. Brent?"

Brent spoke before picking up his glass. "I think whoever broadcast the information about Jack Mulligan could be connected in some way to the killer of Danielle Myers."

"I see," said Ramapo in concern.

"I'm going to check everyone on the list you give me and see if I can find out anything."

"You're doing this on your own?" asked Ramapo, frowning.

"Yes."

"Have you told the police?"

"No."

Ramapo smiled, "You're very ambitious, Mr. Brent."

Brent nodded in agreement.

The professor lifted his glass, "Well here's to your efforts."

Brent clinked his glass with Ramapo's and drank deeply feeling the liquid scorch his throat. The brandy was excellent.

"Did it ever occur to you, Robert, that Jack Mulligan may not fit in with the students at Mt. Sidney?"

"Yes, but you know how it is, change is going to happen. Even I finally had to realize that."

425

"But do we want to see our culture—the Afro-American culture—destroyed by an interloper and just for the sake of change?"

Robert was feeling dizzy in the heat of the room. Sweat was forming in large drops on his forehead, "Maybe we should realize that we all have to live together anyway."

Brent's tongue was getting thick. The oppressive heat was getting to him. He felt lightheaded and sick.

What was going on? What was happening…to him?

Ramapo continued, "Yes but we should fight for our place. The white devils such as Jack Mulligan are a scourge that can easily destroy us."

Robert could now only see Dr. Ramapo swimming in front of his eyes. He looked at the glass on the table. He drugged me, came as a dull thought to his mind.

Robert's eyes looked for help from Ramapo.

Ramapo, however, had no help to give.

"Now Robert, you must join Danielle Myers," he said smiling. "Be thankful that you are going in an easier way than she did."

Brent slumped, falling onto the floor in front of his chair. His arms wouldn't move. His eys couldn't focus. What the…He could still vaguely make out Ramapo and even with his mind fogged, he now realized who had killed Danielle Myers.

"You're much too nosey, Robert," Ramapo whispered as he leaned over him. "I couldn't let you continue poking around."

Robert tried desperately to lift his arm but found it impossible. The room was getting dark. His last thought was how joyless Ramapo's laughter was in his ears.

CHAPTER 48

Monday afternoon Sam Bergman gave Dean Jans a call. The Dean's secretary put him through immediately.

"Detective, may I help you?" spoke Jans over his speaker phone.

"I think you might," said Bergman quizzically. "Do you have photographs of all the professor's and other full-time employees presently at Mt. Sidney College?"

"You mean grounds keepers, janitors, maintenance men, etcetera."

"That's right."

"Sure," said Jans emphatically. "Are you on to something?"

Bergman hesitated to discuss the case, "It's routine. We're just checking your employees. When could I pick up those photos?"

"Well actually, they're all in the annual yearbook. I'll have one of my assistants drop a copy by your office."

"That would be great."

Jans continued, "Detective Bergman, I've been debating calling you about another matter."

Bergman's ears perked up, "What's that?"

"Do you remember Robert Brent, over at Lincoln Hall?"

"Yes the large young man with the big mouth," sneered Bergman.

"Yes, well," sputtered Jans, "He called me a few days ago and informed me he's sort of carrying on his own investigation."

"What!"

Bergman hated amateurs. They all seemed to have watched too much TV. The damned fools.

"I thought I'd better let you know."

"Shit," grumbled Bergman, his voice getting an edge. "Who does he think he is Sam Spade? This is serious. There's a killer loose out there. He could get himself killed. Dammit!"

"I didn't see any great harm at the time."

"Are you insane?" screamed Bergman.

"Well…"

"Dean Jans, call Brent immediately and tell him to stop playing detective. I don't need more corpses in the morgue."

"Certainly I…"

"Please do it. NOW!" Sam ordered and then hung up.

***

Nathan used a garden rake to smooth out the soil on the spot where he had buried Robert Brent in his back yard. A little grass seed in the spring and nobody would ever know that a body was resting there.

Why had this young idiot decided to intrude into his business? Didn't he know that racial purity was never achieved without bloodshed. Once again, Jack Mulligan was at the root of another death. A sense of urgency came to Ramapo. Mulligan had to be eliminated soon to prevent more deaths such as this one.

The shame of this school's administration was unforgivable, thought Ramapo, putting his shovel and rake away in the potting shed. Shame and more shame on all of them.

***

As the days had passed, Jack and Keysha's love blossomed as they took long walks, ate together and studied next to each other. They touched more and more often and their kisses lingered more passionately with each passing hour together.

Juleel noted a dramatic change in Jack. His roommate had a nicer, lighter attitude. Jack talked more easily and revealed more about himself. He even managed to laugh occasionally.

On the Tuesday evening before Homecoming, Jack went to Keysha's room and tapped softly on the door. Keysha opened the door with a mischievous smile and a caressing soft look. Jack was always amazed at how she could melt him on the spot. He couldn't get enough of her.

A single candle lit her room, as she drew him in. Words seemed useless, only their bodies needed to communicate now.

They kissed with long, hot, wet kisses. She was only wearing a tee-shirt and her breasts were outlined with their erect nipples pressing the material. She wondered if he could feel them as she felt his growing erection. Gently she opened his old blue work shirt and pulled it away. His heavily muscled body was like something from a Roman statue. However, she could see scars, some heavy, on his chest, stomach and to her disbelief, on his back.

"What are these?" she whispered, as her fingers slowly tracing them.

"Nothing," he said, looking away.

She wanted to know, and she wasn't going to take his answer as a resolution to her question, "Please, Jack tell me. How did this happen?"

Jack swallowed hard before speaking, "I angered a guard, Inside. I talked back too much. I was young."

Jack then recalled in a far away voice, as if picturing it, "The guard and two others tied me to a pole in the basement of Building C. They…they had this leather thing, sort of like a riding crop. I don't remember too much. It was Christmas eve. They thought it was fun."

"How old were you?" Keysha said tears welling in her eyes.

"Twelve."

How could grown men do such a thing to a child?

Keysha put her arms around him and kissed his chest tenderly; then his hungry mouth. She pulled his hand, guiding him to her bed.

"I think I'm falling in love with you, Jack," Her voice became husky but gentle.

Suddenly Jack froze, then whispered, "Keysha I've never…"

"I know…don't worry, baby."

Their clothes disappeared as if by magic. Her great beautiful breasts were firm and loose in the dim light. Their animal smells mingled as each pleasured the other with their hands and tongues. Keysha's long dark hair swept around her and hung like a shroud surrounding her head.

Their love making had a gentle but desperate edge. She took his hard erection in both her hot hands and trembling, guided him in. The black hair curled wet and hot between her luxurious thighs as full and rich as a mane. She was liquid and her need was great.

Then he was inside.

"Ohhhh."

They both screamed in ecstasy as their bodies tensed with passion. At first Jack felt awkward but soon he moved hot and slippery in an age old rhythm. Keysha's body drew him deeper and deeper and deeper. They climaxed together. All legs and arms and sweat and the deep, soft, warm places sang when they came, surging and straining and then sinking into thick, heavy bliss.

Afterwards in the glow of the candle, Keysha lay on the edge of the bed, her eyes closed, her hands folded on her breasts. Tears of happiness washed her cheeks and Jack gently kissed them away.

"Did I hurt you?"

"No silly," she whispered.

"Why are you crying?"

"Because...I know I love you so much," She said looking away.

Jack yearned for her in the same way. All his life he had only wanted one thing—to be loved and now here was Keysha. Her dark, olive flesh was like satin to his touch and her hair fell past her shoulders accentuating her waiting breasts. He had never felt like this before. His love for her not only encompassed her body, but her soul and even the way she breathed and smelled.

Jack touched her gently on the cheek and kissed her there, "You remember the first time I saw you?"

"Yes."

"I loved you then. But now...now I'm just...lost."

Keysha laughed and answered him by rolling on top of him and covering his brutal face with wet kisses.

They made love again trying in every way to please each other. Then, they fell into a deep silent sleep, holding each other tightly.

***

Raymon was beyond pissed off. Between the nagging Coach Dunn was giving him and Tyrel's indifference to his racial slurs, his ego was taking a beating. Keysha was gone. Even he couldn't deny she was Mulligan's woman. This galled him. He had seen them together, and it was sickening. Mulligan didn't even own a car.

The morning after Jack and Keysha stayed together, he saw Juleel in the cafeteria finishing his breakfast. Raymon patiently waited until the smaller man had eaten his last morsel and followed him out.

Predictably, Juleel headed back to his room. His arm was still in a soft cast from their last encounter.

Raymon caught up with Juleel in the hallway and without reservation or warning, slammed him against the wall. Raymon stuck his face close Juleel as he laughingly asked, "Hey motherfucker, where you think you're going?"

"To my room, asshole," spat back Juleel. "Let me go."

"You know, I'm hearing disturbing news about Mulligan."

"Oh?"

"He's trying to steal my woman," Raymon sneered.

Juleel struggled to shake Raymon's iron grip. "Are you that slow?"

Raymon shot a sharp right backhand to Juleel's face that sent him to the floor. Then he bent over Juleel. "Listen faggot, don't dis me. You know what I'm sayin'?"

Juleel's eyes were glassy.

"Fuck you."

With this, Raymon kicked Juleel; then hissed into his contorted face, "I've got some shit going on for your boy, faggot. Check it out. Tell him he'd best be ready."

Raymon marched off, his blood pounding in his veins, hatred written on his face. He'd get revenge for his loss—his woman.

***

Jack was ready to take a shower when the door opened and Juleel staggered in. Jack ran to catch his roommate before he collapsed. Swelling showed around his cheek where Raymon had struck him.

Jack guided Juleel to his bed and ordered him to lie down. Then, he dashed down the hall to the cafeteria for ice. One of the cafeteria workers gave him a large plastic tumbler with crushed ice, and he raced back to Juleel's side. Using a wash cloth to hold the ice, Jack applied it to Juleel's cheek.

"Who did this?" asked Jack, already suspecting the culprit.

As if in answer, the phone started ringing and Jack picked it up, "Hey motherfucker, I guess you can see it's payback time."

"Jackson, you're a punk. Why don't you come here and try something with me."

"Punk! Listen motherfucker, you've moved in on my woman, turned my best friend into a fuckin' chickenshit and gotten away with murder. You got to pay, boy, and I'm going to be the one dishin' on your sorry ass. You understand?"

"You fool. You have no idea," whispered Jack.

"We'll see, motherfucker. We'll see," then the connection was slammed off.

***

Raymon's next call was to Keysha.

She had just put her eyeliner away and was getting ready for her nine o'clock class when the phone rang. Maybe it was Jack, she thought whimsically.

"Hello."

"Hey, bitch!" shrieked Raymon. "You better say goodbye to that white motherfucker. You know what I'm sayin'."

"Go to hell, Raymon."

She pushed the receiver down, and then gazed angrily at the phone as if more would come out of it.

***

Dean Jans called Lincoln Hall and waited as the phone rang repeatedly. Finally a young woman's voice answered in a bored tone, "Yeah."

Jans was ready to hang up on what he felt was a wrong number, "Is this Robert Brent's office?"

"Yeah."

Jans felt an anger building, "May I speak with Robert?"

"No."

"Is he in class?"

"No."

"This is Dean Jans, young lady."

"So…"

"So would you give him a message?" he asked in exasperation.

"You and everyone else," said the girl impatiently.

"What do you mean?"

"Robert, he been gone for four days. I ain't seen him and no one else has either. People keep callin' leavin' messages. I don't know."

A chill went up Jans back, "You haven't heard from him in four days?"

"No, not a thing," she said with a long breath.

"Oh my God!" he exclaimed.

"What's your message?" asked the befuddled girl.

435

"Never mind," snapped Jans and hung up.

Was he too late? Had Brent found the killer? Oh Lord, no.

His hands shook as he called the police.

CHAPTER 49

Jack was relieved to see the swelling go down on Juleel's face after a few hours of ice packs. Juleel was still cursing and feeling foolish for being so easily ambushed. He realized that he should have been more cautious, especially around Raymon. Juleel, however, was gutsy and more resilient than he gave himself credit for.

It was a funny thing about bravery. For Jack, being gifted physically, anyone would think of him as courageous and to his credit Jack indeed was. But, Jack knew it took considerably more fortitude to stand up to a bully such as Raymon Jackson when you had no prayer of winning. That took real bravery. Juleel, in his estimation, was truly courageous and Jack deeply respected him.

"I should have seen the sonuvabitch coming," Juleel cursed bitterly.

"Sometimes you don't."

"Damn, would I like to get that guy."

"Don't even think about it," said Jack. "We'll talk to Brent again. Let him handle it."

"Sure," said Juleel sarcastically. "He'll probably reward Raymon with a medal."

"I don't know," said Jack. "Maybe things will change."

Juleel regarded Jack in amazement.

The phone rang then and Jack crossed the room to pick it up. An upset voice met his ear.

"Jack, I just got a call from Raymon Jackson," Keysha said crying. "He threatened to do something if we see each other."

"He seems to be on a roll," said Jack calmly. "Jackson punched Juleel a while ago and threatened him, too. Then, he called and laid a threat on me. I think it's time to have a talk with him."

"No!" screamed Keysha and Juleel at the same time.

"That's exactly what he wants," said Keysha. "If you do that, you'll be back in jail by tonight."

"But…"

"No buts, baby," Keysha said in a now calm voice. "I'm going to Dean Jans' office today. If he won't do something, then I'm going to the police. What he's done to Juleel and you and me is called terroristic threats and it's against the law."

"I don't…"

"Please Jack, don't do anything foolish. They're looking for any excuse to send you back."

Jack clenched his fist in frustration.

"You go, Keysha, and take Juleel with you. Let Dean Jans see Raymon's handiwork," Jack said in resignation.

"Okay, I'll be down in a few minutes," said Keysha, relieved. "Tell Juleel to be ready and please let me do this for us."

Jack got off the phone and hurriedly relayed Keysha's message to Juleel. Juleel straightened from his fetal position on the bed, a humorless smile came to his face and his small chest swelled.

"I'm ready," he crowed. "Let me at that sonuvabitch."

***

Sam Bergman entered Lincoln Hall with Dean Jans in tow. They marched into Robert Brent's office unannounced and startled the very student assistant who Jans had spoken to earlier. She was a voluptuous young woman who was dusting the furniture and carefully cleaning and straightening up the office. A plastic garbage bag in front of the desk was filled with trash and papers.

"What are you doing?" demanded Bergman.

"I'm tidying up," said the wide-eyed girl. "I didn't want you to see a mess."

"Stop now and get out!" shouted Bergman and then turned on Jans. "From this point on, I don't want anything touched in here."

The frightened girl, who was a duty-filled assistant put her hand to her mouth and ran from the room in fear. She just wanted to help.

"Jans go to her," directed Bergman, bitterly. "Calm her down. I'll need to get a statement from her."

"She's upset," said Jans, astonished at Bergman's lack of sensitivity. "Can't you see?"

"She just tampered with a possible crime scene," explained Bergman. "There could have been something she cleaned up that could have told us where young Brent disappeared to."

Dean Jans shook his head in grudging agreement and went off to speak to the girl. Bergman, meantime, pulled on a pair of rubber gloves and proceeded to meticulously sift through the papers on top of Brent's desk. He didn't precisely know what he was looking for, but he knew it would strike his eyes when he saw it. It could be a scrap of paper with an important clue scribbled on it or maybe a photo or any of a hundred miscellaneous items.

An hour passed as he carefully picked up, then read each piece of paper on the desk. Then he started on the drawers where he finally spotted what could be considered something pertinent. He had been moving aside the bag of trash and other office supplies when he spied a legal pad stuck under a stack of reports. It had a list of names written on it, alongside each name was a phone number and beside some of these were check marks. What caught his attention most was a circle drawn around one name, Professor Nathan Ramapo.

Bergman walked out into the lobby where Dean Jans was talking in a low, concerned voice to the student assistant who had straightened the office. With his approach, her eyes widened once again, and she seemed on the verge of bolting. Jans placed a hand on her shoulder to calm her.

"Dean Jans, do you know a Professor Nathan Ramapo?" asked Bergman.

"Why yes. He teaches English literature here at Mt. Sidney."

"I see."

Jans frowned, "Why do you ask?"

"His name is on this list," said Bergman, showing Jans the legal pad.

Jans appeared shocked—too shocked. "Robert said he was going to talk to Nathan Ramapo last Friday when I last saw him. Do you think it means anything?"

"We'll know soon enough," said Bergman, then turning to the shaken girl. "I'm sorry I scared you, Miss. What's your name?

"Thelma Parks," she said shyly.

"Well Thelma, did Robert Brent say anything to you about visiting Professor Ramapo?"

Thelma's brow furrowed in thought, "No, not a word."

"Okay," replied Bergman. "When did you last see Brent?"

"Last Friday morning. I worked till noon and got him a cup of coffee about ten o'clock."

"You didn't see him after that?"

"No. Robert asked not to be disturbed. He was studying or something, I think."

"Did he leave before you left work that day"

"No. He was way too busy," she said.

"Do you know if he made any phone calls?

The girl thought for moment. "He was always talkin' on the phone."

Bergman looked at Jans, "Where does this professor live?"

***

Just at that moment, Keysha Jordan and Juleel Washington entered the lobby and saw a policeman cordoning off Robert Brent's office, while another two were taking statements. Over by one of the couches Dean Jans was talking to a piain clothes detective. With combined surprise, they surveyed the scene and hurried to where Dean Jans stood.

Keysha noticed that the plain clothes cop speaking to Dean Jans was the same one who had questioned her a few days after Danielle was murdered. Detective Bergman was his name. He had also been the cop who arrested Jack.

Keysha and Juleel waited as Jans talked to Bergman about Robert Brent. Had something happened to the Head Resident? She sensed serious trouble and dread filled her. Keysha saw Brent's co-ed assistant finish her statement to a uniformed policeman and start to walk their way.

Keysha touched the girl's sleeve as she came close. The girl turned, her bemused face spoke of confusion, "Yes."

"Excuse me," Keysha said. "Is Robert Brent okay?"

The girl, who was dabbing her cheek with a tissue, sobbed, "He's disappeared. Nobody knows where he is."

"Brent's gone!" Juleel exclaimed in disbelief.

"Yeah, I should have known…" Thelma wimpered and ran off leaving Keysha to watch her departure.

Juleel stepped up beside Keysha, "This doesn't sound good."

"Yes, I know, but we still have to see Dean Jans. We've been threatened. We have to do this, Juleel."

Juleel found himself admiring the strength of Keysha Jordan. She was the type who didn't back down to anyone.

He nodded in agreement, "He'll be done with the police soon. We'll wait."

***

Unseen by Keysha and Juleel, Raymon Jackson peered around a support column at the other end of the lobby. He had observed Keysha and Juleel standing to one side of a group of cops and Dean Jans. Talk had reached his ears about Robert Brent's disappearance. He had to laugh. Good riddance as far as he was concerned. Raymon hadn't forgotten Brent's threats from a few weeks before. Brent could go fuck himself. But right now he had another problem.

What were Keysha and the little fag hangin' out beside Jans and the cops? Were they going to run their mouths about him to Dean Jans? Motherfucker. He had tried to be nice; now this. Damn, nobody was going to let him do what was right.

Raymon kept in the shadows and watched. He had been rash in telephoning them. That had been a mistake. But, if they caused him any problems, he'd use his unimpeachable character to accuse them of lying. It was their word against his. What a fool Keysha was and as for the faggot…shit. He'd be one dead queer.

Raymon Jackson was no one to fuck with.

***

Jack raged. He had actually thought of cutting Raymon Jackson a break. Why should he risk expulsion to teach an arrogant asshole, such as Jackson, a lesson? After he had established a relationship with Keysha, humiliating Raymon had momentarily seemed far less important than his feelings for her. In fact, the plan he had so carefully crafted had suddenly felt childish.

But now…

Raymon Jackson was in trouble. Big trouble.

Jack had left Keysha and Juleel to seek their justice from Dean Jans. He wished them luck. They'd need it. He realized Raymon would just lie and deny any connection with them. The running back was the darling of the sports page and the campus. Raymon would fall back on his popularity. No one could touch a football hero or so Jack figured Raymon would think.

Tonight, however, was going to be Raymon Jackson's last night of good press.

In the late afternoon, Jack left Lincoln Hall by the back door and caught a bus to the brick yard where he slipped through a wide place in the back gate. He didn't want to run into Stu Ableson. The older man would try to talk him out of what he knew he must do. As he crossed the yard, a few guys saw him but paid him no mind. Jack was their co-worker, a regular.

Jack retrieved the bag of clothes and other items from his locker and quickly retraced his way through the rear gate and back to the campus. His steps went directly to the Biology Building. He had discovered a hiding place in the basement several weeks before. It was an architectural fluke at the top of one of the decorative pilasters along the wall next to the zoology lab. The pilaster was made of brick and apparently had not been finished off when the building had been constructed. Thanks to the laziness of the builder, it concealed a two foot deep pocket at the top.

When Jack arrived in the hall, a few students were talking here and there; so he waited patiently until the hall cleared. Then, Jack jumped up and grabbed the top of pilaster with one hand and with the other hooked the bag of goodies he'd need for Raymon's surprise into the hole.

Juleel had earlier told Jack that the official Homecoming unveiling of Bob Morgan's statue would be the next morning at eleven o'clock. Jack would be more than ready by that time.

Jack's idea became a vision in his mind, and he managed a small smile. This school would be shown something that they and Raymon Jackson would never forget. What a surprise it would be.

Oh yeah.

He smiled wider. The scars danced on his face making him appear sinister. Nobody fucked with Jack Mulligan's friends.

Nobody.

***

Keysha and Juleel waited until Dean Jans was done speaking with the police and was ready to leave before they approached him.

"Dean Jans," said Keysha boldly, "may we have a word with you?"

Jans turned and took in the exquisite beauty of Keysha Jordan, and then saw she was with a frail looking companion who appeared to have a swollen face.

"Yes, may I help you?"

"Dean Jans, my name is Keysha Jordan and this is Juleel Washington. We are both freshmen here at Mt. Sidney. Today, both of us were threatened by a fellow student."

"Threatened?" Jans asked with a frown.

"Yes, by Raymon Jackson," said Keysha. "In fact, he even assaulted Juleel here. You can see his face is discolored."

Jans pointed to Juleel's face and examined it closer. "Raymon Jackson, the football player, did this to you?"

"Yes sir," said Juleel politely.

"Why?"

Keysha came back, "He threatened me because I won't go out with him, and he threatened and assaulted Juleel because he's Jack Mulligan's roommate."

"Mulligan," Jans' eyes rolled in disbelief. "Not him again."

"Jackson is a bigot, sir," piped in Juleel.

"Well I'll certainly look into this," said Jans frowning impatiently. "But you must understand, I've got another situation going on this minute."

"Of course, Dean Jans," said Keysha triumphantly. "But please do something soon."

"I assure you, young lady, I will."

Then as if on cue, Raymon appeared behind them. He strolled casually through the lobby and then stopped next to Keysha and Juleel as if nothing was wrong. Keysha couldn't believe his audacity.

"Dean Jans, I'm glad you're here," said Raymon in his most polite manner. "I heard that my dear friend, Robert Brent, is missing, and I wanted to say how shocked I am. Is there anything I can do?"

Dean Jans smiled. At last someone with manners, "Thanks for your concern, Raymon. We hope young Brent is okay. The police and especially Detective Bergman are handling the situation."

Jans glanced distastefully at Keysha and Juleel; then changed tone, "By the way, Raymon we have a problem here," he said pointing at Keysha and Juleel, "that involves you. This young lady…"

"Keysha Jordan," interrupted Juleel not liking how the conversation was proceeding.

"Yes, Keysha Jordan and Jamal…"

"Juleel Washington," he corrected again.

Dean Jans glared at Juleel, who glared back. "They say you threatened and assaulted them today."

"What!" exclaimed Raymon in insincere shock. "I hardly even know these two people."

"That's a lie!" snapped Keysha.

"Young lady," warned Jans. "Let Mr. Jackson speak."

"This girl has had this thing for me, which I've tried to discourage. As I've told her, I'm already involved with another girl," said Raymon, who played at indignation. "As far as this guy, he's a liar."

"No, I'm not," said Juleel in indignation.

Dean Jans gestured to Juleel for calm, "Let Raymon talk, son."

447

Keysha noticed Jans and Raymon were on a first name basis.

Raymon continued, "His roommate is Jack Mulligan—the ex-con—and both of them have given me trouble since they came here. If you'd like witnesses, I can produce them."

"This is outrageous," said Keysha.

"He's lying," injected Juleel.

"Enough! I'm going to look into this matter," said Jans coldly. "Something, for sure, is going on here. I don't have time to deal with it this minute. But, I intend to see all of you in my office early next week. Do you understand?"

"Yes, sir."

"Yes, sir."

"Good," concluded Jans. "For now stay away from one another. And Raymon, good luck on Saturday. Make us proud."

"I will, sir."

With that Dean Jans walked away. Raymon's All-American smile faded into an ugly sneer as he gazed at Keysha and Juleel.

Keysha and Juleel both felt a sense of dread spread through them. They knew Raymon had won and that Dean Jans didn't believe one word of their story.

"Good try, but a big mistake," laughed Raymon. "We'll see who Jans believes when I produce forty or so people to testify how you've been giving me a hard time and you Keysha have been stalking me." He then leaned close to Keysha, "Cause you're so jealous of my stardom."

"Oh spare me, Raymon," said Keysha almost in tears.

Raymon wagged a finger at her, "You shouldn't have crossed me, bitch."

Laughing again, Raymon walked away leaving Keysha and Juleel dumbfounded and licking their wounds.

Keysha was speachless, as she glared at Raymon's retreating figure. Juleel realized her angst but had no answers.

"Is there no help for us?" Juleel asked in disgust as he started back to his room.

***

Nathan Ramapo saw three cops, two in uniforms and one plain clothes, start up the sidewalk to his house. There was no way he wanted to talk to them today. Somehow, they must have discovered that Robert Brent had come to visit him and was now missing. He had to hide. Who could tell what they would ask?

Nathan ran for the broom closet in the hall and slipped in just as the door bell chimed. He could tell they'd be looking in the windows to see if he was there. Now was not the time to answer their stupid questions. Sweat poured in rivers from every pore of his body. After Mulligan was found dead, he'd be able to give them all the information they needed.

Predictably, they stayed on his porch for close to an hour. Apparently they had no search warrant or they would have been inside. Christ, what kind of information could they possibly need about that nosey idiot, Brent?

Two hours later, Nathan Ramapo finally crawled out of the closet and shuffled to the front window. Carefully, he peeked around the blind. Sure enough, there was an unmarked police car across the street with two cops posted for surveillance. If they didn't see him by tonight, they'd have a search warrant and be inside by tomorrow. Nathan knew he had to leave.

He spent the next few hours gathering weapons and putting together a change of clothing for Friday night. There wasn't much to carry. Two gym bags contained it all. When the cops came, all they'd get would be notes for his classes. Maybe they'd finally learn something, he thought in amusement. Damn the fools.

When Nathan was finally ready to go, he made a last call to Raymon Jackson. The running back would need final instructions. Two rings transpired before Raymon's voice sounded.

'Whatchu want?" blasted Raymon smartly.

"Mr. Jackson, this is Professor Ramapo. I wanted to touch base with you before our rendezvous this Friday evening to take care of Jack Mulligan."

"I got him goin' already, Professor," said a confident Raymon in a wise-ass voice.

"You what?"

"Check it out," said Raymon gleefully. "I slapped his faggot roommate up side of the head today; then called Mulligan and got in his face."

Don't!" exclaimed Ramapo.

"What's a matter?"

"Stay away from Mulligan until Friday night, Mr. Jackson. Everything is planned. If you engage him now, it could ruin the final outcome and don't tell anyone what you're doing. Understand?"

Raymon could be heard breathing a sigh of frustration. "What the fuck?" he said.

"Don't screw this up, Mr. Jackson," shouted Ramapo.

"But…"

Ramapo interrupted in a quieter voice, "Mr. Jackson, this Friday that white bastard will have the biggest and nastiest surprise of his short, pathetic life."

"Well hallelujah," said Raymon coldly.

"Mr. Jackson, please. I implore you, stay away from him until Friday. Just make sure you're near the phone that evening."

"Yeah, yeah, yeah. I'll leave the motherfucker alone," said a disconsolate Raymon. "But you'd better have something good planned for him."

"Oh I do," said Nathan emphatically. "You can count on that. And Mr. Jackson, you'll get your licks in too."

Before Raymon could say another word, Nathan hung up the phone and grabbed his bags. He checked the back yard and slipped out into the early evening darkness. The police, at this point, probably wouldn't be guarding the alley. He cautiously opened the back gate and checked. Nothing. Then, sticking to the shadows, he stealthily slipped down the alley.

It was time to go into hiding where no one would be able to find him.

CHAPTER 50

Once things broke, they broke quickly. Action on a case, Sam Bergman had discovered long ago, came quickly sometimes, like a house of cards falling. A hunch told him that if photos of Mt. Sidney's personnel were compared to the FBI photos from thirty-four years before, someone was going to drop out in front of him. Methodically, he began comparing the photos taking in consideration how age could change Thaddeus Brown.

His desk became a staging area for the procedure. Bergman had heard years ago from an experienced detective in New York that a person's ears and nose didn't change with age. So, Bergman was careful to observe those features in particular.

While deep in this study, the phone rang, startling him. He irritably picked it up on the second ring, "Bergman."

"Lieutenant Bergman this is Steve Bachmann. We've been busy with a lead we have that Thaddeus Brown spent several years in a Seminary in Quebec. The Canadian Mounted Police questioned a Father

Charles D'Vesso, but he hasn't been very cooperative."

"Did anyone explain to him that murder was involved?"

"Yes, but he claims all his knowledge is confidential," said Bachmann. "The Mounties told us D'Vesso is a hard nut to crack. However, they think he knows our man Brown."

"Do you have a phone number, Steve, for D'Vesso? Maybe I can take a crack at him."

Bachmann exhaled, "What makes you think you'll do better?"

"I may not," said Bergman. "But, I'd like to try."

"Well okay," Bachmann relented, "but don't expect much."

Bachmann repeated the number twice, wished Sam luck and hung up. Bergman immediately dialed Canada and waited as a phone rang. A voice came on the other end of the line with a heavy French accent, "*Bon Jour*."

"Hello, I'd like to talk to Father Charles D'Vesso."

"This is he," came the reply in perfect English.

"This is Lieutenant Sam Bergman with the Mt. Sidney, Ohio, Police. May I have a minute of your time?"

"But of course, Lieutenant."

"Father D'Vesso many years ago you had a man working at the Catholic Shelter named Thaddeus Brown. Do you remember him?"

A moment passed in silence.

"Father are you still there?"

"Yes I'm here," said D'Vesso in a subdued tone, "but I know no one by that name."

"Father," warned Bergman, "please don't lie to me."

"I don't lie, Lieutenant but…"

"But what?"

"I'm a priest," said D'Vesso softly. "What people tell me in confidence, I keep in confidence."

"I understand Father, but this man may be a murderer."

Now it was the priest's turn to ponder, "I'll take your word for that, Lieutenant."

"That's fair."

"But I'm not sure I would have any information that could help you," D'Vesso said in a kindly voice.

"Father, we've traced this man to you," Sam said emphatically.

"Lieutenant, if you need a name, I'll give you some names of some past workers from the soup kitchen. Would that be of help?"

Bergman would have liked more but settled for this scrap. "Well if that's the best you can do," he said.

"Maybe one of them would fit someone you know of. But may I warn you, that's as far as I can help."

"Okay."

D'Vesso immediately rolled off twenty names from the top of his head. Bergman wrote them down frantically.

"That's all I can do, Lieutenant," said D'Vesso. "Please don't ask me for more."

"You've been a big help, Father. Thanks."

Sam Bergman hung up the phone and sat back. The Father had helped much more than he could have imagined. One of the names near the top of the list was Nathan Ramapo.

***

The night was cold and dark on Wednesday with no moon shining. Jack couldn't believe his luck. If there was one thing he didn't want, it was a full moon.

He stood at the window to his room and sensed an uncertain edginess in his gut from the slow rise of adrenalin. It was a welcome feeling to him for it meant his sensory processors were coming into total focus.

He had been quiet at dinner, listening intently to Juleel and Keysha complain of their failures with Dean Jans and the cockiness of Raymon Jackson. Little did they know what he planned for Raymon. They didn't need to know either. Tomorrow would be a new day for the football player and not a happy one either.

After dinner, he took a walk with Keysha, and they talked about everything and anything but Raymon Jackson. Jack deliberately steered the conversation into safe areas with a lighter tone. He wanted Keysha to harbor no suspicions about him when all was said and done. Upon their return to the dorm, he told her he had to study for a test and would see her at breakfast. They kissed and he nearly decided not to do what he knew he must. Fortunately, the thought of Raymon Jackson continuing his unbridled reign of terror kept him on track.

Jack studied dutifully till ten-thirty and said goodnight to Juleel at eleven. He needed an alibi, and Juleel was going to give him one. Juleel yawned too and was soon getting ready for bed. Tomorrow, Juleel would only be able to say Jack was in the room all evening and went to bed early. Jack didn't want anyone knowingly lying for him.

By eleven-thirty he could hear Juleel's even breathing as he slept. Jack slipped from his bed and quietly got dressed. He watched Juleel's face to make sure he wasn't faking sleep. Jack was taking no chances. He then crossed the room and slipped through the door, closing it without stirring Juleel.

Now he had to hurry.

Jack went out the back entrance and stood in the darkness to let his eyes adjust. From where he stood, he could see the parking lot behind the building. He had overheard students say that Raymon Jackson was out every night with a different girl and that he didn't walk. As Jack figured, Jackson's car wasn't in the parking area. Good, he needed time to get to the Biology Building, change into dark clothing and get back.

Darting from tree to tree, he made sure he wasn't seen by any students on a late evening stroll or worse, by campus security. Since Danielle's murder, they had doubled their patrols.

Jack crossed one of the main sidewalks and moved up to a two story brick building. This was the Biology Building, and it sat like an overweight bulldog, squat and modern having only been constructed ten years before. It had rounded corners on the basement level, all concrete and no windows at all, but on one end, there was a single steel door. He crept up silently in the night and listened. No odd sounds came. He had earlier in the day taped back the lock on the door. Jack prayed that no one had spotted his work. He breathed a sigh when the door opened easily.

Inside, he moved cautiously down the hallway to the unfinished pilaster. Jumping up, he grabbed the top of the block wall pulled himself up and grabbed the bag of clothes. Somewhere far off, Jack heard voices. It was probably graduate students working late. The voices were coming closer, just ahead near the stairwell. This wasn't good. Jack had thought he could change in the deserted hallway.

Someone laughed, another door clanged. He saw a door ahead on the right wall and ran for it. Fortunately, it wasn't locked. Jack slipped through into a dark cubicle smelling of strong disinfectant, closed the door and leaned against it, listening.

Footsteps came closer and stopped. Had someone seen him? He held his breath and finally he heard the footsteps move on.

Jack waited three or four minutes in the dark, listening. Perspiration beaded on his forehead and ran into his eyes almost blinding him. The closet was oppressive and stuffy. Finally, he let his breath out and felt around in the dark until he found a chain for the closet light. The single bulb ignited in 100 watts of brightness. He squinted and looked around at the brooms and cleaning supplies. Thankfully there was enough room to change into the dark clothing.

His movements were economical and rapid as he changed. He finally donned the black ski mask to complete his ensemble and within a minute had packed his other clothing back into the bag. Carefully, he opened the door, and the cool air in the hallway immediately refreshed him. The hallway was empty, but Jack stood listening a moment. Then he ran to the pilaster, jumped up and stowed the bag once more into opening in the top.

Then, from a distance, he heard footsteps.

Jack whirled and raced down the hallway to the outer door. Easing it open, he stepped out, glancing back one more time, he saw no one and silently closed it.

Hopefully, nobody heard his footsteps or saw him.

A moment later, he clambered across the top of the wooded slope, crossed the lane and moved into the shadowy, wooded area next to the back parking lot of Lincoln Hall. Raymon's space was still empty. He must still be visiting his girlfriend, Jack thought.

There was a huge boxwood bush twisting out of the ground only thirty or so feet from where Raymon always parked. Jack squatted behind it and waited. With any luck, Raymon would be back shortly. Jack was patient, incarceration had taught him that.

His wait wasn't long, however. A few moments later, he saw Raymon's BMW cruise into the lot, its lights speared the dark but didn't penetrate the boxwood's dense branches. Still, Jack laid flat and waited. The car pulled into the parking space, and the lights and engine went dead together.

Jack gathered himself. He reached into a pocket and took out a roll of quarters and placed it firmly in his right hand. Why hurt his hand? He was about to start forward when once again lights illuminated the night. A security car, with a glaring searchlight rolled into the parking lot. Its search beam came to rest on Raymon's car as he got out. Raymon held up a hand to shield his eyes, and the light was pulled away.

Jack flattened on the ground and listened as the car stopped and the campus police spoke, "That you, Raymon?"

"Yeah man, I'm seein' spots now. That light is bright."

"Sorry," said the voice from inside the car. "We're just patrolling. With the Myers girl dead...you know how it is."

"Yeah," said Raymon irritably.

"Well have a good night and good luck on Saturday," said the cop doing the talking.

"Yeah man, thanks."

The security car then slowly moved off.

Jack scanned the lighted windows of Lincoln Hall and satisfied himself that nobody was watching. He figured now he'd have to take Raymon out in the open. The security car had eliminated any element of surprise. It would have been so much easier to have stepped up and ambushed Jackson. Then, as if a prayer had been answered, Raymon ducked back into his car to retrieve his keys.

That was all Jack needed.

He raced forward gliding like a big cat. He was behind Raymon who suddenly turned at the sound of footsteps.

Raymon's eyes widened at the tall black shape. Jack struck with everything he had. The first blow was wicked and unexpected. His fist nailed Raymon flush on the chin, and the running back fell backwards his knees sagging and hitting the pavement.

Christ, the guy must have a glass jaw, thought Jack. Raymon was knocked out cold.

Jack picked Raymon up by the shirt front and slung him over his shoulder. He then ran behind the boxwood bush and placed Raymon out of sight. Quickly, he ran back to the car and shut its door and returned to Raymon.

In the bag, Jack retrieved the duct tape. He tore strips and bound Raymon's hands and feet, plus one over his mouth.

Now came the tough part. Jack would have to carry Raymon a quarter of a mile to the Homecoming statue.

Watching and listening again with caution, Jack assured himself that no one had seen him. He picked up Raymon and started off. The football player was heavier than he had thought he'd be.

Breathing deeply, Jack moved in a wary crouch through the deep shadows of the trees, trying to stay in the dark and watch out for security cops and other students. Ahead, he saw an open area with some baseball diamonds. He avoided that, and took a more circuitous route which skirted it and stayed close to the trees.

Suddenly, Jack could feel Raymon regaining consciousness and begin to struggle. He edged forward behind a tree and unceremoniously dumping Raymon. Then leaning down, Jack pulled Raymon's head around by the ear till the running back was looking directly into his masked face.

"Stay still punk, or I swear I'll kill you right here. Do you understand?"

Raymon's eyes were wide with fright as he nodded.

Once again Jack picked Raymon up and tossed him over his shoulder. Jack clenched his teeth and adjusted Raymon's considerable weight.

Jack started forward picking up the pace. Time was wasting. He ran in a squatted position around the last of the clearing, keeping his eyes open. The only sound he could make out was the strong breeze rustling the tree branches. The brittle winter limbs swayed in the dark sky, and Jack lowered his head and kept going. His legs screamed with exhaustion from the weight.

He could now see the bulk of the Homecoming statue ahead.

The last twenty yards or so were the longest. Jack's legs churned as he sprinted the distance and ducked under the tarp. There was little space to stand, so he gently laid Raymon down and squatted to catch his breath. His legs felt rubbery.

Between the opening in the tarp, Jack could now see on his radium watch it was twelve-thirty. He had a lot of work to do and had to get started. Since this was Raymon's big moment, he wanted the fool to enjoy every second of it.

***

Sam Bergman arrived at Nathan Ramapo's rented house with a dozen uniformed cops. He had made record time, having awakened a beleaguered local judge for a search warrant and had driven at high speed to the residence.

After knocking on the door, two burly uniformed cops broke it down with a ram. The cops—guns drawn—fanned out. Bergman barked out orders with practiced precision. A thorough search of the house revealed that Ramapo wasn't there and that nothing of immediate value was evident. The stacks of books and papers were in such disorganization, Bergman knew it would take days to sift through them.

Bergman sent one of the uniformed cops out for two large coffees and sat down to have a look at Nathan Ramapo's digs. It was going to be a long night. How could this guy function in this mess? Every room was cluttered. Sam couldn't tell which stack of paper or which of the thousands of books lying on the floor might reveal some shred of pertinent information.

Bergman and two other detectives began searching. It was like trying to find a needle in a haystack without the benefit of knowing what the needle looked like. Hours passed and more coffee was consumed. Towards morning, Bergman and the other men had to conceded that Ramapo had left nothing of value.

Jans had said Robert Brent was bent on talking to Ramapo about who could possibly have leaked word about Mulligan's past. It was Bergman's guess that Ramapo himself was the person. But, who would he have used to disseminate the information around campus? Another faculty member? Or, maybe a student? The latter made more sense. Ramapo could control a younger person easier. Perhaps the student could even work a deal for a better grade.

If it was a student, he probably would have met the young man or woman on campus. And, if his new hunch was valid, Ramapo would have had all meetings with the student in his office.

His office, yes…

Suddenly his Uncle Saul came to mind. He had been the bachelor brother of his mother and had kept an apartment a few blocks away from his parents. The apartment was somewhat like this one, with papers and books stacked high and garbage in the sink. Saul was a slob. Ironically, Uncle Saul's office was immaculate and well organized. Could it be that Ramapo's office was where he really conducted business.

It made sense. They were wasting time here. He'd wake up Dean Jans immediately.

Bergman noted the first gray light of morning easing through the window and looked at his watch. It was still early, but Jans would probably be up by now.

Just then, a uniformed cop came in from the back of the house. "Sir, could you come with me. I think we found something."

Sam followed the uniformed cop around the outside of the house, to a wooden potting shed where a thick overgrown hedge fought with the grass for space. Several policemen were gathered around a barren spot in the otherwise thick, unkempt grass.

"Sir, we think you'd better look at this," said a big Polish Sergeant named Mohowski.

Sam could see that the bare spot had been dug recently.

"It looks like a grave," Bergman muttered, a chill of dread running down his spine.

"That's what we thought," said Mohowski.

"Let's dig it up," Bergman ordered.

Two men grabbed shovels and ten minutes later they stepped back. In the dirt, lying limply, was an uncovered hand. Bergman's stomach tightened, especially when with a few more shovelfuls of soil, it was confirmed. The body in the shallow grave was the rotting corpse of Robert Brent.

Bergman made calls to the coroner, State Police and to the DA and twenty minutes later a manhunt was set in motion to apprehend Professor Nathan Ramapo a.k.a. Thaddeus Brown.

CHAPTER 51

Nathan Ramapo observed the police from down the street, while crouched behind a large maple tree in old man Simons' front yard. Simons, he knew, was inside sound asleep. Nathan could tell by all the activity that his days in Mt. Sidney were now definitely over. He had a sinking feeling. All he had worked for—everything—was now destroyed. Where would he go; how would he live? The questions festered in his demented mind.

He was too old now to run and start over. It wasn't like years before when, as a wanted man, he could escape unnoticed from one region of the country and flee to another. Now with improved communications, the Internet and even those blasted TV shows that highlighted men and women escaping the law, it was hard to slip through the cracks. The long arm of the law had gotten longer.

What could he do?

Nathan pondered his situation as he headed into town. He realized, of course, he had to get off the street. The cops would be setting up an all points

465

bulletin and a manhunt would tighten to a street by street search. He knew that all the bus stations, airports, hotels and motels in a fifty to seventy mile radius would be searched. Nathan had an ace, however.

Years before, a now-retired maintenance man had shown him a hidden room in the basement of Woodburn Hall, the oldest structure on Mt. Sidney's campus. As a former part of the Underground Railroad, this hidden room was virtually unknown to most of the campus. To get inside, a person had to crawl through a three foot high passage in the stone wall of the foundation to a musty room that measured no more than ten feet square.

This was where he would hide, but first he had to get a few days worth of food and water to take with him. Once he was inside, he knew he wouldn't be able to leave until Friday night.

There was a convenience store just off campus where he could get supplies. If he hurried, he'd have a chance. The window of time was closing. Soon the cops would have all avenues of escape sealed off, and everyone would be looking for him. He had to hurry.

Tears, angry frustrated tears, came to his eyes. He'd never truly see home again. He'd never feel love or peace of mind ever again. Had his last experience with that feeling really been his parent's home in Kentucky? That was so long ago.

Jack Mulligan would pay for this, truly pay.

***

Jack checked his handiwork with a measure of dark humor and pride. Under the tarp of the Homecoming statue, unseen yet by the public, was what some would call a true piece of art.

This one would indeed make history.

Except for a large adult fitted brief which looked like a diaper, Raymon was now strapped naked to the statue of Bob Morgan. To anyone who would observe the running back at this critical juncture, they could have observed Raymon hugging the big statue as a baby would embrace its mother.

That's how Jack perceived Raymon as a loud-mouthed, spoiled baby. This one, of course, was in dire need of a lesson in manners. It was time for the public to see the same thing. To hell with all the sport's hero shit and the God-like persona the press had built for this bigoted, self-centered idiot.

Just as a finishing touch, Jack had a message of school spirit for good ol' Mt. Sidney College printed on Raymon's brief. "Rah, rah, rah," smiled Jack at the thought.

Because of the cold, Jack had carefully enclosed Raymon in a blanket, like a protective cocoon. The blanket was crudely sewn into the tarp so it would come off when it was raised. It would not only protect "baby" from the elements, but unless some nosey fool really checked, it would keep Raymon hidden until the tarp was pulled off at the eleven o'clock ceremony.

Jack checked his watch. It was three-thirty. He had to get back to the Biology Building, change clothes again and slip back into his own room.

Jack climbed a step ladder one of the work crew had left and leaned next to Raymon's ear, "This is payback, Jackson," he whispered coldly. "If anymore shit happens to Juleel or Keysha, I'll snuff your sorry fucking ass permanently. *Comprende*, motherfucker?"

Raymon's eyes showed true terror. He understood.

***

A half hour later, Jack and Nathan Ramapo passed within sixty feet of one another. Both were on separate, but related, clandestine missions: one of hate; the other of revenge. These two operations would merge someday. Destiny called for that.

Nathan kept to the shadows of the trees and bushes, till he reached a side door at Woodburn Hall. All the department heads had universal keys to the buildings of Mt. Sidney College. Nathan let himself in and went directly to the basement.

He carried a large bag of crackers, peanut butter, cookies and bottled water he had purchased at the 7-11 just off campus. The time inside the store had been stressful as groups of police cars with sirens barreled by on the way to his house and the body of Robert Brent.

Thankfully, the cops hadn't gotten hungry along the way and stopped at the store. The clerk, a dark Indian man, must have wondered why Nathan was perspiring so much. He kept looking at Nathan's deranged appearance and assessing his nervous manner. Maybe the clerk thought he'd pull a gun. Nathan's shirt clung dark and wet to his body on what was a cold evening. Sweat rolled down his cheeks. Fortunately, the clerk asked no questions.

Ramapo was glad to leave the store and head off across campus at a fast clip. Time was running out.

The police were everywhere, patrolling. His eyes darted around as he sought shadows and hid behind trees to avoid detection. When he finally came to a side door to Woodburn Hall, he breathed a sigh as he slipped his key in and entered the deserted structure.

He stood motionless for a moment listening for any human sounds but none came. The cleaning crew had already gone home. He was blessedly alone.

Quickly, he ran for the nearby stairwell, and descended the steps into the basement.

Along with the groceries, Nathan had a gym bag with his two .45's and a dozen clips. In the dusty basement, he saw the small wooden door at the foot of the foundation that the janitor had shown him years ago. It was the entrance to the tunnel and the stone room. Nathan felt no hesitation about entering the dark passage, the hell hounds were on his trail. He pulled the door open, peered into the dark and then crawled in. A musty smell hit his nose. How he hated closed spaces, but there was no choice. He closed the door behind him, and then, on all fours, he dragged the bags until he knew he was inside the inner chamber.

Nathan searched his pockets and found the pack of matches he had picked up at the store. Lighting one, he looked around with a chill. The place reminded him of a medieval dungeon. The stone walls were windowless and the air was dank and stale. Cobwebs hung everywhere and here and there were remanants of old wooden crates. He could sense the fearful spirits of slaves who had huddled here before the Civil War. They were his ancestors and very much like himself—desperate and hunted.

Nathan blew the match out, and total darkness suddenly surrounded him. Like death, it grasped him, enveloping him as if inside a heavy cloak. In this place of isolation nothing could penetrate the eyes.

He could withstand this, he told himself and much more if need be. Witness what he had already endured, so far. This would be a piece of cake. After all, Friday night was only two more nights away.

Death, he smiled, lay in the wings.

***

Meanwhile, Jack Mulligan silently crept back into his dorm room. Juleel never stirred. He lay sound asleep. Jack noted his roommate's even breathing.

His mission was accomplished. Raymon's fate was sealed.

Jack climbed silently into his bed and fell into a deep, sound sleep.

CHAPTER 52

Thursday morning dawned sunny with a heavy, late autumn frost. Keysha was up early, showered and dressed. It was going to be a wonderful day, she determined. Raymon could threaten all he wanted but nothing would spoil her day with Jack. She was in love, and all was right with the world.

Keysha decided to stop by Jack's room and see if he'd like to have breakfast with her. Going down the hall on his floor, she saw Juleel leaving with his book bag slung over his shoulder.

"Hey Juleel is Jack awake?" she said smiling.

"Actually, he's still asleep."

"Asleep!"

"Yeah," said Juleel, shaking his head. "That's unusual. He's most times awake before I am."

Keysha smirked, "Well, Mr. Sleepy Head had better get up. I'm having breakfast with him."

With that she crossed in front of Juleel and stepped into the room. There was Jack fast asleep and snoring softly.

Keysha sat down on the edge of his bed and began kissing his neck and cheek ever so softly. Jack stirred, his eyes opening to her touch.

"This is the best wake-up call I've ever had," he said hoarsely as he rolled over.

"Well I should hope so, Mr. Mulligan," Keysha said softly. "Are you going to have breakfast with me?"

"Can you give me five minutes?"

"Oh I guess so," said Keysha playing at impatience. "I'll meet you in the cafeteria. Remember five minutes."

Actually twelve minutes passed before Jack sat his tray down across from her. His eyes were puffy from lack of sleep.

"You look exhausted," she said.

"I know…I studied late."

"Well rest up today. We have a date tomorrow night."

"I won't forget."

Keysha then waved at someone in back of Jack. He turned to see Tyrel come ambling up.

"Mind if I join you?" he asked.

"Have a seat," said Jack.

"You guys going to the Homecoming presentation today?" asked Tyrel, putting his tray down. "You know Bob Morgan is going to be there."

Jack gave a puzzled expression.

"Coach of the Buccaneers," filled in Tyrel as if asked.

"Oh," said Jack, embarrassed.

"Don't worry, Jack, I didn't know either," added Keysha.

"You're not a football fan, Jack?" Tyrel asked.

"No, I never had a chance to get into sports."

Tyrel gave an expression of disbelief, "Man you should have. You look as strong as an ox. And I know you're quick. You could have been a real good football player."

Jack shrugged unconvinced, "Well maybe."

"Anyway, the statue is going to get a lot of press," said Tyrel as he buttered his toast.

"I'll see if I can get there," said Keysha. "This guy Morgan sounds important."

"He's in the Football Hall of Fame. I don't know why we have to have a statue though," Tyrel said.

"I do," said Jack to everyone's surprise. "I mean, I saw a lot of people working on it."

Keysha was surprised, "Well good for you Jack. I guess you appreciate all that hard work. Are you going to be there?"

"Sorry, but I have to be in the library. I'm doing a paper."

Tyrel smiled, "Well still, I think Jack is starting to get some school spirit."

Jack answered by shrugging and sipping his coffee.

"What time will that unveiling be?" Keysha asked.

"Eleven."

Jack spoke first, "That's early."

"Yeah, I guess they don't want it to interfere with afternoon practice."

"Will you be there, Tyrel?" asked Keysha.

"Yeah, I have to be. Coach Dunn says so."

"Well, I'll try to be in the crowd," Keysha said in support.

"I think Juleel said he would be there, too," added Jack. "He loves football."

"Or the players," laughed Keysha and the others joined in. "We're going to be at the game Saturday."

"Homecoming at its best," smiled Tyrel, then as if he were feeling guilty for a happy thought, "I only wish Danielle was here."

Keysha placed a hand on Tyrel's arm. She could tell he was still hurt by Danielle's murder but he carried on.

"Try to enjoy it, Tyrel. She'd want you to."

"I will," he said. "Or at least try."

"Hey good luck, Saturday," said Jack trying to lighten the moment as he prepared to leave.

"Yeah, it's going to be a rough game."

Jack looked into space as if his mind was far away, "Yeah, I heard you are playing a tough team."

Keysha wondered what Jack was thinking of. His part of the conversation had seemed strange and nearly surreal. There were still pieces of him that seemed to remain a mystery.

***

The dragnet grew tighter and tighter around Mt. Sidney as Sam Bergman coordinated every available man to search for Nathan Ramapo. The "Mad Professor," as his men and the press now dubbed him, had to be somewhere nearby. All the airports, bus depots, taxi and train stations were notified. Every building on Mt. Sidney's campus was searched. Police patrols were now doubled.

The morning paper had run a large, recent photo of Nathan Ramapo, and was setting up a hotline. Dean Jans was helping by putting together a reward for any information. Bergman applauded his actions. Maurice Jans seemed an odd duck. He was a planner who weighed every move he made. Bergman figured he only performed an action if there was something in it for himself. In this case, he was facing the college's alumni and parents who were very angry. His job and reputation were on the line. Two murders would do that.

Steve Bachmann had sent a contingent of FBI men to Mt. Sidney, and they were putting together a five state task force in the search effort. Canadian police had been notified along with Interpol in case Ramapo tried to flee the country.

A search of the professor's office had indeed turned up a list of names that included, Keysha Jordan, Jack Mulligan and Raymon Jackson. Bergman wondered if Nathan Ramapo would try to murder the people named on the list. In addition, a number of hate publications concerned with black power were found and an essay on the black man's struggle in a white, bigoted world.

He sent a cop out to inform those individual's on the list to be extra careful.

Now came the long wait. This was the worse part of police work, especially during a man hunt. Everything hinged on Nathan Ramapo making a mistake and Bergman knew he would.

Bergman sensed that the professor was nearby. Ramapo would show. Bergman could feel it in his bones.

***

Raymon struggled against the multiple layers of duct tape to no avail. Because of the blow to his chin, he was now completely disoriented. His mental faculties were too dull to put together a definitive plan. All he could figure was that he was stuck in a dark place with his body strapped to a pole or something.

But what?

If he could only yell for help, he could get out of here, but the duct tape was wrapped tightly around his head and covered his mouth. Panic set in but came in waves that peaked and ebbed.

Where was he?

Despite the ski mask, Raymon knew the mugger was Jack Mulligan. The white boy's rock-hard fist had once more caught him on the chin. Raymon felt it must be just luck. Just once he'd like to get a good shot at Mulligan. He'd beat the white off Mulligan's sorry, pale ass. In fact when he got out of this, he was going to personally stomp Mulligan into the dirt.

At day break, the sun started warming the plastic tarps and the blankets around him. The temperature inside was stifling. Raymon itched, as sweat slowly—oh so slowly—rolled down his back. It was maddening. If the torture didn't stop…

Time seemed to crawl in this eternity. Would anyone ever discover him bound in the dark?

The hours of the morning slipped by, and he could hear voices as people gathered for the official unveiling of the statue. When in the hell would someone find him? Would he die here before they saw him trussed like a Thanksgiving turkey?

How much longer?

How much…?

Motherfucker!

CHAPTER 53

By ten-thirty, a crowd numbering in the hundreds gathered around the cloaked Homecoming statue. The Wildcat marching band and cheerleaders were poised and ready for their cue to start the school's fight song. On the edge of the gathering, reporters stood chatting together, ready to catch a picture of Bob Morgan and Coach Dunn or better yet Bob Morgan with Raymon Jackson next to the unveiled statue. The old order next to the new order made good copy.

Two days before, a series of cables had been rigged and tested. On a signal, four students would pull the massive blue tarp upward to reveal the statue. Then, the band would strike up the fight song and Homecoming would officially begin.

Tyrel was among a small group of football players standing at the side of the podium. He eyed the growing crowd apprehensively, since he had to say a few words about Saturday's game. No matter how he felt inside, this was part of the school's tradition and he owed the school enough not to spoil the event for others.

"Hey Tyrel, have you seen Raymon?" said Coach Dunn, who suddenly appeared at his side. "He knows he's supposed to be here already."

"I don't know, Coach," Tyrel drawled. "I ain't seen him."

"Damn, that kid," said Dunn bitterly. "I'll have his hide if he doesn't get here soon."

Dunn then stalked off angrily into the crowd.

"Man, the Coach looks pissed," said Damian Redman, the huge tight end.

"Yeah, Raymon's suppose to be here," said Tyrel.

"Shit man. The Superstar. He gonna catch it this time," said Redman with delight.

"Yeah."

"Hell, Tyrel," Redman smiled, "with all these newspaper cats, it'd seem to me Raymon'd be doin' a break dance."

"Tyrel!" came a voice behind him.

Tyrel turned and saw Keysha working her way through the shoulder to shoulder crowd with Juleel just behind her. Both looked excited by all the fanfare.

"Hey Tyrel," she shouted looking around at the festivities. "This is great."

"Yeah, except Raymon was suppose to be here and isn't."

Keysha rolled her eyes, "Maybe 'god' had a more important event on his calendar."

Tyrel laughed, "Yeah, but the Coach is going to have god's ass if he doesn't show up. The Coach has Bob Morgan ready to talk about the team and especially Raymon, and he isn't here."

479

"He'll show up I'm sure," said Keysha, who figured Raymon would come waltzing in any minute. He was too self-centered to miss this.

"What did you think of Professor Ramapo being charged with murder?" asked Keysha.

"What!" Tyrel said in shock.

"It's been in the paper and on TV all morning," piped Juleel, who pulled a newspaper from his back pocket. "Here. Look at this."

Tyrel unfolded the newspaper's front page to a photo of Nathan Ramapo. The headline and the first two paragraphs said he was being sought for the murder of Robert Brent and considered a prime suspect in the murder of co-ed, Danielle Myers. In addition, the FBI was being called in because Ramapo, whose real name was Thaddeus Brown, was wanted for the murder of a Marine Corps Drill Instructor.

"Oh shit!" he muttered in shock.

Keysha saw Tyrel pale, "You look more than surprised, Tyrel."

"Shit, why didn't I think?" he whispered.

"Think about what?"

"What's wrong, Tyrel?" Juleel said.

Tyrel slapped the newspaper in his hand and gasped.

"Tyrel…" said Keysha.

"The night that Danielle was murdered," exclaimed Tyrel, "I saw Professor Ramapo come wandering out of some thick bushes close to Lincoln Hall. He acted funny, but I thought he was just weird. You know what I'm sayin'? He said he was just out for a walk."

Keysha and Juleel looked at each other.

"You have to tell the police this, Tyrel. You know that cop, Detective Bergman," Keysha suggested.

"I'll bet I know why he was there," said Tyrel in sudden revelation. "I'll bet he was planting the knife outside your window, Juleel."

"Of course!" exclaimed Juleel.

"Want to hear something else," said Keysha. "A cop came by this morning and told me my name was on a list that Professor Ramapo had in his office. Juleel said the same cop came later to warn Jack, too. That's scary."

"You'd better be careful," warned Tyrel. "Ramapo could be anywhere."

A stir in the crowd caused the three friends to look up. Reporters were rushing across the grass to Dean Jans who had just appeared walking toward the podium. The Dean appeared gray and tired, and his normally straight shoulders were slumped.

The reporters surrounded him, yelling questions about Nathan Ramapo. Jans held his hands up and only said, "No comment." Then he continued on his way.

The band raised their instruments and struck up a march tune, and the dignitaries, which included Jans, Coach Dunn and especially Bob Morgan, took seats on the stage in front of the veiled statue. Conspicuously absent was Raymon Jackson.

"I've got to go, but I'm calling the cops as soon as this is over," said Tyrel, who turned and weaved back through the crowd to join a group of players beside the stage.

The speeches soon began starting with Dean Jans' who droned on for twenty or so minutes. There was the usual praise for the school and the football team.

481

Raymon's name was mentioned and Coach Dunn could be seen scanning the multitude, desperately trying to spot his star player.

Everyone wondered where the Raymon could be on such a momentous occasion. How could he not be here? Didn't he possess true school spirit?

Jans introduced Coach Dunn who, in turn, spoke a few brief sentences about homecoming and school spirit before introducing Bob Morgan. Morgan was a large, gray-haired man with a slight paunch and kindly eyes. Dunn praised Morgan for his incredible years at Mt. Sidney when Morgan was an All-American, and then elaborated on the All-Pro years in the NFL. Now, Bob Morgan was the Head Coach of the Buccaneers and chairman of several impressive charities.

With roaring applause, Coach Dunn said his final words, which echoed in the cold autumn air, "We can all be proud as students at Mt. Sidney College and as African-Americans for the gigantic achievements of Coach Bob Morgan. Ladies and gentlemen, I give you retired number 38, Bob Morgan."

At a signal, the four students who controlled the ropes and pulleys attached to the tarps went to work. Simultaneously, the marching band struck up the Wildcat fight song, Bob Morgan pulled out a prepared speech from his jacket and slowly walked to the podium. On the way, Coach Dunn smiled and shook hands with him.

The blue tarp lifted foot by foot as the four young men hauled it up. Then a collective gasp escaped the anxious crowd as they stared in disbelief.

Bob Morgan saw their faces and turned.

Keysha and Juleel's mouths dropped. Tyrel's eyes widened in disbelief. The band's fight song dribbled off into a few sour notes. There on the Homecoming statue of heroic Bob Morgan was another football hero. Raymon Jackson was naked except for a bright white adult brief. On the diaper-like brief, a message was scrawled in bold black letters for all to see.

"BABY SAYS, "Go Wildcats!"

Coach Dunn was the first to react, followed by Dean Jans as they rushed to Raymon's side.

Camera flashes erupted as a hundred cameras took the same picture.

Other team members stared in disbelief as Dunn pulled the duct tape from the running back's face. Raymon screamed with each yank of the tape. He could be heard above the rising din of the crowd.

"Motherfucker!" he screamed over and over.

Coach Dunn then spoke into Raymon's ear to can the obscenities.

From somewhere in the crowd, the first lilt of laughter started and grew. More and more students and general onlookers chuckled and guffawed. Humor, a reaction like crying, comes at odd times and is indeed contagious. This crowd suddenly couldn't stop. Although cruel, the people clearly disguised their discomfort and self-doubt by laughing.

The news reporters, for their part, snapped photos from every angle. They ran to the statue to get close ups and any kind of quote from Coach Dunn, Dean Jans or the now stricken Bob Morgan.

Once Raymon was released, his legs wobbled from hours in a cramped position. Coach Dunn and Dean Jans held Raymon under the arms and helped him from the podium. Raymon's teammates stood slack-jawed but unmoved. They were not fans of Raymon Jackson. They knew what a self-centered braggart the arrogant running back was. It was ironically perfect seeing him get his. Why help him? They knew he'd never stand up for them.

Meanwhile, the flashes of the news cameras and whirring sound of camera motor drives was more audible than the chatter of the crowd. This was a story that would run on the front pages of all the regional papers. Even newspapers such as the *New York Times* and *Washington Post* would carry an article due to Bob Morgan being nationally known. Like it or not, shocking items such as the downfall, or in this case, the stumbling of a celebrity was the fodder the press loved to print. It made human, the once infallible, and brought all-stars to the same playing field as the rest of humanity.

The photo of Raymon Jackson in an adult fitted brief would be everywhere by evening. Then, everyone could join in the laughter and enjoy seeing Raymon's embarrassment. He'd forever be known for this, and not for anything he'd ever do on the gridiron.

Keysha and Juleel caught each others expressions of disbelief. Then something told both of them that Jack was at the bottom of Raymon's malaise. How had he pulled it off?

"Are you thinking what I'm thinking?" asked Juleel.

"Yes I am," said Keysha laughing. "I usually don't like seeing this kind of thing. But…" her face turning to laughter, "It couldn't have happen to a nicer guy."

Keysha then grabbed Juleel by the arm and pulled him out of the crowd. She stopped when she was out of everyone's ear shot. "Did Jack do this?"

"He couldn't," said Juleel. "He was in our room all night."

"Are you sure?"

"Yes," Juleel said shaking his head.

Keysha shook her head and asked again, "Couldn't he have slipped out? Remember how unusually tired he was this morning?"

"No, I would have heard him. I'm a light sleeper."

Actually, Juleel slept heavily. A bomb couldn't have awaken him once he dozed off.

"Then who?"

Juleel shrugged his shoulders.

"Maybe Raymon has more enemies than we know."

"Maybe," said Keysha still skeptical. "I'm still going to ask Jack. He's the only one I know of who could have done this."

***

Jack, meantime, watched from the window of Dunleavy Hall. He had a paper bag containing the dark clothing and leftover duct tape. During the morning, he had retrieved it from the cavity in the pilaster. Now it was time to dispose of anything that could be incriminating.

Raymon could accuse all he wanted, but as he had said to Keysha, "It's your word against mine." Jack would deny everything. There was no proof of his involvement. Juleel would swear he never left the room the night before.

When he saw the multitude of camera flashes, Jack knew Raymon's moment of glory was forever being recorded. Now, maybe Raymon would at last feel what it was like to be totally humiliated. Embarrassment was a bitch. Raymon would now realize what it was like to have dignity torn away.

If Raymon Jackson was smart, he'd learn something from this experience. Jack figured it all depended on what kind of man Raymon Jackson really was.

CHAPTER 54

Raymon was in a murderous rage. His anger aspired to dark, unchartered areas of insanity he had never visited before.

He sat in the school's clinic being checked out by a studious-looking doctor with large glasses and a thin goatee. After fifteen minutes of prodding, Raymon shoved the doctor away.

"Quit touching me, motherfucker. Find me some clothes!"

The doctor sputtered, "Mr. Jackson, you've been exposed to the elements. We must…"

"FUCK YOU! Get me some clothes!"

The doctor backed away unable to believe his ears. Raymon glared at him, "MOVE!" he ordered.

The doctor, who was shaking in fear of this insane man, ran for the door. Where was Security?

Raymon's eyes then grew cold.

They had laughed. All of them. He had heard them. They had laughed at Raymon Jackson. He'd been their fool, their clown. Didn't they remember the touchdowns? Didn't they remember how cool he was?

He dressed to perfection, drove a hot car and only hung out with beautiful women. Sure he had an aloof attitude, but he'd sacrificed for them every Saturday, and they had the nerve to laugh.

Mulligan, that white motherfucker, had caused this. Raymon now wanted him dead. Ramapo had been right. It was now time to cap the sonuvabitch.

***

It was totally dark in the stone room. The dry, musty air was foul, and the hours stretched on in silence.

Nathan awoke from a restless sleep in panic. For a moment he thought he was in a grave. Then he remembered he was in Woodburn Hall. Orientation settled painfully as he found his focus again.

He checked his radium-faced watch for the time. It was one o'clock in the afternoon—but it was midnight in here. His stomach told him he was hungry; so he dug into the grocery bag for the packages of peanut buttered crackers. How he hated processed food. But, today, he had to admit, it tasted good.

Nathan toyed with idea of crawling outside for just a few minutes but knew it would be too risky. All he needed was for one person to see him.

Suddenly he froze. His ears picked up something. What? Tiny…but a sound. His ears perked up. Was it a whisper or maybe a rat? Rats terrified him. No, it was a whisper.

"Dammit, don't tell me I'm losing my mind this quickly," he admonished.

As if in answer, Nathan heard the imperceptible whisper again and froze. It came from the opposite corner. What was over there? Who was over there?

Nathan laughed nervously. In his pocket was a packet of matches. He pulled them out and struck one. The light hurt his eyes as he held it aloft to see better.

Nothing. Nothing anywhere in the room. His mind must be playing tricks.

Sitting on the cold, dirt floor, Nathan finished the crackers and followed it with deep swallows of bottled water.

Only a little longer and he'd be the hunter once again and not the hunted. Then, he heard the whisper, the insistent whisper.

CHAPTER 55

Jack made it back to his room that afternoon at four o'clock. He had spent the late morning and afternoon in classes and at the library. He convinced himself, he had to work harder and not get too distracted by Keysha. That wasn't easy. She was so beautiful. Thoughts of her caused his pulse rate to increase and his legs to go wobbly. It was hard not to think about her voice and her touch.

The morning's events began to trouble him. Keysha would surely ask about Raymon. What would he say? He hated to lie to her, but his instincts told him the truth would have consequences. It was better to deny everything. After all, his alibi was solid.

Juleel came into the room five minutes after Jack arrived. He could hardly keep his words in restraint long enough to tell Jack what had happened in his absence.

"Jack where have you been?" he exclaimed.

"I've…"

"Have you heard all that happened?" he interrupted excitedly.

"Well, I…"

"Raymon Jackson was found in a diaper strapped to the Homecoming statue. It was hilarious. You should have seen him."

"You're joking," replied Jack in mock surprise.

"No, it's true," said Juleel excitedly. "At first I thought maybe you did it, but that couldn't have been. You were here all night, and I'm a light sleeper. I'd have known if you got up."

"Of course," Jack said facetiously.

"Anyway, he's going to most likely miss the Homecoming game, and I hear Coach Dunn is very angry. He says that if the mugger is found, the college will seek legal action."

Another reason to deny everything.

"With Jackson out, can the Wildcats win tomorrow?" asked Jack solemnly.

Juleel smiled, then laughed, "No, but who cares."

"What's funny?" said Jack. "You don't seem upset about it."

"I'm not," chuckled Juleel. "If anyone deserved a come down, it was Raymon—Mr. Big Shot—Jackson. Now maybe he'll know what it's like for the rest of us. You should have seen his face."

"Was he angry?"

"As a hornet in a downpour," laughed Juleel.

Jack raised his eyebrows, "Good."

His plan had worked to perfection.

"What'd you think of Dr. Ramapo being charged with murder?" said Juleel, instantly changing the subject.

Jack snapped around, "What did you say?"

"You and Tyrel."

491

"What?"

"Don't you guys ever read a newspaper?" asked Juleel shaking his head.

"Newspapers are usually a waste of time."

"Well not today," said Juleel. "Dr. Ramapo is being sought all over the country. They found Robert Brent's body buried in his back yard."

"Brent!" Jack said in legitimate shock.

"Yeah, I know. I hadn't seen him in few days, but I never thought much about it. It's scary."

Jack was stunned. So Ramapo was a killer. No wonder he had trouble in the professor's class.

"Wow. Brent's dead," said Jack in disbelief. He suddenly felt guilty for the way he had treated the Head Resident.

"The guy never made a lot of friends around here," Juleel said. "He was always—all business. He hated us, of course. I guess if no one cares, no one notices."

Jack considered how, in a way, he was much like Brent. Since coming to Mt. Sidney, he hadn't put much time into socialization. He'd been segregated by most of the students and had devoted himself to his studies. If he died, however, how long would it take before anyone noticed or cared? Maybe never.

He looked at Juleel. He was a friend who would care. Keysha would care, too. Two good friends, one his lover. He was lucky, so lucky.

"The police think Ramapo may have killed Danielle Myers, too," continued Juleel.

"But why?"

"Who knows? The guy is sick."

Jack nodded and thought back to his first day in Ramapo's class and the strange reaction when the professor saw him.

"Tyrel said he saw Ramapo just outside this dorm on the night Danielle was murdered," Juleel said.

Jack frowned as he thought of that. The news made his own recent problems clearer, like clouds parting on a bright blue sky. Jack recalled now the cold looks and the strange behavior displayed by Ramapo all during the semester. He knew how he had struggled in the professor's class, working extra hard with no visible results. All because of Ramapo's hate.

"You think he planted the knife to frame me?" Jack said.

"Sounds probable."

"Dammit, I should have seen it coming."

"How could you know?"

"Gut feelings, Juleel. Sometimes you just have to go with them," Jack said angrily.

Juleel looked confused by the answer, then brightened as he remembered something else.

"Oh Jack, I almost forgot," he said pulling an envelope from his desk. "Helen in the mail room called me over today and said there was a letter for you. She said its been in your box for several days."

Jack stared at the letter.

Juleel handed it to him. "Since you don't seem to get mail, I thought I'd bring it up to you."

Jack looked at the floor. The old adage came to mind, "No news is good news." He didn't know anyone who would want to write him. He purchased nothing, had no credit and didn't join organizations. Who then would write him?

James Ankrom

Jack sat down at his desk and scrutinized the envelope. The pre-printed letterhead said it was from the Ohio State Parole Board. What now? Had they changed their minds about this college program? Would he be going back to jail? He had talked to his parole officer by phone not long ago and nothing had been said.

Jack tore the envelope open and unfolded the single page letter. He squinted at the flowery official seal and read.

Dear Mr. Mulligan,

We regret to inform you that this office has been notified that your mother, Mrs. Emily O'Connell Mulligan, passed away in the East St. Louis Mental Health Hospital on November 5th...

Further on it said the official cause of death was breast cancer. His mother had died with no will and had no known possessions, except a small photo of him, which was enclosed. Then official condolences were given. Jack was informed that the body would be held for ten days for disposition and then would be cremated at public expense.

Jack dropped the letter. His throat felt thick, as if he'd choke. He clenched his fist and tried to sort through his conflicting emotions and comprehend the words and sentences in the letter. They were now branded in his mind. Jack numbly stared for a while out into the growing darkness with sightless eyes. He tried to tell himself he didn't care, but he knew it wasn't so. He could still remember the young woman who had played with him in the snow.

"Are you alright, Jack?" asked Juleel.

Jack said nothing. He stood up, put on his jacket and without answering Juleel, left the room. It was debatable if he had even heard his roommate's question.

Juleel, his jaw slack, sat stunned. What had just happened? What was in the letter that had so affected Jack?

For two hours, Jack walked aimlessly. He took out the first grade photo of himself that had been enclosed in the letter, plus his one picture of his mother from his wallet and studied them. Did the picture of him mean she had thought of him from time to time? If so, why hadn't she ever written? He'd never even received a Christmas card. Maybe her mind had been so muddled from years of physical and mental abuse, alcohol and drugs, she couldn't remember him. Who could tell? But now, she was dead.

Jack bit his lip until his jaw ached. What a hellva' world, he thought. Some people just get eaten up by it. As for his mother, she had been a small, insignificant morsel for the beast.

CHAPTER 56

Nathan had been listening to the voices coming from the other end of the pitch black room for several hours. They were so clever, the beings—ghosts, ghouls, whatever. When he would strike a match to get closer look at them, they would hide and not speak for awhile. Was their plan to scare him as he sat in the dark? Jump him when he least expected it. Well it wouldn't work. He was too alert and he wasn't a coward.

A few minutes before, Nathan had begun to recognize some of their voices. The first had been his old Drill Sergeant, Warren Whitaker. He could hear Whitaker's hoarse southern drawl spewing threats. The Sergeant had not changed his tune a bit in thirty-four years. The fucking bastard had deserved what he had gotten.

Then came the soft pitched voice of the girl, Danielle Myers. She joined the Sergeant as they harassed Nathan. Did she expect him to stray from his mission, be paralyzed by remorse or perhaps see his collapse in fear? She could forget it.

Her voice brought sorrow to the table, however. Nathan knew she shouldn't have died. He hadn't planned to kill her. It had been a mistake. Nathan tried to explain but only meaningless grunts came out. Didn't she know she would be considered a martyr from now on? She should be thanking him for the honor.

Then her voice reached out as an anguished scream that froze his blood. He could feel the cold chill of her fetid breath permeating his marrow and paralyzing his body down to his toes.

"You murderer! You animal! I could have been someone's mother," she echoed over and over.

That thought hung with him as she berated him.

Finally, he shouted, "SHUT UP! Leave me alone. I did this for you, not to you."

Sergeant Whitaker started laughing in an evil cackle. He laughed and laughed, louder and louder. "You stupid nigger. Wait till we get through with you. Hell will be paradise by comparison."

***

Keysha tapped on the door to Jack's room and heard a voice say, "Come in." When she saw Juleel, she knew something was very wrong. He was slumped forward at Jack's desk with a piece of paper in his hands. His expression was lugubrious, his big eyes drooped in sadness. John Coltrane played lonesomely on the portable CD player, and the room had a melancholy feel.

"What's going on, Juleel?"

He turned his head and gazed up and at first didn't reply, "Jack got this letter a while ago and left. I didn't want to be nosey, but I could tell he was upset when he read it. Jack never gets mail. You know what I mean?"

"What kind of letter, Juleel?"

He held up the letter.

Keysha could now see tears welling in Juleel's eyes. She sat down opposite Juleel on the edge of Jack's bed and put her hand gently on his shaking shoulder.

"You love him, Juleel. So do I."

"He left here...I could tell he was upset," sobbed Juleel. "He left this letter on his desk, so I decided to read it. He just...never gets mail."

With that he handed Keysha the letter. Keysha debated whether she should invade Jack's personal world. Did she really have that right? Whatever was in the letter was his private business, but she wanted to know. Screw it. This was the man she loved. Keysha picked up the letter and in silence read it. The news concerning Jack's mother was terrible and sad. A tear crept down her soft cheek as she returned the piece of paper to the desk.

"Where'd he go?" she said wiping the tear away.

"I don't know, Keysha. He's been gone for over an hour."

"I'll wait here with you, Juleel," said Keysha in a hoarse whisper and the two friends hugged each other.

Keysha knew that Jack's mother was his last living relation. Now he really was alone. For some people, she decided, trouble just followed them everywhere. Maybe they were born into horrible circumstances, maybe events just soured their lives or maybe a combination of factors labored to destroy their spirit.

For Jack Mulligan, Keysha thought, the rain just kept falling, and the clouds just kept rolling in.

***

Tyrel called Sam Bergman that afternoon and left a message, but it wasn't till after football practice that he saw the detective standing outside the locker room. He was wearing a wrinkled overcoat and his face displayed a weariness that centered around his dark, sunken eyes and day-old beard. He was hunting a man, plain and simple, and needed to capture him soon before more people were hurt.

Tyrel approached him, "You got my message?"

"I came as soon as I could, Tyrel."

"Good."

"What's going on?"

"I saw in the paper, you're trying to find Professor Ramapo," said Tyrel. "I just wanted you to know, I saw him outside of Lincoln Hall on the night Danielle was murdered."

"Why didn't you tell me this before?" snapped Bergman angrily. His exhaustion was showing.

"I'm sorry," said Tyrel, apologetically. "It just never occurred to me that he would have had anything to do with murder. I mean...he's a professor, you know."

Bergman did know. He realized that most people have an inherent trust of authority figures. As a society, we like to think that policemen are always honest, that doctors are always skilled and caring, that teachers and clergy can be absolutely trusted around our children. Those notions were taught to us by our parents whom we unconditionally loved and trusted. It was terrible when a trust such as that was betrayed or broken.

Bergman put his hand on Tyrel's shoulder, "Sorry I yelled, kid. I'm just tired. You, of course, wouldn't have any reason to think this guy would harm anyone."

Tyrel looked up into the sky, "I want him caught."

"So do I, kid," said Bergman resolutely. "Can you recall anything else?"

"Only that he was coming from the direction of Jack Mulligan's window and was acting jumpy."

"Jumpy?"

"Yeah, you know, agitated. Shook up."

Bergman's forehead furrowed, "Yeah, I guess you would be shook up too if you'd just murdered someone."

Tyrel nodded.

***

Jack stayed in the library until it closed at eleven o'clock. He had the photo of his mother on the desk in front of him. Every small portion of it had been hammered into his memory.

His body ached with a bone-deep tiredness.

Why did he keep scrutinizing the photo. His mother had been for all intents dead to him for years. The letter today only made it official. Not once had she ever written or visited him. The trial and his time Inside had left deep emotional scars. Now he was supposed to care. Well, he didn't, and he wouldn't cry one damn tear. None.

He left the library and started back to the dorm. A misty rain had moved in with a cold front that evening soaking everything including Jack's spirit. Marked by the light of a lamppost, his shadow cut a stark silhouette across the sidewalk and into the trees along the path.

How strange his life had been so far. Unlike most people his age, Jack's fortune was grounded in little that was solid or predictable. He was constantly victimized by myriad circumstances outside his immediate control and seemed to always be playing on a foreign field far from his own rational connections with reality. Killing his father had been the last voluntary action he had ever taken. Since then, he had been beaten, stabbed and abused but not by choice. Taking the SAT's Inside and eventually coming to school here hadn't been his choice either. Why couldn't he have some say in his life—a nickel's worth of control? Could it be he wasn't worthy of the cards dealt him. These thoughts plagued him, and he hated himself for having them.

He should feel lucky to be here. Why couldn't he celebrate that? His mother had probably had it a hundred times worse. She had never had any good luck and had snapped and never recovered. At least he was free.

As he trudged up the rise to Lincoln Hall, he saw a figure coming down the steps of the main entrance. His heart leaped as recognition came. Keysha's long legs and trim figure made him unconsciously increase his pace.

She ran to him and jumped into his arms, wrapping her legs around him. Grabbing his face in both hands, she began kissing him hungrily. Anguish drained from him as he wrapped his arms around her. The moment stood still with frightening intensity, and he only wanted her to hold him, forever. A page was turning to a brighter chapter in his life. The beginning of a new life with Keysha.

But what about the past?

Jack was distantly aware of his mother's whispering voice. He thought he could hear her calling his name, but it was far away, so far away. The voice faded in the rain like a dying ember in the soft evening breeze. Then something broke inside him like a tortured dam bursting forth.

Keysha's embrace was the spark, the fire. The only thing real was her touch.

Then he cried—at long last—his hard uncompromising body shook with convulsions.

Keysha's lips gently touched his eyes as she whispered, "I'm so sorry, baby. It's okay."

Tears rained down his cheeks, and he couldn't stop them. They weren't being cried for what was or for what could have been. But, instead, to say a long and final farewell.

CHAPTER 57

It was early morning in the dark tomb. Across from Nathan Ramapo, they all sat. A few hours before, they had suddenly materialized. They were hideous beings. Apparitions draped in rotting, bluish-pale flesh. All had been victims of Nathan's murderous hands. Nathan found it amazing they knew each other or that they possessed their own light, an aura that burned through the darkness.

Sergeant Whitaker was to his left, flanked by the man Nathan had slain in Detroit; then Danielle Myers and finally, Robert Brent.

Maggots swarmed in and out of their eye sockets, mouths, noses and ears. Their skin oozed with festering sores as they decomposed. Nathan's pores produced a cold rank sweat. His fear was palatable. His stomach turned, and he wanted to vomit but instead was frozen in terror.

Finally they spoke. Words coming without emotion or life. Nathan could hear them plainly even though the being's mouths didn't move. Theirs was a collective message that portended eternal doom and revenge. He

503

had taken their lives before their time, and now they were here to make him pay—pay with his soul.

The one hellish feature the four visitors shared in common was their eyes, which glowed red inside the dark, empty sockets. Nathan had heard from a funeral director, that the soft parts of anyone's body decayed and rotted away first after death. But the eyes...the eyes of his victims had no pity, no mercy. Nothing for a life gone wrong.

Nathan tried not to look at them, but everywhere his face traveled in the dark, they were there. No escape was possible. They were accusing him, blaming him. Was there no escaping them and their laughter?

Sergeant Whitaker seemed to have the clearest voice. His strength in life must mirror his equal voracity in death.

"Brown, you nigger bastard," hissed Whitaker. "I've been waiting so long for you."

"Don't...please."

"Your begging doesn't cut it with me, nigger. Your ass is going to be mine. The others will have to wait in line."

"Leave me alone," whimpered Nathan.

"What's wrong, nigger? Are you going to cry?"

"No!" screamed Nathan angrily. "I..."

"Oh, you're going to give me pleasure in hell, boy."

"Please..."

"He's pleading," came a female voice.

They all laughed.

"You bastard," piped in Danielle as a milk-white maggot fell from her putrid, rotting nostril. "I'm going to rip your fucking cock off and feed it to you till you choke. Guess how long you'll gag on your own flesh?"

"I...I...don't..."

"Centuries will pass as you suffocate on your own cock," she grinned and laughed until the sound echoed in never ending waves of thunder. Then her companions joined in, adding to the inhuman shrieking.

Nathan held his ears with his hands and screamed, "Leave me alone. Do you hear me? Leave me alone!"

When the sound finally subsided, Robert Brent spat at him. "You poisoned me, Ramapo. Look at my tongue. When I get done with you, nigger, you'll have the same problem I have."

Nathan peeked over his arm. A big rat was eating Brent's rancid tongue, which hung to the ground. Suddenly, a yellowish glowing regurgitation from inside Brent's throat flowed down and covered the large ravenous rodent. The rat then began to writhe and squeal in pain as it dissolved as though consumed by acid. Brent, for his part, started sucking the mixture of yellow mucous, blood and hair into his mouth.

Then the four apparitions stared at Nathan with fixed grins and glowing hellish eyes.

"There you have it, nigger," said the coarse voice of the dead, nameless man from Detroit. "But don't forget me."

"No, I never..."

"SHUT UP!"

Nathan fell against the wall, cringing in fright, paralyzed to move. His eyes were wide and insane. He mopped the cold sweat from his brow to keep the salt from blinding him.

"You thoughtless motherfucker," the dead man shrieked. "You killed me, but you couldn't be bothered to find out my name or who I was in life."

"Yes, I..."

"SILENCE! I've waited long and hard for you. Because I was a murderer myself, I've burned for twenty years in the flames of hell. Do you know what the pain is like to burn on and ON?"

Nathan was now on his side in a fetal position, shrieking in fright. He screamed for his soul for over an hour—until exhaustion consumed him and his eyes became glassy and unseeing.

The apparitions continued to reveal the tortures that were in store for him. Nathan had no reason to doubt them. Their combined hatred was an eternal promise they would fulfill.

Sleep finally came as death's brother—unexpected and sudden.

***

Jack and Keysha made love and talked till nearly morning in her room. They slept in each others arms. Jack wished this feeling of happiness and belonging would last forever. Keysha was in love with him, and all he wanted to do was shout it from every roof top.

She was still sleeping when he left her the next morning. There was something he wanted to do before he saw her next. Jack wanted to give her something small but infinitely precious.

Back in his room, he showered and dressed in some fresh clothes. Juleel was at class, but Jack, for once, couldn't wait to see him and tell him how much he loved and adored Keysha. Although, he figured Juleel already knew as much.

Jack left Lincoln Hall and raced into town. His first stop was the same florist shop he and Juleel had visited before. He bought two long-stemmed roses and found it hard to keep from smiling.

"They're for my girl," he said haltingly as he received his change from a matronly woman with silver hair.

She smiled, "Good for you, young man."

Jack felt foolish for telling the woman, but the words just slipped out. He had to watch out, people would think he was looney.

Jack departed the shop as if he were floating on air. Nobody could bring him down. His love was burning so bright that even God must be smiling.

Although Jack was enough of a realist to know that anything could happen in a capricious world to break up a relationship, he wanted Keysha to know how deeply he felt for her at this moment in time. Moments of wonder were so few. This was a special love they had. It was a joy that could never be duplicated.

He only had fifty dollars when he found himself outside Colson's Jewelry store. He realized so little money wouldn't buy much, but he went inside anyway.

He entered to the dazzle of high priced diamonds mounted in rings, bracelets and necklaces. All were expensive—way too expensive for his meager finances. The atmosphere even spoke of money and not just jewelry. Classical music played from hidden speakers, and Jack's feet sunk in rich, thick pile carpet.

A tall, gaunt man in a grey suit with a red tie came forward. "May I help you?"

"I hope so," said Jack. "I want to get something, maybe a bracelet or necklace, for my girl."

"What would you like to spend, sir?" asked the clerk in an aristocratic voice.

Jack stared for a moment, dumbfounded. He had never been regarded to as a "Sir." He found the mantel of respect pleasant.

The clerk continued to wait for a reply, "Sir."

"Oh yes," mumbled Jack. "I have fifty dollars."

The clerk suddenly looked bored, "I see. Well, we usually don't have anything in that price range. However, let me check with Mr. Colson."

This was a mistake, he thought. Suddenly, Jack felt shabby and inadequate. He shouldn't have come here where the carpet was too thick and the prices too high. A sign should have been placed outside to warn guys like him away. "Poor Idiots DO NOT enter" it could have said. Then, nobody would go away humiliated or embarrassed.

The tall clerk disappeared into the back room, and a moment later a short, portly man with a round, humor-filled face came out to replace him. Jack instantly figured that this man was either a nice guy or he was wanting to laugh in his face.

"Hello, son," said the man. "My name is Hiram Colson. May I help you?"

Jack looked down, "I came here hoping to buy a bracelet or necklace. I've only got fifty bucks."

Hiram Colson smiled, "Who is this for, young man?"

Did it make a difference, thought Jack. He shifted his feet before he blurted, "It's for a girl. She's special."

The man raised his eyebrows, "Really."

What a stupid answer to give the jeweler. The guy probably thought he was retarded.

"Yeah."

"You realize fifty dollars won't go too far."

"Yes sir."

The jeweler considered something in his head then said, "I do have some silver chains and charms that might be of interest."

Jack brightened. Maybe there was hope.

"That sounds good."

From under the counter, Colson brought out a tray of charms, "Pick one of these."

"Okay," said Jack who had already spotted a small heart shaped charm. He scrutinized many of the other charms but his eye kept coming back to the heart.

"I'd like the heart," said Jack holding it up.

"An excellent choice," Colson said in congratulation.

"Can you engrave something on it?"

"There's not much room, but I think we can do that. It'll cost you five more dollars."

"Great," exclaimed Jack.

"Write down what you'd like to say on this paper," said Colson, shoving a pad across to Jack. "No more than three words."

What could he say in three lousy words. His love for Keysha could fill volumes. Three words weren't nearly enough. What, what, what?

"How about, 'I love you,'" said Colson noting Jack's dilemma.

"That's nice but…I want to say more."

"Oh."

Keysha wasn't just Jack's first love, she was his only love. All he wanted was for her to be with him always. He'd never let her down, and she would never have to wonder if he loved her. Keysha would know what was in his heart every single day.

"I have it," he said and wrote down the words.

Colson read the piece of paper when Jack was done, "She must be pretty special. These are great words."

Jack swallowed, "She is."

***

Keysha had felt Jack give her a gentle kiss that morning. It almost seemed like a sweet dream but somehow more real. He had then softly closed the door as he left.

Her schedule was packed on Friday's, so she carried a candy bar in her purse in case she got hungry. When she entered the library at two o'clock it was packed, but she did manage three hours of solid work before she left at five o'clock.

Keysha hurried back to her dorm room and quickly showered. Then she started the arduous task of fixing her long dark hair. By six o'clock, she called down to Jack's room and Juleel answered, "Keysha, please take this crazy man away for this evening. He's obsessed."

"That bad, huh." she said smiling. "What's he doing?"

"He's in the shower right now. But during dinner all he could talk about was you and how wonderful you are."

Keysha laughed, "But it's true, Juleel."

Juleel joined her laughter, "It makes me crazy. Why don't I have someone who loves me that much?"

"You will, silly."

Keysha's heart flew in fits of ecstasy.

"Get him ready Juleel, and tell him to come to my room at seven-thirty."

"I will do that. Then maybe I can get ready for the concert, too," said Juleel in faked exasperation.

CHAPTER 58

Nathan Ramapo pushed the door open to the stone chamber and staggered out into the basement hallway. The dim light of the hall was enough to blind his wild, unfocused eyes. Sweat and dirt were matted on his hair and body like a second skin, and his face had a deranged intensity written on it.

For a moment, he couldn't remember where he was. He was completely disoriented, but then his haunted mind cleared just enough. Yes, he had a mission. He had to kill Jack Mulligan. His legacy depended on it.

Nathan's raised his hand to his forehead. It hurt. He suddenly remembered the men who had castrated him so long ago. Why hadn't they killed him? It would have been so much better if they had. How he hated those men. White men. Devils.

Now was the time for revenge. Tonight was his. He'd have help, of course. Raymon Jackson would serve his purpose. After he completed his revenge on Mulligan and the girl Keysha, it would be Raymon's turn. Nathan couldn't think now of why he wanted to kill Raymon, but he knew he would.

Sacrifices had to be made.

***

The newspapers ran the photo of Raymon strapped practically naked to the Homecoming statue. Although it was shocking to some, generally the public chuckled at the thought of a college prank being played on the big time running back.

On the nightly TV sports shows, the reporters all had their separate jokes about it. None seemed to elicit sympathy for Raymon being assaulted. This wasn't some defenseless person, this was one of the most physically gifted athletes in the country. Surely he could take care of himself. Besides, maybe this was a publicity stunt, or just a "boys will be boys" joke.

Coach Dunn, for his part, took it seriously and when interviewed, stated that authorities were investigating the incident and would prosecute those responsible. He also reported that Raymon would miss the Homecoming game on Saturday.

Raymon sat in his room and stared blankly at the TV set and pondered his once brilliant football career slipping away. He was now a nationally known laughing stock—a complete joke. Nobody would ever forget this.

His father had called him three hours before and had told him what a shameful idiot he was. How could his son have dishonored himself like this? How could a Jackson have allowed something so undignified to happen? Now his father was totally ashamed of him. Raymon had disgraced the family name.

Raymon had always tried to please his father. His father had been the one who pushed Raymon to excel, even when Raymon wanted to quit football. His ol' man's approval was like a drug to him, and now his father was ashamed of him. His father told Raymon he had caused this and accused him of being a wise-ass fool and then said the words that burned in his head. "I don't want to see your face in my house ever again."

His father hated him, the fans were laughing at him. They'd never let him forget what happened yesterday. The photo would continue to be published everywhere he went. Other players would chide him about it. The humiliation would never end.

Raymon's gaze narrowed as he remembered what had happened. There was no doubt that the dark figure who had hit him and bound his hands was Jack Mulligan. Nobody else had the physical strength or courage to face him that way. The ski mask hadn't fooled him one bit.

The phone rang, and he listlessly answered it, "Hello."

"Mr. Jackson."

"Professor."

"Are you ready to help me with the white boy?"

Raymon had to make a decision. This was Ramapo, the Mad Professor the cops were seeking. He had killed Danielle Myers, they said, and Robert Brent; now he wanted to kill Jack Mulligan. The guy was a maniac.

Then he thought of Danielle Myers, who never really respected him and Robert Brent, who had interfered when he was straightening Keysha out. Raymon had not liked either one of them. Maybe they ultimately needed killing.

"You bet!" Raymon said sharply.

"Good, walk towards the Creative Arts Center in fifteen minutes. I'll meet you along the way."

The phone clicked off.

Raymon quickly dressed and was ready to leave when he heard a knock on the door. Who could this be?

He opened the door and there stood Tyrel Friday.

"What do you want?" Raymon asked coldly.

"Thought you might want to talk," said Tyrel calmly.

"Got nothin' to talk to you about," said Raymon. "You're no friend of mine, so just leave me alone."

Tyrel looked hurt, "Hey, if it's about yesterday."

"It's got nothin' to do with yesterday."

"Come on, Raymon…"

"Don't come on, Raymon to me, motherfucker. You chose to be friends with that white sonuvabitch. You can leave me alone."

Tyrel shook his head, "You're the one, Raymon, who wouldn't let it be. You couldn't get it out of your system. I told you to leave Jack Mulligan alone."

"So now he's Jack to you."

"Yeah," said Tyrel. "He's a decent guy."

"Fuck you, Tyrel. The white man has enslaved us, berated us, and you want to suck up to the motherfuckers."

"Hate isn't going to get you anywhere," Tyrel explained. "You'll see."

Raymon pushed past Tyrel's bulk and turned, "No, you'll see. Tonight is that motherfucker's last. Me and Ramapo going to take care of his white ass."

"Ramapo!" Tyrel screamed. "The law's lookin' for him. He murdered Danielle. Do you know where he is?"

"I don't know nothin'," said Raymon regretting his outburst.

"Do you know where that sonuvabitch is?" shouted Tyrel.

"Never mind!" said Raymon and hurried off, leaving Tyrel standing, staring after him.

CHAPTER 59

Keysha heard the light tap on her door at exactly seven-thirty and ran to open it. Jack stood looking awkward in his white shirt and tie and the dark blue dress pants. He had a blue sweater pulled over the shirt, and the overall appearance was one of a conservative, prep school boy. In one of his hands was the flowers and in the other his jacket.

She gave him a long, soft kiss and pulled him into the room.

"Are the flowers for me?" she asked playfully.

"Yeah," Jack said as his eyes scanned her from head to toe.

"What's the matter?" Keysha said as she noted Jack's gaze.

Jack's eyes were indeed wide, "You look fantastic. I've never seen anyone as beautiful as you are tonight," he whispered. "If everything ended now, I'd at least have you to remember."

Keysha beamed at the remark. She had a black silk evening dress that was cut low in front and did nothing but enhance her innate elegance. She wore matching black satin pumps and sheer black stockings. Her hair hung to her slim waist and the whole effect was breathtaking.

"Thanks," she said coyly. "And you look so conservative…in a very nice, sexy way."

Jack blushed. "Is that a compliment?"

Keysha gave him another long, wet kiss in answer.

Jack assessed her with amusement, "I guess that's yes."

Keysha laughed, "Are you ready?"

"No, not yet." he said. "I have something for you."

"What?"

Jack pulled out a small, oblong box and handed it to her.

"Flowers and a gift. My, my." she said.

Her eyes expanded as she opened the box. Then, her breath caught as she pulled out the necklace with the silver heart.

"It's beautiful, Jack."

Then, she turned the heart over in her palm to read the words. "My love eternal," she whispered.

"Do you like it?"

"Love forever. That's a long time, Jack."

"I thought…I mean I wanted you to have this. It's not much," Jack stammered.

Keysha kissed him and smiled, "If I waited a hundred years, I could never find another like you, Jack. I love you so much."

"I love you, too," Jack said shifting his feet.

Keysha rushed to the mirror and attached the necklace, "It's perfect," she said. "I'll wear it forever. But, right now, we'd better get going, we'll be late."

Jack helped her with her black leather coat, and he pulled on his worn tweed sport jacket and hand in hand they departed for a perfect evening.

A moment after the door closed, the phone rang insistently.

***

"Come on, answer," pleaded Tyrel frantically. "Where are you?"

He returned the receiver to the phone's cradle and pondered, once again, Raymon's parting words. What was he up to? Did Raymon really know where Professor Ramapo was hiding, and did he have some relationship with the professor?

Tyrel had first called Jack's room but didn't get an answer; then he tried Keysha's room with the same result. Ten to one they were out and had probably gone to the concert. Raymon was up to something, and whatever it was it would probably happen tonight. Tyrel didn't dare to speculate on the outcome.

He quickly dialed the number for Lieutenant Bergman and waited, "Come on." he whispered impatiently. Finally on the fourth ring it was answered, "Homicide, Detective Clark."

"I'd like to speak to Detective Bergman."

"He's not here. May I take a message?"

"Well, Detective Clark," said Tyrel, "there's going to be a murder on the campus of Mt. Sidney if you don't get Bergman on this line, now."

"What's going on?"

"It's Nathan Ramapo. He's here."

"Okay, we'll page Bergman. Stay by the phone," said Clark hurriedly. "What's your name?"

"Tyrel Friday."

He gave Clark his number and hung up. Forty seconds later the phone rang. Tyrel snapped it up.

"Tyrel, it's Bergman. You've seen Ramapo?"

"Not exactly, but he's here."

"How do you know?" asked Bergman anxiously.

Tyrel quickly explained what Raymon had said.

"I'll be right there, Tyrel. Don't you move."

"I'm going to stop Raymon," said Tyrel.

"No don't."

Tyrel slammed the phone in reply and ran for the door.

CHAPTER 60

Jack and Keysha wandered across the campus under the tree-lined sidewalks toward the Creative Arts Center. They chose a longer path that would afford them more privacy and time together. Jack's hands were entwined in hers, and he could feel Keysha's warmth even through her gloves. The passion of their new and unexplored love held a promise of joy and sweet anticipation.

Jack's spirit couldn't have been higher. His life had turned a corner. Before this day, he had thought that his background, the years he spent behind bars and his scarred face would preclude him from ever finding someone to love. His resignation to loneliness had covered him like a dark blanket.

Now, his euphoria buoyed him to a place where nothing could go wrong. Tomorrow would naturally be brighter and more fulfilling than today. Love was the key, he now knew. The love of friends and of a girl. In his case, a girl named Keysha Jordan. He knew his love for her was the one illusive ingredient he had secretly always sought and prayed he would find.

They paused by the stand of hemlocks where they had first kissed, and Jack drew her into his arms. This would always be their place. Always was such an ominous thought. Keysha's breath was so sweet and her lips so soft with longing as they kissed there in the dark.

Then everything came to an abrupt end. A voice shattered the night, "Hey motherfucker, get your hands off the sister."

Time froze in horror.

Jack and Keysha turned to the sound. There stood Raymon, his face a study in cold fury. A gun was leveled at Jack's chest.

"Raymon, leave us alone," declared Keysha fearfully.

Jack admired her courage, but his focus was on the gun.

"Too late," came another voice to the right as Nathan Ramapo, his hair matted with dirt and stale sweat came from behind the trees. "We have a little something in store for you two, and it doesn't involve classical music or a symphony orchestra."

Jack's skin crawled. Ramapo's eyes were wild and deranged. He had changed as if a metamorphosis had occurred. He appeared as a living corpse. They stared at him, but he examined them with expressionless dead regard. The dirt caked hair clung to his gray face that looked old enough to have worn out two bodies.

Both Ramapo and Raymon had their guns aimed at Jack. That gave him some hope since Keysha wasn't the main target.

"Let her go," said Jack in an even calm voice. "You really want me, you got me. But, she's done nothing."

"That's very brave of you, white boy," hissed Ramapo. "But, the good sister has crossed a line and has become your whore. She needs a lesson to be taught to her about her heritage."

"Yeah, baby," laughed Raymon demonically. "We going to learn you right from wrong. Maybe next time, you'll know how to treat your man, bitch."

"Don't call me that, Raymon."

Raymon's hand shot out as he backhanded her. Keysha fell to her knees. Jack started forward, but Ramapo's gun came into his forehead and stopped him, "Where do you think you're going?"

Raymon's face leaned inches from Keysha's, "Don't ever tell me what to do...bitch."

"Enough!" ordered Ramapo. "Let's take a walk to the stadium."

Jack glanced at Keysha with concern. How had a perfect evening suddenly turned into this nightmare?

"Move!" shouted Ramapo.

Jack started across through the woods and down a slight ridge and swore to himself. He could see Keysha's fists were clenched in self-anger, too. Why had they taken a longer way to the Creative Arts Center. Damn. Worse than damn...a lot worse.

This could be the end, Jack surmised. Why hadn't Keysha stayed away from him?

Both Nathan Ramapo and Raymon Jackson were completely nuts and dangerous. Jack couldn't figure where Ramapo had been but from his smell and the filthy appearance, he wondered if the man had hidden in a sewer, a grave or literally under a rock. Jack decided Ramapo was the more dangerous man. Raymon might hesitate to pull a trigger, Ramapo wouldn't. He was stone cold crazy.

Raymon was gorged with hate and jealousy—a potent combination no doubt. The football player was a spoiled child. He had never really lost, and he was pouting with a gun in his hand.

Think, think Jack admonished himself.

Why hadn't they shot them when they got the drop on them? Ramapo obviously wanted something and probably thought he could wrap it all together at a chosen location.

Think!

How much time did they have? Where were they going? Whatever Ramapo had in mind for them, they wouldn't do it in sight or sound of the public. No, the Professor was taking them somewhere private to shoot them. Jack stared ahead at the looming football stadium. They walked with a slow stride that rapidly ate up distance.

These two idiots were angry, no doubt about it. Maybe their anger would cause them to make a mistake. Right now that was his and Keysha's only hope.

Jack suddenly got an idea. "Hey, Ramapo, is the stadium your favorite place to murder students? Isn't that where you so bravely killed Danielle Myers?"

"Shut up, you bastard, or I'll shoot you where you stand."

Raymon eyed Ramapo with suspicion but kept walking.

"By the way, Raymon," Jack continued, "when this maniac kills us, do you really think he's going to let you live?"

Ramapo answered with a strong prod in Jack's back and sharp reply. "Don't listen to him, Mr. Jackson. This is the same kind of rhetoric white people have been using on black people for centuries. He's just trying to save himself."

They soon were outside the entrance to the Wildcat's locker room. Ramapo took out his master key and opened the door. With his pistol, he motioned them inside.

So this is where they'll execute us, thought Jack. He had better do something soon—very soon. Only his actions could save Keysha from death.

***

"Get out of the way, you bastard!" shouted Sam Bergman, as he moved his car in and out of traffic. He cursed the other drivers who didn't yield from his path soon enough. Why were they going so slow?

Although only minutes had passed, the breakneck trip felt like eternity. Up ahead were the gates of Mt. Sidney. Sam slowed down. There could be students walking. He didn't need a vehicular death on his hands.

Moments later, Sam pulled up directly in front of Lincoln Hall and raced into the lobby. It was deserted, except for a skinny kid with a sketch pad who was doodling on a couch.

Sam flipped open his badge. "Hey kid, I need to ask you a couple of questions."

"I didn't do nothin'," exclaimed the started kid. "My name is CQ, and I'm not even from around here."

Bergman read the terror in CQ's face. Many black kids were frightened of the police. The cops weren't known to them as saviors or protectors.

"I'm not here to arrest you CQ," Sam replied in forced calm. "Do you know, Tyrel Friday?"

"Yeah."

"Have you seen him in the last ten minutes?"

"Yeah, he left here two or three minutes ago. He ran out that door," he said pointing to the main entrance.

"Shit!"

"Is Tyrel in trouble?" asked CQ, but Bergman was already running at top speed.

***

Nathan Ramapo stood in the middle of the brightly lit locker room with dirt, dried sweat and filthy clothes clinging to his rancid body. His body odor was pungent. A deadly smile was frozen on his face, and his glassy eyes danced with a scary intensity.

Jack well knew that he and Keysha's lives were now hanging by a thread. Moments were all they had before Ramapo and Raymon would kill them. He focused on Ramapo, praying that something, a look, a gesture, anything, would allow him an opening to attack. When he went after Ramapo, he'd have to trust that Raymon wouldn't shoot Keysha.

Ramapo then swung his pistol toward Raymon. "Drop the gun, Mr. Jackson."

"Say what?"

"I said, drop the pistol."

Raymon appeared confused and strangely hurt. It was the ultimate betrayal. Hadn't they been partners, fellow travelers in hatred.

"DO IT NOW!" shouted Ramapo.

Raymon's lip curled angrily, "Fuck you I've got a gun, too."

"An empty one I'm afraid, Mr. Jackson," Ramapo laughed. "Did you really think I'd let a moron, such as yourself, have bullets?"

Raymon's face flushed angrily as he pulled the trigger and only heard a dead click.

Jack smiled at the irony, "Hey Raymon, I told you he wasn't going to let you live."

"Shut up!" exclaimed Ramapo. "Get over there, Mr. Jackson."

Raymon, dejected and feeling foolish, dropped the pistol and walked over close to Keysha.

"Now I have you all together," said Ramapo placidly. "I'm not a religious man, but you may, for a moment, address your maker."

Raymon screamed, "You can't kill me. I'm going to be a football star. These two are nobodies. They're nothing. You can't do this to me."

Keysha shook her head at Raymon's words.

"Please don't," begged Raymon tears rolling from his eyes.

"I feel sorry for you," said Keysha angrily to Raymon. Then she pointed to Ramapo. "And for this sick bastard."

"Be quiet you whore," spat Ramapo coldly. "What would you know about me, You rich little bitch? Before you were born, I fought for the black man.

527

Before you were born, I was mutilated physically and spiritually by the white devils, but I endured to keep some pride in my race. I didn't sell out like you."

Tears of hate dropped from Ramapo's eyes, "What would a whore like you know about me?"

Keysha didn't back down an inch, "I know that Jack and I didn't do any of those horrible things to you. Neither did Robert Brent or Danielle Myers."

"Sacrifices. Just like you'll be," Ramapo spat. "This white boy expects some kind of redemption for murder but there isn't any."

Suddenly he looked confused as if someone else in the room was talking to him but no one else could hear. "That's where we are alike Mr. Mulligan. For killers such as us, there is no atonement."

"Then let these others go," said Jack.

Ramapo blazed with insanity. He started to speak.

"I'll give you money," begged Raymon in a pitiful voice.

The gunshot was deafening.

Ramapo pulled the trigger of the .45 with no emotion, putting a bullet through Raymon's knee. Raymon screamed and fell to the floor writhing in excruciating pain.

Jack saw a mere second in which Ramapo studied his next target on the running back's body and laughed at his handiwork. It was the only opening he was going to get.

Ramapo saw Jack's movement and barely had time to swing the pistol around. He fired into Jack's shoulder but was hit full force by Jack's bulk and knocked backward over a bench. Ramapo still had his gun clenched in his fist, but Jack kept coming.

Ramapo rolled and started to regain his feet. Jack was nearly on him when Ramapo fired again putting a slug into Jack's chest. This bullet chopped Jack from his feet.

Then an object hit Ramapo hard in the head. It was a football. Jack saw Professor Ramapo jerk sideways from the impact and stumble backwards. Excruciating pain kept Jack from turning to see who threw the football with such force.

Who was their savior?

The pain intensified. Jack's eyes now were unfocused, but he could make out a huge bear-like man. It was Tyrel Friday.

"Look out Tyrel!" screamed Keysha, as Ramapo aimed at the big man. The bullet, fired off-balance, caught Tyrel in the upper arm but the impact sent him to the floor.

Nathan Ramapo straightened up and carefully aimed the pistol at Keysha.

"Drop it!" shouted a voice from the door. Sam Bergman had his gun poised.

Nathan screamed his anger as he quickly readjusted his aim at Bergman and pulled the trigger. Two shots blasted in unison and a hole instantly appeared in Nathan Ramapo's forehead. He fell hard to the floor. Blood surged out of his head and down between his dead eyes.

Bergman, had been shielded by a support post, which had caught Ramapo's bullet. He ran into the room and assessed the situation, pulling a cell phone from his pocket. A call was placed for an ambulance and back-up that Sam knew had better come very quickly.

"Are you alright?" he asked Tyrel.

Tyrel nodded. "I'll be okay. See to the others."

Bergman walked over to Keysha who was bent over Raymon. The running back was passed out from the pain of his shattered knee but he looked as though he would live.

Bergman checked Ramapo's body. The blank, open-eyed expression on the Professor's face told him that the shot to head had done its job. Professor Nathan Ramapo—a.k.a Thaddeus Brown—was dead.

Jack Mulligan, however, lay sprawled on the floor, blood was gushing from his chest. His breathing was labored and coming in rasping gasps. His legs flexed with waves of pain.

Keysha instantly ran to him.

"Help him!" she shouted in tearful desperation to Bergman. Her face was now a mask of helpless agony. "Please, help!"

Bergman bent down to Jack but could see the boy was losing blood much too fast to stem the advancing tide of his coming death. How he respected Jack Mulligan's courage. A world-weary expression spread on the detective's face; one that deflated Keysha's hopes of survival. Bergman could have said it was too late for Jack Mulligan, but that would have been cruel. Instead, he shook his head and put his hand gently on Keysha's shoulder.

"An ambulance will be here shortly," he whispered.

Keysha turned to Jack, "Baby, help's on the way. Hang on."

Blood dripped from Jack's mouth as if in answer, and Keysha's hopes faded instantly. No ambulance was going to be in time.

Keysha realize she could only make Jack's last moments as comfortable as possible. His ravaged face had now grown gray and ghastly pale. His rough, labored breathing was coming harder and harder as blood filled his lungs. Tears rained down from her eyes as she gently placed his head in her lap.

"Don't cry,…I," he winced and coughed. "I want you…to know, how happy…happy."

Jack had been terrified all his life of dying alone. Now he knew the end was near. Death was beside him. He was ashamed of his fear. He had brought this sort of end to others, now it was his turn. What if all the others were waiting for him somewhere? He prayed that Keysha wouldn't see his cowardice. Was it possible that everyone became a coward just before death? He had faced so much in his life. He couldn't let Keysha know how lonely it was here at the end.

"I love you, Jack," she whispered breathlessly.

He tried to speak but could only cough. It came out as a ragged convulsion.

"Love…you too. Always will…love," he said with great effort.

Keysha could see a dull glaze coming into his eyes. Panic gripped her heart.

"Hang on, baby. Don't leave me," she pleaded.

Jack's eyes widened in terror, as he whispered, "Keysha…help…me."

She grasped him tighter, as if her life force would be enough to sustain both of them. Her cheek came to rest on his. Her lips felt so warm to him.

James Ankrom

Jack suddenly arched his back to fight for one more precious moment.

"JACK, PLEASE! Stay with me!" Keysha screamed in desperation.

His body relaxed.

"So cold," he said softly.

Jack could now only see Keysha's face. There was darkness around the edges—everywhere darkness. He was having trouble getting air. Then, as if by magic, he felt a cool breeze. Fresh air, mountain air.

Keysha saw his expression become placid. His voice then came as the faintest whisper, "I have to go, Keysha. We all…go."

Those were his last words.

He sank into black emptiness that seemed endless and forever. Keysha's voice, calling his name, echoed then faded away into silence. He was again frightened. Even the fearless had to walk alone to eternity.

Then, little by little, in all the darkness came a light. He looked around but could no longer see Keysha, though his eyes searched for her everywhere.

Instead, there in the distance, Jack saw the log cabin he had dreamed of so often. It sat placidly across a meadow full of bright, spring wild flowers. A rushing mountain stream splashed diamonds of clear, cold water into the air where the sun caught each drop and sent out prisms of color everywhere.

The flowers swayed lazily in the gentle breeze and emitted a fragrance as rare and as subtle as an exotic perfume. To Jack, the details of the cabin and the meadow had always alluded him, but now they were different. It was as though the painter had decided to, at last, finish his canvas by filling in the details. Everything was complete and perfect.

532

Jack started walking toward the cabin. His feet felt light and he was smiling. He'd make it to the door this time. It wasn't far away at all.

Jack Mulligan had, at last, come home.

EPILOGUE

(*Eight years later*)

Keysha Jordan Friday examined her face in the mirror and fingered the silver necklace holding the small silver heart. The night that Jack Mulligan and Nathan Ramapo had died seemed long ago. The river of tears she had once cried was now gone, and she grudgingly accepted the past in its final form. She was older, more mature, somewhat wealthy, and through marriage and motherhood, had found lasting fulfillment.

Two years before, she had married Tyrel Friday. Their union surprised even themselves. They had met at a Washington D.C. party by accident, having not seen each other for many years. She was an attorney working for the ACLU. Her specialty was in race law and civil rights.

Tyrel had just been elected freshman Congressman from Pennsylvania's Seventh District. He had had a successful career as an All Pro defensive end for the Pittsburgh Steelers, but a career ending injury had cut short his gridiron fame. Tyrel was resilient, however, and had quickly rallied his sports notoriety into a promising future in politics. Tyrel's easy going manner and patience were a winning combination with the blue-collar constituency back home.

Keysha could remember well how they had talked well into the night after the Washington get together. It was so good to see Tyrel again. They reminisced, but both avoided, mentioning Danielle Myers or Jack Mulligan. There was simply too much pain connected with their names.

On that night long ago at Mt. Sydney, Tyrel had frantically arrived in the locker room just in time to save Keysha. It was a fluke that he had seen Jack and Keysha being herded by Nathan Ramapo and Raymon Jackson toward the stadium. Tyrel had been rushing toward the Creative Arts Center when he spotted them. He trailed them at a safe distance, desperately trying to figure out what to do.

When they went inside and shots were fired, Tyrel threw caution to the wind and burst into the locker room. What he saw stunned and frightened him. Jack and Raymon were both lying on the floor bleeding, and Ramapo was leveling his gun at Keysha.

Having no weapon, he grabbed the only thing within reach—a football—and heaved it with all his strength at Ramapo. It caught the professor flush in the side of the head and knocked him off balance. Ramapo fired at Tyrel but it only scratched him in the arm. Then Sam Bergman came to the rescue, and nailed Ramapo before he could get a better shot.

Tyrel had watched helplessly as Jack Mulligan died in Keysha's arms. She had cradled his head and talked to him long after he was gone. Tyrel could tell that Jack was dead by the blank stare in his eyes and the limp repose. Keysha's dress was soaked in his blood, and she was sobbing.

Sam Bergman gathered up the scattered weapons glanced at Tyrel and could only shake his head. Tyrel painfully walked over to Keysha and bent down, "Keysha…Keysha."

She moaned in a low voice and couldn't seem to hear him. Her eyes were glazed, and she kept sobbing.

"Keysha, he's dead."

"No," she said wimpering pitifully. "No, no, no."

"He is, Keysha."

He put his good arm around her. She gave no indication that he was present. All she could do was hold Jack.

Hours later he led her back to the dorm after a doctor had given her a sedative. A large crowd of students and the press were outside the locker room and parted as she left the bloody hell inside. She was in no shape to answer any questions.

For days, Keysha came in and out of drug induced bouts of sleep and hysteria. Everyone feared for her. Would she take her life? Her parents came from Pittsburgh the day after the shooting, and, following some brief questions from Bergman, they took her home where she stayed for eight months. Her parents called in therapists and doctors who finally were able to help her deal with the enormity of the tragedy.

After transferring to Penn State the following autumn, she worked hard for the next four years and graduated with honors. Then followed law school at Yale.

Although she had many friends, she dated little. No one seemed to be able to replace the magic she had had with Jack Mulligan. Although they'd only known each other for a few, short weeks, Keysha knew in her heart their love was indeed eternal.

When she graduated, she was offered positions in several lucrative firms in New York and Washington D.C. She chose instead to work for the American Civil Liberties Union. Something akin to Jack's spirit told her it was the right thing to do.

She had worked hard. Fourteen hour days were the normal routine. Her fellow attorneys started calling her the "iron woman." Her home life, however, was dull and empty.

Then an invitation to a party changed everything. It was from a lobbying group headed by an old and trusted friend. She owed the friend many favors and simply couldn't refuse to go. Besides it had been months since she had even gone to a movie.

She was shocked when suddenly she bumped into Tyrel Friday at the bar. He looked older and somewhat thinner than she remembered. But his kindly warm smile beamed when he saw her.

They had not stayed in touch, but after talking with each other all evening, they promised to get together. Keysha thought it would be nice to occasionally see him as she did many of her other friends, but to her surprise, Tyrel wanted more.

The day after the party, he called her and they met for lunch. Then they went to an opening at the Kennedy Center and to dinner. Gradually, they started seeing each other on a more regular basis. Eight month later, they were married, and a year after that, their little boy was born.

Motherhood had not harmed Keysha's figure. She was an incredibly gorgeous woman, and Tyrel didn't have to be told by his colleagues in Congress, what an asset she was to his budding political future.

Keysha had taken a year off from her practice to be with her baby, but was returning to work in a week. She missed her work, and the challenge of standing up for those who had no voice in the System.

She scorned the attacks by the conservative right on the poor and detested the bending of rules by the wealthiest to benefit only a handful of Americans. The ACLU fought for the rights of all citizens and tried to ignore the constant attacks on the American government and its laws by religious fanatics and staunch conservatives. The labeling as "too liberal" was something Keysha took as a compliment.

The ACLU was, indeed, liberal. They shared the same sense of values that had guided the founding fathers who risked everything for freedom and change. The ACLU didn't fight for self interest like the conservative right. Instead they fought to keep the hard won purity of the Constitution.

Jack Mulligan would have liked that. He had fought and died for Juleel, Tyrel and for her. Keysha had survived what the press dubbed the "Wildcat Massacre" for a higher purpose. From time to time, she would get a phone call from a journalism student at Mt. Sidney asking her to comment on that night. She was always forthright and honest in her assessment and spoke clearly of how all the death was a testament to the ultimate destruction caused by unbridled racial hatred.

The other survivor, Raymon Jackson, had recovered from his wounds and went to prison for three years after being charged with conspiracy to commit murder. While behind bars, Raymon found God and religion and became a preacher. When he was released, he started an evangelistic crusade that caught the attention of the media. The ex-running back, who was now, "running for God." So said Raymon's pamphlets. That slogan had caught on, and the media had spun Raymon's actions as courageous. Keysha only remembered his cowardice.

Now, Raymon was seen on over one hundred TV stations nationwide. He had, to his sorry credit, gotten what he sought most and that was wealth and fame. Raymon owned a ranch, cars and was married to a buxom, born-again recording star. Keysha knew the real truth though. Raymon was a gutless, conniving weasel and nothing more.

Juleel Washington quit school and moved to San Francisco where he flourished. He found he had a talent for business and opened a restaurant with his mother, who finally agreed to leave Walnutburg. The restaurant, called Jack's, was located near Haight Asbury and attracted a Bohemian crowd of straight and gay artist's.

Juleel found a friend in another young black man named David. Love followed, and now they lived together happily in a town house overlooking the bay.

Keysha looked out her window and thought of her old friends.

Today was going to be a special day. The memories came flooding back as Keysha prepared herself for a special visitor. Just yesterday, she had received a call from Stu Ableson, Jack's old boss. Ableson had paid for Jack's funeral and interment in a cemetery in Mt. Sidney. He had truly considered Jack as a son. Tales of Jack Mulligan were still told at Sparkies Tavern and with each telling became more and more the stuff of legend.

Ableson was now sixty-eight years old and had just sold his business to two young guys from Cleveland. Stu contacted Keysha to tell her he would be in Washington for a week and would be honored to take her out to lunch. The old man had also indicated he had some business to discuss with her.

Keysha had asked what his business was but Ableson told her he would tell her when he saw her.

This bit of mystery intrigued Keysha as she put on a casual skirt and blouse. Jack came to her thoughts again as he did sometime during every day. What would her life have been like if he had lived? Would it have been more passionate than her present knowing, successful existence? Would they still be in love? She had to stop herself there. Going on with some thoughts wasn't good.

Maybe that was the problem with death. All those questions starting with, "what if," could never be answered.

Keysha definitely loved Tyrel. He was an honest, decent man, a great father and certainly well-respected. But, down deep, Keysha knew that something special and romantically poetic had died with Jack Mulligan, and that she would never possess it again.

Keysha was looking at the clock when the door bell rang. Stu Ableson was ten minutes early. Rushing, she hurriedly put away her make-up, gave herself a glance in the mirror and ran to the door. When she pulled it open, she saw a stocky, gray haired man standing with some flowers in hand. He was slightly stooped from years of hard physical work, but looked fit otherwise.

"Mr. Ableson," she said smiling.

"You're Keysha," said the old man. "Jack always said you were beautiful."

"Well thank you," she said blushing. "Come in."

Keysha escorted the old man into the spacious living room.

"It's so nice to meet you after all these years," said Keysha.

"You've done well for yourself, young lady," Stu said looking around. "Your home is very nice."

"Well thank you. Have a seat," said Keysha pointing to a comfortable, overstuffed chair.

"I brought you some flowers," said Stu handing them awkwardly to her. "I love flowers myself."

"Well thank you. They're lovely." Keysha then recalled the roses from Jack.

Ableson sat down and winced painfully at the touch of arthritis in his hip. Keysha took a seat opposite him.

"May I get you something to drink?"

"Sure. A Scotch and water if you please."

Keysha rose and fixed the drink at a small wet bar across the room and returned.

"So, you've piqued my interest by what you told me on the phone," said Keysha.

541

"I suppose I do have a bit of the dramatic left in me. But please indulge an old man," Ableson quipped, while taking a sip of his drink.

Keysha nodded.

"Eight years ago, when Jack was killed," began Ableson, "was one of the darkest moments of my life. Jack was the son I never had."

Ableson shook his head as if he still couldn't accept it, "I had been taking money from Jack's paychecks, a small amount, to save and invest for him. In addition, I had added some money to it, myself. He was such a good boy and hard working. But, when he was killed, I didn't have a clue as to what to do with this money. Jack, as you know, didn't have a family. So, I let it ride in a stock account.

"When I sold the business, my accountant said I should do something with the money, which now had accrued to almost twenty thousand dollars. I thought and thought about it and finally I came up with an idea."

Keysha sat forward with interest.

"If you and Jack had eventually gotten married, you would probably have had some little ones who would have been the best of both you. In this society, sometimes children of interracial marriages have a rough time. It shouldn't be that way but it often is.

"So, I went up to Mt. Sidney College and set up a scholarship fund with that money. I think it's going to help a lot of deserving kids. I'm going to add money to it every year, and it will be awarded to a deserving young person for their education."

Keysha smiled, "That's fantastic."

Stu Ableson continued, "The name of the scholarship is the Jack Mulligan Memorial Scholarship. I think Jack would have approved. I hope you don't mind that I hadn't contacted you until now. You see, I want you to be the Administrator for the scholarship."

Keysha was shocked. Here was a small piece of her past with Jack. It was something positive that might live on. "I don't know what to say, Mr. Ableson," she said in astonishment. "I would be, of course, honored to do it. It's fantastic, and you're right, Jack would have approved."

"Please call me, Stu. You know Mt. Sidney now has about twenty percent white and Asian kids going there. It's good to see."

"Wow. I haven't been back there in years. Has it changed much?"

"Everything changes," said Ableson. "I think that's the key. We can legislate against bigotry and discrimination and frown on those who behave badly, but positive change comes from understanding. It happens when boys and girls no longer hold suspicions and fear of one another because of skin color. It happens when we don't look at one race as gifted in certain ways and ungifted in others. These are the stereotypes that give small minds and souls their opening to feel superior. Then bigotry festers in the wound."

Ableson took another sip of his drink. He looked old and weary but his eyes were bright and alive.

"It's people like Jack, Malcolm X and Dr. King who had to pay the ultimate price for hate. We all suffer when it happens. But there will be a new and better world. It's coming and it won't be stopped by bigotry, and it won't be built on a cornerstone of hate."

From another room, Keysha's baby started crying. Ableson perked up at the sound and smiled, "I hear one of the new world's citizens, now," he said with a laugh.

"I'll be right back," said Keysha as she left the room.

Ableson sat back and enjoyed the sound of Keysha and her child. A mother talking to her baby was one of the sweetest forms of music to an old man. It was a symphony to be savored.

Keysha reappeared a moment later carrying the baby who was sucking loudly on a bottle. Stu rose from his chair and stood beside Keysha looking at the innocent perfect face of the baby.

"Girl or boy?" asked Stu.

"Boy," she said proudly. "He's a hungry guy. And, his father and I love him very much."

"You have a right to be proud. He's beautiful"

Keysha looked from the baby to Stu.

"Stu, I want you to meet Jack Friday."

"Jack!"

"Tyrel and I decided it was a great name," She said proudly. "Jack Mulligan was strong and intelligent, and Jack Friday will be, too, and maybe—just maybe, he'll be a leader in your brave new world."

Stu nodded in agreement.

And so it was.

THE END

ABOUT THE AUTHOR

James Ankrom has been a journalist for over thirty years. He is an editor for *Railroad Model Craftsman* magazine and lives in northern New Jersey. Currently he is working on his second novel, which he hopes to publish in 2004.

Printed in the United States
1310500001B/3